CAUGHT

A Historical Romance

Christina J Michaels

Names: Michaels, Christina J., author.
Title: Caught : a historical romance / Christina J. Michaels.
Description: San Francisco, CA: Finfolkaheem Publishers, 2017
Identifiers: ISBN 978-0-9995904-0-9
Subjects: LCSH Great Britain--History--1714-1837--Fiction. |
Man-woman relationships--Fiction. | Love stories. | Historical
fiction. | BISAC FICTION / Romance / Historical
Classification: LCC PS3613.I34418 C38 2017| DDC 813.6--dc23

2 3 4 5 6 7 8 9 0
First printing November 2017

Font Essays 1743 creator John Stracke
Cover artist Elena Karoumpali (Lıgraphics)

For Carmen Jackson

and everything she loves

Thank you for believing.

CHAPTER I

LONDON, 1772

The chill of late spring crept through the ill-laid brick. The weather, like all of Viscount Charmaine's life, was demoralizing. Attempting to shake away his negativity with a yawn, Charmaine departed his cramped bachelor quarters. Tepid sunshine crept through the morning haze to light the relatively unoccupied streets. Most of the City's occupants were either elsewhere or hard at work inside. The neighborhood leisurely changed during his half-hour walk. Trash vanished from the streets, as dilapidated boarding houses became modest townhomes and then turned into sprawling estates.

Charmaine reached the fashionable part of Town without noticing the route there. His family's London residence was impossible to ignore. Columns dominated the façade of the ostentatious stone building. Ornate marbled statuary overwhelmed the neatly manicured garden. His mother's touch was everywhere, each detail announcing the wealth and power of those who lived within. Charmaine found the presentation more than a trifle overdone.

A familiar butler ushered the broad man into a drawing room. Tea was waiting. Handing over his coat, he sank into a chair to await the doctor's announcement that the Lord Donahue was ready for visitors. Once summoned, Charmaine took the stairs to his father's room quietly and slipped through the large open archway. Ceiling to floor windows drenched the room in sunlight. The room was decorated in light colors in an attempt to create a light, cheery air. Charmaine thought it looked as sterile as an asylum.

Charmaine's father, Ambler Anderson The Earl of Donahue, sat propped on a large white bed. Although his long, wispy gray hair was neatly brushed and his nightgown was of the finest clean linen, they adorned a man who was little more than a husk. Skin hung limply from his massive bones. His withered limbs had long since left his control. The doctors had given into despair, but Lord Donahue refused to die. Charmaine smiled slightly. All the members of the family were fighters and his father was the greatest of them all. Lord Donahue's vacant blue eyes stared aimlessly at the white wall.

Familiar frustration raged through Charmaine at seeing his father helpless. Taking the old man's hand, he sat by the bed and prayed. When he looked again, his father's eyes were closed. Depositing a kiss on the wrinkled forehead Charmaine stole quietly from the room. He would have time to go over the financials with his father later. Perhaps it made little sense to update the unresponsive man, but Charmaine held on to the hope that his father would wake. When the Lord Donahue resumed his duties he would be up-to-date on every part of the estates.

Charmaine's steps remained muted as he walked from his father's rooms. He halted to examine his appearance in a large gilded mirror before entering his mother's domain. Charmaine watched his reflection's jaw unclench and its mouth fight to achieve a neutral appearance. God, he wished his father were healthy again.

With a deep breath, he forced his attention back to the mirror. His un-powdered chestnut hair was tied neatly at the nape of his neck. His mother would likely bemoan his lack of wig, but he found no use for such frivolity unless Society demanded it. She would be hard-pressed to find anything wrong with his garb. His clothing was cut simply but with the well-made elegance that spoke of quality and expense. His man had tied his cravat in a fashion so new Charmaine did not yet know what it was called. He momentarily regretted handing his overcoat to the butler, as it was of an excellent cut and its navy color set off the sapphire of his eyes. Visiting his mother was a bit like going to war, except his clothing was the only arsenal he had against her.

Lady Donahue awaited him in her airy sitting room. Charmaine suspected she picked the moss green with pale rose accents colors of the room for how well they complimented her light blond hair and soft green eyes. Even long after the prime of her youth, there was no doubting she was once the catch of the Season.

Charmaine's first sign of trouble was her shimmering green silk day dress. Bushy eyebrows furrowed as he realized she too had dressed for battle. The gown was a childhood favorite. Charmaine remembered her wearing it while laughing at a joke his father told and the answering softness of his father's smile.

Charmaine stepped forward and bowed to his mother. Standing, he took her delicate hand and deposited a perfunctory kiss. "Mother, you look brilliant today."

A delicately arched eyebrow rose at his words as she withdrew her hand. "What a charming liar you are."

Knowing it was going to be a difficult meeting provided no comfort. Charmaine was doomed to play it through. "In truth, Mother, you look lovely. You glow in that gown."

"For shame! This rag is hopelessly out of fashion, Robert. Everything I own is out of fashion. How am I supposed to help you find you a wife if I cannot even leave the estate without risking utter humiliation?" Lady Donahue's voice was already rising, a slight hint of hysterics entering her mannerisms.

Charmaine took a moment to consider his mother. He expected a charade of emotion, but this was not feigned. His mother was overcome with nerves. He set aside the typical Donahue bickering and closed the space between them. Charmaine held his mother tightly as she broke down in his arms.

There was nothing ladylike or polite about her sobs. The initial crying subsided quickly, but Lady Donahue stood quietly in her son's arms for several long moments. Charmaine could feel the deep, shuddering breaths coursing through her body.

Lady Donahue stepped back from her son's comfort and wiped her eyes. She took a deep breath and raised her chin, once again every inch The Countess of Donahue. Charmaine stumbled for something to say and finally decided on silence. In the awkward

3

moment that followed, Lady Donahue poured herself and her son tea. Charmaine took it gratefully.

"I wish for you to wed." It was a command, not a request.

"I hear your words." Charmaine sounded resigned. "Perhaps it is time."

The first hint of spring, Charmaine remembered. His father said the dress, and his mother's eyes, looked like the first hint of spring. God's teeth, he wished his father would wake. He wished his mother would smile again.

Those spring eyes currently displayed Lady Donahue's skepticism. "What devious trick are you planning now?"

Charmaine fought a smile at his mother's automatic suspicion. "No trick. The traditional solution to monetary issues is to marry rich. A wife with a large portion will solve our quite-temporary dilemma. I created this predicament and I should be the one to extract us from it." His voice was firm. "And, to be clear, I require you compliance with your lowered allowance. I do not lie about our resources, Mother, and I will not access our entailments."

She flipped her hair, an action that made the older woman look girlish. "Not even to relieve our genteel poverty?"

Charmaine's expression was flat. "We have not yet tasted genteel poverty, Mother. I will hear no more on this subject."

With a look of grave irritation, Lady Donahue returned to her second favorite topic. "I am glad you have decided to wed."

Still standing, he sipped his tea as his generous lips curved into a small smile. "Can I truly claim to have decided if I was bullied into it?"

"There is no need to be insulting. No one can bully you into anything." She gave him a critical look. "Have you chosen a bride? I sent a post with several suggestions."

"No. At this point, I have little care to who it will be. She must come with a generous dowry and be willing to wed quickly. No fashionable yearlong engagement. I would prefer a woman with a pleasant temperament. Other than that, I see no reason why one pair of skirts will not do as well as another."

"All women are not the same, Robert. While I agree with your priorities, should you not also look for a partner who will match your character?"

"What wrought this change, Mother? You no longer wish me to rush to the parson with the first petticoat who flutters her eyelashes at me," Charmaine smiled.

"You are being foolish, Robert. I have not changed my position."

"Mother." His flat tone indicated his disbelief.

She grew sober, her façade falling away. "Yes, you should wed and wed soon. But there can be happiness in a marriage too, Robert. A great happiness that…" Her words trailed off.

"Mother?" He repeated himself, but this time his voice was gentle and questioning.

"I miss him, Robert. Your father." Her voice was fragile and oh-so-quiet. "More than I imagined was possible. I can see him. I can touch him. But he is not there. His awareness—he is gone." A single tear rolled down her cheek.

Tentatively, Charmaine stepped forward and took his mother's hand. They stood there in silence for a long time before Charmaine leaned forward and kissed his mother's cheek. "I will wed, my bride's dowry will save us and things will be put right."

She looked at him, her pastel eyes brimming with tears. "Your father is dying, Robert. Nothing will ever be right again."

He stood there, feeling helpless, before she waved him away. Retreating while his mother sorrowed felt impossible. He relented as Lady Donahue repeated her dismissal. Reluctantly, Charmaine retrieved his coat and cane and walked out into the cool sunshine. Frustrated and helpless, Charmaine decided to do something he reserved for only very special occasions.

He decided to get exceptionally drunk.

Charmaine's childhood friend, Edward Ambler Collins, Lord Stanton deliberately purchased a London home near the Donahue townhouse. Thus it was only a short time later that Charmaine arrived outside Baron Stanton's elegant manor. He found himself reluctant to approach.

Collins and Charmaine were the best of friends as youths in the country, but life in London (and specifically the shrew Collins married) forced them apart. Yet, Collins was not only conveniently located but he also knew the story of Lord Donahue's illness. Sharing family secrets with him would not feel like betrayal, since Collins was more like a cousin than a shunned friend. Nevertheless, reestablishing contact with Collins meant dealing with his wife, Elizabeth.

Charmaine deliberated outside the Stantons' ostentatious drive for the better part of an hour before grudgingly approaching the door.

The door to the estate opened before Charmaine finished traversing the stairs. He handed a footman his hat and cane before asking after his friend, "Is Collins in?"

Collins had never adhered to the traditional naming scheme of the *ton*. Rather than being Edward to his friends, Collins to his mates from college, Stanton to his peers, he managed to simply be Collins. It irritated Charmaine, not for the lack of proper etiquette, but rather that Collins maintained such simplicity. Being Robert, Charmaine, and, some day, Donahue seemed unnecessary to Charmaine - why not have only one name?

The footman took the items with a bow. "I will inquire, Lord Charmaine. Would you care to wait in the front parlor?"

Charmaine acquiesced with a nod and escorted himself to a champagne sitting room. A crystal vase on an ornately carved table dominated the room. The hearty floral sent of cream roses filled the air. He smiled at the distinctly feminine touch to the room. His rough and ready friend would never have chosen a table carved with cherubs.

Charmaine's broad shoulders and rugged looks were currently out of fashion. Collins' tall, lithe frame wore the current long tailed coat as if the trend was created specifically for him. His cream breaches were tightly cut and the green of his coat was so vivacious Charmaine had trouble imagining what was used for dye. His hair was styled *à la mode*, curled and powdered several feet above his head. His appearance was far removed from the friend he remembered. Charmaine's eyes widened unintentionally.

Collins grinned as he lifted the glass of brandy. "Go ahead. Say it."

Charmaine held up his hands defensively and searched for a neutral reply. He remembered Collins as they often looked after climbing trees. That scrawny boy was no more. Baron Stanton stood in front of him. Charmaine chose to remain silent.

His friend answered as if Charmaine had spoken, "I know. I should be wearing ripped clothing covered in mud and have sticks stuck in my hair." He took a sip of his brandy while one side of his mouth curled upwards in amusement. "Times change. Elizabeth taught me that I enjoy extravagance. Aside from admiring my dress, what brings you to my doorstep?"

"I beg your pardon, Collins. That was not a polite greeting, was it? I was surprised to see you looking so…"

"Foppish?" Collins offered helpfully.

"Noble, actually." Charmaine grimaced. "Not that you were not before…"

Collins smiled. "I forgive you, Charmaine. I know I was far from the height of fashion as a youth. However, now I am considered a paragon of appropriate attire."

Collins sat on a chair that looked too delicate to support him. "What brings you to my home? I would invite you to my study, but," he looked at the ceiling as the sound of shattering glass echoed down the stairs, "I fear it may be in the process of being redecorated."

"That is quite fine. I do not wish to further upset Lady Stanton. I am aware she is not fond of me."

Collins gave Charmaine a scolding look. "Considering you have been open in your belief my marriage to her was the worst thing I have ever done, I cannot imagine why you would expect her to enjoy your company."

Charmaine avoided his friend's gaze by staring at his large hands. "I did what I thought was right. I stand by that. If you are happy, I apologize."

"I am happy." A muffled clunking noise radiated down the stairs. "And I will accept your apology if you will stop evading my question."

Charmaine glanced inquisitively over at his friend, "What question?"

"Why are you here? I have not seen you in over a year and now you are unexpectedly at my doorstep. Anyone would find this curious."

Charmaine ran his hands over the top of his head, smoothing out his unpowdered queue. "I need to get foxed with my childhood mate."

It was Collins' turn to raise an eyebrow. "You do not drink."

"This is a situation where allowances are called for," Charmaine explained.

"I see." Collins leaned back in the chair and considered. The Lord and Lady Stanton maintained a full social calendar. Tonight was no exception. There was a play, followed by a dinner that would last late into the night. He calculated the social implications of canceling his plans. "Do you wish to tell me what this is about?"

"No," Charmaine replied.

Stanton' lips tightened as he considered his mate's request. If he missed the play, it might be possible to still make dinner. Charmaine made quick work of talk. Hopefully Elizabeth would understand. "I will meet you at Brooks's at nine o' the clock."

"I am not a member. White's?" Charmaine suggested instead.

"I should have pegged you for a Tory, Charmaine. Lucky for you, I am a member of both. Brooks's may have my crowd, but White's has better whist players." Collins chuckled. "Then again, the man of no vices does not gamble."

Charmaine stood with a wry smile. "Oh, I gamble. But only with notably large quantities of money." He bowed. "I will see you at nine."

Collins found Charmaine tucked into a rear booth, hunched over a decanter of whiskey. Several finger-lengths were already missing. Collins sat without invitation and poured himself a drink.

Charmaine remained focused on his beverage, apparently oblivious to Collins' arrival.

Collins adjusted his long waistcoat and leaned back in the booth. "Fine weather we are having."

Charmaine nodded. "Yes. I found today remarkably pleasant."

"Elizabeth is especially fond of afternoon rides in the park while the weather is still cool. As the Season progresses she finds them tedious."

"For once I find myself in agreement with Lady Stanton." Charmaine shifted and pushed himself up so that he was sitting straight in the booth, "The days grow quite warm after The Ascot. I much prefer the first half of the Season myself."

Collins shrugged to indicate his dissenting opinion, "On the other hand, I am not fond of rain. I would rather face the heat than the damp. Lucky for me, Candlemas was bleak and dreary this year."

"Yes. How does the rhyme go?"

Collins attempted a slight Scottish burr. "If Candlemas day be dry and fair, the half o' winter to come and mair." He shrugged. "The rest is lost to me."

Charmaine emptied his tumbler suddenly. Slamming the glassware forcibly onto the table, he grumbled, "This conversation is foolish."

"Yes," Collins replied equably, "it is. Do you want to tell me what is bothering you, or shall I go back to remembering the rest of the rhyme? I know it has something to do with Yule."

"Yes. No." Charmaine's eyes fell to his glass. "I do not want to tell you, but I want to tell you."

"I understand."

"You do?" Charmaine frowned in surprise. "I am not sure I do."

Collins refilled Charmaine's tumbler. "Something is bothering you. You have never been one to disclose your personal feelings. Although you want to share you do not know how."

"Exactly." Charmaine took a large gulp of whiskey. "I intend to wed."

"Considering a year gone you swore off marriage, this is indeed a change. Pray tell."

Charmaine turned his drink as if examining the honey colored liquid. "This is the part I do not wish to reveal. But also, why I requested your company."

"I contemplated your earlier visit. You are the only man I know who would plan to get foxed as a form of escape. You plan everything. I know you have friends here in London, so why would you turn to me? The choice was deliberate. The only reason I can think of is there is something wrong with your family," Collins concluded.

Charmaine nodded.

Collins fell quiet, sounding troubled. "Is it...Lord Donahue?"

"No, no. Well, nothing new, anyway." Charmaine said, "And my mother is well."

"Good. I was worried. Is it too much to hope Lord Donahue's health has turned for the better?"

Charmaine frowned as he refilled his tumbler. "My father is still the same. His eyes open and shut, but he can do naught else. We still meet weekly to discuss financials." His brow furrowed as he shut his eyes for a moment. Charmaine's voice was gruff as he continued speaking. "I'm not really sure why. I don't believe he can hear me. Hope, I suppose."

Collins raised his tumbler. "To the health of Lord Donahue."

The two men clinked glasses. Charmaine put his drink down and scowled at the table. "He's not going to get better, Collins. Or, if he does, it will not be in time. I need to do something now."

"Why? What's wrong?" Collins leaned forward conspiratorially, speaking in same plotting whisper Charmaine remembered from their childhood.

Collins had designed most of their ill-advised adventures. He also never failed to conspire and improve Charmaine's plans. Best, he'd stay and get whipped with the inevitable parental ire at the end. He was a true mate and one worth trusting.

"It is," Charmaine paused before continued fatalistically, "money."

"I heard you were up the river Tick. How bad is it?"

Charmaine swirled his drink before answering. "Bad."

The two men sat in silence for a few moments. Collins spoke first, deliberately keeping his voice even and level. "Are you asking to borrow money from me?"

"No." Charmaine's reply was firm, even a bit heated. "Not at all."

"God's teeth, Charmaine, speak plainly. Either confide in me and tell me how I can help or let us leave this topic and drink ourselves into a stupor."

Charmaine looked at the whiskey decanter as if seriously considering the latter option. "My shipping investments have been delayed or destroyed. The investments in the Virginia plantation defaulted. My liquid assets are almost spent. My debt is exorbitant." He finished his whiskey again. "The only answer I can see is to wed. I need a wife with capital. Land or title does not matter, nor if she is pleasant in temperament or unsightly to look upon. The only thing that matters is a sizable dowry that can be accessed immediately."

Collins refilled both their glasses as he considered the situation. Charmaine was particular about women. More troubling, Collins knew under Charmaine's callous exterior he dreamed, or at least had dreamt, of love. "I am sure there are a plethora of such women who would be pleased to have your suit."

His friend replied by grunt.

"Robert, listen to me," Collins leaned forward over their drinks, "finding the right woman is important. There is more than one girl with money, you need to find the right one."

"Otherwise I will end up with an Elizabeth?"

"You are foxed, so I will graciously forgive the insult to my wife. What you overlook is Elizabeth, for all her faults, is exactly what I want in a partner." Collins voice was steady but filled with passion. "She is frisky, determined, interesting, fashionable, caring, and, most importantly, someone I am proud to call my wife. Do you want any less from Lady Charmaine?"

"Bloody hell, Collins, certainly I want someone I am proud to call my wife. But the truth is what I want no longer matters. What matters is that I am tempting ruin! I cannot pay my creditors. If I have to marry a poxy shrew to do so, I will!"

"Let us try to avoid that." Collins analyzed his friend. "Are your estates secured?"

"Yes. Father's solicitors entailed the land last year. The amount of capital I have squandered could launch and dowry a duchess." Charmaine gave him a foul look. "I have all my teeth, too."

Collins ignored Charmaine's foul temper as he continued, "Then I fail to see the difficulty. If we dust off these country manners that you use so rarely, you are a fair looking man and a Viscount."

"A courtesy title," Charmaine objected.

"Yes, Charmaine." Exasperation crept into Collins voice. "The courtesy title held by heir of the Earl of Donahue."

"I do not..." Charmaine paused. Sentences were rapidly becoming difficult to form. "I do not want someone who wants me for my title."

Collins stared silently.

"I know. I want the chit for her money, but I want her to want me for me." Charmaine set his empty tumbler down. "But I want— oh piss and bother what I want. Need is more important than want."

Silence fell over the booth. Collins attempted to refill the glass but Charmaine waved him away. With a rueful grin, Charmaine shook his head. "I think I am done."

Collins smiled. "Foxed?"

"Three sheets."

"Will you even remember this in the morning? Never mind. I already know you have no head for drink." Collins gestured over to a servant and gave whispered orders. The man returned with ink and a quill. Collins jotted something down and handed it to his friend.

"What is this?" Charmaine unceremoniously crumpled the paper without waiting for it to dry. He shoved the smeared mess into his pocket.

"A reminder you will be joining Elizabeth and myself for dinner Thursday night and attending the opera. We have a box."

"I have no interest in the opera, Collins. It is indulgent nonsense," said Charmaine.

"Whether or not you like the opera is irrelevant, Charmaine. Opening night at Covent Gardens is one of *the* events of the Season. If you are on the hunt for a bride, it is where you need to be."

Charmaine frowned slightly. "Fine." The wrinkles on his face abruptly faded. One bushy eyebrow perked up, "Does this mean you are going to help me?"

"Yes." Collins stoppered the whiskey decanter. "Did you honestly think otherwise?"

"I did not ask," said Charmaine.

"I know." Collins smirked. "Do you remember when we were playing on the ruins and you pushed me off the wall?"

"You broke your leg and never forgave me."

"Correct. This will be my revenge."

Charmaine's brow furrowed. "Seeing my family slip and lose their fortune?"

"No, my foolish friend, not that." Collins smirk grew into a full-fledged smile. "Seeing you suffer through a full London Season will be all the revenge I have ever needed."

CHAPTER II

"**M**iss?" Abigail's voice cut through Miss Alison Brooke's daydream. She put down Burns' latest work and gave her maid her full attention. "Miss Brenda Boswell has come a calling. Are you in?"

Miss Brooke's face lit up with a smile. "Certainly I am! Please send her right up. And it would be lovely if you would bring refreshments."

Miss Boswell careened into Miss Brooke's sitting room in a whirlwind of limbs. Miss Boswell spent most of her life being told how lovely she would be once she grew into herself. At two and twenty, it seemed unlikely such fortune would ever come. Her freckles were bright enough (Alison was kind enough to call them radiant) that hiding them required the thickest of pastes. Wildly curly copper hair crept out of almost any style, unless plastered under a wig or caked with powder. Today was no exception. Miss Boswell's hair made good on its escape from her straw bonnet as she flew into the room.

The two women were a study in opposites. Miss Boswell's whole person gave the impression of wild, reckless freedom that refused to be contained by laces or pins. Miss Brooke's peach morning gown was perfectly pressed, and her hair was arranged in a deceptively simple mass of curls on her head. She smiled at her whirlwind of a friend and stood to offer a hug. It was fiercely returned.

Miss Boswell's excitement overflowed into her speech, "Why did you not tell me, you sly cat?"

Miss Brooke settled into her wingback chair with an amused sigh. "What did I forget to tell you this time?"

"Look!" Miss Boswell pushed parchment at Miss Brooke and waited for her to read it. Miss Brooke's smile crashed as her bright blue eyes scanned the document. Miss Boswell recited out loud,

> *The Season starts with a bang! Lord F announced his intention to seek Miss B's hand in marriage. Shall he find happiness or be yet another reject⸱⸱⸱*

Miss Boswell stopped mid-word as she noticed her friend's expression. "Oh. Dear."

"You thought we accepted." Miss Brooke's voice was quiet.

"Lord Farrington is a Marquis! God's own truth, what more do you want?" Miss Boswell flopped onto the sitting room couch with only the slightest regard for dignity.

"You know this is not about what I want, Brenda." She lifted her chin again. Concealing the hurt, she composed herself. "Lord Farrington spoke to my father. He, as always, refused."

"You are of age, Alison! Your father's permission is not needed to wed!" Miss Boswell sounded as exasperated as Miss Brooke felt.

Miss Brooke lifted her teacup and gave a dainty shrug in reply. "There is the matter of my portion. My grandmother's will explicitly states he must approve my suitor or I will receive not a tuppence of it. I will not be tied to my husband's purse strings."

"This is not about pin money and you know it." With a frown, Miss Boswell took a scone and continued, "Besides, not all men are tedious creatures. Take Lord Farrington for example."

"Yes," Miss Brooke nodded primly. "He was very charming. I am pained he and my father could not reach an accord."

"La, Ali!" A copper brow shot up. "He was very charming? Last week you thought you might be in love with him!"

Miss Brooke shut her eyes for a moment. She spoke with a soft voice. "Brenda, you are not aiding my humors."

"I am sorry. When I read the Society papers I thought…" Miss Boswell pressed her narrow lips together. "No matter what I thought. We will have to think ahead."

"Think ahead?"

"Well, if you can capture a marquis," Miss Boswell continued with overly forced cheer, "why not a duke? It is a new Season full of new chances. Who wants to get engaged at the start of the Season anyway? Think of all you would be missing!"

"What is the point, Brenda? Prince George himself could ask for me and my father would still say no." Miss Brooke successfully fought to keep her voice even and eyes dry. "This is my third Season. Lord Farrington was my seventh offer. What new chances are on the horizon?"

"You could elope," said Miss Boswell.

"Not only would I lose my inheritance but such scandalous action would ruin my social standing. And my father would be furious." Miss Brooke's serious expression faded as a small smile crept through. "I have considered it though."

Miss Boswell chewed on her lower lip as she frowned. "I cannot help but think if you truly loved someone, none of this would stand in your way."

"You have been reading Milton again. I have worked too hard to become the darling of the Court and a diamond on Almack's floor to throw it away for a flight of fancy."

"Mayhap." Miss Boswell twisted her face up. "I still do not like it. I worry you are holding on too hard to the idea of being what Society wants."

"Mayhap," The blond mimicked before sighing. "But, really, what else do I have?"

"Me?"

Miss Brooke laughed brightly. "And I do not know what I would do without you. I am sorry to be so dour. Lord Farrington was so— I thought Father would yield."

"I know. Lord Farrington is quite a catch." Miss Boswell fiddled with her tea. "We should talk about something else, otherwise, we will become maudlin again. What are you wearing to the opera?"

"I was considering not going and hiding in my rooms until the Season was over. I do not suppose you will grant me such leisure?"

Miss Boswell's curls further escaped her bonnet as she shook her head no. "Never."

"In that case, I was planning on wearing my new dark rose and cream silks. The stomacher arrived from the seamstress early this week. I had the embroidery supplemented with pearls. It should be lovely." Miss Brooke spoke with the confidence of an expert. "And you?"

Miss Boswell's whole answer was a shrug.

"Are you asking for help? I know you have to have something." Miss Brooke was smiling now that her friend's cheerful demeanor successfully distracted her.

"This is my third Season as well, Alison." Miss Boswell shrugged again. "Unlike you, I have yet to receive an offer. Maybe *I* should wear the pink silks."

Miss Brooke laughed. "With your hair they would look almost as terrible as that yellow does on you!"

Miss Boswell threw a pillow at her friend. Still laughing, they turned their energy to the problem of planning Miss Boswell's outfit.

Charmaine, feeling like a buffoon dressed in courtly attire, peered over the balcony to see whom Lady Stanton was gesturing at. "Her?" he jerked his powdered head at a rather plain woman below, "The one with two blue feathers in her hair?"

It was halfway through the first act of the opera. Collins leisurely reclined towards the back of the booth leaving Charmaine and Lady Stanton to peruse the crowd. The well-lit audience allowed a perfect forum to analyze the gems of court in relative privacy.

"No, next to her." Lady Stanton indicated whom she meant with her pointed chin. "The one with the birds in her wig."

Charmaine waited until the lady in question turned and provided a clear view of her profile. "Lady Stanton, that creature is no catch. Are you certain?"

An elegant shrug preceded her answer, "Lady Teresa is among the largest heiresses in all of England. She is heavy in the purse. You stated the other qualities were irrelevant."

Charmaine frowned. "I suppose she has a compassionate personality?"

"No, she is a termagant. But, she is both rich and sister to an earl with no heirs," Lady Stanton replied.

"I do not like this," Charmaine admitted.

"Let me direct you to the woman in the pale green in the third box from the left." They both looked. "The Honorable Miss Rebecca Linder is fair in the face and also has a sizable dowry."

"She is still in pastels." Charmaine sounded disgusted.

"Youth is supposed to be an asset, Lord Charmaine." Lady Stanton sipped her champagne. The expensive bottle was arranged so visitors would be forced notice the label. "There are only five or six women on the market that are going to be of acceptable breeding for your mother and with enough of a dowry to please you. All other available ladies that match your criteria are highly problematic."

"Problematic?"

"Do you see the woman in the rose silks?"

"Adorned with pearls?" Charmaine took a good look. She was lovely, the light from the theatre reflected off her periwinkle eyes. Her dusky rose dress hugged her torso tightly, displaying breasts that would fit perfectly in the palm of his hand. Large panniers hid any evaluation of her lower curves. A large cream feather arched over her wig and draped tantalizingly down her back. "Lovely. Truly lovely."

"Indeed. A true diamond, with a dowry to rival even Miss Linder's." Lady Stanton agreed. "More remarkable, under all that paint there seems to be a warm soul. One of the sharks of the court would have eaten her long ago, if not for her father."

Charmaine continued to watch Miss Brooke. "Hm?"

"Her father, The Honorable Daniel Brooke. Lord Sanders' youngest brother. He is a tad—ruthless."

"And he is the reason why she is problematic?"

The plumage in Lady Stanton's wig bobbed as she agreed. "I would assume so. She made quite a splash on the scene. The

Brookes have, so far, refused all suitors. After three full Seasons I am unsure what they are thinking."

"Perchance she has yet to meet the right man." Charmaine watched the woman in question. She was intent on the opera. In an auditorium full of people gossiping and watching each other it seemed odd to encounter one so engrossed in what was on stage.

"La, Lord Charmaine." Lady Stanton tapped her fan on his arm. "Do not be foolish. This is about finding the perfect match, not a nursemaid's tale. Even a girl like her cannot afford to pass up every offer! She has to be at least one and twenty by now."

He shrugged, dismissing the topic. He did not want to be distracted from their purpose. The sooner they finished examining the candidates, the sooner he could be free of Lady Stanton's company. "What was the child's name? The one in pale green?"

"Linder. Miss Rebecca Linder. I can arrange an introduction if you would like."

"Please do." He leaned back into his chair. The crowd held no further interest for him once the decision was made. "Nothing formal, though. I would meet the girl before marrying her."

"Certainly." Lady Stanton made a mental note to add Miss Linder to the guest list of their upcoming dinner party. "Her youth means things inherently will go slow. Luckily, her birthday is upcoming."

Charmaine smiled slightly at Lady Stanton's use of 'we.' "You are being extremely accommodating. My thanks."

Lady Stanton laid her fan on Charmaine's arm and looked at him with large autumn eyes. Her tone was unexpectedly serious. "You are Collins' friend."

Charmaine hesitated, considering what to say. After a pause he replied simply, "I am."

The serious moment lingered, and Lady Stanton shifted uncomfortably. "It is almost intermission. You and Collins must stay here in the box. Sit close to the railing and talk about something. And try to smile."

He graced Lady Stanton with a false smile that looked much more like a grimace. "How is this?"

Lady Stanton smiled charmingly at him. "Perfect. Maybe you could cross your eyes, too?" She flicked narrow fingers at Collins.

He heeled obligingly. They shared a conspiratorial smile before she turned back to Charmaine. "If you have any doubts, follow Collins' lead."

After helping his wife up, Collins took her chair next to Charmaine. On the floor below the women flocked to gossip in tight circles while the men concealed their rumormongering behind cigars and brandy. Lady Stanton quickly burst into one of the colorful clusters below.

Charmaine looked skeptically at Collins, "What is she about?"

"The most powerful thing in Society, Charmaine." Collins poured them both whiskey and handed one tumbler to his friend. "Gossip. The right people need to know Lord Charmaine is looking for a bride."

"I want this done with." Charmaine took the tumbler and set it to the side.

"Try to have a little enthusiasm," Collins said.

"Why? I am selecting my future bride as one would a racehorse and my only criterion for selection is her fortune. I find the situation repugnant. I feel like a scrub."

Collins raised an eyebrow. "A scrub? Charmaine, this is how Society selects brides."

"Picking carefully wrapped packages while the details of their breeding, fortune, and reputation are weighed and analyzed?" Charmaine shook his head in disgust. "I want a person, Collins, not a package."

With furrowed brow, Collins answered, "They are people. Each woman is different. We all know that."

"Yes, but we do not shop for a wife based on them being people, but rather on certain indicators. This feels like considering an investment rather than a wife."

"A wife *is* an investment." Collins was looking at him curiously. "Your ideas are terribly out of fashion, my friend. Marriage is about money and power, not love. If you are lucky, love will come with time." Collins toasted his drink towards his wife below, "If not, there are always mistresses."

"Practicality be dammed, Collins, this is the one part of my life I did not want to approach as a businessman." Charmaine's voice was low as he leaned in to keep their conversation private, an unnecessary gesture in a hall loud with laughter and conversation.

"Then do not." Collins pushed the tumbler of whiskey at Charmaine again. Grudging, Charmaine wrapped his large hand around the glassware. "You need to find peace with yourself, Charmaine. Either marry for money or hold out for whatever it is you are looking for. It will bring no one happiness if you to insist on marrying for money and then resent yourself for the necessity."

"I do not resent myself," replied Charmaine.

Collins pointedly ignored the inaccurate rebuttal and observed the crowd. "Look, Elizabeth has encountered Miss Linder." The gentlemen fell silent as they watched the gaggle of women below. Miss Linder looked interested in whatever Lady Stanton was saying, while her chaperone seemed suspicious.

"Who is the dragon in red behind her?"

"Covered in paste and feathers? That would be the mother, Lady Vassler." Collins smirked at Charmaine's expression. "The dress is indicative of her personality."

"I am charmed already." Charmaine's dry tone was thick with sarcasm. Below them Lady Stanton's azure fan flittered and folded as she chattered at the gaggle around Miss Linder. The gentlemen watched the throng below until the footmen indicated the second act was about to start. Charmaine tried to turn his attention to the opera, but it held little interest for him. His eyes wandered back to Miss Linder and he found himself trying to imagine her as Lady Charmaine. She was a slight girl with a delicate bone structure. If her personality was passable he supposed she would do.

His dark blue eyes continued to investigate the girl examining the way a few loose white curls dangled down her elegant neck. Rebecca Linder was blooming into womanhood. Her light green dress was modestly cut. The dress and her bearing reminded him of grain fields in the spring. A *fichu* covered any hint of her breasts. He forced his mind to consider her as a prospective mate. He sighed at his lack of interest. There were no plush bosoms to discover or even daydreams of the warmth of her embrace. His musings halted on the fact he did not know her, she seemed scarcely more than a girl, and, most of all, he truly did not want to wed.

Collins looked askew at his friend and refilled the tumblers. Good old Collins, Charmaine thought, whenever there was doubt or confusion, his answer was to drink it away. Charmaine picked up the whiskey and continued his morose contemplations. While he did not keep a mistress or partake in the whoring like many of his London friends, he certainly had a great enjoyment and respect for the female form. With a sense of relief, he felt himself grow hard as he visualized a friendly widow from his past. He imagined her arched below him while her body shook with the force of their moans. Yet, he looked at Miss Linder and thought only of—grass. He stared into his glass as he contemplated the nature of money, need, and passion.

Miss Boswell stayed seated at the end of the opera and watched the gaggle quickly ensnare Miss Brooke. The gentlemen of Court encircled her, looking like garish weeds strangling a dark pink rose. Miss Boswell reminded herself that Miss Brooke did not mean to leave her waiting, rather it was easy to get caught up in the laughter and chatter of so many suitors. Some days it hurt to be trapped on the outskirts. It was better to wait for Miss Brooke to finish socializing. Out of the corner of her eye, Miss Boswell caught another staring at the effervescent blond.

Miss Boswell smoothed the brown silk she was wearing and nervously patted her curls. Brown, or "earthen loam" as Miss Brooke called it, was not a color she would normally wear. She much preferred highly saturated shades of red or orange, but Miss Brooke was continually horrified by how those colors clashed with her bright copper hair. Since hair was always powdered at formal events, Miss Boswell did not see why it mattered. Miss Brooke tried to explain it in terms of skin tone but Miss Boswell had little interest. She wanted to wear what she liked. Yet, three Seasons without an offer weighed heavily on her, so Miss Boswell relented to her friend dictating her closet. Putting so much effort into her appearance when no one noticed her except as Miss Brooke's shadow felt pointless.

Miss Boswell was pulled from her musings when she noticed a certain gentleman standing in the shadows staring at Miss Brooke. Suddenly Miss Boswell was glad that she followed Miss Brooke's advice. Timidly, she made her way to where he was standing.

"Lord Farrington." Miss Boswell smiled brightly at him and then bit her lip. She hastily curtsied. While his coloring – with his midnight dark eyes and ebony hair – was unfashionable, his hawk-like features were sharp and strong enough to sweep even the most callous woman off of her feet. Miss Boswell was far from callous. "What are you doing here on the outskirts? This is my place, you know."

He smiled politely at her attempt at humor and averted his eyes from the gaggle. "Good evening, Miss Boswell. It is, as always, a pleasure to see you."

"You are, as always, kind. Did you enjoy the opera? I'm afraid my French was weaker than I thought. I lost everything after intermission."

Farrington looked at her critically for a moment and then dismissed whatever he was thinking. "Perhaps because tonight's selection was Italian."

Miss Boswell grimaced. "Is it not rude to correct a lady when she makes such an obvious blunder?"

He remained expressionless. "Indeed, it is. Pray accept my apology."

"Please, I took no offense. I was looking to make light of my mistake and perchance make you smile. There is no hope of that, is there?"

"I, again, am forced to beg your pardon. I shall take my rainclouds elsewhere, Miss Boswell." He bowed formally to her. "By your leave?"

Miss Boswell's copper brows furrowed together as she ungracefully chewed on her lower lip. "I wish I could say something. She is truly fond of you. Her father..."

"It is of no consequence, Miss Boswell. The past is simply that– the past." He paused at her expression of distress. Farrington's calm exterior had yet to show emotion. "You will save a dance for me at the next Almack's ball, will you not?"

Her curls bobbed excitedly as she shook her head yes. "I suppose I can manage to fend off all of my prospective suitors long enough to save one dance."

"Do that." He extended his gloved hand and she automatically put hers into it. He kissed the back of her hand formally, stood, nodded at her, and walked out.

Miss Boswell leaned back against the wall and rapidly fanned herself. A small smile flickered across her face and her hand curled into a ball tightly held to her chest. There was something about Anthony that made a flock of happy, audacious birds struggle for freedom inside of her. It was impossible to not smile when he was near. She knew he asked her to save a dance because he was polite. He always made an effort to entertain Miss Brooke's wallflower friend. Even a stickler like Miss Brooke was forced to admit Farrington's manners were impeccable. Miss Brooke commented more than once she wished he was more expressive or lively, but Miss Boswell thought his stoic nature made him handsome.

Miss Boswell's admiration of Lord Farrington started her first Season. At first, he was nothing more than a strikingly handsome man she could daydream about from across the ballroom. She was dismayed when he showed intent towards Miss Brooke, positive that their courtship would expose reality's inevitable flaws. Yet as Miss Boswell paid attention to every little detail about him, she had come to realize he was even more amazing than she imagined. If Miss Brooke had accepted his suit, then he would have been around forever. Now he would fade out of their lives and Miss Boswell would be denied even the pleasure of his company. It was, indeed, a sad day.

Miss Boswell approached Miss Brooke's entourage. Most of the finely dressed gentry ignored her. Miss Boswell's progress stalled as the mass of gaily socializing humanity thickened. The men seeking beauty and money surrounded Miss Brooke and the women seeking husbands surrounded them. There were a few who truly enjoyed Miss Brooke's company, but both Miss Boswell and Miss Brooke knew those were a minority. Miss Boswell found it awful, but Miss

Brooke claimed it was all a part of the game they played, a part of the painting the gentry created every day.

Several long moments passed before Miss Brooke noticed her friend on the periphery. Miss Boswell's normally vivacious demeanor was wilted. Miss Brooke mentally frowned as she flapped her fan in Miss Boswell's direction. "Miss Boswell, please, come join me!"

Miss Brooke turned her charming smile on a member of her flock. "Mr. West, would you please make a spot for Miss Boswell? She is such charming company. I know we would both love to have her near."

West, whom Miss Boswell did not know, quickly swept her through the crowd to a place of honor at Miss Brooke's side. The chatter continued around them. In some ways, Miss Boswell thought, this was worse. Now she was standing in the middle of a circle of popularity while the conversation moved around her as if she did not exist. After what seemed like an eternity, Miss Brooke placed an ivory-gloved hand on Miss Boswell's arm.

"Do you mind if we depart, Miss Boswell?" Miss Brooke looked around and smiled conspiratorially at everyone. "I am afraid these shoes are going to be the death of me. Miss Boswell, we simply must acquire new pair from the cobbler before the next ball. Otherwise, I will simply be unable to dance at all!"

Miss Boswell nodded her acquiescence amid the objections and laughter. Several of the more determined gentlemen pressed Miss Brooke for dances at upcoming balls. She handled them all gracefully with a smile and a flutter of her fan. Finally, they were free of the throng. The man Miss Boswell did not know, Mr. West, had gone ahead to call for the coach.

"Mr. West, what a thoughtful gesture!" Miss Brooke seemed genuinely grateful. "I cannot tell you how delighted I am to have the carriage waiting. Such a delightful evening has left me weary."

The gentleman bowed. He was a tall man, dressed in a slightly plainer fashion, both in cut and color, than most of those present. With a charming smile, he gently captured Miss Brooke's hand and brushed his lips to it. Miss Boswell could not help but notice how powerful his hands were. "My pleasure, Miss Brooke."

"Please forgive my lack of manners." Miss Brooke gestured towards Miss Boswell with her fan. "Miss Boswell, may I present Mr. Donovan West. Mr. West, may I present Miss Brenda Boswell." She left her hand in Mr. West's for a second or two longer than was necessary before pulling away.

Mr. West took Miss Boswell's hand in turn. "Miss Boswell. Your servant."

Miss Boswell dropped into a polite curtsey. "Honored, Mr. West. Is this your first visit to Town?"

He nodded. "Indeed. I have only recently returned from my holdings in the Leeward Isles."

Miss Brooke smiled politely while Miss Boswell grew animated. "Truly? I have heard stories of the splendor and beauty of that part of the New World. The beaches are supposed to be as white as snow and the weather like the fairest summer we could ever imagine."

"In American colonies?" Miss Brooke asked curiously.

"Aye, specifically, the Caribbean." He turned his attention to Miss Boswell. "The islands are lovely. The water is an amazing blue, a color I thought existed nowhere else in nature until I saw Miss Brooke's eyes. But the weather is not as perfect as you may have heard. There are fierce storms, which flatten islands and disrupt shipping."

Miss Brooke blushed prettily while Miss Boswell continued the conversation. "Do you have the cold winters of England?"

"No, we do not." He smiled at Miss Brooke's blush as he answered Miss Boswell. "I admit I find the weather here uncomfortably chill."

"But it is the end of April, Mr. West. Spring is upon us and the weather has been unseasonably warm," Miss Boswell replied with a slight frown.

"Perchance that gives you some idea of the weather of the tropics." He offered Miss Brooke his arm, "May I escort you ladies to your coach?"

At Miss Brooke's nod, he led her to the waiting coach. West assisted Miss Brooke into the coach and stepped back as a footman helped Miss Boswell. Miss Brooke drew the curtains as Miss Boswell collapsed back into the seat, "I thought that would never end. The bit about the shoes was brilliant."

27

"Sometimes I fear I overuse that particular ruse," Miss Brooke confided. "London must think I have a horrible cobbler. You looked so withdrawn I could not imagine staying one second more."

Miss Boswell smiled sincerely at her friend. "You are a saint. I wish I had your tolerance for these things."

Miss Brooke shrugged delicately. "I remain glad you have enough tolerance to come with me at all! Imagine what sort of chaperone my family would burden me with, if not for you."

"Not to mention, I am on the prowl for a husband of my own," Miss Boswell reminded her friend gently.

"Certainly you are. And that gown looks simply dashing on you. The seamstress was right, raising your bodice two inches makes you look amazingly elegant."

"And helps hide my 'overabundance' of charm." Miss Boswell made a graphic gesture at her dainty chest so Miss Brooke had no trouble determining her sarcasm.

Miss Brooke covered a laugh with her fan. "So improper. But, yes, it does help draw attention away from the fact we both were not graced with…" Miss Brooke made a similar gesture as she groped for words.

"Nature was not kind to us." Miss Boswell cocked her head, pretending she was deep in thought. "I suppose I can add small breasts to my list of things to trade in when I complain to The Almighty. I already need to get rid of my robin-red hair, my infestation of freckles, and my unnaturally long limbs."

"So blasphemous! You are lovely."

"You are kind, Ali, but the truth is I do not attract men. I am not pretty like you."

"This is what your withdrawal at Covent Gardens was about?"

Miss Boswell nodded and looked at her hands. "I do not begrudge you anything. I wish you all the happiness in the world. But some days, I would like to be in your shoes."

Miss Brooke lifted her skirts to point at her shoes. "Here. Take them. They hurt."

"You are as mad as a March hare. You know what I mean."

Tucking her feet back under her skirts, Miss Brooke nodded. "I do. We have talked about this before. There is not much I can do except make you feel as welcome as possible. If you will simply try…"

"You have been saying that for three whole Seasons. I am trying. I am wearing the dress you wanted me to wear, I have changed my style, what more do you want?"

"Yes, and you look amazing. But there are two problems, my dear." Miss Brooke's voice was low and caring. "The first is Society remembers and holds on to its judgments. Time is required for them to forget the shy wallflower and see you as the lovely woman you are. Second, you did not engage anyone all night."

Miss Boswell's posture stiffened and she crossed her arms. "I conversed with several gentlemen tonight!"

"Yes, you did. And when you talked to Mr. West you were animated and beautiful. I am sure you left quite a good impression on him."

"I could have been a waltzing horse and he would not have noticed. He was noticeably smitten with you."

Miss Brooke smiled. "What a charming fancy. Still, I think you are being genuinely unfair to yourself. Expecting change after one outing is unreasonable."

Miss Boswell looked over at her friend, almost allowing herself to believe. Her voice was vulnerable and childlike. "Do you really think this could work?"

Miss Brooke leaned forward and took Miss Boswell's hand. "I do not think it will work. I know it will work! Unless every man in London is blind, deaf, and dumb, we will find the perfect husband for you."

"If you say so." Miss Boswell sounded skeptical. "Although, with my luck, we may have better success trying to court men who *are* blind, deaf, and dumb."

Miss Brooke rolled her eyes. The chatter turned to more pleasant things on the ride home.

CHAPTER III

Unceremoniously throwing open the door, Charmaine arrived at home. Wilhelm stopped his impatient pacing long enough to scowl at his employer. Throwing his hat and jacket on the seat of his chair, Charmaine gave his man a skeptical look. "I cannot help but notice my well-behaved servant is irritated. I am sure it is not at his lord."

"It is almost eight of the clock." Wilhelm spat back. He picked up Charmaine's jacket and inspected it before carefully hanging it over the back of the chair.

"So?"

Wilhelm's cheek twitched. "The Stantons' are picking you up at nine, my lord. You are attending a ball with them tonight? Remember?"

"Indeed. It slipped my mind. That means time is tight." Charmaine picked through a tray of fruit Wilhelm offered him.

"Yes, my lord. It is." Wilhelm gestured in the direction of the basin. "Go wash. You smell of horse. I have your clothing laid out."

Charmaine headed to the other room and started undressing. He was, he supposed, more than marginally dirty. "I was out riding with Farrington. We went to the races."

Wilhelm's voice came from the other room. "Win anything?"

"No. We did not gamble. Farrington seems upset."

"That seems to be epidemic in your group of friends," Wilhelm mocked.

"You are truly a terrible servant."

"When you can find another servant who will work for the promise of future pay, and help you handle your investments, I will worry about my attitude, my lord." He paused, but Charmaine only grunted in reply. Wilhelm continued, "What bothers Lord Farrington?"

"He did not say. Knowing him, he would stay silent even if his horse died under him." Charmaine considered the matter, "If I had to guess, I would say it was a woman."

"He was recently rejected by Miss Brooke. Do you wish to wear brown with silver braid or navy velvet with bobbin lace?"

"Navy. Someone rejected him? How do you know that and yet I do not?" Charmaine walked into the bedroom where Wilhelm was waiting with his clothing.

"Because I read the Society papers and you do not."

Charmaine tossed the towel on the bed and put on his smallclothes, "Why would anyone decline a proposal from Farrington? He would make a perfect husband."

Wilhelm shrugged and handed Charmaine a pair of tightly cut black knee breeches. Charmaine grimaced but put them on anyway. Wilhelm came over to tie his cravat. "You may be biased in the favor of your friend, my lord. Who knows the whims of a lady?"

"Well, whomever Miss Brooke is, she is a fool." Charmaine stepped forward to examine himself in the mirror. "Much like I feel in all this."

"Sit." Wilhelm pointed to a stool. He reached for the rouge pot and, forestalling Charmaine's objection, ordered, "No complaints."

Charmaine sat quietly through the makeup and application of the wig. Finally, Wilhelm stepped back and nodded in approval. Charmaine snorted, "Will I do?"

"Yes. You cut a sharp figure when I can force you into evening dress." Wilhelm handed him his engraved dragon's head cane and a large brimmed uncocked hat. "Although you would cut an even sharper figure if you let me put you in fashionable colors."

Ignoring the comment about his preference for dark shades, Charmaine gave the new hat a skeptical eyebrow. "What happened to my bicorn?"

"Nothing. This came into fashion at the end of last Season and is emerging into popularity now. Not so new that you will feel uncomfortable, but still avant-garde enough to be the cutting edge of fashion." Wilhelm's ladylove was apprenticed to a popular tailor in London. Her influence and assistance kept the country lord in style on their shoestring budget.

Wilhelm adapted to their reduced circumstances quicker than Charmaine believed possible. He could not imagine surviving poverty without him. Charmaine fiddled a bit with his hat and wig before heading towards the door. "Is there anything else I should know?"

Wilhelm considered. "Your mother sent another letter, which is essentially the same as the last three. She is running out of creative phrases for poverty and doom. Your father's health remains unchanged. There has been no news from the country or the New World. The price of grain is up, coal is down, and we remain within our meager budget. So, no, not really. Off with you, my lord."

"Yes, yes." Charmaine opened the door, oblivious to the heat rushing out into the drafty hallway. "I may be late. Do not wait up."

The Stantons' carriage was already waiting below. A pair of matched grays perfectly accented the blue and silver monstrosity they pulled. Charmaine's stark outfit looked out of place in such frippery. The inside of the carriage was empty, leaving Charmaine alone with his thoughts.

As the coach arrived in front of the Stantons' large residence and waited for its owners, Charmaine considered the past few days. The dinner party with Miss Linder had passed muster. For her age and inexperience, she had managed adequately. Charmaine remembered how Miss Linder scrutinized him. Her eyes had brimmed with a mix of hero-worship and terror. The memory of her gaze unsettled Charmaine.

Lady Stanton's entrance to the coach brought Charmaine out of his musings. As there was no room to stand, he nodded politely before he noticed her gown. "Lady Stanton. You are in prime looks tonight."

She beamed at him, caught off guard by his compliment. "Bless you, Lord Charmaine. Now, I have the confidence of a queen."

The dress required confidence. Her gown was made from a metallic silver silk embroidered with a darker silver thread. Her whole outfit had bits of clear crystal beads and what appeared to be silver metal woven into it. The panniers were so large they filled one entire bench. The style of the season was large wigs and Lady Stanton's was no exception. White curls spiraled above her head with silver wire braided throughout. It was ostentatious, yet somehow suited Lady Stanton perfectly.

Collins' outfit did not receive the same warm reception from Charmaine. Every detail glittered. His embossed shoe buckles were especially radiant. "You, my friend," Charmaine commented lackadaisically as Collins entered, "have become macaroni."

Collins sniffed disdainfully. "You, my friend, have become bilious with envy."

The absurd comment pulled Charmaine out of his worries. "I am caught, Collins. I apologize."

"Forgiven. It is hard to have friends who look this good."

Lady Stanton shook her head in amusement at the two of them. "You look prime yourself, Lord Charmaine."

"Not my fault, I assure you. My man, Wilhelm, has taken an interest in fashion since we arrived. I believe he thinks I will embarrass myself without him."

While Lady Stanton laughed prettily, Collins looked thoughtful. "Wilhelm? The foundling raised with Anderson?"

Charmaine nodded. "He came with me to the city last Season."

"I thought he wanted to be a steward, if he could not marry up." Collins frowned as he searched through old memories.

"He does. And he is. We, ah, need to get through this current period in our lives before I can have a staff, much less a steward."

There was a slight awkward pause before Lady Stanton launched into a recital of the current drama of the *ton*. Charmaine listened halfheartedly as he stared out the window. For the first time he could remember, he was grateful for Lady Stanton's nineteen to the dozen chatter. He was tired of conversations that revolved around two topics: his lack of money or his need for a wife.

Lady Stanton's gossip halted only because she exited the carriage. Collins smiled tolerantly as he extracted her and guided the group towards the door. Charmaine waited until his friend was announced— Edward Ambler Collins and Elizabeth Collins, Baron and Baroness Stanton—before approaching the queue to enter the ball.

The foyer was crowded with the brightly clad nobility of the *ton*. Charmaine handed his card over to a liveried manservant and promptly heard himself announced, "Robert Anderson, Viscount Charmaine."

Sudden murmurs filled the room. Charmaine strode deliberately through the crowd to stand in front of Collins. "What are they whispering about?"

Collins smirked as he lifted two glasses of champagne off of a tray. "Elizabeth does very thorough work. Mamas and their darling daughters are sizing up the latest prey brought before them."

Charmaine took the second glass of champagne and glowered at his flamboyant friend. "Reassuring, Collins."

Collins' smirk grew. "Not my intent. Have a good time, do no violence, and for the love of all that is holy, do not dance with any woman twice."

Discarding the full champagne glass, Charmaine prowled the large ballroom. He spied Farrington speaking with a tall woman in a heather gray gown. She had long limbs that seemed to go on forever and a captivating sparkle in her smile. As Charmaine advanced he noted with surprise that his taciturn friend was engrossed in the conversation. The stranger abruptly stopped speaking as he approached and folded in on herself.

"I apologize," Charmaine interjected, feeling suddenly awkward and intrusive. "I did not mean to interrupt."

The unknown woman bobbed her head and mumbled through an answer, "Oh, ah, there is no interruption."

Farrington clasped Charmaine's hand warmly. "Lord Charmaine, may I have the honor of presenting Miss Brenda Boswell. I made her acquaintance last Season. I can safely tell you she is a charming conversationalist."

Charmaine bowed to Miss Boswell. "Miss Boswell, from Farrington that is high praise indeed."

"Miss Boswell," Farrington continued his introductions, "may I present Robert Anderson, Viscount Charmaine."

Miss Boswell gave him a surprisingly low and graceful curtsey for her height. "I am delighted to meet a friend of Lord Farrington, Lord Charmaine."

"I doubt that," Charmaine countered with what he hoped was a soothing smile, "you will soon learn friends of Farrington are troublemakers of the worst sort."

"Not at all!" Powdered curls shook vigorously in objection. "If you are a friend of Lord Farrington then you must be upstanding indeed."

"What lies have you been telling this poor woman about us, Farrington? Upstanding? Next she will be calling us honorable." Charmaine directed his smile at Miss Boswell, trying to include her into the joke. She replied with a small smile of her own.

"Leave the girl her delusions, Charmaine."

"They are not delusions," Miss Boswell objected. "Lord Farrington, you *are* honorable and upstanding. I know this."

Both Charmaine and Farrington bowed their heads in acquiescence at her firm statement. Charmaine spoke, "You are, certainly, correct. Farrington is the highest order of man. His friends are only poor imitations of such perfection."

Farrington's eyes narrowed slightly at his friend. "I am afraid I must escape before the two of you continue on this path and I further become the object of your mirth." He turned his attention to the lady in front of them. "May I have your dance card, madam?"

With a slight blush, Miss Boswell handed it over. After Farrington signed it, Charmaine took the card from his friend and signed as well. "I hope you do not mind?"

"Not at all, Lord Charmaine. I am delighted." She took her card back with a smile.

Farrington bowed to her again. "Would you excuse us, Miss Boswell? I am afraid I have some unsavory things to say to my friend about his portrayal of my character in front of such a lady."

Miss Boswell beamed at them both. "I will see you both anon."

Farrington smiled slightly as Miss Boswell departed, "I enjoy Miss Boswell. I wish her nothing but the best."

Charmaine cocked an eyebrow. "You are pursuing her?"

"I am not fond of her in a romantic sense, if that is your question. I find her to be a remarkable woman who deserves better than the *ton* gives her. It would be," Farrington paused to consider his phrasing, "impolitic for me to court her."

Charmaine nodded, choosing not to press the issue. They stood in comfortable silence before a question fluttered across Charmaine's mind.

"Do you know Miss Linder? Young girl, first Season?"

Farrington shook his head no. "Only in passing. I would not think you interested in one so young."

"In truth, her youth does not appeal. Her fortune does."

Thick, dark eyebrows turned downward in a frown. "How unlike you, Charmaine."

"Yes." Charmaine fought to keep the bitterness out of his voice. "How unlike me."

Silence stretched between the two friends before Farrington gestured to the card room. "Come, let us await Miss Boswell's dance at cards."

"I do not gamble, Farrington."

"The man I know also does not throw away his ideals and marry for money."

"Reality is a harsh mistress."

"I understand, Charmaine. More than you know." Their eyes locked and a serious current passed between them. For half a second, Charmaine thought Farrington was going to disclose what was bothering him. The moment passed, although Farrington's distress was still visible in the wrinkles around his eyes. "Come play cards with me."

Charmaine nodded, understanding the request was the closest thing to an explanation he would get. Wilhelm may have been correct about Farrington and this Miss Brooke. The Season was progressing unsatisfactorily, at least as far as women were concerned.

CHAPTER IV

Miss Brooke watched Viscount Charmaine twirl Miss Boswell on the dance floor. Miss Boswell's smile split her face as they hopped and bobbed through the complicated steps of the quadrille. More than once, Lord Charmaine lost his place in the dance and Miss Boswell had to rescue him with laughter-filled instruction. Miss Brooke smiled at how lovely her friend looked and sincerely hoped she was not the only one noticing. Miss Boswell deserved more attention than she was getting.

Miss Brooke's examination of the room halted when she noticed how close Mr. West stood next to her. She automatically accepted the champagne he handed her. It was her fourth or fifth glass—she had lost count—and she knew she should slow down. Yet, for some reason, she took the delicate stemware anyway. Normally, Miss Brooke drank lemonade, but when Mr. West proposed champagne she readily accepted. She was consciously suppressing the knowledge that she was drinking to escape.

Farrington was present and as handsome as ever. He looked remarkably dashing tonight in cornflower blue silk heavily embellished with cream lace. His outfit would be improved if she were on his arm, Miss Brooke regretted. Yet now Farrington and his friend, Lord Charmaine, ignored her. She was Farrington's past, not his future. Miss Brooke took a steadying drink of her champagne and turned her attention back to Mr. West.

"Careful there, sweetness. Champagne should be sipped, not guzzled." West teased with a playful smile.

"Tut, tut. I know what I am doing." She smiled at him coyly. "Sometimes even champagne needs to be guzzled."

His dark eyes widened in an approving smile. He tapped his glass to hers in a toast, "To guzzling."

She giggled emptily, "To guzzling."

As they placed their empty glasses on a footman's tray, Miss Brooke stared petulantly at Farrington's dance partner. Was he enjoying the woman's company, or merely being the consummate gentleman she adored? Her own dance card was normally overflowing, but she was not in the mood to dance. So far, her claims of being under the weather kept her off the floor. Mr. West was so kind as to keep her company. She looked at the tall tan man next to her and saw a shadow of someone else. "I do not want to watch the dancing anymore."

He nodded. "Then let us not watch the dancing anymore. Shall we walk in the gardens?"

Miss Brooke shook her head vigorously. A carefully glued and powdered curl fell loose. She was too taken with drink to notice. "It is not proper for a lady to wander through the gardens with an unrelated escort."

"What happened to the bold lady who guzzles champagne?"

"You are charming, Mr. West, but my answer remains no. Some cool air does sound lovely, however. It is hot in here!" Miss Brooke felt flushed and a tad reckless. It *would* be lovely to walk in the gardens with Mr. West. The air would be so delightfully cool outside after the heat of the candles. With a sigh, Miss Brooke recalled that horrible scene last Season when an heiress had taken a garden walk with the wrong gentleman. Risking her impeccable reputation for a moment's worth of fresh air was foolish.

"Miss Brooke?" Mr. West looked at her with a quizzical expression.

"I apologize, would you repeat your statement?" Miss Brooke smiled charmingly at him while wondering about the stability of the room. She decided she was finished with champagne.

"I asked you to call me Donovan, if you would not mind."

"Of course, Donovan. You have been so kind." Miss Brooke put her hand on his arm and leaned on him slightly. Changing angles removed Farrington from her view.

"Perhaps a brief walk. This ballroom is quite stuffy." And *Farrington is quite handsome,* Miss Brooke added internally.

Mr. West nodded and steered her through the crowd. Miss Brooke noticed his direction and stopped short. "Not the gardens. Nowhere improper."

"Would you like a tour of the portrait hall? The upper levels should be much cooler."

Miss Brooke scrunched her face as she looked for another objection, "I would not want to intrude on the family."

"The gallery is public and well-lit. The family is justifiably proud of their old Masters," West said.

"Yes, but—I should at least acquire Miss Boswell for company?"

Mr. West smiled at her. "This, from the lady who guzzles champagne?"

"Ha, yes." Miss Brooke gave in to his charm, "If anything looks too private, we will leave."

"Certainly. This is not a clandestine mission, rather a quiet respite." Mr. West guided her through the crowd and up the main staircase.

≈♦≈

Miss Boswell clung to Lord Charmaine as he swung her around in a country dance. She was ecstatic. It was her third dance of the night, more than the past two balls put together! Miss Boswell knew better than to assume either Charmaine or Farrington was interested in her but, for once, she was not standing on the wall watching the dancing. She was one of the dancers.

She hid a slight frown as an elaborately dressed gentleman in silver escorted a lovely young woman in cornflower silk towards them. The music stopped, but Miss Boswell was still holding on to the whirlwind of dancing. Her companion bowed slightly the newcomers. "Miss Boswell, this is Collins, Baron Stanton and The

Honorable Miss Rebecca Linder. Collins here is a childhood friend of mine."

Miss Boswell curtsied deeply in response. Collins smiled at her. "Miss Boswell, your dress is lovely. Such a daring shade of marigold makes your eyes glow like warm amber." Unused to such compliments, all Miss Boswell could do was blush. Collins continued, "I do not suppose you would do me the honor of a dance?"

"But, sir," Miss Boswell stammered, "we have not been properly introduced. I do not know you."

"I know him," Charmaine interjected, "and Farrington knows me. By proxy, it is as if you are childhood friends."

Miss Boswell was swayed by his smile but more by the prospect of another dance. "And what of you, Lord Charmaine? Shall I leave you without a partner?" For some reason Miss Boswell did not comprehend Lord Stanton gave her a wink of approval.

The young woman in pale blue spoke up, "I would not mind dancing with such a fine gentleman as Lord Charmaine."

Charmaine bowed to her. "Then I am at your disposal, Miss Linder. I suppose this dance suits our needs?"

The four of them took to the dance floor. Collins smiled at the woman across from him. Despite rumors of her gracelessness, she handled the country dances with ease. When the dance brought them together for a moment Collins smiled at her, "Well done."

"Pray pardon?" Miss Boswell asked, confused.

"The way you excused yourself from Lord Charmaine and left the perfect opening for Miss Linder. I could not have planned it better." He took her hand as they twirled around another couple.

"Ta." Conversation was hard as they weaved through partners. "I must admit I did not plan it as such. Would it not be rude to abandon him?"

Collins laughed. "As the woman, that is your job. To run away and leave the man chasing—a game we have perfected here in our painted costumes and pretty Palaces."

Miss Boswell had time to consider her reply as the line of dancers separated them. "I hope there is more to life than that, Lord Stanton. Then again, I am clearly not skilled at courtship."

"You sound like Lord Charmaine." They spun to the left, and back to the right, before he could continue. "And I am uncertain why you say you are poor at courtship. You shine tonight."

"You are kind."

"I am not. I am a ruthless, backstabbing gossip dancing with the most vivacious woman on the floor. Except for my wife, certainly."

Miss Boswell was at a loss for words. When the dance ended he escorted her off the floor, but she stayed silent. He cocked an eyebrow at her and reached for two glasses of champagne on a footman's tray. "Did you lose your tongue?"

"Oh, no, my lord." She took the champagne with a small smile. "Your kindness simply leaves me at a loss for words."

Collins frowned at her. "I clearly stated I was not being kind. Why do you not believe me?"

"I am not lovely." It was a statement said without self-pity or bitterness.

"Perhaps not." Collins looked her over intently. Miss Boswell blushed. She had never felt so inspected in her life. "But you are far from an embarrassment. Your freckles come out through powder, your smile is lopsided, and you are much too tall. But your manner is quite charming. You possess a quiet warmth that is pleasant to be around, a smile that is inviting, and a laugh that welcomes others to enjoy merriment with you. I stand by my statement. You are one of the most radiant women here."

Miss Boswell was bright red. Speaking was impossible.

"It seems to me, Miss Boswell, you should stop dreaming of being what others want and try being yourself. I think you will find being radiant is quite a bit more fun than being beautiful." He took her unresisting hand and kissed it. Miss Boswell stood there and stared at him. With a bow, Collins turned and walked towards what could only be his counterpart in a wide silver gown.

Miss Boswell was at a complete loss of what to do with herself. She finished her champagne and went in search of the washroom. A cool compress on the back of her neck helped her skin change from bright scarlet to its usual pale coloring. Several glasses of lemonade later she could almost accept a fancy gentleman called her the most radiant woman on the dance floor. Still not daring to believe, Miss Boswell sought out her closest friend.

Yet, no matter how hard she looked, Miss Boswell could not find Miss Brooke. Their normal crowd mentioned that Miss Brooke was sitting out the dancing. Miss Boswell searched the card room, the washroom, and anywhere else she could think of. She checked with the footmen, who reported their carriage was still in the stables. Miss Brooke had to be somewhere at the ball.

Charmaine was maneuvered into dancing with Miss Linder. She was not a bad dancer, he supposed. She was more interested in making sure her footwork was correct than enjoying the dance. Charmaine once again tried to picture her as a wife and was left with an image of a child doing exactly what she was told. He knew he was not being fair to her—Lord knows, he had physically enjoyed women when he was her age—but he could not help his reaction. Their dance took place in almost complete silence. Charmaine walked the young woman off the dance floor to her waiting mother.

"Lord Charmaine. Thank you so much for gracing my daughter with a dance."

Charmaine forced himself to smile at the gaudily dressed woman. "Dancing with Miss Linder is a pleasure. I am honored you allowed me such an opportunity." Watching Lady Vassler prepare for another sally, he attempted to retreat. "However, my dance card beckons me to my next partner. Perchance I will see you anon?"

Miss Linder nodded gracefully. "I would like, my lord. Mayhap you will call on us on the morrow?"

Drat, thought Charmaine. "I would be absolutely honored, Miss Linder." He bowed deeply. "By your leave?"

Charmaine did not wait for an answer from either woman before departing. The fake smile stayed plastered on Charmaine's face until he was well clear of the two women. His racing mind needed a break, a quiet place without the dangers of the ballroom. Privacy was unlikely in such a crowded event. The gardens were filled with couples looking for dark alcoves and Charmaine had no desire to stumble across lovers.

He had a vague memory of a billiards room on the third floor that he and Farrington had fled to at some picnic or garden party last Season. At a ball, it would likely be empty.

He was correct. He did startle the occasional servant, but the flippant life of the *ton* was safely ensconced below. Charmaine found the library and sat in the leather chair behind the desk for some time. There was no reason for his reaction to Miss Linder. She was a fine girl, from a fine family, with a very fine fortune. She had done nothing wrong, nor even done anything to upset him, and yet after only two encounters he was already wildly bored. The thought of years with her made his skin crawl.

He recalled the conversation with Farrington. Could he give up what he believed for money? The family still had assets. He could break the entailment and sell off the estates. Yet, with the recent credit collapse in New England the market was flooded with such properties. He'd be lucky to get a third of the value. Marriage was the safest.

Restlessness overcame him and he began pacing the hallways. His father had inherited the Donahue title when it was nothing but a decrepit shell of the ancestral home surrounded by overworked tenant farms. The family soon dripped with both riches and power. Within a year of coming into control of the family fortune, Charmaine stood to piss away his father's success. He shook his head in disgust. These were his poor investment decisions and it was up to him to shoulder the consequences. Charmaine did not know how to stop blaming Miss Linder for being the woman he would marry for money.

Mr. West kept up a light stream of conversation as he escorted Miss Brooke through elaborately decorated hallways. They poked their heads into the library and ended their tour of the house in a sitting room on the third floor without finding the portrait hall.

"Here is our place for air, Miss Brooke. I apologize for the wild goose chase." West escorted her to a wooden-framed chaise and offered her a seat next to him. Attempting to curtsy and sit at the same time, Miss Brooke stumbled and almost spilled over his lap.

Blushing, Miss Brooke quickly righted herself. "It is of no moment. I apologize myself. I seem to be rather ungraceful tonight."

West shifted his weight forward with an amused smile. She again thought he was too close but pushed it from her mind. "Quite acceptable. I am with drink, too. Champagne is for guzzling, remember?"

"Perchance." Her blush spread. "But it is not ladylike to be foxed."

He leaned in even closer. "I find it very ladylike. I find you ladylike."

His breath was warm on her ear, sending shivers down her spine. Miss Brooke startled as he cupped her delicate chin and brought his mouth down hard on hers. She pulled back quickly and looked at him in shock. "What are you doing?"

"Kissing you, Miss Brooke. A woman like you deserves kisses. The way you have been leaning on me, the way you look at me, you beg for my kiss with everything you do."

Miss Brooke scooted away. The arm of the chaise dug into her back. "Not true, Mr. West. This is not proper."

"Proper, sweet? We are upstairs on the other side of a closed door. There is nothing proper about us being here. And since we are already improper, what is the harm of a little kiss?" He pressed his mouth on hers again, this time jamming his tongue between her lips. She pushed hard against him until she was able to squirm away once more.

"No. Leave me be." Miss Brooke rose unsteadily and started walking towards the door.

West interposed himself in front of the door and flicked the lock. He towered above her, halting her progress. Trying to keep space between them Miss Brooke retreated. He moved forward, slowly, methodically, until Miss Brooke's shoulders were pressed against the slick wallpaper. His meaty hands rested on the wall on each side of her shoulders.

"But, sweetling, you are like fine champagne." He lifted her jaw again. She shook her head, trying to free her chin, but he paid her no mind. "I was going to sip you slowly, but you convinced me otherwise. Sometimes champagne needs to be guzzled."

She again shook her head no and attempted to slip under his arm to freedom. One large hand on her shoulder stopped her easily. A calloused finger traced the front of her throat. "Please stop," she whispered.

"Stop what, sweet?" He moved his hand inside her bodice and found her nipple. Rolling it between two fingers, he repeated his question. "Stop this?" He pulled aside her *fichu* and lifted her breasts so that they jutted out over the top of her chemise. The back of his hand rubbed across both her nipples.

West's smile grew as he let the rough hair on the back of his hands scratch across her breasts. "Stop this?"

"Yes, please. All of it." Miss Brooke was almost crying, still struggling against him. Miss Brooke pushed against him with all her might, but he remained firmly against her. His touch felt rough and gross. She had never felt so helpless in all her life. All she could do was tuck her skirts tightly around her legs and struggle against his huge frame, but there was no escape from his harsh caress on her nipples. A scream started in her throat and died when she realized that she would be bound to this wretched thing forever if anyone saw. The stomacher of her new dress ripped as he dug for more of her breast. Glass beads scattered all over the floor.

West chuckled slightly as he mumbled something incoherent into the nape of her neck. He raised his mouth back onto hers and forced his tongue passed her lips. Miss Brooke bit down as hard as she could on the invading object and kicked out at his shins. He jerked back in pain. Miss Brooke made a mad dash for the door. A vase fell with a crash as she rushed. She had not taken more than two steps before he grabbed her shoulder and flung her back against the wall.

"You dumb fucking whore." He roared and spat blood out of his mouth. West advanced upon her with malice in his grimace. Miss Brooke straightened herself and looked directly into his eyes. West smiled meanly and raised his open hand his chest and up above his opposite ear. She stared defiantly at his slow, deliberate action. With a mighty backhand, he wiped the dignity off her face and she let out an involuntary cry.

The door burst open.

When Charmaine heard a feminine shriek down the hallway he sprinted to a locked door and kicked it in. The wood splintered and shattered at the latch. He burst into the room prepared for a fight. Charmaine expected to find an abused maid, so he was momentarily shocked at the pile of peach silk lying on the floor. Her panniers and disheveled skirts hid the lady from view. Charmaine's attention snapped to the tall man in rather plain clothing standing above her. Charmaine recognized the man as a minor Whig in the House of Commons but lacked knowledge of his name. Regardless, West could have been Prince George himself and it would not have stopped Charmaine's wrath.

The man turned as Charmaine approached. "Get out," West spat, a long arm pointing Charmaine towards the door.

Charmaine's eyes narrowed in response. "I shall leave with the lady or not at all."

"You are interfering. Leave now or prepare to pay for the insult."

Charmaine rushed forward and punched the taller man in the jaw. He followed his assault with a quick, hard jab to the gut. The man dropped like a stone. A slight moan from the woman on the floor tore Charmaine from his moment of masculine triumph.

The woman was wedged in the corner of the room with her head at an odd angle. Charmaine felt a moment of panic before she moved slightly and raised her hand to her jaw. He rushed towards her and knelt in the large mass of skirts. Charmaine tentatively reached down to assist.

"My lady," Charmaine coaxed softly, "Are you injured?"

She tried to nod and then winced. The muscles in her cheek tightened as she bit lightly down to test her swelling jaw. "Hurts a bit. But I think I am well."

A rustle behind them demanded Charmaine's attention. "Your pardon for a moment." Without rising from his knees Charmaine turned around to look at the other man. West uncurled himself and was slowly rising to a standing position. Charmaine addressed him curtly, "You will leave now. I will see you at dawn."

A weak objection came from the female voice on the floor in front of him, "No. No. Please no."

Without turning his attention from the other man, Charmaine voiced his confusion. "Why?"

"There must be no scandal. Please," Miss Brooke whispered.

The weakness in her breathy and strained voice convinced Charmaine to respect the lady's wishes. If nothing else, he could always call the cur out tomorrow. "The lady pleads for discretion. You, cretin, will leave now. I suggest you take an extended holiday from Britain. If I so much as see you on the same street as," Charmaine's threatening delivery faltered as he realized he did not know the name of the woman on the floor, "this gentlewoman, I will send you straight to the Devil."

The other man straightened and made the most dignified exit he could. Charmaine fought the urge to rush after him and give the man the full strapping he so richly deserved. Instead he turned his attention back to the woman on the floor. She was trying to pull her stays up and hold the ripped fabric of her bodice together, but each movement created small gasps of pain.

There was a large purple bruise spreading across her cheek. Her ripped dress exposed a good portion of her undergarments. The room was quiet except for her ragged breathing. Time stretched. He knew he should talk to her but Charmaine had no idea what to say.

"I am Robert Anderson, Viscount Charmaine."

"Miss Brooke," she paused, automatically returning the greeting. A wry smile tried to emerge. "Under the circumstances, I suppose my Christian name applies. I am Alison." Any forced cheer faded as she took in the broken door. "Thank you for saving me."

It was his turn to nod. "I wish you would let me shoot that worthless cur."

She smiled weakly at his vehemence as she gently shook her head no. "I am truly sorry to stop you. The scandal must be avoided.

If we are the only ones who know then the situation can vanish. If you duel, all of Society knows why."

"That seems like a poor reason for me not to shoot him." His voice was disapproving. "Do you have a chaperone or a parent present?"

Miss Brooke looked as if she would cry. "I know. It is my fault. I should not have gone off alone."

"Stop that. What foolishness. This is not your fault."

A tear leaked out. "But I was drinking…"

"We can go through recriminations of your guilt later. Right now, you must believe me when I say none of this is your fault. He did this, not you. Now, tell me whom I can fetch to get you out of here." He frowned at her again. "You are a defensive little thing."

"What? I am not."

Now he smiled. "Yes, you are. Who should I fetch?"

"Oh, Lord, I know not. My father is in the country for several weeks, I suppose Miss Boswell."

"Miss Boswell?"

"She has a marigold dress on with cream…"

"Yes. We danced earlier." Charmaine started to rise. Miss Brooke's words stopped him.

"Do you have to fetch anyone? If you get me on my feet and we can act like nothing happened. I think I can manage."

He looked at her ruined dress and the rapidly growing bruise on her face. Charmaine was amazed she could talk at all. There were handprints on her shoulders, each finger clearly visible. "I find that unlikely."

"Please?"

Charmaine nodded assent, it was, after all, her choice. He leaned forward and put her arms around his shoulders. He cradled her neck carefully as he raised her up, as he still did not like the angle it was at when he first found her on the floor. She smiled gratefully into his eyes.

The door squeaked open.

When she could not find her friend, Miss Boswell decided she had a catastrophe on her hands. Miss Brooke was absolutely impossible to lose. She was a splash in every room she was in and everyone remembered her passing. How could Miss Brooke vanish? Hoping she was not about to make a fool of herself, Miss Boswell sought out the Duchess of Castlemire. Her grace was a Lady Patroness of Almack's. She knew everything about everyone.

Miss Boswell approached her timidly and curtsied deeply as the mighty, wrinkled gaze fell upon her. The duchess was an imposing figure even the most carefree of the *ton* took seriously. "Well, girl, what do you want?"

"Um, I, ah," Miss Boswell cleared her throat and started over. "Have you seen Miss Brooke, Your Grace?"

With a glance at the tiny watch on her sparkling chatelaine, the matriarch frowned. "Not in the last hour. Gossip has her with Mr. West."

Rather than meeting the fierce, disapproving gaze, Miss Boswell stared intently at the floor. "I cannot find her."

"Then you have not looked. Perchance she left."

"I checked, your Grace. Our carriage is still here. And I looked everywhere. I really did. I am sorry, but I…"

"You what, child?" the Duchess barked. Miss Boswell felt like a mouse in front of a hawk. The Duchess had a beak-like nose that forbid any other comparison. "Waste not my time."

Miss Boswell curtsied again. "I lost my friend and I am worried. It is not like Miss Brooke to go off alone."

The towering figure pursed her lips together. "You have something there. Girl knows what is proper and what is not. Very few of the rest of you do."

"Yes, your Grace."

"Do not be cheeky with me. Away with you."

Miss Boswell curtseyed deeply and backed away from the imposing presence of the Duchess. Duchess Castlemire beckoned over a servant. People rushed off in all directions and then trickled back to the duchess. Finally, a collection of matrons clustered in conversation. Miss Boswell risked drifting close in the hopes of eavesdropping. The duchess' penetrating gaze enveloped Miss

Boswell. "Girl, you come with us. Your Miss Brooke has found herself a spot of trouble."

A thousand questions popped into Miss Boswell's mind but the duchess halted any further conversation. "Not another peep out of you, girl. Follow along and keep out of the way. If you cannot comply, stay here."

Miss Boswell nodded mutely and followed four older women as they headed up the back staircase and towards the rear of the estate. They stopped in front of a white door on the third floor. The door, while mostly closed, was hanging off its hinges and the latch area was shattered. A boot print marred the door's paint. The women took it all in. After a moment, the platoon of matrons looked at each other and, as if by some communication Miss Boswell could not hear, decided to enter. The Duchess walked in first.

The first thing Miss Boswell noticed was the crystal beading on the floor. She remembered how delighted Miss Brooke was when the dress came back from Madame Bontecous. Miss Brooke modeled it in both the afternoon sunlight and in candlelight to share the wonderful sparkle of the beads to her friend. Now those beads were scattered all over the floor, crunching under the curved heels of the older women.

A pair of broad, navy-clad shoulders hid Miss Brooke from view. Miss Boswell could not tell who was kneeling on her friend's peach skirts. Whoever it was gently cradled Miss Brooke's head. Her arms were wrapped around his shoulders. Miss Boswell could not believe her eyes. The couple on the floor froze as the door opened.

"Lord Charmaine." The duchess's voice was coldly disapproving, as if she had caught a child stealing sweets.

Charmaine turned his head to look at the conglomeration of woman in the doorway, "Your Grace."

Miss Boswell shivered at his voice. It was flat and full of violence.

The duchess looked over her shoulder at the other women present. "Leave us."

They nodded and bustled out of the room, filled with the latest gossip. Miss Boswell scowled at how gleeful some of them looked at being the first to know about such a scandal. The duchess turned her intimidating gaze on Miss Boswell. "You, too."

Miss Boswell considered objecting, but thought better of it. She could not, however, abandon her friend. "Ali?"

"I, yes." Miss Brooke's voice sounded weak, shaky. "I am fine, Brenda. Verily, I, yes…" Charmaine returned his attention back to the woman in his arms.

Duchess Castlemire's glare increased. Miss Boswell curtsied deeply in a wave of dark gray silk and beat a hasty retreat. She sincerely hoped that involving the duchess was correct. All of this was so unlike Miss Brooke. The last thing Miss Boswell expected was to find her in the arms of a man they only met recently. More bizarrely, why would they be coupling on the floor of a sitting room? Answers would come. Miss Boswell waited and fretted, then waited some more.

❧◆❧

Inside the room, the duchess shut the door the best she could. Her step was quiet as she moved to a seat. "Lord Charmaine, explain yourself."

There was a long pause. The only sound was Miss Brooke crying into Charmaine's chest.

"No."

The duchess blinked. "No?"

"I have nothing to say on this matter. I believe I was clear." Charmaine's voice was firm and steady.

"Young man, are you aware of who I am?" The duchess sounded extremely taken aback.

"Yes, Your Grace. You may socially ruin me, send me running to the country in disgrace, or whatever other horrors I cannot even imagine, but I will still have nothing to say."

There was a long moment of silence before Miss Brooke spoke. "He saved me, your Grace. That thing tried to, tried to, tried to," she took a shaky breath and skipped over the words, "but Lord Charmaine saved me."

"I believe that. I knew Ambler and Amelia in their courtship."

"My parents," Charmaine whispered quietly to Miss Brooke.

The duchess nodded. "The idea of their son being the sort of scrub to destroy a woman's dress while at a ball is unthinkable. The beads on the floor told me everything I needed to know. Now, tell me the rest of the story."

"That is Miss Brooke's choice." Charmaine turned his attention to the woman in his arms. "May I move you to the chaise?"

Miss Brooke nodded and he lifted her with great care. Her disheveled hair fell away from her face. Duchess Castlemire gasped when she sighted the rapidly spreading bruise. The Duchess's cold demeanor melted away. "Dear child, tell me what happened."

Miss Brooke tried to start the story several times and finally broke down in tears. Charmaine walked to the other side of the room to give the two women space. He picked up a bead off the floor and examined it. In retrospect, standing up to the duchess was bluster. He needed Court connections to gain beneficial trade contracts. More so, his work in the House of Lords gave him purpose.

Charmaine flexed his fist as he replayed the events in his mind. Certainly, this was not how he intended to spend his first ball of the Season but, for some reason, he felt inordinately proud of himself. Nothing had gone right, recently. His investments were failing, his father was dying, and his mother was oft in tears. For the first time in however many months, he felt like the sun had come up. If only Miss Brooke would let him shoot the wretch, then the evening would be perfect.

Charmaine frowned at himself. He felt guilty about feeling so grand after what happened to Miss Brooke. After a moment's consideration, he decided to be pragmatic. He had done all he could and would punish the wicked if allowed. The threat was over. Feeling elated was acceptable. Besides, he reminded himself wryly, the events of the evening were not complete. He was still in a room with one of the most powerful women in London while gossip ran rampant down below. Yes, he thought, it was best to enjoy this moment for he was unlikely to enjoy the repercussions. Unless it meant killing that man. He would enjoy that.

The duchess interrupted his thoughts. "Lord Charmaine. Tell me what happened. All Miss Brooke will do is cry."

Charmaine walked back over to the two women. Beads crunched under his every step. "I do not know the whole story. I had come upstairs to get some air. While I was pacing I heard a struggle inside this room. I entered, found Miss Brooke on the floor with some creature standing over her, and dispatched him. I was checking on her when you walked in."

"Did he...?" The older woman made a graphic gesture towards her crotch.

Charmaine glanced at Miss Brooke before answering. "That did appear to be his intent, but I do not believe he was successful." Miss Brooke nodded in agreement, her lips pressed tightly together. Her tears slowed and her formal composure wrapped around her like armor.

The duchess's large nose quivered in outrage and anger. "Still crime enough. Who is the man in question?"

Charmaine shrugged. "A dead one, if Miss Brooke will allow it."

"A good reply, but not an answer to my question."

"His name is unknown to me."

"Miss Brooke?" the duchess asked.

"I," Miss Brooke took a deep breath and shut her eyes for a moment. Both Charmaine and the Duchess waited as she struggled to compose herself. With another deep breath she continued, "Your Grace, my head is spinning. I feel like giving out information means I have made choices before I intend to."

"You will tell me." The duchess commanded.

"When I am ready?"

"When you are ready." The duchess rose, gathering her voluminous skirts around her. "You will, additionally, join me for tea on Thursday."

Miss Brooke inclined her body forward in an attempt at a seated curtsey. "I am honored. Thank you."

"Hmph." The duchess started to head towards the door. "Lord Charmaine, let us be off."

Charmaine frowned, "Allow me a moment alone with the lady, Your Grace? I," he stumbled on his words, "do not wish to see this situation go unresolved."

"Hmph." Duchess Castlemire gestured at a female staff member who was quietly arranging pieces of the broken vase in the far corner. "Stay with them. And be quick, boy. I cannot have my maid chaperone you all night."

Looking at the mess of Miss Brooke's dress and the shattered beads everywhere, Charmaine swallowed his reply. There was no need to hold to formal propriety when the lady's skirts were already lifted. Ignoring his silent commentary, the Duchess swept out of the room and, once in the hallway, took Miss Boswell downstairs with her.

Charmaine ignored their new chaperone as he waited for Miss Brooke finished adjusting her dress. Finally, he looked at her. "Now what?"

"We return to the ball?" She smiled at him, drawing her courage and dignity around her once more. She paid the maid no more notice than he did. "I suppose I should be glad you come with a sterling reputation. The duchess was exceptionally kind."

"I did not find her exceptionally kind. Nor was I aware I had a reputation for not ravishing women."

"She invited me to tea. She is a Patroness of Almack's and the Duchess of Castlemire, for goodness sakes. She is protecting me from scandal. Society cannot shun someone she accepts."

"I suppose that is kind." Charmaine reluctantly agreed. "However, all of this really depends on how we get you out of this room."

"I will walk out like it is my own ballroom."

"Pray tell how that will occur, considering your dress is in tatters and half of your face is purple?"

Miss Brooke frowned at him. "I am not sure that I like you."

"In addition, I suspect you cannot yet stand."

"Certainly, I can stand." Miss Brooke was indignant. She stood in a huff and promptly sat back down.

Charmaine's brow drew together at her expression of pain. "I want to get you out of here and have a doctor look you over." His expression softened at her suddenly worried look. "I am sure you are fine. Prudence requires us to be certain."

"I suppose." The edge faded from her voice as she absently touched her jaw again. His concern cut through her defenses. "But first things first, how do you suggest I get out of here?"

"I will carry you."

"With my dress in tatters and a purple face?" She mimicked back at him.

He smiled at her. Her spirit after such an ordeal was remarkable. "Your dress will stay on because I will be carrying you. Your bruised face will be resting on my shoulder. Painful, yes, but at least it will not be visible. And, as for all those people, I am sure the entire ballroom downstairs knows something happened here."

"How? Only Brenda and Her Grace know we are here."

Charmaine frowned. "I am sorry, Miss Brooke, but that is not true. The Duchess' cronies were with her when she first entered the room."

Miss Brooke paled. "Oh, dear God." Her hands clenched and she looked like she might faint.

"I thought you knew."

She shook her head as her mouth made a silent no.

"What is done is done. Let me get you out of here." Charmaine moved towards her.

"You do not understand, I am ruined! Her Grace could keep scandal quiet but if her friends know they are already downstairs gossiping!" She looked close to hysterics. Charmaine was surprised they had not come sooner. If he had his jaw nearly broken, part of his clothing ripped off, and then conversed with one of the most powerful women in London, he would have lost control much earlier.

"Shush, now." Charmaine's voice was soft and reassuring as he sat next to her. "I may not understand, but this is not the time for us to determine what I do or do not know. We need to stay focused on the current problem."

Miss Brooke nodded, composing herself. The quick control of her emotions impressed Charmaine. "While your solution has a certain flare for the dramatic, I much prefer acquiring a cloak and leaving through the servant's entrance. I can take a hack and no one will even know I have left."

"You think running off into the night is less scandalous?"

"Then being carried through a ballroom?" Miss Brooke asked incredulously.

"You could have swooned, fainted, or any of a half dozen other things. At least it does not make it look like you are hiding anything or ashamed to show your face."

Miss Brooke considered. "You may have a point. If we were caught doing something unspeakable, we would not leave together through the main ballroom."

Charmaine shrugged. "I would so assume. I should warn you I am far from the master of social intrigue."

"Hm." Miss Brooke's eyebrows squinted together in thought, "We can do it your way. I fainted and, you are taking me to my carriage. If you use the side stairs we will only have to face the foyer. There will be enough people present to serve the purpose of being bold."

"I can do that." He paused for a moment. "Miss Brooke, have you considered the benefits of being honest? Name your accuser and explain what happened? Lady Castlemire believes you. The Duchess' approval would sway most of the *ton*."

"I think you want me to agree to your duel."

"While I would enjoy meeting that creature at dawn, my suggestion is, in and of itself, a serious one."

Miss Brooke searched for words for a long moment. When she answered, her voice was somber. "Lord Charmaine, our world is not kind to women who are ravaged. Gossip would say I led Mr. West on, and that I encouraged his advances by being alone with him. At best, Society would pressure West to marry me for his actions. At worst, it would blame me for the transgression and shun me. I want neither of those things."

"As long as you have considered it." Noting the villain's name, Charmaine stood and reached to scoop her up. Duchess Castlemire's unobtrusive maid stepped forward and cleared her throat. Charmaine gathered Miss Brooke in his arms and lifted her anyway. He glared over at the reminder of propriety, "We should be off. We have been 'alone' for long enough as it is."

Charmaine cradled Miss Brooke and carried her down the stairs. She was much lighter than he expected, even sprawled gracefully in a faux faint. A sudden feeling of protectiveness washed over him as she rested her head against his chest. Charmaine encountered a footman midway down and sent him to fetch Miss Brooke's carriage.

An expectant silence fell over the foyer when they came into view. Charmaine felt as if every eye was upon them as he attempted to casually walk through the room. Collins quickly rushed to his side. "Good God, Charmaine, is she injured?"

"Yes, the lady is fine. She fainted. I am taking her to her coach." Charmaine noticed Collins spoke louder than necessary. Despite not knowing the reason, Charmaine followed his lead.

"Oh, excellent. Gossip had me worried."

"You should not listen to gossip, Collins. It is almost always wrong." Charmaine continued towards the door and then paused. "You bring up an excellent point. I would see the lady home safe, but I would have no harm come to her reputation. Perchance you and Lady Stanton would care to escort her? No one could question your motives."

Collins made a face. "And leave the party early? Charmaine, you must be joking. The night is still young! You take her. No one will question your motives. You worry too much!"

"Still, it seems wrong. Perhaps I should send her alone."

Lady Stanton floated up to them in a cascade of silver fabric. She tapped her fan sharply on Charmaine's forearm. "Do not be a brute. You will do no such thing! I will go with you while Collins stays and plays cards."

Charmaine nodded. "Let us be off. The sooner I see the lady home the sooner I can join Collins at cards."

Collins bowed to them both and watched them walk out of the foyer to where the carriage awaited. Charmaine had quite a challenge getting Miss Brooke's unresponsive form into the carriage while still hiding her cheek from the crowd. Eventually he succeeded. Drawing the curtains shut, Charmaine signaled the driver and they were underway.

Back at the ball, Duchess Castlemire ushered Miss Boswell back to the dancing with a no-nonsense manner. Feeling lost, Miss Boswell took her normal place on the wall and watched the dancing around her. The whole evening made absolutely no sense.

Taking a glass of lemonade, she strolled casually through the clusters of gossip. Three Seasons as a wallflower meant almost everyone knew her and allowed her into the outskirts of their circles. It was, Miss Boswell thought with irritation, as if she was no more than a dog. Miss Brooke and Lord Charmaine were the hot item of gossip for the evening. The rumor was the established matrons of Society caught them in an exceedingly compromising position. Details varied wildly. That relieved Miss Boswell somewhat. Until the *ton* settled on a story they would not pass judgment as a whole. Each story seemed to have its own supporters. The game of 'who saw what when' was underway.

Returning to her original place on the wall, Miss Boswell had no clearer idea of what happened. Yet, she became more and more certain whatever transpired upstairs was not intentional. She knew Miss Brooke better than she knew anyone else. If Miss Brooke were to do anything reckless, she would have done it for Lord Farrington. As for Lord Charmaine, Miss Boswell knew nothing of him except for his camaraderie with Farrington. Their banter seemed to indicate a close friendship and, as far as Miss Boswell was concerned, any chum of Farrington must be an exceptional human being. Even more interesting was the lack of uproar from the established ladies of the Court. Miss Boswell pressed her lips together deep in thought. Something was amiss.

As the dances wore on, Miss Boswell became bored and then tired. Surely her friend would eventually return. As she mingled, rumor informed her Miss Brooke departed almost a full two hours prior in her own carriage. Miss Boswell was stranded. She frowned as she tried to decide what to do. At worst, she could take a hack home, but even her absent-minded father would object to that. A woman of quality did not ride in a common hack, especially not unaccompanied in the dark of night. She frowned as she mulled over her options.

"Worry haunts your face. Are you well?" Farrington's voice surprised Miss Boswell and she jumped involuntarily. He reached out to steady her. His expression remained impassive but his voice was warm as he continued, "I apologize. I did not mean to startle you."

"Ah, no. I should apologize. I was so lost in my thoughts I was unaware of your approach." How, Miss Boswell thought to herself, is that even possible? Anthony, as always, shown like the sun. A dark sun, maybe, as it was hard to relate his deep brown hair to any form of yellow, not to mention his amazingly dark eyes. Miss Boswell pulled her mind out of its admiration of the male form next to her and tried to focus on his words. It was not easy.

"Understandable. It is loud in here." He stood next to her, so they were both looking out over the crowd. "Tuppence for your thoughts?"

Miss Boswell blushed slightly and then mentally cursed herself. She could not even talk to Farrington without reverting to schoolgirl behavior. "They are of no matter. Thank you, Lord Farrington. How is your evening?"

"Abominable. Yours?"

She blinked. It was the first time she heard Farrington deviate from formulated replies of the polite world. His evening must be bad indeed. "Mine started out lovely but has encountered a small hitch."

"Ah." He looked out over the crowd. "I shall press and again demand to know what worries you. Normally you are all smiles or hiding in the shadows."

"Am I so easy to read?"

"Yes."

There was no harm in talking to Farrington, she supposed. He was far from the type who would mock her problems. "I came with Miss Brooke. She and her carriage have departed."

Miss Boswell could not see Farrington's expression as he was standing directly beside her. She thus missed his eyes tighten and lips compress. His voice, however, did not change. "Without you, clearly."

"Indeed. And I find the events of the evening fatiguing."

His slight chuckle had a bitter undertone. "A common occurrence, I assure you." Miss Boswell's breath caught in her throat as his dark eyes looked at her. "Take my carriage home."

"My lord! I will do no such thing. Then it would be you who was stranded."

Looking back over the crowd, he answered in his same calm voice. "Nonsense. I can either ride home with a friend or walk. My home is close." Certainly, it is, Miss Boswell thought. They were in the most upscale area of town. Where else would a Marquis live? When she did not answer, Farrington continued. "Or, if you wish, send the carriage back. I will be at the card tables for several more hours."

"Only if it is no inconvenience to you." Her voice dropped a little. "I am tired."

"It is no inconvenience at all. In truth, it would be my pleasure."

She smiled at him, trying not to let her adoration shine through her eyes. Miss Boswell held on to hope Anthony did not know how she felt. It would only lead to embarrassment for them both. "I would be grateful."

He nodded. "I will send for my driver. A footman will fetch you when the carriage is ready."

Miss Boswell curtsied as he walked away. She leaned against the wall and attempted to ignore the delightful warmth coursing through her.

❧◆❧

As the carriage pulled away from the ball, Lady Stanton instantly turned on Charmaine. "What in God's teeth is going on? The gossip is outrageous. And did I not tell you that she is a problem?"

Charmaine leaned back on the seat of the coach. "Baroness Stanton, may I present Miss Alison Brooke." Charmaine pointed at the unconscious form next to him. "Miss Brooke, this is my friend's wife, Lady Elizabeth Stanton."

Miss Brooke peeked opened an eye. "I take it I can cease playacting?" She sat up slowly and leaned cautiously back on the padded bench. The lighting was extremely dark in the coach.

Lady Stanton glared at Charmaine. "You failed to mention she was pretending."

Charmaine shut his eyes. "There was no opportunity."

The tense silence broke when the carriage hit an especially rough piece of cobblestone. Miss Brooke winced. Lady Stanton looked at the younger woman with concern. "Oh, dear me. Charmaine, what did you do?"

Charmaine took a deep breath and tried not to snap at his friend's wife. How ironic a stranger could believe he would do no harm to a woman, but the wife of his childhood best friend automatically accused him. He gathered his breath to retort but Miss Brooke spoke first. "Lord Charmaine? Lord Charmaine did not do this."

"Someone clearly hurt you and now…"

"Please," Miss Brooke interrupted softly, "do not worry yourself on my account. Lord Charmaine intervened. I assure you everything is fine."

Lady Stanton's frown deepened. "Everything is fine? Girl, let me look at you." She knelt forward in the carriage to inspect Miss Brooke's face. Her gaze traveled lower and Miss Brooke blushed slightly, moving the hanging fabric to shield herself from Lady Stanton's prying eyes. "There is bruising coming up from the rip in your dress. Are you in pain?"

Miss Brooke smiled softly. "It is of no moment."

"Lord Charmaine, I think we should get her to a physician."

"Please, Lady Stanton, I appreciate your concern, but I will be fine." Miss Brooke drew back from Lady Stanton's attentions.

Charmaine opened his eyes and stared openly at Miss Brooke's chest. There were dark purple lines starting to form from under her left side. "You have a point."

Miss Brooke turned to look at Charmaine. He noticed how drawn and pale she was becoming but she still sat tall and proud. "I am fine. Please. I wish to go home."

"Do you have a doctor at your house?"

"Who on earth keeps a doctor at their home? It is almost one in the morning!" Miss Brooke was vexed at the turn in conversation.

Charmaine considered the situation for a moment and then rapped on the roof of the carriage with his cane. "Driver. Fifteen King Street, St. James Place."

There was a muffled reply of assent as Miss Brooke started at him. "You cannot simply appropriate my coach and ride off with me wherever you please."

Lady Stanton's fan flipped open. "As much as it pains me, I must agree. Where are we going?"

He leaned back and shut his eyes again. "The Donahue townhouse."

Charmaine missed the downright dangerous look Miss Brooke gave him. "I am not going to your home and that is final."

"I agree. You are not. My parent's mansion, however, has a doctor on staff at one in the morning. I pay the man enough for his services, I might as well use them." He opened his eyes again. "Now, unless either of you has any more pressing concerns, I would ask for some quiet. I have to figure out what to tell my mother."

Lady Stanton laughed cruelly. "There is no argument I can have with you, nor ruckus I can create, that will match your mother."

Charmaine glowered at her. "You are not a nice person."

"No, Lord Charmaine, I am not. And I am quite vexed at your highhanded behavior without the slightest explanation or justification. Since nothing I say will change that, I will take solace in your mother's likely overblown hysterics." Lady Stanton's voice was acquiring the shrill edge Charmaine particularly hated.

Miss Brooke stopped paying attention to the conversation. Once it was clear she was not going home, she curled into herself. In what seemed like a matter of moments, they arrived outside of the elaborate townhouse. The ever-vigilant staff escorted Miss Brooke out of the coach before she could do much more than object. She was surprised to hear someone call for a doctor.

Charmaine watched as the household absorbed Miss Brooke. He exited the coach and looked at the still seated Lady Stanton. He offered her his hand, but she did not take it.

"I think I shall return to my own home for the evening. This much excitement is not good for the blood."

Charmaine frowned. "Are you truly offended?"

"No, Lord Charmaine, I am not."

"Good. I," he stumbled awkwardly on the words, "would not like to give you offense."

Lady Stanton smiled at him. "You have not. But since your Mother has this well in hand, I will retire. I think I have intruded on your melodramatic evening long enough."

Charmaine bowed and stepped back from the coach doors. A footman closed them. Lady Stanton pulled back the fabric and gave Charmaine a small, honest smile. "The next few days may be difficult. Know Collins and I are here for you."

"Do you know something I do not?" Charmaine frowned slightly, concerned.

"No. I know even less than you do. Get some sleep, Lord Charmaine. I will likely call upon you on the morrow." The coach drove off leaving a confused Charmaine to stare after it. With a shake of his head, he walked towards the elaborate residence.

His mother was impatiently waiting for him. He was amazed at how she was woken from sleep only moments before and still look composed. Charmaine bowed slightly to her before kissing her cheek. "Mother. You look younger than ever."

"No thanks to you." The caustic reply was quick in coming. "You have delivered the girl, now you can go."

"Ah, pardon?" Charmaine blinked.

"The story will come to me sooner or later. What I know now is my son will not spend the night under the same roof as an unmarried woman."

"Mother, there is no better chaperone than you. No improper behavior would occur under your roof."

"Exactly." Lady Donahue pointed at the door. "Now, out."

"But..."

"Out."

Charmaine sighed. In reality he was glad to leave Miss Brooke in his mother's care. He had no idea what to do, or even what he was doing. He hoped the morning would bring more answers. "Yes, Mother. I am leaving."

"Good. Call on me on the morrow, I am already *dying* of curiosity."

Charmaine smiled at his mother's last statement as he started the long walk home. He was fairly sure that his mother would be absolutely frantic for information when the morning arrived. The walk home gave his mind plenty of time to run in circles as he tried to piece the evening together. He gained nothing for his efforts but a headache. All he could do was hope sleep sorted it out.

CHAPTER V

As usual, Charmaine woke early. He lay in bed for several long moments, luxuriating in the warmth of his sheets and the peace of the morning. Dragging himself reluctantly out of bed, he shuffled over to a warm basin of water to freshen himself. Wilhelm was leaning on the doorframe of the room. Drying himself with a towel, Charmaine glanced at his impatient valet. "What?"

"Three notes have come for you, my lord. And it is still before nine of the clock. The polite world is supposed to be asleep." Wilhelm thrust Charmaine's shirt at him.

"I had a busy night."

"Clearly, my lord." Wilhelm's voice dripped with mockery. "Do you wish to discuss what occurred?"

Charmaine fought a yawn as he ran his hands through sleep tousled hair. "I still do not know how I feel about it myself."

"While understandable, it makes lying for you impossible."

Charmaine's voice was muffled as the shirt slid over his head. "What makes you think you will need to lie for me?"

"Three messages before nine, my lord. Tell me."

Charmaine glared as he buttoned his waistcoat. "You truly are a wretched servant."

"Servants get paid."

"Fine." Charmaine stopped dressing and sat on the bed. He folded his hands in front of him and considered the events from the previous evening. "It is complicated." Charmaine was silent for a long set of moments as Wilhelm continued preparations for the morning. "I do not know where to start."

Wilhelm handed Charmaine his freshly polished riding boots. "You arrived at the ball…"

"…and it was a ball. Nothing special. Miss Linder was pressed upon me for a dance and afterwards I needed space. I went upstairs and encountered—an imposition from a gentleman upon a lady of Quality. I intervened. The lady and I were interrupted while I was helping her regain her composure. It created gossip."

Wilhelm considered. "And Lady Donahue?"

"My esteemed mother sent one of those early morning letters?"

"Your assumption is correct," the servant replied.

Charmaine stood with a frown. "I suppose I should not be surprised. There was harm done to the lady's person. It was imperative she receive medical attention. I took her to my parent's townhouse."

"Society found you alone with a ravished woman and you took her to your mother's estate?" Wilhelm did his best to keep his expression steady. He had the impression he might be failing.

"I could not leave her at the ball," rebutted Charmaine.

"Why not?"

Charmaine shot a disapproving glance at Wilhelm, "Because it would not have been the right thing to do."

"You would know best, my lord. What is the right thing to do?" Wilhelm asked.

"Unknown." Charmaine stretched before picking his jacket off the bed. The letters were already tucked inside a pocket. He paused and looked at Wilhelm seriously. "I do not want to regret rescuing her."

"Who is she?"

"Miss Alison Brooke."

Wilhelm's eyebrows rose. "My lord! Miss Brooke! She is rich, beautiful, and at the center of polite Society. Lord Charmaine, that is…."

"That is what? What is it you were going to say?"

"Pray consider my words before becoming angry?" Wilhelm spoke rapidly, indicating his quick mind had a plan.

Charmaine nodded, "Go on."

68

"This is excellent news." Charmaine glared at Wilhelm. This time it was the valet's turn to hold up his hand. "Lord Charmaine, Miss Brooke is wealthy. Her dowry is large enough to eliminate all your debt. Best of all, none of it is land. Some of it is in the Exchange, but most of her capital is liquid."

"I do not care about her monetary status, Wilhelm. She was going to be raped and you are talking about her net worth!"

"Yes, yes, exactly." The younger man stood and started pacing. "I know you had all the right reasons, but the woman you saved also has everything you need. You are trying to marry for money, my lord. Miss Brooke is a much better catch for you than Miss Linder, but Mr. Brooke has refused seven suitors for his daughter's hand already. With her reputation on the line, she will be forced to marry you. It is perfect!"

"You have a very interesting definition of the word perfect." The whole conversation left a bad taste in Charmaine's mouth.

Wilhelm ignored him. "You did get caught in a suitably compromising position, did you not?"

"Kneeling between her legs with her skirts lifted and her stays ripped open. Compromising enough for you?" Charmaine's reply was caustic.

"Oh, yes." Wilhelm smiled. "Miss Brooke would make an excellent countess. Only you, my lord, could make silk purses out of sows' ears."

"I have no desire to profit from the infringement upon her person." Charmaine jerked his arms through the jacket and roughly shrugged it onto his shoulders. "I have not decided to wed Miss Brooke nor will I use this situation to force her to the alter. This is my life, Wilhelm, not a shipping venture or canal investment."

Wilhelm started to retort, but Charmaine silenced him with an angry hand gesture and stormed out of the flat. Perhaps, Wilhelm admitted to himself, he could have handled that conversation better. However, he knew his lord. No matter how much words initially upset him they would be carefully weighed and considered. Dismissing Charmaine's anger, Wilhelm set about discovering as much as possible about Miss Brooke.

꙳◆꙳

St. James Park was a good distance from Tower Hill. Charmaine was glad for the long walk, as it gave him time to cool his mind. He hated the idea that Wilhelm might be right. Miss Brooke was, for the brief time he had known her, a much better match than Miss Linder. He had seen Miss Brooke at a terrible disadvantage and had found her to be truly remarkable. It was impressive how composed she was throughout the whole ordeal. He had not realized she was hurt until Lady Stanton mentioned it. He smiled at the memory of Miss Brooke's poise.

Charmaine planned his destination based on the letters in his pocket. There were two from his mother. The first was a polite calling card informing him his presence was requested as early as possible, while the second was a personal letter begging for information. Most of the World was still asleep or, at best, leaving for their morning rides, yet somehow gossip already started to reach his mother. The third note was from Lady Stanton, also requesting his presence first thing in the morning. The letter indicated in strong terms he should do nothing, nor talk to anyone else, before he visited the Stanton household. Charmaine was happy to accede to Lady Stanton's starchy request. The Stanton family had indicated an extraordinary willingness to help. It would be foolhardy to discount them now.

Charmaine trotted up the Stanton's grandiose steps. Their home was smaller than his parents' townhome, but what it lacked in space it made up for in stature. The decorations of the three-story residence were ostentatious and the large glass panes on the windows were of the highest quality. The doorman showed no surprise when Lord Charmaine presented himself at such an impolite hour. Lady Stanton came down promptly.

Charmaine automatically bowed when she entered. Lady Stanton's gown caught his attention immediately. The warm blue day dress conformed to the strict rules of fashion and looked almost matronly. Charmaine cocked his head as he took in this new Lady Stanton. "You look—different."

She wrinkled her nose at him. "I suppose you approve."

"You know I do."

"I am glad you like this gown, as I am wearing it for you."

"For me?" Charmaine's eyes narrowed in confusion, "Lady Stanton, you make less sense than my mother."

A disapproving wave greeted that statement. "Do not offend me today, Lord Charmaine. I am about to have several long days on your behalf. Go back to telling me how lovely I am."

He smiled. "Yes, ma'am. If I am properly obedient will you tell me what this is all about?"

"There is no great mystery, Lord Charmaine. After we talk, I am out to pay calls on my friends. I will spend the morning with my inner circle and then the afternoon working my way outward." She frowned. "Keep your late afternoon free. I may want to drive with you in the park."

"I will be free after Session lets out. We start at two and thirty today, but it still should be no later than five."

She sighed. "You can skip, can you not?"

"No." His voice was firm. "Unlike many of my brethren, I take my duties in the House of Lords seriously. Sometimes I think most of the *ton* forgets the real reason why we are in London. The Season's purpose is not parties, but government. England is the premier…"

Lady Stanton cut him off. "Yes, yes." She waved a gloved hand dismissively. "So, you will be available to drive with me in the afternoon if I deem it necessary? I will send a note." She pursed her lips. "See if your mother will drive with you in the park. That would be better."

"I take it you have a plan?"

"Several, actually. It depends on what you want to do." She sat daintily on the cream chaise and rang for tea.

"I do not know. Do I need to do anything?"

Lady Stanton considered. "No, you do not. However, if you do nothing, Society is likely to dictate your next few actions. You are an honorable man and unlikely to leave a woman with a ruined reputation behind you."

"Miss Brooke's reputation is not ruined."

"Not yet. You are lucky, indeed. The Society papers do not come out until tomorrow. You have one whole day to dictate the path of gossip." She smiled at his uncomfortable expression. "We have one whole day, rather."

The tea service arrived and Lady Stanton poured for Lord Charmaine. He took the fragile china with care. The cup looked toy-like in his rough hands. "What are my choices?"

"Marry her, admit what happened, or ignore the situation." Lady Stanton seemed to think this was an adequate summary of the options.

Charmaine waved for her to continue, "Go on. Expound."

"Really, Lord Charmaine. Did you grow up under a rock?"

"Yes. The same one your husband did, actually."

"That explains much." Lady Stanton set down her tea so that she could gesture with her expressive hands. "We will take them in reverse order. Ignoring the situation means very little for you. You may gain some notoriety as a rake but, frankly, most of the men of the *ton* are more likely to be jealous you tasted Miss Brooke's charms. Miss Brooke's reputation will be damaged, but it is possible Society will overlook it. She has powerful patrons and a good deal of money."

"To be clear," Charmaine interrupted, "I did not 'taste Miss Brooke's charms.'"

Lady Stanton waved him to silence. "Your second option is to play the hero card and admit what happened, whatever that is. This allows you to gain admirers and softens the blow to the lady's reputation. No matter the reason, nor what truly happened, she was compromised. Her reputation is still damaged. More, your unreasonable refusal to discuss what you intervened on will have to be lifted."

"I will honor Miss Brooke's request not to discuss the situation."

"If you do not intend to marry her, the appropriate mode of address for the lady is Miss Brooke." Charmaine nodded his head in acknowledgement. "Now, marrying her is a viable option. She is what we have been looking for. Pretty, well connected, and as rich as even I could want. You have compromised her," again Charmaine tried to object and again Lady Stanton held up a hand to stop him, "so it is unlikely she will be able to refuse you. More, it is the right and honorable thing to do."

"You clearly have a preference."

"Yes." Lady Stanton lifted her teacup and took a sip. "But this is not about my preference. We are discussing you. As you are so fond of reminding us, this is indeed your life."

"Of all the people in the world, you seem to be the only one listening to that." Charmaine smiled gently to indicate the words were a compliment. "I suppose one heiress is as good as another and I do need to wed. However, I dislike feeling I am forcing her into anything. It feels—dishonorable."

Lady Stanton shrugged. "If you are willing to marry her, then it will not be you forcing her. Society will force her for you. Besides, she can always refuse."

"I..." Charmaine frowned. "While I am willing to marry her, I would greatly like to avoid being her eighth rejection."

"You left your pride behind when you decided to marry for money. This way you keep your honor."

"I suppose that is something."

"Good. If we are finished, I must away." Lady Stanton smiled over the table at him. "I have to go gossip for you."

"I would never stand in your way when you are planning my life."

"Good. I am glad to see you learned *something* from my husband."

❧◆☙

Charmaine's mood was considerably lighter after his meeting with Lady Stanton. Nothing changed, but somehow the catastrophe of the previous night seemed as if it would work itself out. Lady Stanton, he was forced to concede, might have some positive characteristics. He was neither fond of her shrew-like tendencies, nor the way she molded Collins into a fop, but he could see the appeal of having her on his side. She had a way of making Charmaine feel like he was not alone and, no matter how horrible the situation became, they would find a way out. A nagging part of his mind pointed out he might owe Collins an apology.

It took little time to walk from Stanton's to the Donahue home. The residence had changed overnight. The front gardens were immaculate and the large stone building had flowers placed in every window. Charmaine's eyes narrowed as he took in the crisp folds of the curtains and the pristine front steps. Lady Donahue was preparing for war.

The doorman bowed deeply when Lord Charmaine arrived and ushered him upstairs to his mother's dressing rooms. She was still in the final stages of polishing her appearance. Her maid scurried to and fro looking for the exact right pair of earrings. Lady Donahue was dressed in her conservative finest and looked every inch the matron of Society.

Lady Donahue looked in her mirror so her soft green eyes met her son's brooding blue. He bowed at her reflection and waited patiently for her rebuke. Placing the last of her cosmetics away in a small box, she finally addressed him. "Good morning, Son."

"Good morning, Mother. How are you? Other than lovely, certainly."

She smiled in response. "I am mostly well. In all honesty, I feel very alive. There have been more callers before nine than in the past three weeks combined."

"Anyone of interest?"

"How would I know? No proper lady would receive callers this early. I will review them over breakfast and return the visits in the afternoon." She turned on her divan so that she was facing her son. "Now, Robert, tell me what I need to know."

He walked fully into the room and looked around for a place to sit. He seemed to be spending an inordinate amount of time in places with delicate or fragile looking furniture, he thought wryly. He chose a wainscot chair next to a heavily curtained window. As he settled into it, he considered the question.

"Need to know?" He raised his hand and started ticking off his fingers. "I am willing to marry Miss Brooke. Lady Castlemire and her entourage caught us in a compromising position. I have discussed nothing with Miss Brooke. I have spoken to no one except you and the Stantons." He looked at his four raised fingers and then nodded. "I suppose that is it."

74

"I see." Lady Donahue frowned. The expression did not sit well on her. "What should I know?"

This time he curled in his fingers rather than extending them. "First, you should be proud of me."

His mother interrupted him, clearly vexed. "*Certainly,* I am proud of you. I raised you, Robert. If you bring me a battered woman with her clothing falling off in the middle of the night, there could be a million explanations. All of them involve me being proud of you. In addition, if you were to do something horrid to a girl, would you truly bring her home to your mother?"

"I had not considered it that way." His mother's vehemence caused him to pause. "I suppose I expected condemnation, after all, Society assumes I took advantage of Miss Brooke."

"I should hope your own mother knows you better than the tattles of Society." Her frown became a full-fledged scowl. "Do you really expect so little from your family?"

Charmaine stood and bowed deeply. "I did not and I apologize. My words were incorrect. I am—out of my element."

She waved her fan impatiently at him. "Oh, do sit. Finish telling me what I should know."

"Privileged information follows." He waited for his mother's nod before continuing. "I walked in on a man attempting to force himself upon her. I rectified the situation. We were discovered as I was leaning over her to check on her health."

"Did you have an early morning?"

"Not as early as I would have liked. Miss Brooke forbade the duel. She does not want the incident to become common knowledge and feels drastic action would call attention to the situation."

"Who was it?" Lady Donahue's frown deepened, and her eyes grew serious. Charmaine rarely witnessed this side of his mother.

"A man named West. A Whig. He is a recent arrival to London I know little about."

His mother nodded. "That will soon change."

"How is the lady?" Charmaine knew if anything were seriously wrong it would have been the first thing his mother mentioned.

"Still sleeping. The doctor would not let her go to bed until near dawn because of the head injury. Her ribs may be cracked but are otherwise fine. She should be on her feet by Thursday or Friday. The bruising will fade within a fortnight."

"She has tea with Lady Castlemire on Thursday. Her Grace was most insistent."

Lady Donahue's eyebrows rose. "Well, that is interesting and not to be refused. We can put the girl in a chair, if need be. Heighten the drama and the mystery of the incident."

Charmaine's eyes narrowed. "This seems the opposite of the lady's wishes."

"Just because you are uncomfortable being in the center of attention does not mean others do not thrive there. I not speak on what has happened. The lady took a fall and she remembers nothing. You are bound by honor not to speak. Let Society create its own story."

Charmaine frowned. "I shall follow the lead of those who know this dance better. Just, please, Mother, keep my desires in mind. Miss Brooke's choices dictate our course."

"Yes, yes, dear. I will." She batted her eyes at him. "Do you not trust me?"

"To bully a young woman to achieve what you feel is best for the family? In that, I trust you completely. Thus, rein in such instincts. If Miss Brooke will not have me, I will marry Miss Linder."

"If Miss Linder will have you…"

"Mother. My point stands."

"Fine, fine, I concur. If Miss Brooke does not want to wed you, I shall not use my influence to persuade her otherwise." Lady Donahue gave her son a hard look. "Since I am a lady of Quality I do not, obviously, bully."

Charmaine allowed a small smile to escape his lips. "Yes, Mother."

"Excellent. Will you break your fast with me before you run off to whatever den of iniquity consumes all of your time?"

"The den known as the Palace of Westminster. Such language. The Lords are in session," said Charmaine.

"Stuff and bother. Who even goes to those things anyway?"

Charmaine did not sigh. "I do. But I will see you this afternoon, if you will have me?"

"Hm?"

"Lady Stanton suggested I ride with you in the park. She seems as involved as you in my personal affairs."

Lady Donahue sniffed. "Well, it is about time Collins' girl did something to make herself useful. Although, I doubt she will manage well. That woman turns everything into a production."

Charmaine hid a small smile, "Shall I see you at five of the clock?"

"I will beg, borrow, or steal a carriage."

Charmaine allowed his parting bow to hide his wince. He forgot he sold his mother's carriage earlier in the month. He was surprised she was silent on their fall from grace. "Then I will see you anon."

Lady Donahue lifted her cheek for him to kiss. "If you wish it, I will not pressure Miss Brooke. I would see my son happy."

"I try, Mother. I truly do."

She smiled a bit sadly at him. "So much like your father. The easy route was never one either of you could enjoy."

There was nothing Charmaine could say. After depositing a kiss on her cheek, he promptly left the imposing residence.

❧◆❧

The Donahue servants arrived at the Brooke estate to fetch clean clothing for the invalid Miss Brooke. With typical carefree charm, Miss Boswell decided she should be fetched as well. Miss Boswell's bounce faltered briefly as a scowling butler showed her in. She brushed off the disapproving look and scampered up the stairs.

Her friend smiled brightly as Miss Boswell burst into the room. Miss Brooke looked like an angel propped up on blinding white pillows. Her golden hair fell freely to her waist and the white of her dressing gown made her soft blue eyes glow. The green and yellow splotch spanning the side of Miss Brooke's face ruined the beatific image. Miss Boswell settled in the white wicker chair next to the bed and plastered on a false smile. Miss Brooke's expression grew worried.

"What—what is it?" Miss Brooke was groggy from the laudanum.

Miss Boswell leaned forward and took her friend's hand. "Is that any way to greet me? As if something was wrong?"

"Do not act as if you have horrible news if you want to avoid such greetings." Miss Brooke pushed herself up on the mountain of pillows.

"I do not have horrible news. I have great news!" Miss Boswell's false smile was terrible, Miss Brooke thought with amusement.

"I remember your seventeenth birthday."

Miss Boswell blinked. "What does that have to do with anything?"

"My mother confided if we were going to give someone bad news, or news we thought they might take poorly, we should present the information in a positive light. If we excelled at the trick, we might even convince the other person the news was good."

"And then she demonstrated by making your mischievous older cousin play dolls with us." Miss Boswell smiled, sliding into the memory.

"Exactly. So, tell me this horrible news of yours?"

Miss Boswell frowned. "The entire *ton* is talking about only one thing, you and Lord Charmaine."

"Ugh. I suppose it is to be expected, I suppose. But no worries, it shall pass." Miss Brooke sounded confident, but Miss Boswell could see wrinkles form around her eyes.

"I am not sure it will. You see, they are no longer talking about the incident at the ball." Miss Boswell let her words trail off, clearly not wanting to give bad news to her friend.

"Brenda. Tell me or I will break *your* ribs and you can be stuck here."

"Sorry. Lord Charmaine has announced his intention to offer for your hand, as he feels it is the only honorable thing to do after the incident."

Miss Brooke gasped, both her hands flying to cover her mouth. "He did not."

"He did." Miss Boswell's curls bounced around her head as she nodded. "Apparently, he was drinking in White's and announced, quite loudly, no one should worry about your honor for it was safe with him. If it was breached, he would render it whole."

With a groan, Miss Brooke slid down on her pillows. "Does he have any idea what he has done?"

"Which part? The part where he cements in Society's minds something happened the night of the ball or the part where he announced your engagement without your permission?"

"Or my father's."

"La, and then your father."

"Oh, no." Miss Brooke's eyes grew large. "I thought this could not get worse. How does he figure in to this?"

"He does not. Not yet." Miss Boswell leaned back in the chair. The furniture squeaked in protest. She straightened with a frown. "After Lord Charmaine made his declaration in the crowded club, someone—and I wonder if it was Lord Farrington—asked if he had your father's approval. After loudly seeking Mr. Brooke, he found out that your father is in the country. He apparently hired a messenger to fetch him with all due speed."

"I am unsure if I wish to faint or swat him."

Miss Boswell shrugged in an unladylike manner. "Fainting does nothing. And you would be horrified if you swatted him."

"Yes, yes. I would." Miss Brooke wrinkled her nose. "I do not suppose that is all?"

"I feel as if that is quite enough!"

"Oh, yes, plenty! I cannot believe how far out of control events have gotten. I wish Lord Charmaine spoke to me first!"

"That oversight may not have been his fault." Miss Boswell admitted grudgingly.

"How could it not be his fault?"

"His mother is turning away all visitors, according to gossip, and not even allowing her son in the residence. She says the ordeal you have been through is quite tiring and you need rest."

"Sweet heavens. They make it sound like I have been half murdered."

Miss Boswell frowned. "Indeed, you look like you have been."

"Oh, stuff and bother. I took a bad spill. Lord Charmaine was kind enough to help me up and take me someplace he knew there was a doctor. Lady Stanton was with us the whole time, nothing improper happened."

"That is the best you can come up with?" Skepticism was clear in Miss Boswell's voice.

"Always keep things simple. Makes it more believable."

"So, Miss Propriety, how do you explain the multiple reports that Lord Charmaine was intimate with your person?"

Miss Brooke dismissed the question with a wave. "What exaggerations. He was clearly helping me up after my fall. I most certainly do not appreciate he glimpsed my skirts askew, but it is nothing more than he would have seen in a graceless dismount."

"And why were you alone in a room together?"

"Oh, Miss Boswell, you always think the worst of me!" Miss Brooke perked up. Color flooded her cheeks as she animatedly explained the lie. "I was alone in the sitting room on the third floor. It hurt to see Anthony. I was so distraught I must have fainted. I fell over the chaise and knocked over a vase. Lord Charmaine heard the crash and rushed to my rescue."

Miss Boswell raised a copper eyebrow. "You think Society will believe such nonsense?"

"Yes, I do." Her rose-colored lips turned downwards in a frown. "Or I did. Lord Charmaine's proclamation my honor has been damaged makes such a story problematic."

"Why?"

"Because he is indicating something happened, that somehow I have been less than chaste. Society will follow his lead."

"I am not so sure." Miss Boswell bit her lip in consideration. "Lord Charmaine's reputation is so upstanding he might as well be a saint. The Donahue line is apparently synonymous with honor and dignity. I admit I know little about them, but the recent gossip has been favorable to your Lord Charmaine."

"So, you are saying...?"

"He may be the type of gentleman who would marry a woman if Society so much as implied he dishonored her." Miss Boswell spread her hands helplessly. "I wish you were the one hearing all this gossip, you are so much better understanding all of this than me!"

Miss Brooke took one of Miss Boswell's hands. "You are doing wonderfully. I cannot begin to thank you enough. What would I do without you?"

"Become so worried about what is proper and right you would never have any fun?" Miss Boswell squeezed her friend's hand. "No matter, I will always be here."

"Until some devastatingly handsome man comes and sweeps you off your feet!"

"Yes, until then." Miss Boswell's smile turned slightly melancholy at the reminder of her three failed Seasons. "I shall be a spinster and you shall be ruined. How delightful."

Miss Brooke wrinkled her nose. "Do not be dour. You are not a spinster and I am not ruined."

"When will you know if you are ruined?" It was a serious question.

"Soon. Within the week. The Patronesses of Almack's meet on Monday. If they revoke my membership, I am formally a ruined woman. I could be ruined in many other ways, though. If I start being snubbed at balls, or if the amount of invitations I receive drops off drastically, if I am excluded from dinner parties, that sort of thing."

"What if that happens?"

"Well, it will not, but if it does…" Miss Brooke stared at the ceiling for a moment before looking back at her friend. "I marry Lord Charmaine, if he will still have me, or I live in exile with my father until he finds someone who will overlook having damaged goods as a wife. That will be at least nine months from now."

"Nine months? Alison—I do not mean to be impudent, but you and Lord Charmaine did not…?" Miss Boswell's face glowed the same vivid red as her hair.

"No. We did not. Please believe me?"

"Mary's toes, you know I do. But I do not know what is going on." Miss Boswell wanted to know, badly. She genuinely worried for her friend. The situation felt wrong. "Will you tell me?"

Miss Brooke chewed on her bottom lip with downcast eyes. "I, I—please do not ask."

"If you insist." Miss Boswell gave her friend's dainty hand another squeeze. "Can you at least tell me if I am mad at Lord Charmaine or not?"

"No." Miss Brooke gave her the ghost of a smile, trying to brush away the memory of Mr. West's touch. "We are not mad at Lord

Charmaine. We are happy with Lord Charmaine." She sank further down into the pillows with a small pout. "Or we were happy with Lord Charmaine before he decided to announce to the world my honor was breached."

"Do not be unfair. He was likely only doing what he thought was best."

Miss Brooke mock glared at her friend. "Why are you taking his side?"

"Because you told me moments ago I was happy with him. And I am willing to give the people I am happy with the benefit of the doubt." Miss Boswell removed her hand from Miss Brooke's and stood, "We should get ready for Lady Castlemire's tea."

"You are coming?" Miss Brooke perked up, excited.

"Absolutely." Miss Boswell smiled. "Did you really think I would let you get thrown out of Society without me?"

CHAPTER VI

The Castlemire residence was enormous. Miss Boswell could not call it a townhouse, as it was as large as her uncle's country estate! Lady Donahue gave her wide-eyed wonderment a disapproving look. "Close your mouth, child. Ladies do not gape."

Miss Boswell fought the urge to stick out her tongue at the older woman. Lady Donahue made her skin crawl. She was the type of woman Miss Boswell was always afraid Miss Brooke would grow into! Lady Donahue's gown was so shapely that Miss Boswell could not imagine how she breathed. Yet, somehow, Lady Donahue made wearing the constraining outfit seem effortless.

Miss Brooke was in a similarly fashionable getup, minus the restraining undergarments. A sheer muslin fichu sat artistically over her shoulders. Elaborate curls were arranged at a jaunty angle to block part of her face. A heavy layer of paste concealed the rest of the bruising.

Miss Brooke watched the large residence approach with a sense of dread. Her reception here would provide an idea of how serious the scandal was. Did she dare hope the whole thing would blow over? The Duchess of Castlemire had extraordinary influence and Miss Brooke had not done anything wrong. Miss Brooke's cheeks hurt from frowning. Society never cared about right or wrong.

Miss Boswell gasped in delight as the group entered the foyer, with Miss Brooke being pushed in a chair. Each wall was a work of art bespoke with gold leafing and elaborate wainscoting. Before Miss Brooke could admire the myriad of wonders in the foyer, Miss

Boswell leaned and whisper to her, "Look at the floor! Do you know what this is?"

Miss Brooke glanced at the white stone floor crisscrossed with dark orange-brown veins. There was no doubt it was lovely. Still, it looked like a standard marble floor, perhaps with a different color running through it. "Marble?"

Miss Boswell rolled her eyes. "Perhaps. But it has gold veins in it. Gold!"

Lady Donahue silenced the younger women with a firm scowl. The butler arrived to escort them to the back gardens. A modest gathering of brightly colored women sipped tea and casually chatted in the grandiose open gardens. The Duchess made a substantial dark blot in the center of the cheery picture.

The maid wheeled Miss Brooke in front of the Duchess. Conversations stopped as Miss Brooke passed and promptly restarted with vigor once she was deemed to be out of polite earshot. She felt her small hope the incident was overlooked died. Her life was now a full-fledged scandal.

At Lady Castlemire's direction, the maid placed Miss Brooke directly beside her and then retreated. Miss Brooke fought the urge to fidget. The Duchess gave no greeting or acknowledgment. Propriety dictated that higher-ranking members of Society begin conversations. Miss Brooke was unsure if being placed next to the Duchess counted. She decided to wait patiently. And not fidget. The last part was the hardest.

Miss Brooke watched the crowd with the Duchess as her silent companion. Lady Donahue wasted no time in sliding familiarly with a cluster of women close to the patio entrance. Miss Brooke had not seen the Lady Donahue much in her three Seasons in London, but the cream of Society undoubtedly accepted her. Poor Miss Boswell was left standing on the outskirts of the circle, looking like she wanted to be anywhere else. Miss Brooke fretted. She had let her own troubles weigh on her down and neglected her friend. After a striking triumph at the Haven ball, Miss Boswell had reverted to her traditional attire and, worse, color scheme.

Miss Boswell's current dress was overly bright for midday and the cut was practical rather than fashionable. The ruddy orange clashed horribly with her hair and made her freckles glow brightly.

Yet what could Miss Brooke do? It was pointless to talk to her. Miss Boswell would laugh off her concerns and tell her friend the color made her happy. After all, was that not what mattered? Miss Brooke caught herself before sighing. She forced her frustration behind a pleasant expression. It was one thing to dress for comfort and in colors one liked, but Miss Boswell longed for both a husband and Society's acceptance.

Suddenly Duchess Castlemire spoke. "Let us discuss Lord Charmaine."

"Yes, Your Grace," Miss Brooke replied with a nod, "I have little to say as he is a stranger to me."

"Is he now?" Duchess Castlemire glanced at the young woman beside her. "That is unexpected but perhaps true. The relevant details are simple. The Donahue title and lands, not to mention their shipping contracts, are highly desired. These matchmaking mamas would love to get their hands on young Charmaine. For years he has resisted marriage. Yet now he announces he is willing to wed you due to honor."

"Miss Boswell said he and Miss Linder were reaching an accord."

Duchess Castlemire snorted. "The one who cannot dress herself? Consider your information source, girl." Miss Brooke stiffened but bit her tongue. She needed this woman as an ally, but the insult at Miss Boswell rankled. The older woman continued, "Lord Charmaine has kept his intentions, whatever they are, close to his chest. All Society knows is that an eligible bachelor is suddenly involved in a scandal and taking the honorable way out. A bachelor who previously avoided all attempts at matchmaking. Until you caught him."

Miss Brooke did her best not to appear confused. "I am not sure I would say I caught him. As you know, I..."

Duchess Castlemire interrupted her, "My friends admit it was a brilliant plan, sending Miss Boswell to the highest sticklers for propriety and bringing them to you and Charmaine."

"What?" Miss Brooke's eyes widened. "They suspect that I planned to have you walk in on Lord Charmaine and myself in an improper situation? You know I did no such thing."

"I do." The old woman shifted and sipped her tea. "But since you do not wish to announce what happened, there is little that can be done to reverse the perception. You may be right on that decision, sad as it is. A spiteful, conniving woman is more desirable than tarnished goods."

Miss Brooke's shock faded as she considered the latest gossip. She did not expect this. "If I am so husband hungry, why an earl over a marquis?"

"Simple. Farrington seems a nice catch but his title is ceremonial. He lacks a large amount of land and his family is out of favor with the Crown. You likely thought he would make an excellent husband until you were able to look at the financials."

"And the other six?"

"All worse than Farrington. You may have seriously considered Farrington until you met his good friend, Charmaine."

"They are friends?" Miss Brooke frowned. "Oh, poor Anthony."

"It appears you are quite the bold puss." The duchess replied without a trace of pity, "The *ton* was aware that Farrington's heart was badly trampled by your refusal. Now he is the target of histrionic poetry."

"I…" Miss Brooke took a deep breath. "This is overwhelming."

"I know." The momentary softening of the duchess's voice startled Miss Brooke. Her normal caustic tones quickly returned. "But you are a smart girl. Figure it out."

She nodded slowly, smoothing her skirts. "What do you recommend I do, your Grace?"

"Why, you marry Lord Charmaine." Duchess Castlemire sounded surprised at the question. "What else do you think to do, silly girl?"

"And if there are reasons that is not possible?" Miss Brooke did not know how her father would react to the current scandal, but the previous rejections taught her to expect the worst.

"Discount them."

Miss Brooke looked at her hands. "Yes, Your Grace."

"Do not disregard the seriousness of your situation. Almack's will expel you on Monday, yet being part of the unfashionable majority will not destroy you. The Donahues, and, unexpectedly, the Stantons, are giving you the support that is maintaining your popularity. They say firmly that people should not be so quick to judge, and that Charmaine is no fool." The duchess took a sip of her tea and looked over to ensure she had Miss Brooke's full attention. She did. "Reject Charmaine and that changes. The anger of the hostesses at the treatment of Farrington, and then Charmaine, will be your downfall. Invitations to balls will stop coming. Slander will declare you a ruined woman. Gossip will be brutal. You will have to find a husband who does not mind being declared a fool for marrying a cruel woman who gave her charms to another man."

Miss Brooke glared fiercely at her tightly curled fists. It was all so unfair! "This is not my fault. I did nothing…"

"I know, girl." Duchess Castlemire interrupted, her voice brisk. "Pull yourself together. Something horrible happened. Now you must make the best of it. Anger in public helps nothing."

Miss Brooke raised her chin. "I apologize. Lord Charmaine should be viewed as a hero, not as a manipulated fool. This is unfair."

Duchess Castlemire nodded, "We are in agreement. I will not have this man hurt. You may either marry the lad and prove gossip wrong or explain what happened. The choice is yours."

Miss Brooke's brow furrowed. "I," she paused, thinking frantically, "I will do the best I can. But whatever it is, I will do right by Lord Charmaine."

"Good." Duchess Castlemire gestured for the maid to return and take Miss Brooke away. "Because if you do not do right by him, you will discover how unfriendly Society can be when *I* turn on you."

Miss Boswell was bored beyond reason. Lady Whitehall had sixty-three silver beads on the left sleeve of her dress, Madam Bartlet had twenty-seven glass rubies on her left slipper and Lady Vassler had forty-two golden flowers embroidered on the hem of her gown. Normally, Miss Boswell walked around the gardens to escape such tedium, but Lady Donahue had firmly blocked her first attempt at flight. Miss Boswell decided she actively disliked Lady Donahue. The Countess was a reminder of why Miss Brooke needed to be reminded what fun and excitement was. Otherwise, she might end up a dry, crusty matron like Lady Donahue. That was a fate to be prevented at all costs.

Miss Boswell started counting the pearls in Lady Whitehall's hair. She was up to seventeen when a maid approached her. "Pray pardon, Miss, but Miss Brooke requests your company."

Miss Boswell restrained herself from tackling the maid in appreciation. She curtsied to the assembled group. "By your leave?" Lady Donahue gave her an absent nod and Miss Boswell followed the maid over to a remote part of the yard with alacrity.

"La, Ali, I could kiss you." Miss Boswell rushed to her friend's side and grabbed her hand with a smile. She could not help but notice Miss Brooke's distress, but decided to see if she could cheer her friend up before discussing what upset her. "Do you know Madam Bartlet has twenty-seven glass rubies on her left slipper and only twenty-four on her right? Her cobbler must hate her!"

Miss Brooke gave Miss Boswell a wan smile. "I am sorry I left you with them."

"Rubbish, it was fascinating. I heard all about Madam Bartlet's middle son's latest progress at Oxford and the scandal her of her eldest losing their fortune at the tables." Miss Boswell wrinkled her nose. "I do not know how that woman is so heavy. I do not think she stopped talking long enough to breathe, much less eat."

A laugh involuntarily escaped Miss Brooke's lips. "Oh, Miss Boswell, whatever will I do with you?"

"Let me push Lady Donahue off something very steep?"

"Oh, please no, I fear I might be stuck with her!"

Miss Boswell sat on the grass next to her friend's pushchair. "You have decided to marry Lord Charmaine, then?"

"The Duchess gave me little choice." She sighed, choosing to ignore Miss Boswell sitting directly on the grass. Bigger problems were afoot. "I do not know what I am going to do about my father. He will, inevitably, refuse Lord Charmaine's suit."

"Even if it means your social ruin?"

Miss Brooke nodded. "Yes. You know my Father."

"He is rather determined." Miss Boswell considered. "You are of age. There is nothing he can do to stop the two of you from wedding."

"He will withhold my inheritance. The will is written in such a way if I do not marry with his approval I will receive not a whit of it. That seems like plenty he can do."

"Will Lord Charmaine care?"

"Brenda, I know nothing about this man. I believe I have only met him once."

"Well, that will soon be twice."

"What?" Miss Brooke looked surprised.

"A select group of gentlemen will be joining us during the House of Lord's break. Lord Charmaine will be among them." Apparently listening to endless hours of chatter had its uses, Miss Boswell thought.

"I do not know if I am ready to meet him." Miss Brooke was still reeling from all the recriminations Duchess Castlemire had laid upon her. "I do not have a plan."

Miss Boswell smiled. "You do not need one, Alison. Just smile and be yourself. He cannot help but be charmed."

"Yes, but I am not worried about charming him." In a rush, Miss Brooke relayed the conversation with the duchess. Miss Boswell's disregard for the laws of polite Society did not make her blind to the intricacies of the *tons* machinations. In fact, Miss Brooke thought to herself, Miss Boswell was likely the smarter of the two of them. "So, you see, I am worried about how to best handle Society."

"I do not see." Miss Brooke started to expound, but Miss Boswell waved her to silence. "No, wait, please. Society views you as a mercenary beast for what you did to Lord Charmaine. In their eyes, you already did it. Now they expect you to keep being a beast, but, as long as Lord Charmaine favors you, Duchess Castlemire seems to indicate they will accept you. But if you are genial they will still accept you. Being a sinner or saint achieves the same results."

"I suppose."

"So why take a risk and be yourself?"

"I am always myself, Brenda." Miss Brooke sounded slightly vexed.

"No, you are not." Miss Boswell smiled at her friend, trying to take any sting out of her words. "You oft care more about what someone thinks, or more about what you should do than what you want to do. Now you have a chance to throw that all to the wind and be yourself."

"Brenda, I like all of the fripperies you hate. I enjoy my pointed slippers. I know the rules of the fan, I enjoy the dances, and I even like gossip. I am good at the games of the *ton* and I am happy partaking in them. You make it sound like I am trapped in a world I do not love. Well, I do love it, and there is nothing I wish to throw to the wind!"

"Perhaps." Miss Boswell did not seem convinced. "I am sure some of that is true. But sometimes it is not. For example, think about going to the theatre. What do you truly love to do? Watching the play. Society does not go to the theatre to watch the actors or the performance. Perhaps you should just watch the play?"

"I…" Miss Brooke sighed. "If I do marry Lord Charmaine, I will need to make him an excellent countess."

"Viscountess," Miss Boswell corrected with a wave. "He is not an earl yet. Nevertheless, you could no more be a bad countess than you could be out of fashion."

"Or be the center of a scandal?"

"La, that is beside the point. Everyone has a bad day. Ali, you are beautiful, elegant, and affable. How could you make a bad viscountess? This is an absurd worry!"

"Duchess Castlemire told me I had to save Lord Charmaine from the gossip saying he is a fool or else she would personally ruin me."

Miss Boswell hid a smile at her friend's apprehensions. "The Duchess is worried gossip might be correct. She knows it is not, but you are still a stranger to her. Worse, you are a stranger she is extending an umbrella of respectability over." Miss Boswell leaned in and took Miss Brooke's hand. "I mean it, be you! Who could not fall madly in love with you?"

Miss Brooke smiled at her friend, starting to perk up. "You make me sound like Helen of Troy. I am really not all that irresistible."

"Or improper." Miss Boswell smiled at her. "I suppose you are right about it being an unfair comparison. I bet Helen knew how to have fun."

Miss Boswell pushed Miss Brooke's chair out of the secluded part of the garden with the intent to rejoin the crowd. Charmaine was sitting on a small stone bench a goodly way down the path. Miss Boswell halted the chair with a smile. It was clear he picked a spot that would reassure them he was safely out of earshot. She liked his consideration. Miss Boswell considered him critically. He was not as handsome as Farrington—no one could ever be as handsome as Anthony—but his piercing blue eyes and strong jaw were certainly attractive.

Charmaine stood at their approach with a small bow. There was a moment of awkward silence. Miss Boswell broke it with her typical grace and charm.

"La, this is uncomfortable." Charmaine and Miss Brooke gave her identical looks. "Well, it is. Why pretend? I will go over and sit on the bench so you two can talk."

Miss Boswell asked her friend, "Is that acceptable?"

Miss Brooke nodded. "Yes, thank you."

Miss Boswell shot Charmaine another lopsided smile and pranced over to her bench. Charmaine could not help but smile back at her. He looked at Miss Brooke. "I am impressed with Miss Boswell. You are lucky to have her as a friend."

"I would be in Bedlam without her." Miss Brooke noticed she was smoothing her skirts endlessly and relaxed her hands.

"Have you been friends long?" Charmaine looked around for something to sit on. He felt as if he was towering over her. Finding nothing he settled for leaning against a small tree. Parliament would have to deal with a slightly dirty coat. Lord knows they'd seen worse.

"Yes." This was better than talking about the weather. "We met our first Season here in London. We were introduced to Her Majesty on the same day. Miss Boswell was a chatterbox in line and I was perfectly silent. After two hours of endless talking at me she finally got me to open up about how nervous I was about tripping due to having to walk backwards in my huge train."

"Did you trip?"

Miss Brooke flashed him a quick smile. "What a rude question."

Charmaine straightened and bowed. "I apologize."

In that moment, Miss Brooke realized he was as nervous as she was. "No, no, there is no need to apologize." Miss Brooke forced a smile on her face. "I did not trip. The opposite. I was an instant success. Miss Boswell, on the other hand, had a dismal time of it."

"Which I find odd. I enjoy dancing with her. That is not something I can say about most women in Society."

"You were kind to dance with her." Miss Brooke was sincere.

Charmaine gave her an odd look. "Since we will be dealing together for some time, will you permit me to be bold?"

Oh dear, thought Miss Brooke. "Please do."

"That is a horrible thing to say about your friend." Disapproval filled his voice.

"Pray pardon?"

"I was not kind to dance with her. I danced with her because she is a lovely woman who was making a friend of mine laugh. Assuming kindness does her a disservice."

Miss Brooke leaned back into the cushions of the chair. It was not a good day for her pride or self-esteem. She was not sure how many more of these shocks she could take. "I—I do not know what to say."

Charmaine shrugged and leaned back on the tree again. "You do not have to say anything. I ask only you think upon it. Society follows your lead—if she is an outcast and worthy of pity in your eyes, the *ton* will replicate that reaction."

"I…" Miss Brooke straightened and looked at him. Her eyes were a wonderful bright blue. "Can we talk about something else? I will consider your words, but I am not in a place to continue this conversation."

"Certainly, forgive me." He smiled ruefully at her. "I am afraid I am not very skilled in the delicate arts of conversation."

"Well, I am," Miss Brooke offered with a small smile. "So, I will assist."

Charmaine absently ran his hand through his chestnut hair, pulling some of it out of his neat queue. "So, my tutor, what it is I should be saying to you?"

"In honesty, I think you are doing quite well. Talking about Miss Boswell was far superior than discussing the weather." Miss Brooke frowned slightly. "I have had a trying day."

"I will try not to contribute to your stress." Charmaine replied, straightening from where he was leaning on the tree.

"Now it is I who should give thanks." His cadence was so stilted, Miss Brooke thought, so very formal. He would relax and tense from sentence to sentence. She did not know how to put him at ease. "Tell me, what you are skilled at?"

"Pray pardon?"

Miss Brooke smiled politely at him, "You claimed a lack of skill in conversational sallies. What then, are you are skilled in? I know naught about you, you realize?"

"Ah." Charmaine smiled slightly. "What is my worth as a human? Fairly minimal in the eyes of the *ton,* I suppose. I find the gatherings of Society a chore."

Miss Brooke made an effort to equal his smile. "Well, they say something about opposites attracting."

"Society loves you. I take it you love it back?"

"Very much." Miss Brooke considered. "I grew up on a sprawling country estate. Life was solitary, with only my imagination for company. My mother has no interest in children. My father is always in Town. Now, I spent most of my time here with him. I have never truly enjoyed academics or the womanly arts of needlepoint and the like, so I was never good at anything in the country. In London, well, I am good at London."

"A true debutante."

"I suppose, but that sounds negative."

"Forgive me." He was awkward again.

She decided to press the issue. "You find me frivolous and pointless, do you not?"

He smiled unexpectedly. "Now who is being rude?"

"But you do."

"But I do." Charmaine shrugged uncomfortably. "I have a negative impression of most of the nobility. We have an obligation to lead, to use our resources to benefit the British Empire and her people. Our duty, our very purpose, is to serve England."

Miss Brooke looked at him, interested. "So, you are fighting for reform? A Whig?"

"While I am fighting for reform, I am part of Lord North's government. The monarchy continues to lead England to glory. The sun never sets on the British Empire. Success is built through strict control on trade and the ability to oversee our colonies. If we weaken the Crown, we destabilize the system."

"But when the monarch is weak?" The passion in his voice fascinated Miss Brooke. No one spoke politics with her before, as having a brain was considered unfashionable in women. "His Majesty is a fine ruler and all, but…"

"His son?" Charmaine shrugged. "A weak heir is a challenge. But we have survived worse and still prosper. Unless we overthrow the monarchy completely, which as Cromwell showed us, is a horrible idea, we will face these challenges."

"But people say the prince is unfit to rule…?"

"We do not know that. What we know is he is not his father. But he is ten. King George is in fine health. Let us not borrow trouble."

Miss Brooke smiled at him, "We have enough of our own?"

"We do indeed." His brilliant blue eyes softened a little as he looked at her. "You have a quick wit."

"I do. It is part of that useless Society you dislike. We banter and insult with great speed. It is called repartee."

"I have never heard of it." His smile made his sarcasm inclusive. "So that is my passion. I do not know if I would call it a skill, but I come to London for the Sessions of the House of Lords. I also manage our shipping interests, play the 'change, and oversee my family's estates. Not an interesting life, I suppose, but one makes do."

"Compared to mine it seems fascinating. I select dresses, write correspondence, and dance the night away with men who only care about my fortune."

"And your pretty face."

She frowned. "Frankly, I am not sure how much that matters. I sometimes wonder if I would be half as sought after if I did not have the largest dowry on the market."

"Second, actually. Maybe third. Lady Teresa is plum with wealth and Miss Linder has a dowry as impressive as yours. And she has not rejected seven suitors."

Miss Brooke did not like the turn of the conversation. She decided to playfully redirect it. "Perhaps I should increase it to eight."

"I would prefer if you did not," Charmaine remonstrated, frowning. "I am not overly fond of rejection."

This is not where I wanted the conversation to go at all, Miss Brooke thought with a frown. My father is going to reject him! What then? "Rumor has reached me that you summoned my father to ask for my hand."

Charmaine nodded. "I hear that is how things are done. Do you know if I will hear from him soon?"

"You should." Miss Brooke did not add her father would likely be riding horses to death to return to London as soon as possible. "Our country estate borders Cornwall, so it will be at least a week. I should warn you that he is not the easiest man to deal with."

"Neither am I," Charmaine retorted with a smile.

They sat in silence for a bit, each searching for things to say. Miss Boswell, noting the awkward silence descending, bounced over. "No new scandal?"

Charmaine laughed. "In front of your watchful eyes? For shame, Miss Boswell, what a cad you must think me!"

"I can turn around if you like."

"Miss Boswell!" Miss Brooke exclaimed.

Charmaine laughed again. "A charming offer, Miss Boswell, but I fear my companion objects. Will you instead indulge me by accompanying us back to the gathering?"

"With pleasure! I will summon the maid for the chair," Brenda responded.

Charmaine waved her off. "No need. The day I cannot push a chair is the day I hang up my hat for good."

The house felt empty. Miss Brooke drifted from room to room in her father's spacious townhouse without any real purpose. She finally snuggled down in the library. She loved the room. Her father had read to her in this giant wingback chair when she was young. Her thoughts lingered on her father and she chewed inelegantly on her lip. Hopefully he would hurry. The house was quiet and empty without him. More so, he'd be able to tell her everything, no matter what it was, would be fine. The world would be so different if she had accompanied him to visit her mother in the country.

With a sigh she curled further into the chair. The problems of her father and Charmaine did not seem as pressing when confronted with the idea that she might have been a bad friend. Miss Brooke had an endless sea of acquaintances, and a handful of women whose company she sought out at balls, but only one true friend.

Charmaine's comments kept replaying through her mind. Was she being unfair to Miss Boswell? Worse, was she using her influence to project that viewpoint to those around her? Miss Boswell always was forceful about succeeding on her own and not wanting Miss Brooke to use her popularity to include her. Yet, perhaps, Miss Brooke thought, she took that too far. Rather than using her popularity to support Miss Boswell, maybe she excluded her?

Miss Brooke never invited Miss Boswell into the little closed circles because it seemed like listening to endless chatter made her friend unhappy. And she confided now and again to her circle how she desperately wished she could teach Miss Boswell about fashion. Perhaps, Miss Brooke concluded with a sigh, Charmaine was right.

By the time a dinner tray appeared, Miss Brooke's mood was bleak. She gave her maid a forced smile along with a thank you for the food. The maid, a short, chubby woman she knew as Abigail, did not instantly retreat. "You staying in tonight then, miss?"

"I believe so. I am afraid I lost track of time, Abigail. I think a night in would do me good. Perhaps a book and early to bed with me. And, if it would not be too much trouble, a bath?"

"It won't be no trouble at all, miss." Abigail looked at her mistress critically. "Staff is a mite worried about you."

"That is kind of them, but I am quite well. I fell at the ball and the Donahues had a doctor on staff." The words sounded unconvincing even to her ears.

"That ain't all that I mean, miss. Gossip coming back a mite cruel to you lately."

Miss Brooke had no idea how people who were mean or disrespectful to their staff managed to survive in Society. Father raised her alone, without any other children around, so the staff filled the resulting void. From a young age, she knew the invisible help saw everything. More frighteningly, each household talked to the next. The result was a gossip web rivaling even the *ton*.

"I know." Miss Brooke tried not to let her frustration show. "There is not much I can do, however."

"Maybe. Maybe not."

Miss Brooke gestured for Abigail to continue.

"Your Da is going to reject the pup, like always?"

Miss Brooke restrained a smile. The staff's support raised her mood—pup, indeed. "If he rejected Lord Farrington, I foresee no reason why he would accept Lord Charmaine. I suspect you are correct."

"And you gonna to listen to him?"

"Yes." Miss Brooke did not consider her answer. Uncertainty vanished once she was asked so simply. She loved her father and he loved her. If something mattered so deeply to him, well, she would accede. With anger, tears, and objections, but if she was going to defy him, she should have done it for Farrington.

"Then why wait for his Lordship to do it?" Abigail asked as if talking to a child.

Miss Brooke frowned, "You mean reject Lord Charmaine myself?"

"Uh-huh. Think about it. People are saying you are after the biggest fish. Met the current bloke through the last one and you ditched one for the other. Played them both, set a trap, reeled them in. Aye?"

"So they say." Miss Brooke's irritation came through this time.

"And what happens if you let him go?"

"Abigail, you know this. Society treats me like a ruined, stupid woman. I get exiled from balls, I stop getting invitations to dinner parties and I sit at home and rot."

"You is being foolish, miss. Society won't completely toss you out. No one is saying it won't be rough, but it won't be all that. Thems wild bucks still want your money and pretty face." As Miss Brooke sat back and considered, Abigail started to withdraw. "Your food is getting cold. You eat up and then we'll get you your bath. It ain't all bad, you know."

"I know, I do know. One's own problems can seem overwhelming, as I am sure you understand. Would you please thank everyone for their concern? And reassure them I am fine?"

Abigail nodded and backed out into the hallway. She shut the door and looked askew at the several eavesdroppers. They all walked down the hallway a bit before a young footman asked, "You think she's really holding up?"

"Naw." Abigail's answer was prompt. "She ain't and you know it. All that girl ever wanted was to show her Da she was good for something. He ain't ever gave her a chance at nothing, so she showed him she's good at being a lady. Now that's all crumbling around her and it's gonna get worse. Course she ain't well."

Another maid piped up, "Why don't she elope? The master would forgive that girl anything."

"Ain't that easy." Abigail, Miss Brooke's maid, was the expert. "Ali ain't dumb or meek, but she's got a real soft spot for her Da. She won't hurt him. 'Sides, if she was gonna do that, she'd have done it by now. I don't think she even knows this Charmaine fellow."

"Well," Ron spoke up, "we don't know him neither. Billy went by to try to talk to his people but we can't find where he lives. His mail all goes to the Donahue's but he don't live there. His man comes by a couple times a day and picks it up. Dunno."

Abigail paused in her march down the stairs. "Huh."

The conversation continued as they descended on the kitchen. The kitchen helper, a scrawny teenager who had only been with the household for a few months, peeped up from where she was cleaning a pot. "Charmaine lives over on Tower Hill."

The whole gaggle of gossip stopped and looked at the stringy-haired girl. Abigail dismissively replied, "No gentry live on Tower Hill."

"I don't know about where no rich folk live, but my last mistress had a thing with Charmaine's man. They live over by Tower Hill in a little set o' rooms. All run down and stuff."

Abigail's eyebrows flew upwards into her graying hair. "The Viscount Charmaine lives in Tower Hill?"

"Uh-huh. 'Manda says Billy ain't got nothing now cause of somesuch, but when the ships come in he'll be rich enough to make her a princess." The girl stopped scrubbing long enough to shrug. "Bet he's lying to swiv her, but she don't listen to me."

"You saying they're poor?" Ron clearly shared Abigail's surprise.

"Both Billy and his Lordship. Poor as poor. At the dun's door."

"Well," There was a note of sadness in the maid's voice. "That changes everything, don't it? Another one after her money. Poor little Ali."

CHAPTER VII

Miss Brooke looked with disgust at the pile of correspondence haphazardly threatening to spill off her desk. Everyone wanted their fingers in the latest gossip. Yet no matter how many times she looked through the pile she failed to find the neat and proper hand of Lord Farrington. Miss Brooke looked again anyway. Maybe it was stuck to the back of something else.

There was no letter from Farrington, but there was one from Lord Charmaine. The correspondence was brief, asking if she would accompany him for a ride around St. James Park. Miss Brooke frowned. Only couples who were engaged, or about to announce their engagement, rode alone around the park. She was still unsure what to do about Charmaine. He seemed well enough, but if she could choose anyone, she would choose Farrington.

All day she considered Abigail's words. She carefully rearranged her desk, unobtrusively hunting for correspondence from Farrington. If she her reputation was already ruined, why not do what she wanted? Miss Boswell's words from the tea party came back to her clearly. She might as well be herself. Why had she not eloped with Farrington? He seemed like everything she ever wanted. He was charming, serious, and they shared similar interests. She was positive she could grow to love him. Everyone said it was a perfect match. Everyone except for her father.

Finding nothing new in the pile of correspondence, Miss Brooke pulled out stationary and penned an invitation to ride with Farrington on the morrow. While she had yet to make up her mind about what to say to him, it was time to take control of her own life. If nothing else, he deserved the truth of why his friend was now pursuing her. Or, maybe, just maybe, Miss Brooke thought with a small, contemplative smile, it was time for her to do the pursuing.

Charmaine threw his wig across the room as he stormed through the door. It bounced off the wall and sprawled across the worn chair. Wilhelm looked from the ledger he was writing in and raised an eyebrow at his Lordship's undignified entrance. "Something amiss, my lord?"

"My peers are half-witted mongrels who should drown in their own privilege." Charmaine knocked the wig to the ground and replaced it in the chair. He sprawled out and started kicking his boots off.

"A spirited session today then. Taxes, the Church, or trade?" Wilhelm put down the quill and gave Charmaine his full attention.

"Neither. Slavery. I do not understand how someone can bring a slave to England and expect them to remain a slave. Do they not understand we are a civilized country? Are they daft?"

Wilhelm grunted in what sounded like agreement. "Do you want more bad news?"

"Let me guess. We are poor?" Charmaine managed to scrounge a grin from somewhere.

"Right on the money." Wilhelm rolled his eyes at himself. "Pardon the pun. The good news is the 'change has played heavily in your favor. Your man of affairs, me, cashed out several volatile investments. We lost the chance at larger returns, but I assumed you wish to pay your parent's servants until at least mid-summer."

"Any word from the ships?"

Wilhelm shook his head no. "I wrote your brother, my lord. I think it is high time he investigates matters personally. He is in Geneva at the moment. I suspect his contacts and ability to get information will far exceed my own."

"Shipping Michael off with the East India Company was the best investment I have ever made."

"I agree, my lord. As much as I personally enjoy his company, poverty would be impossible to avoid if he was still a rake in the gambling hells. If we can so much as find out the whereabouts of any of the three ventures I will feel much more secure."

Charmaine nodded. "Any news regarding Miss Brooke? Did she answer my missive?"

"Yes and no, my lord. Amanda, my current paramour, previously employed a girl who is now with the Brooke's. She says the household is against you and is attempting to ferret out information regarding your person and intent."

Charmaine frowned. "That is not the sort of information I had in mind. That feels like spying."

"It *is* spying, my lord. This is what the servants of polite Society do. Spy." Wilhelm, as was frequently the case, was exasperated with his employer.

"Did you find out anything I would be interested in? Her preferred flowers, perhaps?"

"Lilies, I did that two days ago. I am working on compiling the reasons Mr. Brooke gave to previous suitors. I suspect the answer to our mystery is there."

"Our mystery? Wilhelm, I think you need to find a hobby."

"I have a hobby, my lord. This is it."

"Ruining my life? And what mystery are you talking about?" Charmaine was having trouble following Wilhelm's quicksilver mind.

"That is running, not ruining, thank you. The mystery is simple. Why would a woman come to London, act like any other, and then refuse all offers of marriage? It is not done."

Charmaine shrugged. "Perchance she does not wish a husband."

Wilhelm frowned in thought. "Unlikely, my lord. Most young ladies are not given a choice. And marrying Farrington would have given her access to considerable prestige."

"In truth, I care not. Her life is her own. I am sure she had reasons for her choices."

"Yes, my lord, I understand. But we need to know if those choices are going to affect you."

"Yes, they are going to affect me. I am going to marry the lass!" Talking to Wilhelm was as frustrating as talking to the Whigs.

"Only if she accepts you, my lord. This has yet to occur."

"She will." Charmaine frowned at a hole in his stocking. "I know this is a fine turn for me, but I feel sorry for the girl. She was not given much choice."

"Some would say the same of you, my lord."

"Irrational. Letting her reputation be soiled hurts me not at all."

Wilhelm nodded. "I agree. However, your mother and Lady Stanton have convinced Society you are a virtuous and noble man who would defend the honor of any young lady."

"Poppycock," Charmaine replied.

"Your mother's doing, my lord. She is preaching you are a paragon of virtue. Society does not know you, so they have eaten it whole. The tale is that the lady laid a parson's trap when she lured you into that upstairs room and had her friend bring several high sticklers to 'accidentally' discover you," explained Wilhelm.

"That sounds overly complicated." Charmaine considered the story once more. He was willing to discount it off as typical fluff when Miss Brooke mentioned it, but Wilhelm's sense of gossip tended to be accurate. "And rather flattering, actually. A woman who creates a trap that complicated and canny has both the intelligence and ambition to make a decent wife. I would be more eager to marry her if it was true."

"You still do not like her?"

"No, the opposite. I find I enjoy her company quite a bit. She seems a bit shy and overwhelmed, but there is a good deal of spirit hiding under that proper façade." Charmaine considered their conversation at the Castlemire tea. "I feel like she could be a good deal more than she is now. As if she is a star that has never been allowed to shine."

Wilhelm leaned back in his own chair. "I will remember that when writing your poetry for you, my lord. Are you truly fond of her?"

"It is more than fondness." He frowned at his boot. "I like how I feel around her. When I saved her from that cretin, I felt—emboldened. Strong. Proud. A primitive, primal feeling. I defeated the dragon and rescued the princess. It felt good." Charmaine ran his hand through his chestnut hair. "Taking joy in such a terrible event feels inappropriate but, I suppose I do."

Wilhelm considered, "Be careful, my lord. No losing your heart to a woman with seven rejections behind her, my lord."

Charmaine stood, laughing. "Worry not. My heart is safe."

Wilhelm watched him walk into the other room and tried to turn his attention back to their expense ledger. He never heard Lord Charmaine speak about feeling primitive for a woman before. The wording might be erroneous, but Wilhelm understood the meaning. Being a hero might be the one thing that could loosen the cage around Lord Charmaine's heart.

Wilhelm grabbed the letter addressed to Hr. Mr. Michael Anderson and quickly added a postscript to his friend.

Miss Brooke's gray mare was restless as they approached Hyde Park. Normally Miss Brooke and Dapple rode every morning, but this was the first time since the incident Miss Brooke felt well enough to make such an excursion. Her groom followed at a discreet distance and she had half a mind to have the man hold her horse and to continue on foot. In truth, she forgot about her ribs when planning her meeting with Farrington. She wished Dapple would stop prancing, as each high-spirited step caused a small twinge of pain.

The day was lovely. London was delighting its tenants with a week of unseasonably perfect weather. Miss Brooke smiled a bit with nervous excitement as she rode further into the park. Her nerves came to a crescendo when she peered Farrington waiting for her. He looked like a paragon of masculinity, his gelding's mane matching his own black hair. The horse and rider moved as one unit towards Miss Brooke. She felt butterflies flapping in her stomach.

Farrington bowed from his saddle in greeting. "Miss Brooke."

"Lord Farrington." Miss Brooke inclined her head, having no way to curtsey on horseback. "You look magnificent."

"All the horse, I assure you. He is a recent acquisition and I am most pleased with him." Farrington patted the gelding's arched neck familiarly. "Shall we ride?"

"I would be delighted." Miss Brooke kept Dapple to a stately walk. Farrington's mount fell in step beside them. "I have something on my mind."

"You are hardly one to call me out to talk about poppycock, Miss Brooke." Farrington's voice was mellow and even. Nothing ever seemed to break the cadence of his speech. "How can I assist you?"

Miss Brooke reined her mount in and looked over at him. He also came to a halt and patiently waited. Except for her groom trailing along behind them, they were perfectly alone. She took a deep breath, lifted her chin, and delivered her well-rehearsed line with great dignity. "We should elope."

"Excuse me?" Farrington's eyebrow moved the slightest smidgen upwards.

"We should elope," Miss Brooke repeated.

"What about your entanglement with Charmaine?"

"There is no entanglement. Nothing happened between myself and Lord Charmaine." Miss Brooke searched Farrington for any reaction and was a bit disappointed at how calm and steady he appeared.

Under his gloves Farrington's knuckles were white from tension. "Miss Brooke, I saw you. When Charmaine carried you down the stairs, I was there. I find it hard to believe nothing happened."

Miss Brooke shrugged. "I do not feel what happened between me and Lord Charmaine concerns you, nor is it relevant to this discussion. I assure you nothing improper occurred between us." She frowned slightly, losing her air of impassive unconcern. "I would hope that would be good enough for you."

"Then why, Miss Brooke, do you wish to elope?" Farrington encouraged his gelding into a slow walk. He was not sure what he was expecting from Miss Brooke this morning, but this certainly was not it.

"This is what I should have done two weeks ago. I am of age and I consent to your suit. It took me time to build the courage to defy my father."

"Or to become embroiled in a social situation where marrying me would protect you from scandal?" Farrington gripped his reins even harder, fighting to maintain control over his emotions.

"Foolishness." Miss Brooke was dismissive. "If I was worried about scandal, I would elope with Lord Charmaine. This is what I want."

Farrington looked into her eyes and winced at the sincerity shining back at him. His heart lurched as he realized she was serious. Everything he wanted was being offered to him, but after the conversation with her father, he knew he could not take it. "Miss Brooke, I thank you for the compliment of the offer, but I am afraid Gretna Green is not in my future."

Miss Brooke blinked. "You are refusing? But you claimed to love me."

"I am, I did, and I do. But marriage is more than love, Miss Brooke."

"You will not marry me without my dowry." Miss Brooke gaped at him.

Farrington would not look at her. "The situation is unfortunate."

She stopped her mare and stared at him. "You only wanted my portion."

"I believe, Miss Brooke, this conversation has progressed to its conclusion." Farrington turned his steed to face her and bowed deeply. "Please accept my regrets and convey my regards to Miss Boswell."

Miss Brooke's mind stumbled. All she could do was repeat herself. "Truly? You will not marry me without my inheritance? But you claimed to love me."

"Farewell, Miss Brooke." Farrington turned his gelding and set off at a barely constrained canter through the park. Miss Brooke sat dumbfounded on her mare and stared blankly after him as her world crashed around her ears.

Eventually, she turned Dapple back towards her father's estate. The mare's buoyant and merry step made a poor counterpart to her rider's bleak mood.

Charmaine was in the middle of his morning exercises when there was a powerful banging on the outer door. The thin walls carried the sound of Wilhelm answering the door, and, curious, Charmaine peered out of his room to identify the visitor. He was startled to find Farrington in his doorway, shoving Wilhelm aside.

"Farrington." Charmaine greeted his friend, deciding to treat this like any other visit.

"Charmaine." There was a rough, unusual edge to Farrington's voice. "Do you have whiskey in this shithole?"

Charmaine directed his attention to Wilhelm. "Get us whiskey. An absurd amount. Then make yourself scarce."

Wilhelm bowed, suddenly a respectful servant when a non-family member appeared, and quickly returned with two decanters worth of whiskey before silently leaving. Charmaine poured two full glasses and handed one to his friend, Farrington slammed the whiskey. Charmaine refilled the glass and sat. "You have words for me?"

"Not yet."

Charmaine sat back to watch his friend throw back another glass. After the third tumbler, Charmaine took Farrington's glass from him and refilled it with water. "Enough. Slow down."

Leaving the glass on the table, Farrington stood and began to pace around the small room. He glared at the furnishings. "How do you live like this?"

Charmaine shrugged. "Not by choice. I suppose I could move back in with my parents. If I did, it announces to the world we are poor or brings attention to the severity of my father's illness. Neither of these is preferable to living in, as you so eruditely put it, a shithole."

"Is it worth it, Charmaine? Is it really? Honor and duty and all such rubbish?"

"Perhaps not. But it is who I am." Charmaine sipped his whiskey and tried not to make a face. He still had not acquired a taste for it.

"And it is who you are."

"Damn it all. I know. But it is not what I want."

"What do you want?"

"I want to marry Miss Brooke. I want to take her to bride, I want to swive her brains out, I want to be her damned world." Farrington's hands were balled tightly into fists. "Do not you understand, Charmaine? I love her."

"Then marry her, Farrington. It is that simple."

Farrington gave him a look of disgust. "It is not that simple. Zounds, Charmaine, how can you even say that?"

Charmaine acquiesced with a rueful grin, "I can say it easily. Living it is another matter. Tell me why you cannot marry Miss Brooke. Her father will not give you permission? If you truly love her, you could elope?"

"True." Farrington's voice drooped. "She offered that very thing on our morning ride."

"I clearly have not made a good impression on the girl, have I?"

Farrington glared at Charmaine. "This is my crisis, Charmaine, not yours."

"Pardon, I was trying to be funny. So, she thinks you should elope. And you think…?"

"I cannot." Farrington finished his water and refilled the tumbler with whiskey.

Charmaine watched in silence. At worst, Farrington would pass out from drink on Charmaine's bed. In truth, Charmaine considered, that might be the best thing. He was not sure he wanted to turn his friend loose on Society in this state. He filled Farrington's glass even higher. "Why not?"

"The same reason you cannot. I need her damn money."

"I did not know you were hurting."

Farrington nodded. "George is furious at our family for supporting the populist movements. He confiscated our largest source of resources and threatened to seize more of our land. I favor

Miss Brooke, zounds, I love the girl, but I cannot give up on what I believe for love."

"If His Majesty is angry at you, no amount of money is going to save your lands. He will find a way to sideline you." Charmaine bit the inside of his cheek to try to stay calm as politics entered the conversation.

"I know." Farrington took another gulp. He seemed to be intentionally trying to knock himself out. "But if I can get enough assets together I am going to move to Virginia. Take Miss Brooke and help overthrow the Crown and empower the people. Do something with my life rather than be a pretty face in Court."

"Anthony! I am part of Lord North's government. You understand you are speaking treason to me?"

"Do not trespass on my misery, Charmaine. You will not break faith with me. Commiserate with me. I cannot marry Miss Brooke."

Charmaine fought a small smile. Many philosophical conversations had occurred between the two friends. Farrington knew Charmaine prized personal honor over the government. "You would reveal me if I was plotting treason."

"Only if it was a government I believed in. Zounds, Charmaine. Alison!"

"What is it you wish me to say? As you know, I am courting her."

"I know, but you cannot marry her either, so it matters not what you do." Farrington glowered. "It should not matter. I should not care. I do. I am trying hard not to care. But, by God's teeth, if you do anything to harm her..."

"Stop being insulting." Something occurred to Charmaine. He tore out a piece of paper, wrote a single word, and handed it to Farrington. "Show me that later. I have something to tell you when we are both calm and sober. Now, why cannot I marry Miss Brooke?"

Farrington took the piece of paper with a confused look but did not question it. "You cannot marry her because her inheritance is locked in a ludicrous trust. Her father's approval is required for any suitor to gain Miss Brooke's dowry nevertheless of her age. And if he does not marry her off, he gets to keep control of all of it. Why ever marry her off?"

"I doubt the legality of that." Charmaine was trying to remember the small bit of contractual law he learned from the House of Lords but drink blurred his brain as well.

"Legal or not, do you have the capital to hire solicitors to challenge it? I do not."

Charmaine was still frowning. "He could be lying."

"I cannot take that risk." Farrington finished yet another drink. "Can you?"

"No." Charmaine took Farrington's cup from him. "You should slow down. You do not drink any more than I do."

"I do not want to slow down. I want to marry Alison. Actually," Farrington leaned in conspiratorially, "I want to see the Colonies free of King George. Imagine, a place with no monarchy. Rule by the people. How it should be."

"There would be chaos, Farrington. The people are not fit to rule themselves. They are an uneducated, uncivilized mass that we have an obligation to protect. The only way I will ever agree with the idea of universal democracy is if all people are educated and have equal interest in the overall wellbeing of the government. Otherwise the farmers only care what is best for the farmers, traders only care about the traders, and the merchants only care about the merchants. The system would be fragmented and inefficient."

"It could work. The people have a right to rule themselves." Farrington looked like he wanted to say more, but he was slurring heavily. Words were difficult.

"And then there is the issue of taxation." Charmaine leaned forward as he became more animated about the subject. "How do you expect people to vote to tax themselves? It creates an unsustainable situation. Unless a government is able to maintain a tax base there is no money to educate. If you do not educate, then there is an elite anyway, but capital and education create the elite rather than birth and training. I fail to see how such a risky transition, with likely the same outcome, would be beneficial to any of the Colonies."

"Social mobility," Farrington replied.

"What?"

"Social mobility." Farrington scowled at Charmaine. "Why can you not understand?"

Charmaine nodded. "You mean the argument that even if an elite is created it will be more fluid. Birth will not control social and economic standing. Rather, education, capital, and ambition will dictate one's status. I find such unrealistic and idealistic. Consider the merchants we trade with. We trade with the same small group every time. You think a pattern of nepotism would not blossom in the Colonies? A new set of ruling elite would be created, one with even less accountability to the masses. Why would these people want to tax, limit, or otherwise burden themselves? At least we have manufactured rules to limit royal power. What limits are there on democracy?"

"People are not like that. People are good. People want what is best."

"Under that stoic nature of yours, you are really an idealist. People are inherently selfish. We need Hobbes's leviathan or else we will consume ourselves." Charmaine frowned as he watched his friend's head bob towards the table. It was irritating to be so far into a conversation he cared about and have the other person fade out.

"You are wrong." Farrington shook his head like a wet dog and tried to stand. He failed, collapsing back into the chair.

"The last argument of the idealist." Charmaine walked around the table and helped his friend stand. "Come, we shall get you into my bed. You can tell me how I am wrong when you wake."

"You *are* wrong." Farrington squinted as they stumbled into the other room. "And I truly love Alison. It would have been a new world, a new life. It would have been sublime."

Charmaine shoved Farrington gently at the bed. "Things will be better when you wake."

Farrington held on to consciousness long enough to give an accurate rebuttal, "Liar."

Charmaine walked back into the front room to find Wilhelm sitting in Farrington's chair. "How much did you hear?"

"All, my lord." Wilhelm's eyes narrowed. "We have a problem."

"Other than my drunk traitorous friend?"

"Yes, other than him. You know I care naught about politics." Wilhelm considered. "It may be in our best interest for him to move to the New World. We have a good captain but having a partner in the Americas would increase profits."

Charmaine grunted. "Then what is the problem?"

"The money, my lord. If Lord Farrington speaks the truth, it seems unlikely Mr. Brooke will give anyone permission to marry his daughter. And, without permission, we will not get a shilling."

"Find a way to circumvent that." Charmaine had become attached to the idea of marrying Miss Brooke, even if she freshly requested to elope with his best friend. He was not sure of his feelings on that matter. Even if he was only interested in her for her dowry, could he pursue a woman for whom Farrington carried affection? Bruised pride aside, he questioned the wisdom of involving himself with a woman his closest friend cared for. Charmaine took a deep breath and attempted to banish such concerns from his mind. If Miss Brooke declined his offer of marriage, he would accept that. Otherwise, the dice were cast.

"I will look into it, my lord." Wilhelm replayed the conversation in his mind. "Are you going to tell Miss Brooke you know she asked Lord Farrington to elope?"

Charmaine shook his head. "No. I am sure Lord Farrington does not want his personal life blathered to the four winds. It is hard enough to be rejected by the woman you love. Having to reject her back seems cruel."

"So, what are you going to do?"

"Absolutely nothing. Stay the course. Prepare to go to battle with Mr. Brooke."

Wilhelm frowned. "You think you can gain his permission?"

"Maybe. Perhaps."

"Have you considered you might overestimate your abilities at persuasion? Miss Brooke's inheritance is impressively large, my lord. No sane man would relinquish control over it." Wilhelm skepticism was clear.

"No sane man places his daughter on the marriage mart and then denies all suitors, much less a tight-fisted one. The expense is obscene. There is more here than we know. I shall go forth as planned until I speak to Mr. Brooke."

"This course of action is not prudent, my lord," advised Wilhelm.

Charmaine's gaze flickered door of the bedroom. "I wish to be alone."

Wilhelm retreated deeper into the small flat with a small bow. Charmaine failed to notice the rare respectful gesture as he contemplated the mess his life had become.

Collins frowned at Charmaine's shoes. They were negligently tossed on an embroidered footrest with their owner stretched leisurely behind them. Charmaine was in an animated discussion with Lady Stanton about the latest developments about how he should handle the courtship of Miss Brooke. Lady Stanton, with her hawk-like perception, noticed Collins distraction.

"Collins, would you please pay attention?" Lady Stanton sounded cross. Then again, Collins thought ruefully, Elizabeth always sounded cross.

"My apologies, beloved. I was considering Charmaine's shoes."

Charmaine arched an eyebrow. "My shoes?"

Collins nodded. "They are quite out of style. The curled toe is on everyone's foot and a jeweled buckle has become *de rigor*. What are those appalling things you are wearing? They look like a peasant's riding boot!"

"I do not believe peasants ride, Collins." Charmaine sounded amused. He glanced at his boots. His primary town shoes seemed serviceable.

"Charmaine, Collins, can you please pay attention?" Lady Stanton was clearly growing vexed. "We are speaking of Miss Brooke, not Charmaine's poor fashion sense."

"Darling, you worry too much. We already know what to do with Miss Brooke. What we need to know is what we are going to do about Charmaine's boots. I fear he will not listen to reason."

"Indeed?" Lady Stanton sounded skeptical. "And what is Charmaine to do with Miss Brooke?"

"Make her fall madly in love with him, obviously."

Charmaine leaned back and let the spouses talk. Their repertoire was so quick it was impossible for him to even get a word in. When they wanted his opinion he assumed they'd ask for it. Lady Stanton responded promptly to Collins' offhand statement. "La, because that will be easy. A woman like that has a heart made of ice. Seven suitors, Collins, Seven!"

Collins looked from Charmaine's shoes. "Yes. And she must have known her father would reject each and every one. She has to stop herself from becoming overly attached so she does not get her heart broken. But she has shown she is frustrated with the situation. After all, she asked Farrington to elope."

Charmaine finally interjected, "Which is a secret, please remember."

They both shushed him to silence with identical gestures. Lady Stanton answered, "Nothing is different between Farrington and our Charmaine. They are both handsome, strong willed men with impressive titles. Farrington has the better court manners. Such things seem to impress Miss Brooke."

"Yes, Elizabeth," Collins patronized, "but Charmaine saved her. He is her hero. And, more than that, he's a fighter. Charmaine can convince her that he will win against her father, and, even if he encounters refusal, marry her anyway."

"Except I am unable to marry her without her dowry," Charmaine interjected.

Lady Stanton spoke over Charmaine. "That seems simplistic. She must be smarter than that."

Collins shrugged. "Almost no one knows of Charmaine's need to marry except for his family and our family. He is an honorable man protecting her from scandal. Where is the difficulty?"

Lady Stanton again spoke over Charmaine, raising her voice so whatever he was going to say was drowned out. "If she discovers Charmaine wants her for her money, the plan fails."

"Not if she loves him," Collins shot back. "Miss Brooke will recover and forgive."

Lady Stanton considered. "Mayhap. She does seem rather tame."

Charmaine shook his head in disagreement, but Collins was already speaking. "Exactly. Charmaine here needs to convince dear Miss Brooke he is committed to marrying her, nevertheless of her father. With her heart and honor is involved, Mr. Brooke will have little choice but to yield."

Lady Stanton frowned. "Do you know Miss Brooke's father?"

"Daniel Brooke, younger brother of Lord Sanders. From Cornwall. An absolutely ruthless individual famed for his wealth, temper, and stunningly beautiful daughter."

"A man you call absolutely ruthless is going to yield if his daughter is ruined and in love?" Lady Stanton was extremely skeptical. "Now who is ridiculous?"

"Not so ridiculous," Collins continued, clearly enjoying showing off his superior knowledge, "Brooke has one flaw, my love. He denies his little girl nothing. There are ludicrous stories floating around from Miss Brooke's youth."

"What about Farrington then, my genius? If Mr. Brooke will give his daughter anything she desires, why oppose a man she cares about enough to elope with?" Lady Stanton turned to talk at Charmaine. "You can never tell that story to anyone else. Getting caught with a man is one thing. Asking to elope? Shameful!"

Charmaine again tried to answer, but Collins cut him off. "I have not once heard that she loves Farrington. And she did not ask him to elope until it was clear she was going to be forced to marry our charming Lord Charmaine."

Lady Stanton's voice was still sharp, "All the more fool, her. Charmaine is a much better catch. Farrington is going to get himself thrown out of Court on his ear. No sane woman would tolerate that."

There was an actual pause in the conversation. Charmaine found himself with nothing to say. Lady Stanton continued, "Besides, I am uncertain if Farrington really loves the girl. He seems more to love the idea of her."

Charmaine spoke, "I think you are wrong. I have never seen him that upset about a woman."

"While that may be, if he loved her, he would have eloped with her." Lady Stanton's declaration vibrated with confidence.

Charmaine again shook his head. "We all wish such romanticism was true, Lady Stanton. Duty is lighter than a feather but heavier than a mountain. We cannot forsake duty because of love."

Collins looked at Charmaine. "If you think that is true, you have never been in love. It is an unstoppable force, Charmaine, something that consumes the very soul. If Farrington loved her, they would be at Gretna Green right now. Mark my words."

Charmaine stared back at Collins. "There is a whole society, multiple generations of nobility who prove your words wrong. How many men have fallen for their mistresses or ladies for a handsome face? We have duty to marry as we should, not as we want."

"Tut, Charmaine, Farrington is not in the same place you are." Lady Stanton was clearly trying to sound kind. She was failing. "He is foolish, blinded by her beauty and wealth. You are blinded by nothing and seek only her money. Eloping with the girl costs Farrington nothing. You are fortunate he declined."

Charmaine could only nod. He was not about to spread gossip that his best friend was a traitor to the Crown and wanted Miss Brooke's money to fund revolution. Both Collins and Lady Stanton were staring at him, waiting for an answer. "You both know how uncomfortable all of this makes me, correct?"

Collins rolled his eyes. Lady Stanton tightened her lips and moved to sit daintily beside him. "Lord Charmaine, can I ask you a question?"

"Certainly, Baroness, I would be delighted to honor your request for information." The snark in the room was starting to get to Charmaine.

"There is no need to be unpleasant." Lady Stanton's gaze was intense. "Will you be a good husband?"

"The best I can be," answered Charmaine.

"Will you care for her?"

"That is two questions, Lady Stanton."

"Answer anyway," snapped Lady Stanton.

"Then yes, I will care for her as much as I am able. More than anyone else in my life," said Charmaine.

"Will you defend her from harm?"

"Yes."

"Will you put her needs equal to or before your own?"

"Yes,." Charmaine repeated.

"Will you take her interests to heart and care what she has to say?"

"Yes."

"Then why the remorse?" Lady Stanton joined her husband in an eye roll. "There is no plan to mistreat the girl. Yes, you want her money. So? Collins only married me because he wanted to bed me."

Charmaine blinked in surprise as Collins sighed wearily. He gave his friend a long-suffering look. "Alas, it was not worth it."

Lady Stanton swatted Collins without even a glance in his direction. "The point is, Lord Charmaine, everyone marries for a reason. What you do after that reason is what matters."

"I am unwilling to lie to her," said Charmaine.

"Then be creative and careful with the truth," said Lady Stanton.

"Lady Stanton, that is the same as lying," Charmaine said.

Collins cut in. "Charmaine, who cares?"

"My apologies, Collins, what?"

"Who cares? You are willing to marry her for money. You are willing to court her. Now is when you guide her through the process of falling in love and then marry her. Self-doubt is pointless. Recrimination gets in the way."

Charmaine looked confused. "Mr. Brooke, for one, cares. I do not understand how your scheme addresses the challenge of Mr. Brooke's control over the dowry?"

Lady Stanton and Collins exchanged a look. Lady Stanton spoke, "My brilliant husband is gambling. He assumes Mr. Brooke loves his daughter and would rather see her wed than thrown out of Society for being a ruined woman."

"I still fail to see how that fixes the problem of the dowry," Charmaine said.

Lady Stanton drew her lips into a line. "I am unclear as well. Collins?"

"You wait until she is madly in love with you, until Society only accepts her because of you, and then tell her father he is giving you his permission, or you are taking her away from him forever." Collins shrugged, "That is where he yields."

Charmaine looked at Collins in horror. "This is how you truly think?"

"Yes." Charmaine's surprise did not seem to bother Collins. "The gentry are naught but players in a game, Charmaine. Who marries whom, who supports what, which coalition rules the House, all of it. Power comes through manipulation and the willingness to use it."

"I—this does not sit well with me."

Collins looked to his wife for help. Lady Stanton took over once more. "I understand. Discard this conversation. Take the girl on a drive and show her kindness and warmth. Can you do that?"

"Not if it has a sinister purpose." Charmaine's voice was firm.

"Is saving her from the scorn of Society sinister? Remember your heroic goals?" Lady Stanton was trying to keep her voice sweet. The irritation was creeping through.

"You make it sound as if not wanting to lie and manipulate Miss Brooke is wrong." Charmaine was getting heated as well.

"In truth," Collins replied, "you are trying to marry her for her money. You *are* using her. Manipulation is a part of that, the same as with Miss Linder. What is the difference with Miss Brooke?"

"Because I like Alison, Collins." Charmaine spat. His anger escaped. He looked at them and stood. "I need to walk. Thank you both."

Unperturbed by Charmaine's wrath, Collins walked with him to the door. Lady Stanton stayed seated behind them. His friends' machinations disgusted Charmaine, but his ingrained good manners stopped him from storming out their door.

"Do you want to know what you truly should do?" Collins voice was even.

"No, Collins, what horrible and manipulative thing should I do to this poor girl? Please, tell me."

Collins took Charmaine's anger in stride. "Take one of our mounts, go for a ride with the girl, and be yourself. No manipulation, no thoughts of the future, only a ride."

Charmaine glared at him. "What scheme is this?"

"Nothing." Collins raised his hands in a defensive gesture.

"Lies."

"Robert, I have nothing but your best interest at heart. Trust in that. I will see you at the Hartford's ball." Collins stepped back with a small bow. The footman opened the door and handed Charmaine his hat and cane. Charmaine took them, bowed angrily at Collins, and removed himself from the estate.

Collins walked back into the parlor and looked over at his wife. She stood at the window watching Charmaine storm off. "We handled that wrong."

Lady Stanton said, "He's conflicted. Hearing the advice he needs to achieve his goals leaves him distraught."

"His goals do not match his dreams, Lizzy. He wanted the fairy tale. Now he is marrying for money."

"But why object with Miss Brooke and not with Miss Linder?"

"Because, as Robert so forcibly growled, he likes Miss Brooke." At Lady Stanton's continued look of confusion, Collins clarified, "I have only heard him say he likes a girl two or three times in a lifetime of friendship."

"Then he does want to marry her?"

Collins nodded. "Yes. But each time he talks to us we paint him as the villain. We tell him how to manipulate her and it breaks his dream even further."

Lady Stanton frowned again. "What dream?"

"The fairy tale. While he is still marrying for money, at least he can pretend he saved the girl, is rescuing her, and the money is his accidental reward. He remains the knight in shining armor," said Collins.

"You know him well." Lady Stanton turned back from the window to look at her husband.

"I do. He's a good man, Lizzie." Collins smiled unexpectedly. "Too bad you are not still on the market. You would have made him an amazing wife."

"Charmaine? Not in a million years. He is indecisive, whiny, and unsure of himself. I'd eat through him." Lady Stanton was quite sure of her position as a premier shrew of the *ton*.

"Well, yes. But Charmaine is naïve as well. He has dreams of saving the world. Without a sharp-minded chit, the *ton* will eventually eat him alive."

"I think we should sup soon. All these eating references." Lady Stanton considered. "Perhaps I shall invite Miss Brooke to tea."

"See if she is shrew enough for Charmaine?" Collins asked.

Lady Stanton's grin matched her husbands. "Exactly."

CHAPTER *VIII*

"**M**iss?" Abigail timidly poked her head into Miss Brooke's room. Miss Brooke returned from her morning ride two days ago and promptly locked herself away. Miss Boswell had repeatedly attempted to drag Miss Brooke out, but to no avail. Abigail was therefore a bit surprised to find Miss Brooke sitting by the window looking calm, composed, and every inch a regal young lady.

Miss Brooke did not turn. "Yes, Abigail?"

"There's an ill-tempered man outside a'callin'. Claims to be Lord Charmaine, ma'am."

"Claims?" Miss Brooke questioned with a raised eyebrow. Quickly, she began to gather her things.

"You described Lord Charmaine as dashing and polite. The man outside is not even-keeled," Abigail sniffed.

Miss Brooke smiled at her maid's tone, "Let the staff know I will be right down. Come, help me into my riding habit."

Abigail's unconvinced gaze burned a hole in her back as she traversed the grand staircase to the large oak front door. Charmaine was waiting for her on the street, mounted on a magnificent ebony thoroughbred. The horse matched his dark clothing perfectly. Charmaine's scowl completed his brooding appearance. Miss Brooke paused for a moment to appreciate his sheer beauty. His blue eyes flashed as they fell upon her and Miss Brooke automatically curtsied.

The groom rushed, leading Dapple. She wasted no time in elegantly mounting and arranging her skirts around the sidesaddle. They rode off towards Hyde Park without Charmaine speaking a word. Miss Brooke was first taken aback by his curt manner, but after consideration, decided it suited her perfectly. Being out in the sunshine was a welcome relief. Moreover, it was a relief a suitor would still come a calling and she had not managed to ruin chance at happiness.

Miss Brooke allowed herself to smile in the sunshine and admire the glorious weather. The other fashionable couples were out, mostly in carriages, looking to see and be seen. Miss Brooke silently examined who was with whom and what everyone was wearing. The normality of Society was a pleasant change from the whirlwind of her thoughts.

"We are getting a lot of attention." Charmaine's voice was crisp, almost harsh.

Miss Brooke gave another carriage a smile and flutter of her fan. "We should. We make a striking pair. We have also been at the center of Society's cruel gossip for a smidge over a week."

"Has it been that long? It seems as if it has been only a few days."

She tilted her head with a small, tight smile. "Time flies when you are having fun."

He laughed. The cloud over his disposition vanished. "I suppose. Although, frankly, I would not call this fun."

Miss Brooke felt an absurd rush of joy at being able to change his mood. "Poor you."

"I suppose you have been having a rough time of it as well. And, for you, it can only get worse." Miss Brooke stayed silent as they rode on. "The worst thing that happens to me is I have to marry a strikingly beautiful, rich, and witty woman."

"I can be a bit of a shrew," Miss Brooke warned with a smile.

"Nonsense. Trust me, I know shrews. Gossip says you

have not an ounce of steel and only flourish due to your father's ill mannerisms."

"I manage perfectly well without my father, thank you." Miss Brooke's tone grew playful, "more likely, no one wants to alienate me since I may become the next Princess of Wales."

Charmaine smiled slightly. "The Prince is ten."

"I am joking." Miss Brooke returned his smile. "Besides," she became serious again, "I would not marry Prince George. The amount of propriety surrounding the royal family is overwhelming. You can do this, cannot do that. I would drown under such restrictions."

"But you are the queen of propriety now." Charmaine glanced behind them. "Notice our groom?"

"Yes, but that is different. I could be much more scandalous. The princesses have no choice. My propriety is chosen while theirs is enforced," Miss Brooke said.

"You choose to be chaperoned and you could choose to be scandalous?" Charmaine sounded unconvinced.

"That is not what I meant and you know it. I can choose, for the most part, who is on my dance card. I am sure you have had a meeting with a lady or two in a dark corner. We have our restrictions, but not everyone chooses to obey them. The princesses have no choice."

"What is the difference between choosing not to dance with a rake and not having the choice at all?" Charmaine was still confused.

"Why," Miss Brooke looked over at him, "I am surprised the man passionate about obligation and duty does not know that answer. Free will. It is what makes us human rather than slaves."

Charmaine muttered something she could not hear.

"I am sorry? What?" Miss Brooke was a bit surprised at her boldness. The whole ride she had left her restrained demeanor behind, expressing opinions, challenging his statements, and truly enjoying herself.

"It is tangential and political. I apologize." Charmaine seemed a bit uneasy and it sparked her curiosity even more.

"Please?"

He sighed. "Slaves are humans, too." Miss Brooke gave him a confused look. "You stated free will makes us humans rather than slaves. But slaves are humans as well. And, like it or not, they have free will. They just have a very rubbish set of choices presented to them."

Miss Brooke grew quiet and Charmaine did not press. The black stallion he was riding had a rough gait and almost no sense. An annoying amount of his concentration was required to steady the mount. He cursed his friend under his breath. Borrowing horses from Collins came with risks. Only Collins would buy a horse with more style than brains. Charmaine strongly approved of the small gray mare Miss Brooke was riding. It had a dainty step and was smartly put together. The dapple pattern shone brightly in the coat, a sign the horse was in excellent health. Charmaine was about to comment to Miss Brooke about the quality of her stable when she spoke again.

"Sometimes you make me feel very…" Miss Brooke let her words drift away.

Charmaine tightened his hold on the stallion's reins and moved the horse closer towards Miss Brooke. "Very what?"

"Stupid? Pointless?"

Charmaine blinked, taken aback. "I mean to do no such thing. I apologize."

"You have done nothing wrong. I simply fail to consider such things. And I could say it was ignorance, but that does not match some of the other things you have mentioned."

"Like what?" Charmaine asked gently.

"Like Miss Boswell. I am afraid you were right. I am not fair to her."

Charmaine shrugged dismissively. "Now you know and thus can change."

Miss Brooke shook her head. "But I was a rubbish friend because I failed to pay attention. The slavery conversation is more of the same. I know there are slaves in the Empire, but I do not think about them."

Charmaine rode in silence for a bit, trying to find the

correct words. Miss Brooke seemed honestly distraught. "Can I tell you a secret?"

She lifted her head and looked at him, curiosity overcoming the furrow in her forehead.

"I cannot dress myself for Court. Or a ball. Or the opera. Or, really, even a ride in the park. I forget little things. I have no idea how to tie a cravat. And I cannot tell you if your dress is in style or out of fashion," admitted Charmaine.

Miss Brooke's brow furrowed again. "What does that have to do with anything?"

"We think about different things. I am passionate about politics, about the rights of man, and the obligation of the gentry to uphold those rights. You are passionate about the affairs of the *ton*, the social life of the selfsame gentry. Not paying attention to politics does not make you less," Charmaine answered.

"And Miss Boswell?" Miss Brooke asked.

"We all have oversights where our closest friends are concerned. I should have known Farrington was deeply attached to you." Charmaine shrugged. "We make mistakes."

Miss Brooke resisted the temptation to turn the conversation to Farrington. "I still feel my life is a bit pointless when compared to yours."

Charmaine shifted uncomfortably. The stallion pranced in response. "I am not sure what to say in reply. My life is as pointless as anyone else in government. We attend sessions, we argue, and I oft feel like nothing gets done. War, chaos, poverty, uprisings, and rebellion—these all happen no matter what we do. Sometimes I feel as if what I do is even less useful than knowing how to pick the correct shoes."

"I did not know men ever felt useless." Miss Brooke smiled to herself and looked around the park. Charmaine lifted her spirits. Miss Boswell was so helpful and supportive, but she had not been able to bring herself to explain what happened to her friend. Miss Brooke held on to the irrational hope that if she ignored her memories and feelings about what happened with Mr. West, then the whole ordeal would vanish. But with

Charmaine she did not have to explain it, he had been there. And, better, he saved her.

Admittedly, he was rather preachy. He did have an annoying habit of pointing out her flaws. Still, he managed to say exactly the right thing to make her feel better about herself. Sadly, her father would come home soon and send away another suitor.

Abruptly, Miss Brooke remembered Charmaine's request she not embarrass him and make him her eighth rejection. Not wanting to make the same absent-minded mistakes she made earlier, Miss Brooke decided to broach the conversation.

"So," Miss Brooke ventured timidly, "I suspect my father will arrive home soon."

Charmaine nodded. "This day or the next. The weather has been excellent."

"And there is a thing I should tell you."

Charmaine's eyes narrowed slightly. From his conversation with Farrington he had the impression the rejection came as a surprise. Or, maybe, she was going to tell him something else. "Yes?"

"My father will reject your suit." There, Miss Brooke thought, it was out. Now he knew.

"Why?"

"Because, because—it is rather complicated." Miss Brooke sighed to herself. She supposed it was too much to ask he could have accepted her statement without a reason.

"My father wants me to be happy, so he requires a suitor gain his approval before I wed. But he is never satisfied with my suitors. And without his blessing I will not have access to my inheritance. Please do not repeat this to anyone. I have not been public about this." In truth, he was the only one she told so bluntly. Miss Boswell knew about it, certainly, but that was because she had been around for all seven rejections. How could she not know?

Charmaine inclined his head in acceptance of her trust. "However, are you not in your majority? You do not need your father's permission to wed, or to access your funds."

"While that would normally be true, my funds are in a trust and are controlled by my grandmother's will. Without my father's blessing, I cannot access the funds after I am wed. They become locked in an entitlement until my eldest daughter reaches her majority," explained Miss Brooke.

Charmaine considered the new information. Previously, he was unsure how Mr. Brooke planned to halt his daughter's inheritance. The stallion tossed his long mane and Charmaine was forced to wrestle him back into passivity. As he did so he happened to glance at Miss Brooke's face. She seemed withdrawn and nervous. "Is something amiss?"

Her answer was directed at her horse's mane, "Now you know you will not gain my father's approval and thus cannot marry me."

"I know I will not gain your father's approval. That says nothing about being able to marry you." His words were automatic, as he attempted to figure out why she warned him but not Farrington. "You have reached majority, so your approval is all I need. We are, after all, a modern society."

They again fell silent, but this time Miss Brooke had a smile flickering about her mouth. Charmaine looked at the dainty blond next to him and felt disgust rising within. All he had to do was tell her that he did not care about her inheritance and she became all smiles. He should have been more careful with his words. He desperately wanted to tell her that he needed her money. Yet, he could not. Riding with her in the park was pleasant. It was the first real conversation he had with a woman in years. Most of the women of the *ton* had less sense than Collins' damnable horse. He did not want to be parted from her company so soon. He hadn't lied yet. And, he told himself firmly, he would not lie. No matter what she asked.

His resolve did not have long to wait. "Does that mean you would still marry me if I had no money?"

Charmaine frowned at her intense scrutiny. "A hard question. Your money is certainly a large part of your appeal." He watched her smile fade and quickly retreated to safer ground. "But it is not all of it. As you know, you are quite beauteous. I have never met a woman who could hold even the slightest candle to you. That appeals to me. And," Charmaine shrugged, "I like how you make me feel."

"But not enough to overlook not having a dowry."

"If I was going to marry a woman for her dowry I would be marrying Miss Linder."

Charmaine's answer was curt. It was becoming harder to deny he was lying.

Miss Brooke paused. "I suppose that is true. I was not exactly your plan, was I?"

"No, no, you were not. I am caught here with honor."

"Oh." Miss Brooke was quiet for a moment and then continued. "If you walked in on—that—last year, would you still have offered to marry me?"

"You like hard questions, do you not?" Charmaine hemmed and hawed as he considered his answer, grateful the money conversation appeared to be behind them. "Last year, I would likely have ignored your wishes, beat West down, and then declared his sin from the balcony of the ballroom. I have mellowed significantly."

"Apparently." Miss Brooke frowned. "You have stopped making me feel good about myself."

"I apologize." Now it was Charmaine's turn to frown. "I was trying to be honest."

"I, I—thank you."

They rode further around the park before Charmaine stopped his addle-brained mount. The gray automatically halted as well. He looked at her, his maple hair falling into his eyes. Earlier Charmaine's eyes flashed in the midday sun, but now they were as soft as morning sky. "Miss Brooke. Alison. I am not well versed in this." Charmaine took a deep breath. "But I think I would not mind having you as my wife." His eyes were wide and slightly vulnerable.

Miss Brooke's voice was soft as she answered, "Thank you."

He smiled a lopsided grin. Charmaine leaned back in his saddle feeling rather pleased with himself. He ran the conversation back through his mind and the smile faded. "That was not very good, was it?"

She smiled. "Worst proposal I have *ever* received. But it will do."

Charmaine grew serious again. "Alison, I am not perfect. I do have problems. But I have never been a hero before and I do not want to ruin that. I promise to try to do right by you."

Miss Brooke was taken aback. She had not even considered Charmaine in those terms. His analysis made everything so much more romantic. He was not trying to save her honor out of any sense of obligation, but rather because he was her personal hero. Miss Brooke smiled to herself. It was rather charming. Farrington was so uptight. With him, she had not felt anything like this whirlwind of emotions. Whatever this feeling was, it was new and amazing. Only Charmaine could take the horrible event with Mr. West and turn it into something where she would get to be a princess rescued from a nasty dragon.

Miss Brooke searched for words. He was, quite frankly, magnificent. Speech failed her, so she settled for gazing at him. Charmaine leaned forward slightly, bringing his head towards hers. His movement stopped at the loud clearing of the groom's throat from behind them. Miss Brooke knew that was her cue for a perfect dramatic exit, but every part of her being begged to stay and find out what happened when his lips touched hers. She wished her groom to the deepest part of Purgatory before backing her mare away and riding back the way they came.

Miss Brooke's buoyant mood carried her throughout the day. When Miss Boswell arrived to prepare for the evening's festivities Miss Brooke was still glowing. Early in their first Season the women began preparing for evenings together at the Brookes'. Miss Boswell's father was an older, absent-minded fellow who took little notice of his daughter, or the events of the household. It gave the place an abandoned, empty feel that Miss Boswell was glad to escape.

Miss Boswell cocked her head at Miss Brooke's cheery mood. She expected to find her friend pulling her hair out over the past week's troubles, but instead was greeted with a smile and obvious good cheer. "What has you so happy?"

"Lord Charmaine." Miss Brooke smiled at her friend as she placed a wedge of cucumber and cream cheese sandwich in her mouth.

Miss Boswell took one as well. "Lord Charmaine? What happened to swooning over Anthony?"

Miss Brooke frowned delicately. "I spoke with Lord Farrington. He is not the person I thought he was."

That's curious, thought Miss Boswell. "But Lord Charmaine is?"

"La, I would not say he is perfect. But he called himself my hero. I have been thinking about it all day. He really is. I genuinely was rescued. Rather than reminiscing about that horrible event, and letting it make me feel helpless and defiled, I have decided it must have been a fated moment to meet a splendid gentleman. A required evil, if you will." Miss Brooke popped another sandwich in her mouth.

She forgot she never told me what happened, Miss Boswell thought with a smile. Eventually, I will piece it together. "What happened to the bit about your father refusing him?"

"I told him, Miss Boswell, I told him the whole bit about my portion and everything!" Miss Brooke was clearly excited. "And he did not seem to care. He said if he wanted money he would have married Miss Linder, but this was about honor and about being a hero."

Miss Boswell stared at the sandwich plate as she considered the conversation. There was a whole pile of little triangular cut sandwiches configured in a pyramid shape. The different types of bread made a circular pattern. "I overheard he was going to marry Miss Linder for her dowry. Miss Linder certainly thought so."

"Then why are they not together?"

"Because Society found him with you." Miss Brooke's excitement troubled Miss Boswell. She had heard these statements before. This suitor would be different. Her father would approve of him. She would finally be able to live the next step of her life. And then it would all fall apart. It was nerve-wracking to watch. "He declared he would save your honor and wed you, if you will have him?"

"Brenda, I would marry a merchant at this point. I love my father dearly, but I want to be out from under his roof and free to make my own decisions," Miss Brooke said.

"A husband does not guarantee such freedom. You may be trading one overly controlling man for another," Miss Boswell cautioned. "And you are ignoring my point about Miss Linder."

"She is a young girl, in the pastels of her first Season. Do you remember your first Season? I do. I thought everyone was about to marry me!"

Miss Boswell hid a frown. She remembered her first Season all too well, yet her memories had no proposals or mistook male attention. They had much to do with standing around while her feet ached.

Miss Brooke noticed her friend's frown and misunderstood the cause. "If it will please you, investigate and tell me what you find? You can ask Lord Farrington." Miss Brooke made an unladylike sound. "Apparently they are friends."

"I will." Miss Boswell could see she was ruining her friend's mood. She decided to change to the topic. "What are you wearing to the ball?"

"My dark blue velvets. You?"

Miss Boswell's autumn eyes widened slightly. "I thought you advised dark colors should be used sparingly and only for dramatic purpose. A lady should stay in midtones with splashes of bright. Why the deviation?"

"I am in mourning for my ideal of Lord Farrington." Miss Brooke flipped her hair.

"Ali, be serious."

"Yes, nanny." Miss Brooke gave Miss Boswell her schoolgirl blush again. "I think Charmaine likes dark colors. I have only ever seen him in brown and navy. It is so very unfashionable of him, but…"

Miss Boswell stopped worrying. Miss Brooke was already lost. Miss Boswell was inexperienced with love but held on to hope the emotion was an unconquerable force. Miss Brooke's falling in and out of 'love' seemed more like a disease. "Then wear your blues, dear. Dance with your hero."

Miss Brooke beamed at her. Miss Boswell could not help but return the smile. Miss Brooke was always pretty, but happy Miss Brooke was beyond radiant. "I will. I am excited. What are you wearing?"

"My greens." Miss Boswell picked a safe outfit of a midsummer green Miss Brooke claimed set off her eyes.

"Your greens? The emerald ones?"

"No." I like those, Miss Boswell added mentally, but you always say they are too dark. "The lighter ones. With the daffodil embroidery."

"You hate those," Miss Brooke said.

"They are not miserable." Miss Boswell was lying. She hated the greens. She had to admit they looked pleasant but they were boring. They made her look like everyone else.

"I think they are prime but that does matter if you detest them. Why are you bringing them out?" Miss Brooke took her last sandwich and walked over to her elaborate dressing area. She absently smoothed out the midnight blue velvet as she listened to her friend's answer.

"Because I promised I would try to dress right this Season, Alison." Miss Boswell sounded slightly annoyed. "You say you will marry a merchant, well, I would too. But even merchants fail to notice me."

"Dear Brenda, I told you I was wrong. Tell me what you want to wear, and I will find a way to make it possible." Miss Brooke was earnest.

"Alison." Miss Boswell hesitated, carefully picking her

words. "I know you are good with fashion, but," she took a deep breath, "I do not want to be a spinster. Eventually, you will have the most amazing husband in the *ton* and I will be your queer friend hanging on the outskirts. If wearing clothing I do not like is the only way to change that, well, it is only clothing, right?"

"No, it is not only clothing." Miss Brooke made an effort to not become passionate about the topic. "It is about how you feel. When you are happy, you smile, and when you smile, even the elite of the *ton* noticed you. You told me Lord Stanton, of all people, noticed and complimented you last week! Stanton!"

"I was wearing a dress you picked out," Miss Brooke replied.

Drat, thought Miss Brooke, she was right. "But you were happy. Will the greens make you happy? At least you thought the browns were marginal."

I danced with Anthony, Miss Boswell thought, I could have been wearing nothing but sackcloth and been happy. "My dress is adequate. Besides, they are all I had the maid bring."

"Well," Miss Brooke adapted, "at least we can accessorize. I have this outrageous fan you will love…"

CHAPTER IX

The ball was the same as any other, Miss Brooke thought with a disdainful sniff. She hated the idea she was succumbing to ennui. She glanced over at her friend and her world-weary commentary came to a halt. Miss Boswell managed to find amazement everywhere. She was currently gaping at a chandelier in the corner.

Speculative eyes followed Miss Brooke and Miss Boswell as they gossiped and curtsied their way across the crowded ballroom. Miss Brooke startled when she noticed Mr. West leaning leisurely against the far wall. His gaze made her feel unclean. She could feel his touch on her skin the second his eyes fell upon her. She shuddered and forced herself to look elsewhere.

Miss Brooke pushed the cretin from her mind and settled down to the important business of chitchat with her circle, quickly becoming current on who, what, where, and when. Since the incident, every time she approached the group Miss Brooke felt a tinge of fear her scandal and rejection would cause her social scene to fall apart. So far, the desire for gossip about Charmaine seemed to outweigh the scandal. It seemed the Duchess Castlemire was right. As long as she proceeded forward with Lord Charmaine, she might be able to avoid being socially ruined.

As they chattered, Miss Boswell tried to fade into the background, but Miss Brooke was on the watch for it. Each time Miss Boswell tried to step back, Miss Brooke would direct a question at her. When a gentleman asked Miss Brooke for the next dance, Miss Brooke refused, saying she would not leave Miss Boswell alone. Shortly, both of them were on the dance floor.

Miss Boswell found herself dancing with a relative stranger in outrageously fashionable court dress. He was handsome enough, she supposed, and was often in the circle around Miss Brooke. She searched her memory for his name and finally found it as they joined hands to circle around, "I appreciate the dance, Mr. Hobson."

The man responded with an expressive smile. It reached his eyes and gave him an overall boyish appearance. "I assure you, it is no trouble, Miss Boswell. You dance exceptionally well."

Miss Boswell blushed, even though she knew it was true. As a teenager, she would beg extra instruction out of her tutors. She loved to dance. Moving with music was a divine feeling. "You are kind. I do so enjoy dancing."

"I find that surprising. I wrongly assumed you sat out due to lack of interest. I would be grateful if you saved a spot for me on your dance card in the future," Mr. Hobson said.

Miss Boswell stumbled over herself for an answer.

Mr. Hobson clearly took her hesitation the wrong way. "I apologize. I had no intent to be forward. I enjoy dancing as well. Most of the ladies of Court seem to do it because it is expected. You, however, are quite skilled."

"In that case," Miss Boswell smiled, "I can certainly indulge you." Miss Boswell failed to mention her dance card was almost always empty, which was the real reason she sat out dances. "I wish I knew earlier, as there is a quadrille tonight I would have loved to dance."

Hobson smiled at her. "I love it also but find it a nightmare with any but the most skilled of dancers. Do you, perchance, know Lord Stanton?"

"I have met him once," Miss Boswell replied with a nod.

"Lord Stanton has as fine of a step of any in Society. I am sure he would be the perfect solution for the quadrille," Mr. Hobson said.

"I have no desire to impose on anyone. Lord Stanton surely has better things to do than dance with the likes of me," Miss Boswell said.

Hobson gave Miss Boswell an odd look but the dance drew them apart before he could answer. They spun and wove through the line of dancers before they were thrust together again. Miss Boswell was bright with color from the excitement of the dance and her earlier objections were forgotten. When the dance ended, Miss Boswell found herself swept away from her traditional spot in Miss Brooke's shadow to stand in front of Lord Stanton.

Miss Boswell thought Mr. Hobson's outfit was outrageous but Collins was even more extravagant. His satin breeches were so tight Collins appeared as if he was poured into them. His cravat flared out like a warbling bird. Tightly curved shoes peeked up at Miss Boswell from under diamond-encrusted buckles. Collins was the height of fashion. Miss Boswell restrained herself from smiling at how ridiculous he looked. She thought Lord Stanton was spectacular for both embracing what he loved and having the courage to wear it in public.

"Mr. Hobson, Miss Boswell, it is a pleasure to see you both." Even Collins' half bow had a flourish.

Miss Boswell curtsied with a smile, pleased he remembered her. Mr. Hobson also returned the Baron's greeting. "Lord Stanton, the pleasure is mine. Your tailor continues to impress. How can the rest of us hope to keep pace with you?"

"You cannot, dear Hobson, you truly cannot," Collins preened. "Although, you manage adequately, Hobson, and Miss Boswell, that fan brings a delightful bit of vibrancy to an otherwise drab outfit."

Miss Boswell was not sure if she was complimented or insulted. However, since she loved the bright yellow fan and despised the green dress she was wearing, she decided to be flattered. Miss Boswell wished she cared much more about clothing. The *ton* seemed to spend an inordinate amount of time talking about it. She ignored the next several exchanges between the two gentlemen, as she had no interest in their cobblers or the changing fashion of men's heels. Eventually, the conversation drifted to a halt and Collins began to excuse himself. Mr. Hobson spoke up, "Lord Stanton, perchance I could beg a favor?"

Miss Boswell blushed. This was not what she had in mind. She did not want to be anyone's favor. Collins noticed her blush and gave her a sidelong look. "That depends. I will at least consider it."

"Miss Boswell reminded me I have no partner for the quadrille. I was wondering if you might know of someone? I would ask Miss Boswell, as she is a divine dancer, but I am afraid I wasted my dance with her on a simple country tune." Miss Boswell stopped blushing out of fear of embarrassment and started blushing from the compliment. Balls stopped being dreadful and started being fun.

Collins considered the request. "I believe Miss Silverage might suit your needs and the two of you are overdue for an introduction. If you will wait a moment while I sign Miss Boswell's dance card, we shall be off."

Collins took Miss Boswell's dance card without so much as a by-your-leave as Mr. Hobson thanked Collins. Collins handed the dance card back to Miss Boswell and the two gentlemen half bowed at her before walking across the floor. The abrupt change in conversation and the corresponding departure left Miss Boswell feeling flustered and abandoned. As she made her way back to Miss Brooke's side, she perused her dance card. Her previous irritation vanished with a smile when she discovered Baron Stanton's mark next to the quadrille.

Miss Brooke was smoothing her skirts in excitement. Miss Boswell gave thanks for Miss Brooke's gloves. Without them, there would be a pattern of discoloration from how often she rubbed her skirts.

"Where have you been? No matter," Miss Brooke continued, "Lord Charmaine and Lord Farrington have arrived. They look grand!"

Miss Boswell followed Miss Brooke's gaze across the dance floor. Farrington and Charmaine had recently entered and were deep in discussion with Lord Stanton. Miss Brooke smiled as they appeared. The magic of the moment faded as she noticed Mr. West withdraw from the room with a scowl. Miss Brooke returned her attention to the scene in front of her, as it would do no good to focus on that unclean slime any more than necessary.

The outrageous evening dress Collins modeled contrasted starkly with Charmaine and Farrington's dark garb. Both lords looked more suited for a hunt than a ball. Farrington's dark brown coat was at least liberally adorned with embroidery, while Charmaine's was unfashionably plain. They looked almost like a pair of matched stallions, Miss Brooke thought.

"I wonder if they share a tailor?" Miss Boswell mused.

A woman standing next to her giggled, "If so, I want to see them get measured!"

There was a general murmur of agreement before Mr. Hobson interjected, "I do not know why you ladies swoon so over those two. They are horribly out of fashion."

There was another round of agreement and the group's attention moved on to more in vogue targets. Miss Boswell noticed the sideways glances directed at Miss Brooke, clearly waiting to see her reaction to her current and former suitor approaching together. Miss Boswell gave Miss Brooke an encouraging smile as Charmaine closed the distance between them. Miss Boswell hid her disappointment as Farrington veered off to the card room.

"Miss Brooke. Miss Boswell." Charmaine gave them both his most charming bow. The gesture did not appear practiced.

"Lord Charmaine," Miss Brooke gushed in greeting. Her smile almost split her face, transforming her from lovely to unbelievably radiant. Miss Boswell smiled to herself as she watched the predictable effect on the poor man. At her loveliest, Miss Brooke could melt even the most jaded.

Miss Boswell was impressed at how quickly Lord Charmaine pulled his gaze away from that smile and turned to her. Most men never even knew Miss Brooke had a redheaded friend with a propensity for outrageous colors. "Miss Boswell. May I have your dance card?"

"Mine?" Miss Boswell asked with confusion as she handed it over.

"Yes, yours." Charmaine frowned at it briefly. "Which dance do you want me to take?"

Miss Boswell glanced at her almost empty card. "The waltz after Lord Stanton." She smiled with a timid attempt at a joke. "It is easy."

"That is good for your feet. But bad for Miss Brooke's." He turned his attention to Miss Brooke again. "And your dance card, my Aphrodite?" Miss Brooke handed it to him with a smile. It was almost completely full.

"I saved the supper dance for you, if you would have me?" Miss Brooke offered with a smile.

"My dear, you underestimate me." Rather than signing Miss Brooke's card, he put it in his pocket. "I intend to dance every dance with you and only let you go when you claim weariness."

"My lord, you will do no such thing!" Miss Brooke sounded truly shocked. Miss Boswell hid another smile. She knew both exactly what Miss Brooke was thinking (how improper!) and was sure Miss Brooke would give in to her hero with only token objection.

As Charmaine swept Miss Brooke away, Miss Boswell could see she was correct. In no time at all, Miss Brooke was lost in Charmaine's vivid blue eyes. There was a set of shared smiles among the group of friends before they quickly descended into gossip again. Without Miss Brooke, Miss Boswell found herself on the outside. She drifted away, floating from one pocket of conversation to another, before making her way into the card room.

The room was crowed. Too many tables overfilled the relatively small room. The crush of people made it hard for Miss Boswell to find her quarry. Eventually, she spotted Farrington playing cards, tucked in the far back. He gestured for her to join him. Her heart skipped a beat at his invitation. She scurried to obey.

Without speaking, she watched him play for several hands. Being accepted felt magical. She knew it was foolish to be in love with a man so magnificent, but she could no longer help herself. Standing beside him was enough. The pile of coins grew in front of Farrington and, after one particularly large win, he pushed himself back from the table. There was an immediate objection from the other card players, all demanding a chance to win back their losses.

Farrington declined with a small shake of his head. "I apologize, good sirs, but I owe the lady a dance. I have kept her waiting long enough."

Farrington offered Miss Boswell his arm. She almost swooned on the spot. With a timid smile, she placed her arm on his and they slowly worked their way through the crowded room. The air of the ballroom was much cooler. "Your dance card is empty, correct? Will you indulge me this dance?"

"I would enjoy that, Lord Farrington." Her voice was soft and timid. She hated how he could rob her of wit. She would have preferred to come back with a witty statement about how people did wish to dance with her, and she was not the wallflower he thought she was. But that might risk the one dance with Farrington. No amount of self-righteous indignation was worth that.

Miss Boswell knew she was supposed to ask Farrington about Charmaine but spinning around in his arms was not the time. She knew Hobson and Collins were more technically proficient dancers but it did not matter. Skill was no substitute for the magic Farrington carried with him. She did not speak for the whole dance. She did not want to ruin the moment and he remained quiet as well. When the dance was over, he deftly maneuvered them to an empty bit of wall. Still silent, he stared out over the crowd.

Miss Boswell stood patiently and managed to acquire two glasses of lemonade from a footman's tray. Wordlessly, she handed him one and he took it with a gracious nod. "I apologize for my poor company tonight, Miss Boswell."

"You are always excellent company, Lord Farrington." Miss Boswell fought a blush as she fretted about sounding like a silly young thing.

Farrington scanned the crowd and deliberately avoided staring at Miss Brooke and Charmaine. They were still on the floor, smiling and twirling in dance after dance. "I will likely be leaving soon. I am up at the tables and the ball is of no interest to me."

"I am sorry to hear that."

Farrington looked at her. Miss Boswell was a tall woman and yet he still towered over her. She loved that about him. But then, she thought to herself ruefully, she loved everything about him, from how his eyebrows were too close together to his overly strong jaw.

As he spoke, Brenda added the steady cadence of his voice to her list of perfections, "Are you trying to say the ball has interest for you?"

"You know it does not," she said. "But it will have even less with you gone."

"I understand and return the sentiment. The company of a friend improves many things."

Miss Boswell worked hard to keep her frown internal. It was well and good that he considered her a friend—she had only heard him refer to Charmaine as a friend before—but she did not want to be only his friend. She wanted to be so much more. "Why are you leaving?"

"Miss Brooke."

The two-word answer was an epic from the normally taciturn man. Miss Boswell decided to press her luck. "What happened?"

"Did she not tell you?" Farrington sounded surprised.

"She mentioned something was afoot, but I decided not to inquire."

"But to question me instead?" Farrington shook his head with a small smile. "You are an odd duck, Miss Boswell. As you likely suspect, I would prefer not to discuss that aspect of my life. Know, however, that Miss Brooke and I are no longer a prospective match."

"I am sorry." Her words were truthful. Miss Boswell knew nothing would ever happen between her and Anthony, but as long as Miss Brooke had his attention, he came around quite a bit more. She would miss his company. Tremendously. After her initial reaction, she bit her lip. Farrington and Miss Brooke's split was old news. Something must have changed and then changed back.

"The matter is of no consequence." Farrington's voice was steady but his free hand balled itself into a fist. Miss Boswell watched as it slowly unclenched and hid a frown. It was wretched to see him hurt.

They stood in silence for a few moments before Miss Boswell remembered her previous conversation with Miss Brooke. "Ta. This is likely terribly rude, but…"

Farrington sounded amused as he looked at her, the previous pain banished from his eyes. "That means Miss Brooke requested it."

"How did you know?"

"Because, Miss Boswell, I have never seen you undertake an inconsiderate action on your own. Miss Brooke does nothing malicious but often fails to consider consequences."

"Miss Brooke is a wonderful person, Lord Farrington, and I will not hear otherwise."

"Miss Brooke is a wonderful person," Farrington agreed. "But that does not mean she does not have faults. Needless to say, what is your improper request?"

Miss Boswell considered how best to approach this and decided the direct method would be most suitable. She wished he were easier to read. One moment Farrington let her see his pain over Alison and the next he was a mask with only polite smiles. "I am concerned about Miss Brooke's attachment to a stranger and how little we know of him. I was wondering if I could ask you about Lord Charmaine?"

"You wish me to gossip about my best friend and the woman who refused my suit? Specifically, you wish to discuss the progress of their courtship?" Farrington shrugged. "Why not? Your company will balance the dismal topic."

"Ah, yes." Miss Boswell shifted her weight from leg to leg. The conversation suddenly made her uncomfortable. Maybe she should not have pressed about Miss Brooke at all. She did not want to hear if Farrington still cared for Alison or not. Crafting her own illusions was safer.

"Do you ride?"

"Ride?" The question was unexpected. Miss Boswell quickly caught herself. "Yes, I do. Not as well as Miss Brooke, but I am a fair horseman. Horsewoman. Horsewhomever."

"Then we can ride in the park on the morrow. Horsewhomever to horsewhomever."

Miss Boswell further melted as he turned her stumbles into shared humor. "I would enjoy that."

Farrington bowed at her. "Then I will see you on the morrow." With that, he turned and walked through the ballroom, eager to escape the sight of Miss Brooke giggling in Charmaine's arms.

Miss Brooke melodramatically swooned the second the groom closed the carriage door. Miss Boswell smiled at her friend. "At least you know you are being silly."

"What a terrible thing to say. I am not silly." Miss Brooke shifted into a normal, upright, seated position. "I am happy."

"Unsurprising. How many dances did you share with Lord Charmaine tonight?"

Miss Brooke blushed. "Six."

"And the supper dance," Miss Boswell added.

"And the supper dance." Miss Brooke shrugged defensively. "But what does it matter? Society already thinks we anticipated our vows, and he has announced his intent to marry me. So, I danced with him too many times. La de da."

Miss Boswell sighed. Miss Brooke had the retention of a small bird. "And what happens when your father rejects him, just like all the others?"

"I told you, Lord Charmaine cares not. He claimed he would court me, money or no."

Frowning, Miss Boswell tried to remember what her friend told her earlier in the day. "Are you certain of that memory? This morning you reported Lord Charmaine's words as something similar to if he wanted funds he would marry Miss Linder. That sounds like avoidance to me."

"You see the worst in everyone." Miss Brooke fought the fear Miss Boswell might be right. She needed the fantasy of being rescued and having a hero. Featuring in a fairy tale was much preferable to surviving a commonplace horror. "Besides, I already told him about the coming rejection and he still danced six dances with me."

"Seven. And one with me. I do hear your point. He is still showing all signs of interest. But, remember what the Duchess Castlemire said. Now it looks like he is wrapped in your charms more than ever. If your father does reject him those mean old ladies will really be displeased with you."

"I know." A slight frown touched Miss Brooke's painted face. "But I do rather like him."

"Enough to defy your father over him?"

"I will marry him without my father's approval, yes. But I will not marry him with my father's disapproval."

"That seems like a thread thin argument," Miss Boswell said.

Miss Brooke shrugged. "There is a substantial difference between approving of something and actively opposing it. Besides, I think I may have made some incorrect assumptions."

Miss Boswell raised an eyebrow in question but was otherwise silent.

Staring at the wall of the coach, Miss Brooke continued. "I suppose I always thought I was making the choice to let the suitors go and obey my father. But, you see, I never made a choice. I simply let my father make the choice for me. I have been thinking about this since Lord Charmaine came into my life. The whole situation made me feel caught, as if I am being forced to marry him. So, I thought about what I really wanted and whom I wanted and then I went and saw Lord Farrington."

"Anthony?" Miss Boswell was no longer sure where this story was going.

Miss Brooke nodded. "I told him I should have taken action when my father rejected him. Then, I asked him to elope. He refused."

"Pardon? Lord Farrington declined?" Miss Boswell was truly shocked. Not only had her incredibly proper friend offered to elope—an act she previously described as deeply shameful—but also Anthony refused. Miss Boswell would have sworn Farrington would marry Miss Brooke no matter the circumstances. After all, he did claim to love her.

Sadness washed over Miss Brooke's face. "For the best, I suppose. He would not marry me without my inheritance. What is it you told me? If I loved someone, nothing like money or my father's approval would stop me? Well, I suppose Lord Farrington does not love me."

"That seems out of character for him." Miss Boswell had never known Farrington to even appear to care about money. His clothing, his horses, and his estate were all of the highest caliber.

Miss Brooke nodded again. "I know. I was surprised, too. I gave the matter thought and decided I would tell Lord Charmaine about my father's likely rejection. I used to think my father was rejecting them, but Lord Farrington made me understand these suitors did not want me unless I had money. Really, they were rejecting me."

Miss Boswell's emotions were a chaotic mess. She was saddened by how rejected her friend sounded, disappointed Farrington would be so affected by money and so immune to love. And yet she was strangely happy Alison and Anthony did not elope. She had no idea what to say. "Surely you do not wish to partner a man who wants you only for your money."

"You are correct, I would not. But," Miss Brooke considered, "my ego, my vanity, my pride were hurt. My suitors did not want me for myself, but rather for my portion."

"Perchance that is not true? You have only talked to Lord Farrington about this, after all." Miss Boswell considered the army of Miss Brooke's former suitors. For the most part, they were fairly stalwart and decent gentlemen. Then again, Miss Boswell had to admit her own knowledge of courting and gentlemanly character was far from what one would call vast.

"Perhaps," Miss Brooke sounded skeptical. "But it does mean I have never questioned. I blindly assumed my father's rejection was keeping men away, not that it was based on my money. It makes me feel lousy."

"I can understand that." There were plenty of suitors that were only charming towards Miss Boswell in order to gain access to Miss Brooke. It had been a dismal day for Miss Boswell when she figured out those people did not care for her at all. "And thus, you have decided Lord Charmaine is a fantastic creature because he has not fled when you warned him he might not get your money?"

Miss Brooke rolled her eyes at Miss Boswell's wording. "Close enough."

148

"And he is handsome, makes you laugh, seems to treat you well, and comes from a very impressive lineage…" Miss Boswell decided the serious conversation had gone on long enough. It was time to bring back Miss Brooke's cheerful mood.

"All of that and more. Although," Miss Brooke admitted with a laugh, "he truly cannot dance."

Miss Boswell smiled. "Believe you me, I noticed. He is graceful enough, but it seems like he is never put any effort into learning. I like him though. His attire is even more out of fashion than mine. He takes all the pressure off me."

Miss Brooke giggled. "You may be onto something with his dress. He manages to be barely formal enough to not offend Society. I would adore seeing him trussed up in Court clothes at a function with the King and Queen."

"He could not avoid formality there." Miss Boswell hated events with the Royals. Miss Boswell felt bad for wishing they would attend even fewer functions, but she strongly disliked wearing heavy powder. There was none of her left, only a courtly creature who bore no resemblance to Miss Boswell. Miss Brooke managed powder with absolute elegance, looking like a living statue. Miss Boswell felt like she was doused in flour.

"No." Miss Brooke smiled slightly. "So, you do like him?"

"I said so, did not I?" Miss Boswell cocked her head while considering her answer. "He is sweet. He always asks me to dance, he does not moon at you like a brainless fop, he seems kind, and we already know he is a man of action. Anthony is a friend of almost no one and the bond between him and Lord Charmaine seems strong. I think Lord Farrington is a good judge of character."

"Good enough that he would not elope with me," Miss Brooke answered in a huff. Seeing Miss Boswell's expression, Miss Brooke waved a dismissive hand. "No, I am not overly upset. I am only a bit bitter. I should not give way to it but I am fatigued from the ball."

"We will arrive at my estate soon enough. Then it is only a short while longer until your big, empty house awaits you." Now that they were talking about home, Miss Boswell could not help but yawn.

Miss Brooke mimicked Miss Boswell's yawn. "Oh, stop it, those are contagious! And you need to tell me how your night was. Enough about me, more about you."

"My night was lovely, in truth." Miss Boswell decided to leave out the part about dancing with Anthony or meeting him in the morning. Miss Brooke seemed rather put out with her former suitor and there was no need to rub salt in the wound. "Lord Stanton danced the quadrille with me. He is a divine dancer. And he liked my fan."

Miss Brooke gave the bright yellow fan she loaned Miss Boswell a dismissive look. There was no doubting Collins was a master of style, but his foppish bright-colored ways were the opposite from Miss Brooke's conservative dress.

"Baron Stanton is an excellent person to cultivate, Brenda. The Stantons may not have the ear of the King, but they have the eye of the *ton*. You are doing well for yourself this Season." Better than I am, Miss Brooke added mentally.

"I do not want to cultivate anyone. I like people who are kind to me. Lord Stanton is charming. Although his dress is a bit…"

Miss Brooke smiled. "The insult is 'Macaroni,' dear."

"I think he is amazing for having the gall to wear it," Miss Boswell jumped to his defense.

"Or blind."

Miss Boswell smiled at her friend's cattiness. "Or blind." The carriage pulled to a halt. "Thank Heavens we are here. Without your banter, I would already be asleep."

Miss Brooke leaned across the carriage and gave her the other woman a kiss on the cheek. "Sleep well."

Miss Boswell hopped out of the carriage with the help of a footman and gave her friend a little wave. Miss Brooke leaned back into the leather and dozed the rest of the quick ride home. She relived the dances with Charmaine and, once again, let herself hope.

CHAPTER X

Charmaine's mood was as light as his step as he sprightly ascended the stairs to his tiny set of rooms. A sliver of light under the door alerted him Wilhelm was still awake. Upon entering, he found his valet carefully transcribing information from a pile of letters into those damnable ledgers. Charmaine frowned at the reminder of money but decided it would not ruin his mood. Nothing would ruin his mood, not Wilhelm, and certainly not reality.

Charmaine pulled off one overly polished boot and tossed it negligently on the floor. Wilhelm gave it a half glare and continued with his bookkeeping. After the second boot joined it, Wilhelm shifted the glare to Charmaine. "Do you mind?"

"Not at all. I pay someone to pick up after me."

Wilhelm hmphed at his lord. "You are in a good mood."

"I would need to be to overcome being scolded by my own staff."

"I apologize, my lord." Wilhelm leaned back in Charmaine's favorite chair. "These numbers make my head ache."

"Assume we are miserably poor. Then you will not have to do any math." Charmaine flung his hose after his shoes.

"How did you survive without me?" Wilhelm seemed to ask the question of the ceiling than of Charmaine. "For once, my lord, things do not seem that dire."

"You have gotten our funds confused with someone else's, then."

Wilhelm refused to be drawn into Charmaine's jovial mood. "Trust I know the Donahue funds, my lord. Word came from the Stiles venture that sounds positive. They should be landing in London within the month. Your brother's ship was spotted roughly a week ago but the message is old. They may appear any day. The tenants are even paying their taxes. As long as something drastic does not happen to Stiles or your brother's ventures, we should see your capital return."

Charmaine grew slightly more serious at the unexpected news. "And the third venture? The gunpowder ships we are sponsoring?"

"Nine months overdue with no word." Wilhelm's shrug contained a good deal of irritation. "We have to assume a complete loss. It was the highest risk of all the investments."

"Yes, but with the biggest return."

"That is rather irrelevant at this point, my lord," Wilhelm countered. "If Stiles is as successful as he is indicating, our financial troubles will soon be over."

Charmaine considered the turn of events. "Does that mean I do not need to marry Alison?"

"The ships are not yet in the harbor, lover boy." Wilhelm smirked at his lord. "But, yes, it does look like you can manage to retain the townhouse without her portion. Still, more money is always welcome."

Charmaine stood and walked into the bedroom. He changed into comfortable nightclothes and brushed his teeth. After pacing the room several times, he returned to the chair in front of Wilhelm. "But I want to marry Alison."

"Then for God's sake, marry Miss Brooke. Money or not, she is certainly the catch of the Season. And I have rarely seen you smile so over a woman." Wilhelm waved a dismissive hand. "Why would you not marry her?"

The viscount shrugged and slouched in his chair. "I began courting her for money. Without need, why should I go forward?"

"Because you enjoy the lady's company?" Wilhelm was always amazed at Charmaine's ability to have truly inane conversations.

"I do." Charmaine stretched. "I assume you will summarize the good news for me?"

"Yes, my lord. I will have it ready in the morning, in time for your weekly visit with your father. I have also compiled a list of ventures Mr. Brooke is involved with and highlighted those of interest."

"Good. I am off to bed. Good night, Wilhelm." Charmaine stood and started to head towards the bedroom.

"One more thing, my lord." Charmaine stopped and turned to look at his valet. "Mr. Brooke returned to London tonight. He is keeping his presence a secret, likely even from his daughter, but he is in Town."

Charmaine nodded with approval. "Thank you. And I thought I told you to stop spying."

"I will get right on that, my lord," Wilhelm smirked. "Sleep well and wake."

❧♦❧

The first thing Miss Brooke noticed upon returning home was the oppressive quiet. The background noise of the servants was noticeably absent. When she normally returned from balls, the kitchen staff was preparing for the day. The house was never fully silent—except for when her father was in residence.

Miss Brooke glanced at the footman who opened the door for her. "He is home?"

The man nodded almost imperceptibly and answered in little more than a whisper. "He has not yet announced his presence, mistress. It may be a surprise."

She nodded and quickly headed to her room. Miss Brooke had no doubt her father would be furious over the events of the past two weeks. Meeting with him as his little girl rather than a polished woman of the court seemed strategic. After putting Miss Brooke in her nightgown, Abigail unwrapped strands of hair and took out the multiple pads and rollers used to create the incredibility tall styles Society favored. There was a snowstorm of white powder on the floor behind her. Soon, her nightgown was covered in dandruff-like specks.

As Abigail worked on her hair, Miss Brooke considered her plan of action. "Abigail, do you think Father will call for me tonight? Or in the morning?"

"You ain't supposed to know he is home, miss."

"I know. But the staff is walking on eggshells." Miss Brooke winced slightly as a pad was unglued from her scalp.

Abigail nodded. "He came in a might miffed."

"I can imagine." She absently brushed powder off her lap. More fell to replace it. "He has reason. He was gone for only two weeks and I became embroiled in scandal."

"You're being too hard on yourself." Abigail frowned at the back of Miss Brooke's head. "No reason for that, he'll do that plenty for you."

Miss Brooke smiled, "I suppose so. But I am still right glad he is back. My heart is warm when he is around."

Abigail held back a snort. It was unsurprising Miss Brooke was so attached to her father, Abigail supposed, considering how distant Mrs. Brooke was from her daughter. Mr. Brooke practically raised the girl himself. "I should not be warning you, miss, but he is in a right fine temper tonight. He'll want to see you, certain, but perhaps you're too tired tonight?"

"No, letting him stew makes his temper worse. But thank you for the warning. I believe I am prepared for his thunder."

Abigail finished brushing out the powder. Miss Brooke smiled in thanks, "Take yourself to bed, Abigail. I can tuck myself in once he is done scolding me."

Abigail curtsied, and Miss Brooke trotted down the stairs. Despite Abigail's warnings Miss Brooke was excited to see her father again. Everything had become such a disaster while he was away, it would be delightful to have her rock of stability back again. Abigail was right, Miss Brooke supposed, in that she was going to get quite a lecture. But, after that, everything would be fine once again. Hopefully.

She stopped outside of her father's study and knocked lightly. The room was tucked into the back of the residence, right against the kitchens. Brooke had a large, pretentious study he used for formal meetings, but preferred this small, cluttered room to handle day-to-day affairs. He claimed the constant heat radiating through the wall from the ovens helped his joints. Maps and other interesting papers were pinned to the wall. Miss Brooke always liked the small room.

Miss Brooke had plenty of time to consider the inside of the room, as her father left her waiting on his stoop. Eventually, he called her in. He was exactly as she remembered, a gruff, slightly balding older man, except for the tightness around his mouth and a determined sparkle in his eye. Miss Brooke ignored the warning signs of his fierce temper and sailed across the room to give her father a hug. He paused, glaring at the top of her head, before returning it.

"I am very mad at you, sunshine."

"I know." Miss Brooke stepped back and moved a pile of maps off a chair so that she could sit. "Thus, hugs first. If I waited until after you banish me to my rooms for a week, I would never be able to greet you properly."

Brooke glared at his daughter but was inwardly pleased. She had grown into a strong-willed woman who rarely was intimidated. "Alison, I give you everything you want, everything I have, and I have asked only this one thing of you. Why is it so hard to obey?"

Miss Brooke looked frankly at her father. "Is that an honest question?"

"Excuse me?" His voice was harsh and curt.

"I am asking if you would prefer to yell at me or know what happened?"

"Both. I rode my best horse to foundering for whatever chaos you have conspired," Brooke replied.

"Then go ahead and yell," Miss Brooke said.

"I should be lucky your mother does not have half your wit." The wind was clearly taken out of Brooke's sails. "Regale me with your story then. Maybe it will inspire me not to throttle you."

Her father's threat was ineffective. He had not raised a hand to her since she outgrew spankings. She doubted he would start now.

More likely, he would curtail her activities. That had to be avoided at all costs. The only thing worse than Society thinking she coupled with Charmaine would be if they assumed she was waiting to see if a child had taken hold. Her father raised an eyebrow at her pause. Miss Brooke struggled for a place to start.

"This story is not what you think, Father." Miss Brooke raised her chin and properly clasped both hands in front of her. "And I have not told it to anyone before. But, before I start, I need you to promise me two things. The first is you will not yell at me while I tell it, no matter how stupid I was. The second is you let me dictate how things proceed from here."

Brooke leaned back into his chair and steepled his fingers in front of his face. "I agree to waiting until the story is over before I pass judgment. I do not agree not to act. You are, after all, my daughter."

"Then I am not telling you. I need to handle this on my own," said Miss Brooke.

He analyzed the strong, proud thrust of Miss Brooke's jaw and considered her demands. Such requests were unusual coming from her. "You do not trust how I would handle this?"

"That is not it. At all." Miss Brooke's voice was firm and steady. "You likely could respond better than I. As could Lord Charmaine. But that is not the point. This is something I need to do."

"I do not understand," said Brooke.

"You will."

"If I will, then I have no objection." Brooke did not like the sound of whatever was unfolding. He liked his daughter's white knuckles even less. "What happened, Ali?"

"I was careless. Everything you want to yell at me and accuse me of is likely true." Miss Brooke tried to keep all emotion from her voice. Maybe if she could stay distant from the event and keep pretending like it did not happen, it would not affect her. "I went to the Haven ball with Miss Boswell."

"I," Miss Brooke tried to find any way to phrase this in a flattering manner. Her father waited patiently, expressionless. "I drank too much."

She glanced at her father, clearly expecting a rebuke. He showed no reaction. "I met a man at the opera, Mr. West, who was standing next to me at the ball. He kept handing me champagne."

"West?" Brooke interrupted. "Tall man, big hands, runs a sugar plantation in the Caribbean?"

"Yes." Miss Brooke queried her father, "You know him?"

"Aye."

"Do you like him?" Miss Brooke hated how timid her voice sounded.

"I do not know. Do I like him, Ali?"

"No." Miss Brooke's chin grew strong again. "You hate him."

"Then I hate him." Her father gestured for her to continue. "Please, go on. You were speaking with this man at the ball and..."

Miss Brooke frowned. "This story makes me sound terrible. I really do not want to tell it to you."

"That option ceased when you started, dear. Tell me what happened so we can fix it." Brooke stood and walked around the table to face his daughter. He put a finger on her chin and moved her face so that she was looking into his eyes. "We will fix it."

Miss Brooke nodded. "I had too much to drink and I knew it. I stopped drinking, but I was still dizzy. I kept watching Anthony dance with all those women and I got more and more upset. It was too much. I finally had to get away. Mr. West noticed my agitation. He suggested we go for a walk in the gardens. I declined. But, still, I really wanted to get away. Finally, Mr. West convinced me that the picture gallery would be public enough for propriety, but empty enough to compose myself."

She dropped her head to look at her hands. Brooke let his hand fall from her chin. "He lied. There was no one else upstairs. We walked around, looked in rooms, and everything seemed pleasant. We got lost and decided to rest in a side room. I did not see him shut the door and then..." Miss Brooke let her voice drift off.

Brooke sat very still and kept a tight lid on his emotions. "And then what, Ali?"

"And then he was very improper with me. I did not want him to, but..." Her voice started to break. "He tore my gown." She balled her hands into fists and stared at them.

Brooke counted to ten, then thirty. His voice was calm and supportive when he replied. "And how does Lord Charmaine fit into this story?"

"I cried out." Miss Brooke brushed a tear away with the back of her hand, "and Lord Charmaine burst in and pulled Mr. West off me. He hit him and threatened to kill him."

"Mr. West still lives."

Miss Brooke nodded. "I stopped Lord Charmaine from challenging Mr. West. If he did the details would be everywhere, in the papers even. He threw Mr. West out of the room and then came to check on me. And then, and I do not even know how this happened, The Duchess Castlemire and her entourage were in the room. I was exposed with Lord Charmaine looming over me. Lady Stanton and Lord Charmaine took me to the Donahue mansion because they keep a doctor on staff and I was hurt."

Brooke's eyebrow rose. "The Donahues keep a doctor on staff?"

"Queer, is it not?" Miss Brooke breathed a little easier at her father's question. It was off-topic enough to make her feel more comfortable, but still showed he was paying attention. "But they do. And I was there for three days."

"Three days! Did the physician find a serious injury? Are you recovered now? We should get our own doctor to look at you." His eyes raked over her body looking for a bruise or scratch.

"I am fine now, I promise. I spent time healing, but it was nothing more than cracked ribs and a sore jaw. My heart, my head, I do not know how to explain it. My body was hurt, but something inside me got hurt more." She shook her head as if to banish bad memories and raised her chin yet again. "But no matter."

"While I was at the Donahue's, I found out that Society decided Lord Charmaine and I behaved improperly. Lord Charmaine claims his honor demands that he seek you out to request my hand in marriage. About that same time, the Duchess Castlemire sought me out to tell me that if I disgraced Lord Charmaine she would ruin me." She bit her lip and shrugged. "I think that is everything."

Her father considered. "Why does Society blame Lord Charmaine rather than Mr. West?"

"My fault." Miss Brooke sighed. "I hoped the event would be overlooked. I could not imagine Mr. West would tell anyone, I was certainly not going to blab, Lord Charmaine promised silence, and the Duchess Castlemire indicated she would stay silent. I thought the event would fade away. I was wrong."

"My poor sunshine." It was hard for Brooke to focus, as all he wanted to do was run out of the residence and harm Mr. West. He was angry to the core of his bones—a white-hot rage that demanded release. Yet he knew giving in to malevolence would not help his daughter. He worked to maintain his rational, calm approach, there would be plenty of time to experience the more primal emotions later.

Miss Brooke watched her father's lack of reaction and became increasingly worried. He was staring at nothing, not speaking. Miss Brooke quietly ventured, "You are disappointed in me?"

"Nay, not at all." Brooke leaned forward again and took her hands. "Listen to me, Ali. You did nothing wrong. It is easy to replay these situations in our heads and find ways to blame ourselves. You should be able to get a little punchy at a ball without this sort of consequence. Do you hear me? You have done no wrong."

"But I must have." Miss Brooke sniffed, determined not to cry again. "If Lord Charmaine had not burst through the door Mr. West would have—he would have…" She could not finish the sentence.

"Would have?" A small hope ignited inside Brooke's chest. "He did not?"

Miss Brooke shook her head. "Lord Charmaine stopped him. Mr. West wanted to, really wanted to. He ripped my dress and when I fought back he hit me. He hit me so hard. I could not stop him."

Brooke watched helplessly as his little girl broke down into uncontrollable sobs. He gathered her into his arms and held her while she cried. He tried to think of anything to say, but the desire to end West's existence blotted out all rational thought. Miss Brooke eventually gained control of her tears and pulled away from her father. She gave him a wan, tentative smile, "Now you can yell at me."

He smiled gently back at her. "Perchance on the morrow. Tonight, you should sleep. I need time to think."

"You promised that you would let me deal with Mr. West." she took another breath, "This is important to me."

"Why?"

"Because," Miss Brooke lifted her chin, "he made me feel helpless. I am tired of feeling helpless. I want to act. I need to be the one to punish him."

"What will you do?"

"I do not yet know. I was going to use my influence to ostracize him in Society, but I am no longer have the social standing. Society is still trying to decide if I am going to marry Lord Charmaine or be an outcast."

"You are not going to marry to solve a scandal." Brooke's eyes narrowed as Miss Brooke started to object. "The last thing I will allow is a husband selected by circumstance."

"But, Father, he saved me!"

"And I will thank him for that. But doing what is right and honorable does not automatically win a prize such as my daughter," Brooke said.

"But Society will throw me out! The Duchess Castlemire will ruin me! Father, you cannot do this to me!" Miss Brooke's knuckles were white as she gripped the arm of the chair.

"I am not doing any of this to you." Her father rose and walked back around the desk to his chair. "Marrying a man because Society is forcing you to do so is not a wise choice."

"But when I have sought to marry a man because I want to, you tell me I am irrational and impractical! This time I have good reasons."

"I will be the judge of whether the reasons are good or not." He shrugged. "And I find them lacking."

"But Father, I *want* to marry him!" Miss Brooke knew her father would reject Charmaine, the same as he rejected all the others, but his kindness when she related the story had given her hope.

"I know." Brooke pulled his pipe out of the desk drawer. "Good night, Ali."

Miss Brooke raised her chin as if she was about to keep arguing but seemed to think better of it. She stood and curtsied gracefully. "Good night, Father." Head held high, Miss Brooke walked to her rooms and punched her pillows in frustration.

❧◆❧

The weather was a juxtaposition of Charmaine's mood. The sun was shining, birds were chirping, and even the grass seemed to be a more striking shade of green then when he entered Parliament. Yet a personal raincloud followed Charmaine. He decided to walk through the park and see if any of nature's good cheer could creep in. There were only two things left on his agenda for the day, writing a speech for the Lords about the need to maintain stability in the American Colonies and visiting Miss Brooke's father. Charmaine thought it likely that convincing the Lords to ban slavery would be easier than gaining Mr. Brooke's approval. The old man did not matter, though. The ships from the New World were due within the next month, thus he would be able to make it through the current financial disaster without Miss Brooke's money. Still, the idea of being rejected stuck in his craw.

Charmaine realized he was stuck with his foul mood. He has spent the morning before Session with his father, telling the unresponsive man how he failed as the head of the family. Then there was the afternoon spent pointlessly arguing in Parliament. He had almost reached his rooms before he decided to methodically ruin the rest of day. Charmaine turned and, with the joyful deliberation of a Bedlamite walking to the gallows, headed towards the Brookes' London home.

The Brooke townhouse sat on the edge of the fashionable part of town. Charmaine knocked on the immaculate white door and leisurely waited for a footman to send him to his doom. The more he phrased the meeting with Miss Brooke's father in apocalyptic terms, the more Charmaine found a grim, sardonic pleasure to the event. He already knew the outcome of the meeting. He might as well try to enjoy it.

A youngish looking footman let him into the foyer and peered quizzically for instruction. Charmaine made an effort to put forth his most formal tone, "Inform Mr. Brooke that Lord Charmaine is here to see him."

"My apologies, milord," the servant meekly answered with a bow, "Mr. Brooke is still in the country."

Charmaine gave the man a flat, unfriendly look. He was starting to enjoy himself. "Tell him anyway."

The butler floundered for a reply and left with a small bow. Charmaine was uncertain if Brooke would even see him, or if the butler would be fetched to invent a convincing excuse. A scurrying movement in the periphery of his vision caught his eye. Charmaine glanced over to see a maid rushing upstairs. Good, he thought to himself, Miss Brooke will know I am here. He would hate to deny her a part in this farce.

After a short period of time the same footman returned. "This way, milord."

Charmaine handed his cane and hat to another servant and followed the butler with a small smile. There was nothing Charmaine could do but be every inch the Viscount Charmaine, with all the mannerisms he tried to avoid. He outranked and outclassed this little man and, by God, he was doing him a favor by offering for his daughter. He would not be denied. Charmaine sincerely hoped Miss Brooke did not eavesdrop on this part of their farce. He disliked making such an ass out of himself.

Charmaine was shown into an ornate library. While the room was opulent, the man behind the mahogany desk managed to overpower it with his very presence. He was rotund and balding, but his crisp manner of dress, imposing manner, and piercing eyes made it clear he was to be taken seriously. Mr. Brooke took a disapproving puff of his pipe and scowled at Charmaine's entrance. Charmaine inclined his head, rather than bowed, and took a chair without being offered.

Brooke's scowl deepened. "Lord Charmaine, is it?"

"Indeed." Charmaine attempted to imitate some of his classmates at Oxford at their most arrogant. "I have come to inform you that I will be marrying your daughter."

A bushy white eyebrow shot up. "I decline."

"I did not request your permission." Charmaine was already proud of the exchange. "She has reached her majority and can make her own choice in this matter. Your consent is irrelevant. With that said, I am sure she would appreciate a blessing if it was given."

"As much as you may think otherwise, young man, my consent is indeed relevant." Charmaine was careful not to let his smile show as Brooke called him 'young man.' He must be getting under the other gentleman's skin. Brooke continued, "There are complications you are not aware of. You are not the first to make such presumptions."

"I am not them." Charmaine came close to telling Brooke how he gave Miss Brooke his word, and nothing would break that, but realized it did not benefit the game they were playing. "I know about the restrictions on her dowry, Brooke. I do not care."

This took Brooke aback. "Without my approval you will receive not a hapenny from her. She would come to you as a pauper. There would be no reason for you to wed her then."

"You do your daughter a great disservice with that statement." Charmaine stood. "Miss Brooke will be my bride. With or without your approval."

"You do not have it." Brooke tapped his pipe. "You may go. I have nothing more to say."

Charmaine nodded and headed for the door. He groped for a witty parting line and settled for his normal straight speech. "Your approval would please your daughter. I seek her happiness. Nevertheless, we will wed. The only approval I need is hers."

Charmaine walked arrogantly back to the foyer and retrieved his hat and cane. The conversation ended with the predictable outcome, but he felt he handled it fairly well. If he was going to get rejected he might as well do it in such a way he did not look like a jackass who only cared about Miss Brooke's wealth. Hopefully, he thought grimly to himself, that never again becomes true.

Walking towards the door, he noticed Miss Brooke standing at the top of the stairs. She was lovely, with her blond ringlets framing her heart-shaped face, but a hint of sadness marred her perfection. Her expression was crestfallen, and her shoulders slumped forward slightly.

Charmaine smiled at his love. "Miss Brooke." She did not answer him, but rather looked expectantly. "I must away. I have a speech to write for the Lords tonight. Perchance we can join the promenade of coaches in the park tomorrow?"

Miss Brooke took two tentative steps down the staircase. "I would like that, but did my father not refuse your suit?"

Charmaine disliked the timid hesitation in her voice. "He refused, as expected. But what does it matter? You are over one and twenty, are you not?"

"I am," Miss Brooke answered, perking up. "But my portion…"

"Will be saved for our daughter, Alison." Charmaine kept is voice soft, level, and tried to project confidence. "I see nothing wrong with that."

Miss Brooke beamed at him, all traces of sadness vanished. She flew down the stairs and appeared ready to leap into his arms. Propriety caught her only inches from Charmaine. She could do nothing but smile at him with excitement.

Charmaine closed those few inches and looked into her sky blue eyes. They were the color of a summer sky that he could be lost in forever. "You will be my wife." Her smile grew even larger.

Charmaine felt inordinately pleased with himself. He did the only thing a sane man could do in this situation, he leaned down and kissed her. He meant for it to be a chaste kiss, but her happiness wanted a form of expression. At the inquiry of his tongue her mouth opened eagerly for him. He broke the kiss off before he wanted to, acutely aware they were standing in her father's entryway, and stepped back. His mouth still tasted like her. Licking his lips set his blood aflame. This woman would be his wife and he could hardly wait to possess her. Miss Brooke's breasts were heaving in excitement, and while it was possible to control his voice and actions, his groin was throbbing from that slight kiss.

He bowed to her with a wicked grin. "I will enjoy having you as my wife." She curtsied with a vivid rosy blush. Smiling, he walked out the door. Yes, Charmaine thought to himself, he was inordinately pleased with himself.

CHAPTER XI

Miss Boswell woke before dawn. Giddy with excitement, she was dressed and ready before the grooms even considered saddling her horse. She paced around her room for what felt like hours before her mare was saddled. Miss Boswell circled The Serpentine at least three times before Farrington approached. Her heart skipped upon seeing him and her stomach tightened in anticipation. He was so gloriously handsome! Farrington's riding habit perfectly matched the gelding's rich brown coat. He rode with such grace he almost appeared to be a centaur. His dark bushy eyebrows drew together in concern as he advanced.

"Miss Boswell, I apologize if I kept you waiting. Am I late?"

Miss Boswell beamed at him, her sherry eyes sparkling in delight at his presence. "Nay, Lord Farrington. I woke early and decided to enjoy the lovely morn." That was a much more politic answer than admitting I am so excited to see you I woke before dawn, Miss Boswell congratulated herself.

"A lovely day, indeed. I plan to spend much of the day inside Westminster, so a morning ride has promise." Farrington nudged his mount into a brisk walk and nodded approvingly at Miss Boswell. "You have a solid seat. I was expecting worse from your comments."

"I enjoy riding. However, my father is a scholar and does not see the point of keeping our own stable."

"A shame." Farrington was known to be a master of horseflesh. "I ride whenever possible."

"I am envious." Miss Boswell looked over at his mount, trying to discern what made it more spectacular than any other. With a slight frown, she had to admit it simply looked like a horse. A pretty horse with a big neck and expressive ears, Miss Boswell thought ruefully to herself. Her own horse was rented from the Palace's livery stables for the Season. She picked it because of the lovely red flecks of color that were splashed across the mare's white coat.

Farrington was quiet for a moment and then continued. "Have you been to the races?"

"No," Miss Boswell replied.

"No?" Surprise was apparent in Farrington's voice. "Not even the Ascot? That is more of a tea party than a race."

"Not even the Ascot." Miss Boswell tried to keep the wistful envy from her voice. "My father views such social events as unimportant and I have found no excuse to go."

Miss Boswell did not add that Miss Brooke had little interest in the races. The proper blonde claimed she found them barbaric. Miss Boswell secretly suspected Miss Brooke thought anything fun was improper and thus the races had to be avoided at all costs.

"The Derby is happening shortly. Charmaine and I will be in attendance. You should join us."

Farrington seemed to have given his proposal little thought, but Miss Boswell found it to be a most delightful offer. "I would have to bring a chaperone."

"I am sure I can find a proper female relative," Farrington replied with a hint of a smile.

"I would enjoy that." Miss Boswell was excited and shy all at once.

Farrington nodded. "Then it shall happen."

They rode in silence. Miss Boswell tried to relax and enjoy the ride, yet a million things crashed through her brain. Did Anthony like her dress? Was she holding her reins correctly? Did he notice the way she kept looking at him? Did he find her to be nothing but an inane wallflower?

They made it almost a fourth of the way around the lake before Farrington interrupted the silence. "You requested my presence to interrogate me, if I recall correctly?"

166

Right. That. Miss Boswell nodded and tried to think of a good place to start. "Do you believe Lord Charmaine will be a suitable match for Miss Brooke?"

"I do. I believe Miss Brooke and I are better suited, but Charmaine will make an adequate replacement. His country manners may irritate our court debutant." Farrington's voice was detached as he looked straight ahead.

Miss Boswell bit her lip. "Did you really love her all that much?"

"Pardon?" Farrington turned and looked at her. Miss Boswell bit her lip, not believing her internal thoughts spilled out of her mouth.

"Nothing. Nothing at all." Miss Boswell turned scarlet, her face more vivid than her hair.

Farrington frowned slightly, but otherwise gave no indication of his thoughts. "I am not sure I believe in love anymore, Miss Boswell. I wanted to wed your friend, yes. I wanted to spend the rest of my life with her. I have deep feelings for her. I believed all of those things to be true of her as well and yet the next week she is in the arms of my best friend. The word love currently rings hollow."

"I am sorry for intruding." Miss Boswell was still blushing. Not only was it an improper question, she received the answer she was dreading. Farrington adored Miss Brooke and was nursing a broken heart.

"Why do you ask?"

Mary's toes! Miss Boswell thought frantically for an answer. The truth—because I wanted to see if you still cared because I am so in love with you—was completely unacceptable. "I was startled you did not press the issue after Mr. Brooke's refusal. You do not seem like the type to be easily thwarted."

"And you believe love can conquer everything, even a father's refusal?" A slight smile tugged at the corner of Farrington's mouth. "That is very you, Miss Boswell."

"And what does that mean?" Miss Boswell was relieved the topic shifted.

"That you are a dreamer. That you see the best in everyone and think everything can work out." His slight smile faded. "That if one tries hard enough, or wants a thing bad enough, it will happen."

"What is amiss with that?" Miss Boswell asked.

"On you? Nothing. Idealism is not practical in politics, trade, and, frankly, love."

"I refuse to believe that, Lord Farrington. Happy endings occur. You are so gallant you cannot help but acquire one of your own." Did I really call him gallant? Miss Boswell thought with another blush. I need to stop talking!

Farrington looked over at her with a smile. "I forget losing Miss Brooke is not the end of my romantic story. I made plans with her in them." He paused. "It is hard to imagine a future without those plans."

Plans? Miss Brooke had never mentioned Farrington and plans. In fact, Miss Brooke admitted she knew nothing of what Farrington desired for the future. Furthermore, Miss Boswell thought to herself, how could he say he lost Miss Brooke when she offered to elope with him and he declined? What *was* going on here? "I think I understand. It will be a bit odd when Miss Brooke does marry." Miss Boswell forced a small smile. "I shall be a lonely spinster."

"You, Miss Boswell, are no spinster."

"I, Lord Farrington, am two and twenty. I am, at most, a Season from being firmly on the shelf. And who is there to meet in my fourth Season that I did not meet in my third?"

"I am nine years older than you. Lord Charmaine is eight. I find it difficult to consider you ancient."

"We both know our world is not fair." Miss Boswell fought to stay in the discussion. It was hard to come up with appropriate things to say when the topic was so personal. The conversation needed to be redirected. "Speaking of Lord Charmaine, how did the two of you meet?"

"Ah, yes, my interrogation." Farrington placed his reins leisurely across his horse's neck and turned to face her. Miss Boswell stared, fascinated. The horse appeared to be directing itself. "Lord Charmaine and I met on a hunting trip the better part of a century ago. My father insisted on my attendance and Charmaine was there to keep an eye on his younger brother. We gravitated together to preserve our sanity."

"I did not know Lord Charmaine had a brother." Miss Boswell was talking simply to talk. She did not care about Charmaine's brother.

"Yes, the Honorable Mr. Michael Anderson. He is a bit wild. Charmaine bought him a commission in the East India Company last year and sent him off to earn his fortune. I doubt you have met him. He does not move in your sort of circles."

"Or yours?" Miss Boswell asked curiously.

"Or mine." Farrington smiled slightly at her. "However, I think you know me well enough to know drinking and women are not the focus of my existence."

"What, then, is the focus of your existence?" Miss Boswell tried to keep the eagerness out of her voice. This is what she really cared about.

"This and that." Farrington shut the question down quickly. "But, to stay on topic, Charmaine's passion is politics. He has been actively involved in supporting Lord North for several years now and he is quite involved in the House of Lords. I do not think he has missed a day in the past two Seasons. He strongly believes the nobility is indebted to the public and has an obligation to perform their duties at the highest level of their capability."

"You do not agree?" Miss Boswell asked, trying to draw Farrington out of his shell.

"Not completely. But Charmaine's ideas have been able to bridge the gap between the monarchy and the populist movements. He is advancing well in government and, it is suspected, has the eye of the Crown. If Miss Brooke wants a politically astute husband, he is a fine choice."

Miss Boswell searched for the question she was supposed to ask, knowing Miss Brooke would expect a full report when she returned. "Do you think he is trying to marry Miss Broke for her portion?"

Farrington raised an eyebrow at her. Miss Boswell flipped her curls back at him. "What? With as rich as Miss Brooke is, it is a valid question."

"But certainly not a polite one." Farrington lifted his reins again but the horse did not seem to notice. "I suspect Miss Brooke's money is a factor in Charmaine's considerations. However, Miss Brooke is not the easy route to wealth. There are currently women with dowries rival to Miss Brooke's. None of those require going through her problematic father."

"How do you know that?" Miss Boswell was curious. She giggled slightly at the image of each of the unmarried women of the *ton* with an amount in pounds sterling listed on their calling cards.

Farrington looked over at her giggle. "Share the amusement?" Miss Boswell told him, and he gave her an indulgent smile. "Not quite that obvious, but it is close. Gossip provides a mostly accurate indicator of what a woman will bring to the marriage. The mamas of the *ton* are quite forthright about the net worth and breeding potential of their daughters. Since I have been dismissed from Miss Brooke's charms, gossip is again making its way to my ears."

The things you miss by not having a mother, Miss Boswell thought to herself with interest. Without Miss Brooke, Miss Boswell would likely have no way of entrance to the *ton's* fanciest parties. "You are still looking to wed?"

Farrington nodded. "I have been told I am not getting any younger. As you know, I am the last direct male of my line. There is pressure to produce an heir."

"I am surprised a man of your caliber has not wed before now," Miss Boswell replied.

"I only just came out of mourning," said Farrington.

"I am sorry."

Farrington inclined his head in thanks and continued. "After meeting a woman like Miss Brooke, I find it hard to direct my attention to any of the mindless youths of the *ton*."

Miss Boswell bit her lip. The last thing she needed was for another accidental blurt to give her feelings away. Screaming 'what about me?' or 'I am right here!' would help nothing. She instead settled for mindless reassurance, "I am sure something will come up."

He nodded. "It must. Is there anything else you would like to know, Miss Boswell?"

A million trivial things popped into her mind, but they were all about Farrington. Charmaine seemed unimportant when she was riding next to her dearest love. "Can I ask you something not about Lord Charmaine?"

"As long as it is not improper. I think our conversation has been adventurous enough for the day."

"What is amiss with your mount?" At Farrington's arched eyebrow she continued hurriedly, "I mean, you drop your reins and it keeps walking. But it does not seem like the broken-down nags at the livery stable."

Farrington smiled at her, a rare, real smile. "I am steering with my knees. I have trained Amsterdam to know he should keep the course he is on when he feels the reins on his neck. I remind him I am paying attention with my legs. I promise you, nothing in my stables is broken-down, or even very calm."

He patted the gelding's neck fondly. "Charmaine claims it is a weakness I like overly spirited animals. But if they do not challenge me they bring to me no pleasure. A horse should have a mind, a spirit. Those nags you mention are barely fit to be called horses."

"Ta." Miss Boswell nodded in agreement, captivated by the passion in his voice. "'Tis a shame he is called Amsterdam rather than New Amsterdam."

"Why is that?" Miss Boswell did not notice the hint of wary curiosity.

"I am sorry, he is your horse. You can call him anything you like." She fidgeted as she blushed and her horse flicked its mane in irritation. "I am so intrigued by the New World."

Farrington nodded at her with his standard expressionless look. "As are our Crown and Country, Miss Boswell. It occurs to me I have a question for you as well."

Miss Boswell nodded eagerly, "Yes?"

"If you overheard Charmaine say the word 'west' to me, what would you assume he was referencing?" Farrington found a piece of paper with Charmaine's handwriting on it when he woke from drink days before. The meaning of wrinkled piece of parchment was a mystery.

She wrinkled her brow in confusion. "West? As in the opposite of east?" At his nod she shrugged helplessly. "He was giving you directions? I really do not know."

Farrington nodded and halted his horse. Miss Boswell had to fumble with the reins to do the same. "It was a pleasure riding with you this morning."

"Yes, thank you." Miss Boswell smiled brightly at him before crinkling her brow. "That was a queer question about directions though."

"Charmaine and I are queer fellows, if you had not noticed." Farrington granted her a small smile. "Now, if I may have your leave?"

"Certainly." Miss Boswell gave Farrington a silly little wave to match her lopsided grin. He returned it with a half bow, turned his horse, and rode the opposite direction back down the path.

Farrington leaned forward to stroke his horse's neck and straighten part of the bridle. While he was there, he whispered into his horse's ear. He always felt more comfortable with animals than people and his favorite mount in the city often got little snippets of commentary. This time, however, it was a question. "How did she know your name, New Amsterdam? Are you telling pretty girls my secrets?" The horse cocked one brown ear back to catch his words but otherwise did not answer. Farrington rode home wondering what it would be like to be able to trust a woman with his secrets.

Farrington took the better part of a week to seek out Charmaine. The American Colonies were an increasingly heated subject in the House of Lords and the two old friends were often at odds with one another. Thus, when Farrington knocked on the door of Charmaine's small rundown rooms, both gentlemen were suitably wary. Wilhelm ushered Farrington in, poured both men a tumbler of whiskey, and left them to their discussions.

"Farrington, well meet."

Farrington nodded at his friend and sat in a spartan chair. "You as well. Do you have a moment?"

Charmaine nodded, putting the papers he was working on to one side of his desk. "For you, always. I was getting eye strain from reading anyway."

"That is what you get for being so involved. I swear you do the work of three men."

"I would do the work of four if time would allow it." Charmaine smiled slightly. "But we both know the dangers of talking work lately. Pray tell what is on your mind."

"Nothing important, or so I would imagine." Farrington reached inside his waistcoat and pulled forth the scrap of parchment. "I found this in my pocket after my undignified morning here. Would you care to explain?"

Charmaine reached over the table and took the scrap. He glanced at it and handed it back. "Indeed."

Farrington sipped his whiskey and raised an eyebrow at Charmaine's enigmatic reply. "Care to elaborate?"

"I would prefer not to but apparently my past self thought otherwise." Charmaine sighed and leaned back in his chair, giving Farrington his full attention. "I suppose it must seem odd to you that I would court Miss Brooke so recently after your rejection."

The direction of the conversation surprised Farrington, "Odd was not the word that entered my mind, but, yes, I did notice my rejection had not even exited gossip before your interest was the highlight of Society's papers."

"I apologize. Such rudeness was unintentional."

"How can pursuing a woman not be intentional?" Farrington swirled his whiskey as he peered shrewdly at his friend.

"Only through landing in a farce." Charmaine scowled and decided to take the plunge. "I walked in on a cretin assaulting Miss Brooke."

"The hell you say?" Farrington leaned forward in his chair, whiskey forgotten.

Charmaine nodded. "I interrupted the cad, but, as I was helping the lady up, some of the gossips of Society walked in on us and decided we had been coupling. I was left with an—unusual set of choices."

"Who was it? I will kill him." Farrington's eyes were uncharacteristically fierce.

"The lady has requested we refrain from action so that she may handle this on her own."

"God's blood, Charmaine."

Charmaine shrugged. "I agree. But it is Miss Brooke's decision. I support her choices. Unless the man steps out of line," Charmaine amended his statement. "Then I will act, nevertheless of her wishes."

"Then why are you telling me this?"

"Two reasons. The first is I wanted you to know I respect you. Secondly, I want to ensure I can rely on your assistance when Miss Brooke decides we can lynch this scum."

"You do not even have to ask. Although, I am sure there are many who would be glad to second you in a matter such as this." Farrington's ever-present calm was returning.

"Perhaps," Charmaine admitted, "but Miss Brooke wishes this whole matter kept quiet. I should not even be telling you."

"Who knows?"

"Me, you, my parents, Castlemire, and the Stantons."

Farrington's eyebrow twitched upwards. "His Grace?"

"No, The Duchess. Her Grace walked in when I was helping Miss Brooke to her feet. She managed to pry the story out of Miss Brooke after sending her cronies away."

"That must irritate Miss Brooke. What an unexpected wrinkle." Farrington was clearly thinking. "What did her father say about all of this?"

"I do not know if he has been told. He rejected me with all due speed, though."

"As expected. So where do your sights turn now?"

Charmaine frowned. "Nowhere. I still intend to marry Miss Brooke."

"You cannot be serious, Charmaine. You cannot afford to."

"Perhaps. But maybe not. I am still waiting on my ships." Charmaine remained stubbornly optimistic. "And, besides, I enjoy her company."

"Do you enjoy genteel poverty?" Farrington's voice was harsher than usual as he took a large gulp of his whiskey.

"No, I do not." Charmaine was growing irritated. "But the ships will come in."

"Dammit, Charmaine, you are not normally this foolish."

"I can, and I will, marry Alison. If you wanted to marry her, you would have eloped with her. You love your revolution more than you love her. Do not take that out on me."

Farrington slammed his glass down on the desk and stood, dark brown eyes flashing. "Do not tell me what I love." Charmaine gazed coolly back. Farrington grabbed his hat and met Charmaine's gaze. "You are being foolish. You are risking your future and you are risking her heart. This will all end in tears. You are a money hunter, Charmaine, and men such as you cannot marry for love."

Charmaine's temper got the best of him. "At least I am not a traitor."

Farrington's hands flexed as he scowled. "Good day, Charmaine."

Farrington walked out of Charmaine's small flat without waiting for his friend's reply. His outward façade was immobile and calm but inwardly he was seething.

Farrington had been certain Charmaine and Miss Brooke's entanglement would fall apart as soon as Charmaine found out about her finances, but still Charmaine persevered. It was impossible. Charmaine needed the money even more than he did. He fought a scowl as he headed outside.

Farrington was almost home before he realized he had not gotten an answer about the scrap of paper. Luckily, it did not take much effort to draw the correct conclusion.

The invitation to take tea with Lady Stanton was unexpected and Miss Brooke considered it carefully. She was unsure if an invitation to tea should be seen as a welcoming into the family or as yet another interview. Still, she could not see the harm in going. Now that she was standing in the parlor of the stately Stanton residence she began to doubt the wisdom of coming.

A footman led Miss Brooke upstairs to a warm wood paneled room where Lady Stanton awaited with tea. Lady Stanton wasted no time in waving the younger girl forward. "Stuff and bother with ceremony, do sit. Tea?"

Miss Brooke smiled in greeting and gracefully slid into the tall wing backed chair across from the baroness. "Please." A servant stepped forward to pour for them both. "Thank you for inviting me into your home. I am honored."

"You are welcome. I am eager to meet the woman who caught Lord Charmaine."

Miss Brooke lifted her tea with a small nod. Apparently, Lady Stanton had decided to ignore their previous meeting. Miss Brooke adjusted quickly. "I am honored by your invitation. Although I will admit I do not feel as if I did the hunting. Lord Charmaine is a determined man."

"Indeed." Lady Stanton nodded with a scheming smile. "Your Lord Charmaine will take careful handling. I am unsure if a girl such as yourself can manage."

Miss Brooke sipped her tea while considering Lady Stanton's words. She was sure there was an insult there but she felt complimented instead. The idea of 'handling' Charmaine's life for him was repulsive. "I am uncertain what you mean."

"Even with a shut-in of a mother, I find that hard to believe. You cannot intend to let him walk all over you?"

Miss Brooke was lost. She was supposed to be a political savant, yet her hostess's purpose eluded her. She could assume the woman was mean, cold-hearted, and digging for insults and information but her previous interactions with Charmaine made that unlikely. "I do not think he will walk all over me. He is respectful of my wishes."

Lady Stanton blinked, startled. "Are you moonstruck? Have you met him?"

"Once or twice." The blonde smiled to indicate her reply was a joke. "He has always been exceedingly courteous."

"Such as when he took you to his mother's house against your will? Or perhaps announcing he intended to wed you before speaking to you?" Lady Stanton cocked her head. "Those things do not seem courteous to me."

Miss Brooke frowned at the other woman's tone. "I find Lord Charmaine charming and do not appreciate implication otherwise."

"But Society itself implies otherwise. It calls him foolish and gullible, wrapped around the charms of the *ton*'s brightest diamond."

Ah ha, thought Miss Brooke, now we get to the point. "I am aware. It is unfortunate but, I assure you, I have done no such thing.

176

To be honest, the selfsame circumstances that caught him have trapped me. This is a web of someone else's making."

"Foolish youth." Lady Stanton rolled her eyes as she vigorously fanned herself. "All webs are of someone else's making. When will you learn no one cares about truth?"

"I do not care what they think, Lady Stanton. Lord Charmaine is an amazing man and I am honored to be his promised." Miss Brooke's voice was steely, and her blue eyes flashed with an inner fire.

"You do not care what they think? The finest diamond of the *ton* and her politician do not care what polite Society thinks of them? Rubbish. A load of stinking rubbish. More likely you do not care what Society thinks of him. After all, you are already ruined. Your membership to Almack's is hung out to dry. Why would you care what Society thinks of dear Lord Charmaine?" Lady Stanton's cruel little smile never faded.

"That is a horrible thing to say. Truly I do care. How dare you suggest otherwise!" The debutant was a bit taken aback at the harsh allegations. Yet she would not, no matter the cost, show this wretched woman how much her remarks stung.

"Why?"

"Because I am not like that, Lady Stanton. Why would I toss the man who saved away like a broken hair plume?"

Lady Stanton raised an eyebrow. "I do not know. Why would you?"

"I would not. I have not."

"Have you not?"

"I have not. If you are attempting to infer something, I invite you to speak plainly. Dancing around the issue does no good." And to think, Miss Brooke thought with anger, at one point I hoped to make a friend and ally of this woman.

Lady Stanton was quiet for a moment as she sipped her tea. "Do you care for Lord Charmaine?"

"I do." Miss Brooke's voice was clear, confident.

"Do you love him?" While the first question had been asked in a detached tone, there was now a note of curiosity in the matron's voice.

"I do not see how that is any concern of yours."

"If you loved him, you would be clear about it. You would be publicly enthralled and it would not be political or manipulative." Lady Stanton sounded like she was talking to a small child.

"What do you want me to do? Pin on a sign proclaiming my affection?"

"Frankly, Miss Brooke, I am not concerned with what you do. All I want to know is, are you are willing to fight for my husband's friend. It is irrelevant if you succeed or if you make a mess of things. I want to know if you are willing to try."

Miss Brooke hid her confusion by taking another long swallow of tea. "I will. I thought I was. I danced every dance with him. My reputation lies in tatters around his neck. Plus, our relationship progresses even though my father has yet to approve. What is it exactly I am failing to do?"

"Does the *ton* still think your petticoats have bewitched him?"

"Apparently." Miss Brooke spat the word out, bitter this conversation kept occurring.

"Then whatever you are doing is not working. I do not care about your success. I care you try. You see, Lord Charmaine is inept in our world. They tell me he has skill at politics, but he cares nothing for the *ton* and, without his parent's connections, the *ton* would care nothing about him. He would be a pretty face with a title to be chased after and then forgotten. A boring man with a boring passion doing a boring occupation."

"I do not see your point."

"Lord Charmaine has no use for a pretty face. He needs a woman with a mind, with a wit, and, most importantly, with a will. He needs a champion who can win in the Society he ignores so he can succeed in what he believes in. That boy has the foolish idea our parties, balls, and politics are not connected. He views them as two different worlds. He can fight in one. He needs a woman who can fight for him in the other." The malicious smile faded, and it was replaced with an intense, serious passion. "I am not sure you are that woman."

Slowly inhaling the aroma of the tea, Miss Brooke forced herself to take the other woman seriously. "I would like to be."

"Then you will be."

Miss Brooke bit back a thousand caustic replies and concentrated on trying to bring Lady Stanton on her side. Being petty would gain her nothing. Perhaps, Miss Brooke considered, the best thing to do would be to play to the other woman's pride. "I do not know how."

"That is because you are not thinking." Lady Stanton leaned forward. "Or you are thinking wrong. You want to handle things in a straightforward manner. You do not try to be crafty or underhanded. Dancing six dances a night tells Society nothing except you are laying claim to the poor boy. Talk. Gossip. Go about things through your friends. You have become so flustered you have forgotten your base of power."

Perhaps, Miss Brooke thought to herself, the battleax has a point. "You want me to create gossip that I love and adore him?"

"How else are you going to fight for him, Miss Brooke? Sabers?"

Miss Brooke was quiet for a long moment. "I will consider your advice. Thank you."

Lady Stanton waved her words away with a flick of her fan. "Now, with that aside, I want you to tell me all about your plans for the King's Birthday. I'll have to get Charmaine ready, and…" The two women's chatter turned to less serious matters. Miss Brooke's mind, however, continued to muse over the conversation. She had never been much of a deep thinker, it was only since meeting Charmaine she was encouraged to be more than a pretty decoration. Yet throughout the rest of the day her mind would not be still. Defeated, she decided to spend the night in. She supped with her father, took a long bath, and curled up in bed.

Miss Brooke had almost fallen asleep when her epiphany came. She was being foolish. The way to ruin Mr. West was not through gossip aimed at getting him excluded from the *ton*. The man likely did not even care. The real way to ruin Mr. West was financial. She had been so focused on her own struggles to not feeling helpless that she not considered directing actions through other people. She would still being in control, just indirectly. That was what Lady Stanton had been trying to convince her to do with Charmaine. Miss Brooke needed to make the *ton* gossips dance and sing that she and Charmaine were a love match. All she had to do was run the same type of show, with very different puppets, to ruin Mr. West.

Society thought she was a manipulative shrew. It was time to see if Society was right. Grabbing the hem of her nightgown with her fists, Miss Brooke dashed to her correspondence desk to create a plan of action. She saw dawn before she again found her bed.

The maids burst into Miss Brooke's room at entirely too early of an hour. She put a pillow over her head and wished them away, but the bustle continued. Peeking one cornflower eye out from her pillow, she fixed Abigail with a sleepy glare. "Why all this excitement so early?"

"Your father wants to see you, Ali. He seems to think you should be awake." Abigail was pulling out a day dress from the armoire. "Pale green?"

"I suppose." Miss Brooke agreed as she sat and stretched. "Do you know what he wants?"

"No. But the post arrived and he called for you. Now," Abigail encouraged, "upsey-daisy. Time to get dressed."

Hunger and lack of sleep made her a mite grumpy. Miss Brooke hoped the meeting would not be a stressful one. The moment she opened the door to the study, she knew her hope was futile. Her father was frowning at paperwork, the wrinkles on his brow pronounced. That, however, was normal. The real warning signs of trouble were the empty brandy glass on the desk and an ashtray full of half-smoked cigars.

Miss Brooke curtsied slightly before taking her favorite chair next to the desk. "You called for me, Father?"

"You received a letter." He did not look at her, still staring at the papers in front of him.

"A common occurrence, I assure you." Miss Brooke smiled, trying to cheer him up.

"I think not." Brooke looked at his daughter. She saw sadness in his eyes. Wordlessly, he handed her a letter. Miss Brooke took it with a frown. She could feel two sheets of paper inside. "Go on, open it."

Turning the parchment over, Miss Brooke blanched. Duchess Castlemire's seal was unmistakable. She took a letter opener from her father's desk and slid it through the wax.

The first letter only had a single line of script:

Chin up, girl.

With shaking hands, Miss Brooke handed the Duchess' parchment over to her father. He read it and frowned.

Brooke unfolded the printed letter. Her name was the only handwritten item. The lady patronesses did not personalize letters to those denied membership.

> The ladies patronesses' compliments to
>
> Miss _____**Alison Brooke**_____,
> and are sorry they cannot comply with her request.

Miss Brooke reread the correspondence. She was expecting the rejection from the most elite of the *ton*, but it still managed to be a shock. The letter was the formal announcement of her ruin. She placed the parchment down and looked at her father.

He struggled to find appropriate words. Failing, he settled for trying to look supportive. With a perfunctory curtsey, Miss Brooke turned on her heel and rushed from the room. Brooke smacked his hand on the sturdy wood desk in frustration. He never wanted to see his daughter ruined. In fact, this Charmaine character was reacting exactly the way he would want a suitor to handle such a situation. And yet, there was that deathbed vow. He was not about to break his word to his mother. Still, each and every time he watched his daughter run from him in tears after dashing her dreams of a happy ending, he considered breaking it. Eventually, Brooke reassured himself, his daughter would be happy. He hoped she still loved him when that day came.

Charmaine, under the command of Lord North, was investigating the internal finances of the Kingdom. His head ached from tracing who was taxing, bribing, buying, selling, or otherwise funneling money throughout the country. Both the Prime Minister and himself were convinced there was a leak. France alone could not funnel enough money to the American colonies to support resistance. The idea these loyal Englishmen would revolt on their own was unthinkable.

Charmaine only left the Palace of Westminster because of his evening ride with Miss Brooke. He missed the ride for two days in a row and was damned if he was going to allow a third opportunity to slip by. Simply speaking to her had become a calming act. She listened to his frustrations and, most importantly, looked at him as if he was worth something. He never knew he was lonely until he met her. It was as if he was a seagull finally meeting the sea.

Charmaine was chortling at his melodramatic metaphors when he arrived at the Brooke's doorstep. They took her carriage for their afternoon rides. Charmaine implied he preferred to leave his free for his mother.

As always, seeing Miss Brooke took his breath away. She was radiant. Her golden hair was hidden under a fashionable bonnet, but the frizz of her curls made it seem as if sunlight poured forth from her. But no matter how pretty she was, it was always the smile that undid him. Every time she spotted him, Miss Brooke smiled. Her expression was shy at first and then filled with unbelieving joy. Her smile inspired him to kill dragons for her or lay the world at her feet. She inspired his mind to poetry—to metaphors about nonsense— and left him astounded at how he could be so lucky.

Charmaine helped Miss Brooke onto the driver's ledge of her phaeton. He took the reins from the groomsman and perched next to her. Cracking the whip, he led them toward The Serpentine. He was still mulling over the events of the day and scolded himself for being distant. "I am sorry I am quiet, dearheart. The Lords irritate."

She smiled and waved a dainty hand in forgiveness. "As they do thrice a week. I was lost in my own thoughts. What have they done now?"

"I do not want to discuss it. I promise, I am not keeping secrets, I am unreasonably frustrated and if I recap, I am afraid my temper will flare," Charmaine wished he was joking. He had the horrible suspicion he was chasing Farrington's embezzlement to the rebels in the New World and was at his wits end on how to handle it.

"Since we are both in such cheery moods, I suppose I must make it better." Miss Brooke's tone was self-depreciating. "I am afraid I am not really in the mood for a drive in the park. Preening and being proper seems very—unappealing right now."

"I thought you loved this. No matter, we can turn the horses around and do this another day." Charmaine already started to rein the horses in. He was determined not to let his disappointment at her withdrawal show. "Let us take you home, then."

"I did not say I wanted to go home." Miss Brooke expected to feel reckless all day. She was positive it would overtake her at any moment. She was condemned. She was a slattern. Yet, no matter how many times she told herself that, nor how many times she reread the wretched form letter, she still felt like plain boring Miss Brooke. If she were to do anything drastic, it seemed she would have to do it rationally and deliberately, rather than wait for fancy to take her. For the briefest of moments, Miss Brooke wished she were Miss Boswell. Her friend would have no problems being reckless.

"I suppose that is true." Charmaine glanced over at her, his brow furrowed. "What is your desire?"

"We could ride elsewhere? Take a picnic in the country." Miss Brooke made a broad sweeping gesture as if to say anything or anywhere was fine.

Charmaine looked at the sun. "It is rather late in the day."

"Surely there is enough time for a short ride and a stop. The days are long," Miss Brooke pleaded.

"It would be improper."

Miss Brooke blinked at him. "Is that not my retort?"

"Alison, your reputation matters to me. I will not tarnish it. Us getting holed up in the country after dark would give those gossiping fools more ammunition."

She nodded, a bit dejected. Here she was, almost throwing herself at him, and he was worried about it getting dark. She had always been told men would take any opportunity given to ravish a woman, yet Charmaine was being the proper voice of reason. Miss

Brooke wanted to explain that she welcomed his advances but the words would not come. All she could do was nod in acquiescence.

Miss Brooke's sudden bright blush confused Charmaine, but he decided not to press for the cause. He took the horses for a turn around the park, smiling and exchanging pleasantries with the various nobles they passed. In the past few weeks, Charmaine had almost become used to being the center of attention, but today the looks were reinvigorated. Rather than making a second pass through the park, Charmaine turned the horses and headed for the Brookes' townhouse. Miss Brooke gave him a grateful little smile. They arrived at her large stone residence a short time later.

"If you wish for a ride in the country, we can go the day after tomorrow." Charmaine did not understand her withdrawal and wished to remove the lingering upset he felt radiating from her. "Miss Boswell will join us?"

That is not what I want at all, Robert, Miss Brooke thought crossly. "That would be delightful," she replied with a smile. "Thank you for the drive."

"My pleasure. Spending time with you always is." Charmaine frowned as Miss Brooke curtsied and promptly swished inside. Her smile was fake, he was sure of that, but there was no hint of what was bothering her. Smoldering with frustration, Charmaine stalked home.

Miss Brooke's irritation led her down a path she rarely took. She paid a call upon Miss Boswell. As much as she loved her best friend, the empty, slightly run-down townhouse depressed Miss Brooke and she avoided it at all costs. The house felt like a monument to the death of Miss Boswell's mother. Miss Boswell's father had withdrawn from the world and remained wrapped in his misery. Oftentimes, it seemed like he did not even notice he still had a daughter. Miss Brooke had no idea how Miss Boswell functioned as well as she did. Miss Brooke would be locked in Bedlam if she were trapped in the same situation.

Her feeling of unease mounted as a footman showed her into a small, sun-filled parlor. It was spotlessly clean and lacked trademarks of the haunted house Miss Brooke expected. The furnishings, however, were at least ten years out of date. Miss Brooke was pulled from her critical examination when Miss Boswell bounced into the room.

Miss Boswell was already talking before she was halfway through the door. "La, Ali, what is amiss?"

Miss Brooke smiled in spite of herself. "Cannot I visit you without something being tragically wrong?"

"No." Miss Boswell's curls shook with the vigor of her nod. "You hate my house. What happened?"

"Nothing." The stress Miss Brooke put on the word made it sound like she was announcing a social catastrophe or risqué gossip. "Nothing happened. That is the problem."

Miss Boswell sat next to her friend. The overstuffed couch groaned slightly under their weight. "What did not happen?"

Miss Boswell was concerned. Not only was Miss Brooke in her drawing room, but she was also acting like a fool girl in her first Season—right down to melodramatic posturing.

"I tried to tempt Lord Charmaine" Miss Brooke made a sexual gesture as she reclined further on the couch. "And he declined!"

Miss Boswell's eyebrows arched. "Tempt him, Eve-style?"

"Yes, what else could I mean?!" Miss Brooke exclaimed.

Miss Boswell paused, a bit out of her depth. "You want to tempt him, biblically?"

"I am ruined anyway! If I am ruined, I might as well sin a little."

"So you asked him to sin with you and he refused?" Miss Boswell needed facts before deciding if her normally prudish friend had gone crazy.

"Brenda! Forsooth, I did not ask him! What sort of bold trollop do you think I am?"

The kind that is on my couch, furious her affianced did not make her a fallen woman, Miss Boswell thought irreverently. "Kindly tell me what transpired, then?"

"He refused to go on a ride in the country with me," said Miss Brooke.

Miss Boswell raised an eyebrow. "Something is amiss with him refusing to ride in the country with you?"

"Because, Brenda, I did not want to go for a ride in the country. I wanted to…"

"… to join him in amorous congress?"

"Brenda, bad form!" Miss Brooke's cheeks turned a rosy pink.

"Sorry, sorry. But perhaps you should tell him rather than me? How on God's green earth is Lord Charmaine supposed to know a ride in the country is the new metaphor for illicit behavior?"

"Because proper behavior is our shield against such sin!" Miss Brooke looked at Miss Boswell like she was dense.

"So, any improper activity you suggest is an offer to couple with him?" Miss Boswell arched an eyebrow.

"You are being unreasonable. I was perfectly clear."

"Ta. Then why did he not go?"

Miss Brooke sniffed. "He blamed the late hour. Some nonsense about it getting dark."

"Seems reasonable." Miss Boswell smiled at Miss Brooke's glare. "Did he reschedule?"

"In two days. I am supposed to ask you to come with us."

Miss Boswell paused. "Is that another metaphor?"

Miss Brooke was so shocked she laughed. "No, I, you are impossible!"

Miss Boswell smiled in return. "You have no sense of humor. So, I agree to come, but I think I am going to get sick—when did you say I was getting sick?"

"In two days," answered Miss Brooke.

"I will get sick and send word I cannot come. You make sure there is a picnic in the carriage with blankets and wine. Direct the driver to a scenic and secluded place, spread the blankets, and become Eve."

Miss Brooke looked at her hands. "He will refuse. He says he does not want to ruin my reputation even if it is already ruined. That the truth matters or some such frippery."

"Seduce him."

"Pray pardon!" Miss Brooke looked at Miss Boswell as if she had grown another head. "I—no. I cannot. I am no Eve. Seducing him is not proper!"

Miss Boswell smiled. "But it is proper to ride into the country alone and persuade him to lie with you?"

Miss Brooke spluttered again. "I, but—I cannot. I…"

"Then you will wait for your wedding night like you have always dreamed."

"This is not what I always dreamed, Brenda. I have been rejected from Almack's. How is that what I always dreamed?"

"Ah, that is what this is about." Miss Boswell took her friends hand. "You are borrowing trouble. Let us avoid speculation."

Miss Brooke shut her eyes. Tears formed on her lashes. "Her Grace sent the rejection personally."

Miss Boswell considered that unusual bit of news. Normally revoked or denied members were informed, and humiliated, at the door. "Kindness from the old crow. Surprising."

Miss Brooke inclined her head in agreement.

Miss Boswell leaned back into the plush couch and blew air out her nose. "Those fools do not know the difference between paste and diamonds."

A sad smile answered the statement. "I do not deserve you. But if those fools no longer matter, then I am free of their rules, yes?"

"Oh, Ali," Miss Boswell huffed, "those people never restricted your actions. Only you do that. They did not stop you from being Eve with any of your former suitors, you did. They did not make you wear fashionable gowns, you did. A membership, or lack of it, to a silly club does not change who you are."

"You are such a romantic. Almack's rejection does not change who I am, but it changes what I have access to and what I can do. And it changes the consequences for my actions. What punitive threats can be applied? Shall they revoke my membership again?"

Miss Boswell shook her head. "Ali, there are worse things than being refused entry to Almack's. Approximately eighty percent of Society tries in vain to gain membership. That other eighty percent can still shun you."

"Mayhap. But I want to be reckless. I always do what is right, am always proper, and, for once, I simply want to live. And maybe," Miss Brooke pushed away the memory of West, "maybe I need to feel in control of my life again. I am done reacting. I want to take action."

"Then take action," Miss Boswell said.

Miss Brooke raised both eyebrows. "Pardon? Truly?"

"What else do you expect from me? A scold? You are my friend and you have considered your actions." Miss Boswell shrugged. "And, perchance you are right. Everyone does think the two of you were caught in flagrante delicto."

"Brenda."

"Sorry. I forgot, biblical references only. Stole his rib? Offered him your apple? Ooo, I have it! Dallied in God's garden!"

Miss Brooke smiled despite herself. "You are impossible."

Miss Boswell returned the smile. "I know."

"So," Miss Brooke asked, "how do I tempt Robert?"

Miss Boswell laughed good-naturedly. "My friend, I have not the slightest idea."

CHAPTER XII

The next two days passed with agonizing slowness. Miss Brooke imagined wild schemes, fantastical manipulations, and discarded each as unsuitable. She knew how to flirt, how to promise more than she intended to give, and all the tricks and tactics of getting a gentleman to propose. The next stage was alien to her.

The same two days flew by for Charmaine. He made serious progress in tracking the shipping operations coming in and out of London's docks. Wherever the supplies being smuggled to the American Colonies were coming from, it was certainly not from London. Charmaine turned his attention to the many other ports, all the while trying to ignore that the Farrington ancestral estate bordered a coastline filled with coves and inlets. Charmaine headed towards Miss Brooke's with a sense of great relief. Perhaps a peaceful ride in the country would clear his mind.

Miss Brooke was ready when Charmaine arrived at her residence. The coach was waiting out front, fully stocked for their excursion. Miss Brooke begged her maid find a discreet driver. The wicked gleam in her maid's eye made Miss Brooke blush to the roots of her hair but a driver who was not on her father's payroll had, nonetheless, been procured. The servants still had their doubts about the mongrel money-hunter but there was no doubt how happy he was making her.

Without a thought for the gossip, Miss Brooke rushed to greet Charmaine as he arrived. Her eyes sparkled with joy as shining sincerity radiated from them. Words spilled out of his mouth at the sight of her, "You are so pretty."

A rosy red flooded Miss Brooke's cheeks, "Some callers might greet a lady first."

"I apologize." Charmaine frowned inwardly at himself. Not only was he a bumbling fool whenever he spoke to Miss Brooke, he could not manage a better phrase than pretty. She was more than pretty: she was extravagantly gorgeous, she shone brighter than the whole Greek pantheon, she was what God had in mind when he created light.

Miss Brooke's smile faded at Charmaine's queer expression. "Is all well?"

"Yes, certainly." Charmaine looked at her quizzically. "Why?"

"You had an odd expression. I hope you do not think I was offended by the compliment."

Charmaine smiled ruefully. "I, no. No, I did not think that. I was thinking 'pretty' does not do you justice."

"And that made you frown?" Miss Brooke put her hand through his arm and started walking for the coach.

Charmaine seemed to blush slightly. Miss Brooke was sure she was mistaken, as she could not imagine what was discomforting him so. "I was describing how lovely you are to myself. The words I generate seem false, like a bad poet trying to flatter for flattery's sake. Yet 'pretty' seems inadequate. Does that make sense?"

"You are afraid of making a fool of yourself by complimenting me?"

Charmaine frowned slightly. "Not quite. I never like to make a fool of myself, but I doubt complimenting you could do that. The level of compliments you deserve can only be given in words that will come across as fake or as platitudes."

"I do not understand."

"It is of no matter." They reached the coach. "Where is Miss Boswell?"

Miss Brooke pouted slightly. She hoped he would overlook her absence. "She is feeling out of humor. She sent a card saying we should go on without her."

"And trust your reputation to nothing more than a maid chaperoning us? Are you sure?" Charmaine seemed genuinely concerned. Miss Brooke hid a sigh. This was going to be much harder than she anticipated.

"I am sure." She held out her hand expectantly for Charmaine to help her into the coach. He did so without question. As he started to pull himself into the coach, he paused with one foot on the rail.

"Where is your maid?"

"Abigail is also not feeling well." Miss Brooke gave Charmaine a cross look. "Stop being prudish. I refuse to have my day ruined because of a silly cold."

Charmaine finished pulling himself into the coach. He pulled the curtains over the windows shut. "Miss Brooke, we have discussed this. Just because you feel your reputation is ruined does not allow for risks. Running around without a chaperone is foolish."

"Why? Because you might take advantage of me?" Miss Brooke asked with a coy smile.

"I would not disrespect you so. But others may think I have." Charmaine sat across from her. The dim lighting made him look overly stern.

"They already think that." Miss Brooke fought her urge to sulk at what felt like his continued rejection. She shook her head slightly to clear her insecurities away. "Will you open the windows? It is stifling in here."

"Not until we are clear of the city. I will not squander what is left of your reputation."

Miss Brooke wanted to strangle him but settled for delicately reorganizing the folds of her skirt. Silence descended on the couple. Miss Brooke felt the carriage change from the bumpiness of cobblestone to the more irregular packed dirt. The clack of the horses' hooves on stone faded into a dull thud.

She looked at Charmaine to vent her frustration with his over-protectiveness and noticed an unexpected look of worry on his face. His brows were deeply furrowed as he rubbed his thumb back and forth across his cane. Miss Brooke brushed her own concerns away. They could wait if something was bothering Charmaine.

"Is something bothering you?" Miss Brooke asked timidly.

Charmaine blinked and settled his attention on her once again. "I am fine. I apologize for my distraction."

Miss Brooke nodded in acceptance and tried again. "You seem worried."

Charmaine was silent for a long moment as he considered his answer. "I am."

"Would you like to talk about it?"

"I cannot." At her unintentional frown, he continued. "It is not I do not trust you, nor is it I do not want to talk to you. Politics are complicated."

"I did not mean to pry." Miss Brooke reached over and pushed a curtain back. "The weather is lovely today."

Charmaine smiled slightly. "The weather, eh?" He looked back at his cane and grew serious. "Mayhap you can aid me with a dilemma. Suppose I was told something in confidence and I will not break trust. Now someone else has tasked me to ferret out that information. I need to make sure I do this right, rather than using my own secrets."

Miss Brooke frowned. "As if Lady Stanton told me in confidence she had an affair and then Lord Stanton asked me to look into if she had an affair? So, if I wanted to help him I could only try to find evidence, rather than using her words?"

"Yes. Exactly." Charmaine smiled. "Exactly."

"But…" Miss Brooke's brow furrowed. "In my example do I like or dislike the Stantons? Or like one or the other?"

"You like them both. Very much."

"Then, even if I told Lord Stanton that Lady Stanton was having an affair, and I discovered that using information she did not tell me, I would still be disingenuous. Not only would I destroy their marriage, but Lady Stanton would think I betrayed her trust."

Charmaine's frown now matched hers. "I think the Stantons could survive a little adultery."

"That is not my point."

"I know." Charmaine scowled at the wall of the coach behind her. "But I am bound to protect Lord Stanton. If Lady Stanton was foolish enough to cheat, then I have to tell her husband."

"If true, then you should have told Lord Stanton as soon as you found out about his wife's indiscretion. But you did not."

"I will not betray Lady Stanton. I will not. I cannot." Charmaine's voice was fierce.

Miss Brooke sounded confused. "But then why would you agree to help Lord Stanton look for the affair? You already know what you will find, you know you will have to tell him, and you know you will betray Lady Stanton. Or, I suppose, you could protect Lady Stanton and tell Lord Stanton you found no evidence of infidelity. Either way, it seems like a rubbish set of choices."

"Duty, Miss Brooke. It is my duty. I believe in Lord Stanton. I believe in what Lord Stanton represents and I believe what Lady Stanton is doing is immoral, unethical, and wrong."

"Does Lady Stanton feel that way?"

"No." Charmaine sighed. "Lady Stanton feels she is doing what needs to be done, she is acting on the side of right, justice, and good. She feels Lord Stanton is being overbearing and cruel but has no chance of affecting change through straightforward means. Thus, she goes behind his back."

Miss Brooke tisked him with a small smile, "Your metaphor is falling apart. Or Lady Stanton is crazy."

Charmaine returned the smile, but the stress never left his face. "She is not crazy. She is making rational decisions I think are foolish in the extreme."

"Do they hurt Lord Stanton?"

"Very much. It is as if she is giving him the clap. Over and over again."

Miss Brooke made an expression of disgust. "Well, assuming the clap is something you can get over and over again, what about your obligation to tell Lord Stanton?"

"I already told you, I will not betray Lady Stanton." Charmaine no longer sounded angry. Now he sounded weary.

"You already said you were going to. You first have to find proof to betray Lady Stanton, rather than using Lady Stanton's words to betray Lady Stanton. Aside from a technicality as thin as embroidery floss, I do not see the difference." Charmaine frowned at her but otherwise stayed quiet. When it was clear he was not going to respond Miss Brooke continued, "Will Lady Stanton see the difference?"

"No. She will not. She will be furious either way."

"Can you talk to her about this?"

"No. If I told Lady Stanton of my ethical dilemma she would know I am about to tell Lord Stanton and thus be able to—I am unsure how the metaphor plays out. Run for the hills, I suppose."

Miss Brooke nodded. "I can see why you are upset about this. You will betray one of them."

"Yes." Charmaine frowned at his cane again. "One of them will never forgive me. I have to do it in a way I am able to forgive myself."

"And, thus, the philosophical bit about finding proof that is not Lady Stanton's confidential confession."

Charmaine nodded. "Exactly." Miss Brooke nodded in return and opened the other curtain. The fresh country air was cool as it tossed her golden hair about. Charmaine watched her for a long moment, awed by how lucky he was. Not only was she beautiful, but she also could talk to him. He frowned suddenly. "You do not know our true topic, do you?"

"Not at all," she promised. "I swear."

"Are you sure? You see, if…"

Miss Brooke cut him off. "I understand. Or, rather, I do not and I do not want to. Let us leave it at that. I am sure Lord and Lady Stanton have plenty of marital problems."

"Thank you."

Miss Brooke nodded. "Go back to brooding, Robert. We should be at a suitable place to stop soon. But, I warn you, I will tolerate absolutely no brooding at our picnic. Get it all out now."

Charmaine smiled. "Yes, my sweet fury."

The driver outdid himself in finding the perfect location. A small path led to a well-tended, rock lined clearing divided by a small, babbling brook. Large pine trees blocked any view from the road. Charmaine helped her out of the coach as the driver placed the blanket and delivered the basket. With a small wink at Miss Brooke, he hopped back up on his perch and drove off.

"Where is he going?" Charmaine asked with slight alarm.

"To water the horses. Apparently, the bank is more gradual a bit further down." Miss Brooke was impressed with the efficiency of her staff. Somehow, she was alone with Charmaine in a beautiful and secluded bit of country.

"I hope he remembers to come back. It is a long walk to anywhere."

Miss Brooke frowned at him. "I thought I told you to leave your grumpy in the coach."

"No, my dear, you told me to leave my brooding in the coach." Charmaine grinned at her. "You said nothing about grumpy."

"Well now I do." She snaked her arm through his. "Shall we go and see what is in the basket?"

They quickly unpacked a spread of grapes, cheese, various hard meats, and puff pastries. The basket contained more food than four people could hope to eat. She smiled when she found several bottles of wine. Pulling one out at random, she tried to uncork it.

Charmaine took it from her with a smile and smoothly uncorked the wine. Scavenging for glasses, he poured them both a small bit of wine.

"To my Lady Miss Alison Charmaine." Charmaine raised his glass towards her.

Miss Brooke blushed. "I am not yet your wife, Robert."

"Name your date. I would, by special license, marry you on the morrow if you would have me."

She smiled at his proclamation as she sipped her wine. "Oh, the scandal that would cause."

"Would you mind?"

"Of a certainty!" Miss Brooke frowned at herself. Here she was, about to try to seduce Robert because she felt cast out of Society, and yet she would not rush into marriage. "Or maybe not. I do not know. So much has happened so soon."

"Oddly, I feel like I have been with you forever. I know it has only been slightly over a month, but already I cannot imagine a life without you."

Miss Brooke smiled. "And you claim your compliments come out as empty flattery."

"That was when I was comparing you to the entire Greek pantheon."

"A bit extreme," said Miss Brooke.

"But honest." Charmaine smiled at her, his blue eyes soft and warm. "You are as glorious as any of Hephaestus' creations, Alison. I never expected I would wed the diamond of the century."

Miss Brooke blushed again. "Why not? You are handsome, titled, and politically connected. You seem quite a catch."

"I have never wanted a wife for the sake of having a wife. I have a brother. Let the title fall to him and his children. I wanted to marry for love. I wanted a wife who would inspire me. I wanted the happy ending." He shrugged. "I never thought it was possible."

"I am sorry you were forced into this." Miss Brooke took a sip of her wine and tried to banish the crushing sorrow his words caused.

"I am not." Charmaine leaned back on his elbow and stared at the sky. "I never would have picked you otherwise. You were supposed to be dramatic, high maintenance, shallow, and of a difficult parentage. Instead, I found a woman whom I can talk to and whose company makes me feel complete."

"I am still all of those other things though."

"In a way. You are dramatic because people watch you. You have a crowd. Everything you do causes ripples. You like attention, but you do not need it only from me. I would not call you shallow, but rather unobservant about details people are reluctant to share. But once you know of a problem, you are caring and concerned about the plights of others. I expected the diamond of the *ton*. But instead, I met the real Miss Brooke, and I like the real Miss Brooke."

She sat in silence for a moment trying to figure out how to respond. She settled for refilling his wine glass.

"I have offended you." Charmaine sat up, his relaxed manner melting into his courtly gentleman mien.

"No." Miss Brooke gestured for him to lean back again and he did, "you have disarmed me. I am not sure if I am flattered or insulted, angry or delighted."

"Can you not be all of these things?"

"I have never mastered delightedly angry."

Charmaine chuckled. "I suppose I have not either. I did not mean to offend you. I was trying to say I feel lucky."

"I will take such as a compliment." Her smile faded slightly. "I am sorry you did not get your fairy tale."

Charmaine moved to sit next to her. His dark blue eyes held her gaze as he crooned, "Foolish girl. I got everything I wanted."

Miss Brooke took a second to understand the meaning of his words. When she did, she leaned forward and kissed him deeply. His lips were soft and gentle and filled with the taste of red wine. Charmaine pulled back with a smile. "Behave, beloved. We are out in the woods alone. And I am no saint."

Miss Brooke swallowed her pride. "I do not want you to be a saint."

"Good. Because I am not." Charmaine pulled further away as he reached for a grape. "Would you like cheese?"

"No." She wished he would allow her to do this with a semblance of subterfuge or dignity. It was impossible to ask him. Gathering her courage, she made the attempt. "I would like you."

His head turned sharply to look at her and he frowned slightly as he cut cheese. Charmaine handed her two slices. "My hearing is playing tricks on me."

"Oh, Robert!" Miss Brooke's rising emotions drowned out shyness, "I said I want you, not 'I want two!'"

"Sorry." He smiled ruefully. "You have me, love. Everything I am and everything I will be is yours for the taking. You will be my wife."

Miss Brooke considered strangling him. "I do not mean matrimony. I mean I want you as a wife desires her husband." Miss Brooke turned a rosy pink and struggled for words.

"And we are to be wed."

"Are you being intentionally woolly-headed?" Animated, Miss Brooke's hair bobbed with her words. "Why does a lady arrange a country picnic with a gentleman? *And* has her friend and maid claim to be sick? *And* sends the driver away? What is amiss with you?"

Charmaine's expression settled somewhere between puzzled and amused. "This is a seduction attempt?"

"Yes!" Miss Brooke almost screamed at him.

Charmaine could not stop laughter from bursting forth. Miss Brooke sat there with her hands balled into fists and stared at him.

She blushed, this time from shame, as he attempted to get himself under control. "Please cease laughing," she asked quietly.

"I must beseech your forgiveness," he managed between gasps for breath. "I am not laughing at you. Or maybe I am. But it is because you are delightful. What were your words? You have disarmed me."

"This does not feel delightful." Miss Brooke's frustration vanished as rejection and shame washed over her.

"I promise you, it is. The most desirable woman I have ever seen is making a total hash of seduction." Charmaine finally had his chortles under control.

Miss Brooke's chin came up. "You are being a cur."

"Again, I am sorry." Charmaine took several deep breaths and regained his focus. "I am honored to have you in my life. While you might find it insulting, your lack of experience in how to entice me to bed charms me to the core. I am sorry if I did not react as I should have."

She frowned at him. "I do not understand."

Charmaine considered how to explain. "You are not a no lightskirt."

"What?" Miss Brooke's eyebrows flew up. "Certainly not."

"I, perhaps, have an unfair view on women."

"What does that have to do with anything?" Miss Brooke was getting frustrated again, a much better place to be than hurt.

"I have experienced several wolves in lamb's fleece. Glowing innocents that I later I found out warmed bedsheets with my so-called friends. You are a shining example of how wrong I am. You are a gift to the eyes yet lack the knowledge of how to get beyond a kiss." Charmaine shook his head slowly and leaned in to kiss her forehead. "I am lucky."

She glared at him. "You make me want to scream. Certainly, I am not warming your friends' bedsheets. Not even yours, as you keep reminding me. I obviously lack the faintest idea how to go about it!"

"I will spend the rest of our lives teaching you, I promise."

"That is all well and good, but what about now!" Miss Brooke was aghast at herself, but too angry with Charmaine to care.

"Why?"

"Because—oh, I do not know. I want to."

Charmaine shook his head negatively. "That is not a good reason, beloved. I want to claim you, too, but we can wait until after you are my wife. I have waited this long for you, I can wait longer."

"I do not want to wait." Miss Brooke's voice was serious. "I have been kicked out of Society because of something we did not even do. For the rest of my life everyone will think I surrendered my innocence at the ball. Except for me. And I want that to change. If I am going to be blamed for it, I want to actually do it."

"You have not been kicked out of Society. There is no need to exaggerate."

"You are impossible. My membership to Almack's was revoked. I have been directly snubbed." Miss Brooke's voice was rising again.

Charmaine fought the urge to roll his eyes. "Almack's is a social club, Alison. The subscription balls are notorious for weak tea and stale bread. Are you really going to miss that?"

"I will. Not the refreshments, the people, the experience." Her hands were balled into fists. "I do not know why you do not care, Robert, but everyone else does. I was a diamond of the first water, the catch of the Season, but now I am in disgrace for lying with you and I did not even get to enjoy it."

"I will lie with you on our wedding night. Things will be well."

"Things will not be well!" Miss Brooke was yelling now. "I want—I want to lie with you now."

Charmaine grabbed her upper arms and shook her until he was looking straight into her eyes. "Why? Do not dissemble with me. Why, Alison?"

"Because…" Tears poured from her eyes. Her yelling vanished, replaced with a breathy whisper. "Because I do not want to feel West's touch on me anymore."

Charmaine engulfed her in his arms and held her while she sobbed. He was again filled with white-hot rage. His voice was soft when he answered. "Alison, let me exterminate this man."

"No." The word was hard to hear through her sobs but her voice was defiant and firm. "I will not have that stain on your soul."

"Then let me do something about him. Anything."

"Perhaps. I will think on it."

"Please consider it carefully" Charmaine stroked her hair. He gently removed her bonnet and started raking his fingers through small snags in her hair. "Things will be well. Cry yourself out. When you are done, I will cut more cheese and then I will teach you the wifely arts?"

"Truly?"

"Yes, truly." Charmaine could not help but smile at the absurd situation. "But first, finish crying."

Miss Brooke nodded into his shoulder. A good deal of time passed before she was ready to pull away. When she did it was with a sheepish smile. "I am sorry."

Charmaine shrugged it off as if she had not spoken. "I cut you two slices of cheese."

She smiled timidly. "I want two."

"I know." He handed her the cheese and watched her as she picked at it. When she was done with the cheese he handed her two slices of meat and then two grapes. A real smile rewarded him when he handed her both glasses of wine.

"I am sorry, I..."

Charmaine cut her off. "You have nothing to apologize for. We can talk about it if you will like, but I suspect it will only make you cry again."

Miss Brooke nodded. "It might. And that is not what I want right now."

"What do you want?"

"I want..." She blushed. "You know what I want."

"I know what you think you want. And I am happy to give it to you. I need to know you have thought this through."

"I have. Brenda and I discussed it."

It was Charmaine's turn to blush. "Miss Boswell?"

"Uh-huh. It was her idea to try to get you drunk."

Charmaine poured himself another glass of wine. "I see. Are you going to tell Miss Boswell about what happened here, too?"

"I do not know. I might. Unless you mind?"

He was still blushing. "I would really rather you did not."

"Then I will not." She smiled slightly at his blush. "But, yes, it means I have thought this through. I have thought about nothing else for the past two days."

"Then let me see if I can measure up to those thoughts." He tilted up her chin and placed a soft kiss on her lips. He traced her jawline with little kisses before pulling back to wipe away her tears. "Tell me you want this."

In answer, Miss Brooke leaned forward and put her lips on his. She opened her mouth and timidly flicked her tongue into his mouth. Charmaine responded by quickly taking the lead. His tongue danced with hers and soon she found herself in his lap. She had always known he was muscular, but it was quite another thing to be fully embraced in his arms at such an awkward angle. She could feel his muscles quiver to keep them upright as she leaned deeper and deeper into his kiss. His tongue beckoned her towards something she did not know. A new feeling deep inside leaped in response.

Charmaine stroked one hand up her back until he was cupping her neck. His hand wrapped around Miss Brooke's golden hair and pulled gently, prompting her to arch into his hand. She whimpered slightly in objection, wanting his lips back on hers. Instead, his lips found the soft underside of her neck as he lightly bit on it. She moaned at the strange feelings inside of her and squirmed on his lap, seeking release from the burning feeling in her stomach. His hand tightened on her hair, pulling her head back further and holding her in place against him. His mouth found her ear and traced it with his tongue. Despite his strong grip, she still writhed against him, grinding her body in response.

"Robert, Robert," she gasped as he flicked her earlobe with his tongue. "Tell me what is happening for I—I do not understand."

Letting go of her hair, he lifted her in one smooth motion and laid her on the blanket. He positioned himself so that he was lying over her but not touching. The muscles in his arms strained as he hovered fully above her. "It is past time for telling. I will show you."

He lowered himself onto her, being careful not to put too much weight on her. His tongue found her mouth again and she instantly began squirming under him. Charmaine tried to nibble her neckline, but she grabbed onto his shoulders and forced his mouth back on hers. With a chuckle, he urged her back down and kept one hand firmly on her collarbone. He again dropped kisses on her neck, and when she tried to force her mouth back on his, he held her firmly on the blanket. Her hands found his hair as he kissed and explored her collarbone and her shoulders. Little bursts of sensation bloomed under his lips. He had to release his hold on her shoulder in order to rub a hand up and down her body. As soon as she was free, she once again pulled and grabbed at him. He chuckled at her frantic behavior.

"Lovely, let me take my time." She pulled him to her by his hair, kissing him deeply once more. He shook free. "There is more than kissing, I promise. It is better."

"Better?" Her light blue eyes were wide and a bit unfocused. She leaned in to kiss him again. He pulled back.

"Alison, tell me you are well."

She rolled her eyes. "I am fine, Robert. Silence your mouth and kiss me."

He laughed, the eye roll providing more reassurance than her words. "I will but I want to take off your dress. Sit up."

She sat and pouted as he fumbled with the laces. "I would like it if you hurried."

"Your clothing is complicated, sweeting. There." He held open the top of her dress and she rose to daintily step out of it. He caught his breath at the intimate view of her in chemise, panniers and stays. Her blush told him he was taking too long to respond, but her beauty left him speechless. He reached for her and pulled her onto his lap. She was timid now that the crest of passion behind her. "Kiss me, Alison."

She dropped a dainty kiss on his lips. It was his turn to grab at her in passion. He pulled her on top of him and plunged his tongue into her mouth. She shied slightly at his passion but kissed him back. He frowned at her response and rolled over, pinning her under him. He kissed her deeply. This time she curled around him, gripping him tightly as she processed the new feelings.

Charmaine smiled at the change as he enveloped her under his body, there would be time to overcome such shyness later. He fought with her again for the right to kiss her collarbone and listened to her moan in pleasure when he succeeded.

Her breasts tempted him like very little else ever had. They were perfectly shaped for his hand and looked as if they were carved from living porcelain. His excitement mounted. Finally, he could wait no longer and let his mouth cover one plump breast. He flicked the nipple with his tongue and felt her shudder beneath him. His free hand found her other breast and he alternated between squeezing and sucking on her soft flesh. The way she squirmed and moaned under him left him with no doubts of her enjoyment. She was frantic again, clawing at his coat and yanking on his hair.

He rolled her over on top of him and this time she had no shyness. She plunged her tongue back into his mouth and pumped her body on top of his. Miss Brooke pushed his head to one side so that she could access his neck. She bit and kissed his brawny flesh as if it was a lifeline. She had no idea she could feel this good. All she knew was Charmaine was her anchor. Her delicate hands ripped at his cravat, attempting to get at the flesh underneath. He laughed and untied it for her, unbuttoning his waistcoat as an afterthought. She wasted no time reaching for the flesh of his chest and covering it with kisses. She gave his nipples special attention and final managed to elicit a slight moan from him. With a smile of triumph, she flung herself back on top of him and kissed him deeply.

"I want more." Miss Brooke leaned over him, her golden hair blocking out the rest of the world. "Show me more."

Charmaine's only answer was to grab her by the back of the neck and roll her over. Using his elbow to support himself, he continued to kiss Miss Brooke firmly. His free hand traced her breasts until she moaned and then traced his fingers lightly across her stomach. He brought his hand down over the side of her hip and played with the top of her stockings. She squirmed into him, trying to get their bodies as close together as possible. Forcing her hips flat on to the ground, he used his thumb to draw spirals on the flesh of her inner thigh. Miss Brooke paused under him and Charmaine drew back to look into her eyes. He expected fear, but instead found curiosity and wonder. He raised an eyebrow in question. She grabbed him by the hair and kissed him deeply in answer. He kept rubbing her inner thighs, moving his hand from knee to hip, over the stomach, then down the other leg. Miss Brooke started to rotate her hips to match his motions, raising her pubis in an age-old demand.

Charmaine felt the motion and moved his hand to rub the apex of her thighs. He moved his hand in a light circular pattern, making sure he was gentle until he knew how sensitive she was. Miss Brooke had no interest in his delicate touch and quickly shoved her hips into his hands. He chuckled into her kiss and pressed harder. She was panting quickly under him, kissing him as she breathlessly gasped and moaned. His touch felt incredible. He could feel her muscles tensing and he tightened his fingers into the back of her hair. Soon she was screaming, her body shuddering with its first release, as she clawed wildly at his face and back. He kept kissing her deeply even after the wave of pleasure passed.

He pulled back long enough to remove his coat. He kissed her lips, chin, chest, breasts, and stomach on his way to sit next to her. With a small smile he removed her chemise and placed his hand on the blond curls underneath. Miss Brooke watched him with lazy, content eyes. He leisurely traced the folds of her flower with one finger, watching Miss Brooke slowly start to squirm again. The hard center of her passion peeked out from her nether lips, and he brought his fingers near, rubbing slow circles around it. He risked touching her once, but she flinched away, too sensitive after pleasure.

His slow circles soon had her panting again and he used his other hand to insert a finger inside of her. She froze for a second and raised herself to look at him with wide, questioning eyes. He paused and met her gaze. After a brief moment she eased herself back down and Charmaine continued working his finger inside of her. Her moans grew louder, and she tensed again in passion.

Charmaine raised himself next to her and her eyes flew open in objection. "You stopped!"

He nodded. "Are you sure you want this?"

"Are not we doing it? Is not this it?"

"Most of it. The main part is still to come. And it might hurt a little." Charmaine frowned slightly. "More than a little."

"Less talking. More of the—the whatever you were doing."

"You sure, sweeting?"

"Yes."

Charmaine smiled and rolled himself on top of her. The clawing helped. The large scratches on his arms and back were the only things keeping him in control. The closer she got to pleasure, the more sweet pain she seemed to cause him. Charmaine approved, considering he was not far behind her in passion. Listening to her moan was invigorating. He opened his breeches and pulled out his shaft, making sure to keep it away from her body. He was afraid of startling her. His hand moved again to the nub of her passion, and pushed her right to the verge of release. Once she was ready he slid his member into her in one smooth motion. He made it about a fourth of the way until he felt her hymen pushing back at him. Charmaine paused, morality and the desire to cause her no pain racing through his head. His love took the choice from him with a powerful shove of her hips. Miss Brooke's thrust tore through her hymen and buried him deeply within her. He could not tell if she was in pleasure or pain as his base instincts took over and all he could do was slam into her. She was hot, tight, and clawing at him, holding him to her as if she would never let him go. It released something primal in him and he thrust into her for all he was worth. He peaked in great screaming groaning gasps and fell forward.

Her little 'oof' and tap on his shoulder made him force himself upwards slightly, trying not to flatten her with his weight. His arm started to tremble, so he rolled back over, still holding her. Miss Brooke quickly curled onto his chest.

Charmaine lay immobile for several long moments before looking around at the picnic site. The open bottle of wine was spilled, the cheese and meat were flattened, and their clothing was scattered everywhere. He smiled at the mess and then chuckled as he realized he was bleeding from the scratches on his arm.

"Something amiss?" Miss Brooke sounded sleepy and content. It warmed his heart.

"You made me bleed." He moved his arm to show her. "You are quite the wildcat, Alison."

"I did not make you bleed. You made me make you bleed." She nuzzled her head further into his shoulder.

"I suppose. We should probably clean up."

"Why?"

Charmaine was hard-pressed for an answer. Caught without any objection, he shrugged and pulled her tighter to him. The woman he chose as his wife was an Amazon in bed. He may be, he decided, the luckiest man alive. Unless her hellcat nature killed him. And then, certainly, he would be the luckiest man alive or dead.

CHAPTER XIII

Daniel Brooke was once again in his warm study. Although it was the end of June, the mornings in London held a damp chill. The unpredictable weather made his joints ache. The small room bordering the kitchen ovens was a blessing. He leaned back from reading the latest update on the prices of beans when there was a knock on the door.

"Come." Brooke creaked his old bones back into a formal sitting position. When he saw it was Miss Brooke, he slumped back again. He waved his daughter in and watched as she picked her way through the clutter. Her morning dress was a light green with emerald trim around the hem. Miss Brooke had always preferred light colors, but now dark hues were appearing in the accent of all her clothing. Brooke hid a smile of approval. She must be truly smitten with this Charmaine fellow.

Miss Brooke settled herself on the singular empty chair in front of the desk. Its partner had become so covered in paperwork and books, the chair no longer resembled furniture. She gave the clutter a disapproving glance and settled herself determinedly. Miss Brooke was nervous about the meeting, but it was an important step to regaining control of her life. "Good morning, Father."

"Good morning, Daughter." He smiled at her formal positioning and properly clasped hands. He prepared himself for another fight about Lord Charmaine. "How fares my sunshine on this damp and miserable morning?"

"Passable, thank you." Miss Brooke smoothed her hair back without a smile. "Thoughtful, if you must know."

"Indeed? Pray tell."

"I have been considering the way power works in the *ton*," Miss Brooke started in a rush, "and if I want something to happen I do not take direct action, but rather use inference or gossip. Even though I never say to my circle directly they must accept Miss Boswell, they still know that truth. Influence can be action without having to being direct. I do not push her into my circle, but she is still there, and it is still my fault, if you will."

Brooke raised an eyebrow as he reached for his pipe. "I suppose that makes sense. Continue."

"Good. I," Miss Brooke paused, "I want you to ruin West. Financially."

He paused mid-reach before recovering and lifting his pipe. The topic was unexpected. "Done. Anything else?"

"No. Thank you, Father."

He lit his pipe, coughing slightly as the aromatic smoke filled the room. "Do you want to plan this with me?"

"No." Miss Brooke shifted slightly. "I do not. I need to know I made this happen. Aside from that—I, I seek to put this behind me. I cannot feel helpless anymore. But no matter how forgiving I try to be, I want him hurt. I know it is wrong, but I cannot stop hating him."

Brooke nodded. "Try to be the person you want to be. But do not hate yourself for being who you are. I do not blame you for hating him." He smiled supportively at her. "If I were to cast blame, I would have to blame myself."

She returned her father's smile with a forced one of her own. "Will you be home for luncheon?"

"Alas, I have errands and will be out past teatime. Supper?"

She shook her head. "Miss Boswell and I are attending a dinner party. It will go late. Breakfast?" At his slight frown she tried again. "Luncheon tomorrow?"

"Luncheon. And we will not talk about West unless you will it."

Miss Brooke nodded. "Thank you. This is—difficult."

"I have no need for your gratitude. You are my daughter. Go ride with your friends or whatever other frivolity you have planned. Take a chaperone and be safe. I will handle West."

She rose and curtsied gracefully. "I, um," Miss Brooke started to stutter her way through another thank you.

"You are dismissed, sunshine." Brooke rebutted. The wrinkles around his eyes indicated his friendly demeanor.

"Yes, Father." Miss Brooke fled.

Once in her room, she sat at her correspondence desk. There was one more person she had to ask, or, more aptly, release from his restraints, to ruin West. She lifted her quill and carefully composed a letter to Charmaine.

Charmaine adjusted his formal attire as he leisurely walked up the steps of the Farrington townhouse. The two friends had grown increasingly distant over the past two weeks. "My fault, I suppose," Charmaine muttered to himself as he stared at the doorway. Associating with a man he was certain was guilty of high treason was becoming harder. Worse, it was becoming likely he would be the one presenting the evidence against his friend. He would not betray the trust Farrington had given him, but he would not stand back and let the American Colonies flaunt the will of the Crown.

Still brooding, Charmaine knocked on the door. A footman showed him in and within moments Farrington appeared downstairs. They flashed grins at each other as they both realized they were both examining the other's dress. Charmaine held out his arms and half turned. "Am I acceptable?"

Farrington snorted. "I do not know how you live in poverty yet still manage to turn out as well as you do."

"My man is walking out with a miraculous tailors daughter."

Farrington actually laughed at that. "Shall we be off? The crush to get into the Palace will be outrageous."

"I abhor these rigmaroles. The King's Birthday more than most. Most of Parliament will be there. Mixing politics and frivolity is always a bad idea," Charmaine said.

Farrington seemed unconcerned. "Treat it like any other ball. Avoid politics and drink, and you will be fine."

Charmaine smiled ruefully. "Except politics is what I enjoy. My plans for tonight mostly center on a few carefully constructed conversations. Several members of the Lords have been avoiding me. I should be able to corner them there."

"Only mostly?"

"Miss Brooke is attending, as well as Miss Boswell. She is far too good of a conversationalist to be a wallflower. Girl needs to assert herself." Charmaine adjusted his cravat in the mirror.

"Leave Miss Boswell alone. She is fine exactly the way she is." Farrington moved gracefully to the front door and down the steps. The carriage was waiting for them. "I will admit to not understanding the *ton's* blindness to her. She is truly an Original."

"An original in everything they hate. She is kind, believes in enjoying life, wears colors she likes rather than what favors her. Our Society forbids all of that. Think, Farrington, how many genuinely sweet girls do you know?"

Farrington grimaced slightly. "Not many. You may have a point."

They settled themselves in the carriage and headed out. Charmaine frowned as they got underway. "Walking would be quicker.

"But completely unfashionable." Farrington answered. "What would the polite World think of Viscount Charmaine and the Marquis of Farrington doing something as common as walking?"

"We had sense?"

Farrington allowed a smile. "Now you sound like Miss Boswell."

A comfortable silence descended between the two friends. The Palace was only minutes from Farrington's fashionable address. The bulk of their time in the carriage would come from the long queue of carriages waiting to drop off their brightly attired cargo. Charmaine fought for patience at the unnecessary wait.

Farrington raised an eyebrow. "You are squirming."

"I hate waiting." Charmaine looked out the window with a frown. "Can I confide in you?"

Farrington's expression grew guarded. "If you wish. I do not think outside the Palace is the best place to confront me, however."

"Not that," Charmaine admonished with exasperation, "we cannot talk about *that*. I wanted to ask a favor."

"Certainly. I will not agree until I hear it, but you are welcome to ask."

"Quite reasonable. But, before I do, since the other topic has been mentioned, I would ask you be particularly careful this eve."

Farrington nodded. "I know. I will. I am. Ask your favor."

Charmaine returned the nod. "Do you know a Mr. West? Tan, Whig, runs a plantation in the Caribbean?"

"I know of him. I had my solicitor investigate after you disclosed what happened to Miss Brooke. For the reasons we are not mentioning, I have more contact with the Americas than most. He is active in trade there."

"Good." Charmaine's eyes grew fierce. "Sink his ships, destroy his investments, paint him as a traitor, blame him for drought, famine, and pestilence. Anything and everything. But lay not a finger on his person."

"That is a complicated favor. I am rather—overextended at the moment. Is it important we not shoot him? It is the significantly more expedient route."

Charmaine nodded. "Yes. Miss Brooke's requests will be honored. I might not fully comprehend her reasoning, but I feel strongly about respecting her wishes."

Farrington frowned, considering. This was not a good time for him to make enemies who were also active in the New World. Then again, one word from Charmaine ensured him a worse fate. "Then it will be done."

"The man is vile, wicked, and a betrayer of the meaning of the word gentleman." Charmaine's passion caused his voice to rise. His hands were curled into fists.

"You are angry." Farrington noted.

"I am beyond angry. I have never wanted to harm someone more in my life."

"Then we will harm him."

"Thank you." Charmaine took several deep breaths to gain control of the adrenaline accompanying his anger.

Farrington waved the gratitude off. "You are my friend. No thanks needed. I suspect we should change the subject. I prefer to avoid undue notice when we enter."

Charmaine flashed a rueful smile. "So much for my mighty control over my emotions."

"It happens. You have seen me angry."

"True." Charmaine eased even more, "And the world thinks you do not even have emotions."

"I do not," Farrington confided. "Now, pray tell me of your life. How is your mother, brother, lands, or anything else that will take your mind off this? We go on stage shortly."

"That is all this is to you? A play? An act?"

"Yes," Farrington seemed surprised at the question, "One false line and I hang. If anyone sees who I really am, I hang. How could it be anything else?" He paused and looked directly at his friend. "I really should have you killed."

"And I really should turn you in. You force me to betray everything I believe because of our friendship. I almost would prefer if you shot me."

"An easier solution, indeed." Farrington paused and then seemed as if he was about to continue. He did not.

"I will not betray your trust," Charmaine answered. "However, if you slip, even once, I will catch you, and you will hang."

Farrington nodded. "I expect nothing less. However, again, I do not wish to have this conversation outside of the Palace. Tell me of other things."

"Certainly." Charmaine took another breath. This evening was not going to be pleasant for his nerves. Using idle chatter to unclench his temper (and jaw), Charmaine informed Farrington of the mundane details of his life. He barely finished the recap of the family and was starting on the details of his estates when the carriage finally arrived at the steps of the Palace.

Miss Brooke had yet to Charmaine in full court dress. His appearance took her breath away. He outshone even Lord Farrington. They moved with such a similar grace that they almost appeared as brothers. Miss Brooke had noticed a rift growing between the two men lately, but tonight it was not in evidence. Farrington was resplendent in a cream suit covered in gold piping, while her Charmaine played the darker fiddle in a royal blue that made his eyes glow brighter than the candlelight. Miss Brooke smiled at Miss Boswell as the two gentlemen made their way through the crowd to them. Their progress was slow, as people Miss Brooke frequently stopped to converse with Lord Charmaine.

Charmaine offered the ladies an apologetic smile as the two men finally traversed the ballroom. "Ladies. You both glow."

It was true. Miss Brooke shone in a new ball gown in dark rose. Miss Boswell wore a gaily-painted silk that more closely resembled a disorganized colony of wildflowers in full bloom than anything else. Charmaine was not sure the dress was attractive, but Miss Boswell's bearing was radiant. She gained much vibrancy in the past month that it was hard to remember her as the wallflower from the Season before.

Identical curtsies greeted his proclamation and Miss Brooke blushed prettily. "You are popular tonight, My Lord."

Charmaine shrugged. "Everyone attends the King's Birthday. My contemporaries from the House of Lords are trapped here with me. However, unlike myself, they do not have a ray of sunshine to keep them company."

Miss Boswell rolled her eyes at Charmaine's comment and Farrington hid a slight smile in return. Miss Brooke blushed, "You are too kind."

"I am no such thing. Now, my sparkling summer's day, you owe me at least three dances before I get dragged into a night of political discourse. Shall we away?" Charmaine bowed to her and offered his hand.

Miss Brooke laughed. "You are ridiculous. As always, I would be honored to dance with you."

Charmaine swirled them both onto the dance floor, leaving Miss Boswell and Farrington in their wake. The waltz was slow and stately and allowed time for them to talk. Charmaine's humor fell as looked at his intended anxiously, "Have you been in good health?"

"Certainly," her smile was joyous. "Your countenance is serious for a night of frivolity. I thought we spoke against such brooding."

"I am not brooding, Alison. I have not had the chance to speak to you since our carriage ride, and I…" The phrase trailed off as his face flushed.

Miss Brooke twirled around him with a pout, "And our carriage ride makes you upset?"

"No. Not at all. But I worry you…"

"La, Robert." Her eyes twinkled as she impishly smiled. "Worry for me? There is no need. I found our carriage ride wonderful."

A goofy smile came over his face and he missed a step in the dance. "Delightful. Let us wed anon and have more such rides."

Her smile widened, "I am sure carriage rides can happen before marriage."

"While they can," he twirled her around, "I will do right by you. Our children shall be born properly, and that may make timing tight. Not to mention, it is much easier to arrange more of these rides you propose with you as my wife."

Her expression grew serious and she looked to watch her steps. "There is no need to worry on account of our last carriage ride. I received my menses."

He was silent for a moment, swirling her through the crowd. "I am sorry to hear that. The idea of our children pleased me."

"Then look to the future. The idea of our children pleases me as well."

"Good," he declared with a mischievous grin, "then let us hurry to the altar so we can begin filling our nursery."

Miss Boswell watched her friend twirl on the dance floor and smiled at the handsome man next to her. "They seem happy."

"Indeed." Farrington frowned slightly. "It pains me to say it, but I do not think I have ever seen Charmaine this pleased with a woman. They make a striking pair."

"Why does it pain you to say it?"

Farrington looked at her for a moment and then resumed watching the dancing. "Because, two months ago, I believed she would my wife. Now, I believe she will be his."

"Time heals all wounds," Miss Boswell timidly suggested.

"Aye, it does. And you are correct. I am not nearly as upset as I was. Now, I am bemused at my friend's apparent success. And, I suppose, envious he has succeeded where I did not," Farrington said.

"You should not brood on the King's Birthday. You may dance with me as a consolation prize," Miss Boswell cajoled with a smile.

"Dancing with you is not a consolation prize." Farrington's dark eyes were serious. "You dance marvelously."

Miss Boswell laughed, finally at ease with the object of her idolatry. "It is a secret only a few know. As you can tell from the number of empty spaces on my dance card."

"Their loss. Choose your evening, a dance now, or a dance later?"

Miss Boswell pursed her lips and looked over the set list. "Later. The second waltz is a favorite of mine."

"Then it is yours." He signed her card and asked, "Will you stand by me at cards?"

"I would be delighted." Miss Boswell walked with him to the card room. Farrington's attention was momentarily distracted when he noticed a tall, powerfully built man in simple dress intently watching Miss Brooke twirl on the dance floor. His eyes narrowed as he identified Mr. West. There was malice in the villain's gaze. Farrington decided to alert Charmaine. If the look in the cretin's eyes meant anything, investment in Miss Brooke's safety might prove worthwhile.

Miss Boswell looked at him with a questioning smile, which he returned with a reassuring nod. Miss Brooke was in no danger while dancing with Charmaine, so Farrington devoted all his attention to the friend at his side. Miss Boswell maintained the firm fiction there was nothing between them. Miss Boswell's hopeless *tendre* continued to grow until it became a thing she no longer had words for. She considered it might be love, but it seemed impossible for true love to be unrequited. More than impossible, it seemed cruel, and Farrington would never be cruel—therefore she was clearly not in love.

Farrington had not considered Miss Boswell, or his reaction to her, as he slowly recovered from his broken heart. Yet, he was aware of how much he enjoyed Miss Boswell's company and how he enjoyed her steady and silent presence at the card table. Other women of his acquaintance, Miss Brooke included, seemed to have a constant need to yap about everything and nothing. Miss Boswell spoke without any artifice or polish and her words always had a purpose.

The night was still relatively early, giving Farrington his pick of the tables. He placed his mark on his preferred rear table. The two men already present nodded in greeting. Farrington returned their nods and leaned back on the elaborately gilded wall to wait for enough players at the table to start. Miss Boswell stood next to him with her head cocked to one side. "I was wondering..."

"Yes?" Farrington answered, hiding a smile. He was sometimes positive she could read his mind, as he knew a direct and purposeful question was coming. He enjoyed how she unconsciously proved him right over and over again.

"How goes your courtship of Miss Linder?"

Farrington raised an eyebrow. "I am not courting her, nor have I claimed to be."

One of the other men at the table, Mr. Hobson, leaned in to listen intently. Miss Boswell gave him a shy smile of welcome. She was never one to forget a man who danced so well.

"You mentioned it as a possibility." Miss Boswell answered Farrington a bit timidly.

"In passing. I am not pursuing her, or anyone, at the moment." Farrington did not give reasons. His involvement with the rebellion in the American Colonies had become even more serious in the past few months. He had little time to court anyone, much less find someone who would be blind to his activities. He had no intention of being hanged.

Miss Boswell looked back over the gaming room, seeking a way to change the conversation.

"Why do you ask?" Farrington continued.

"Oh, no reason." Miss Boswell waved across the room. "Look! There is Lord Stanton!"

Farrington pondered her dodge. He had not thought Miss Boswell the type to gossip with the women attempting to gain his favor, but perchance he was wrong. Collins pranced over and derailed his line of thought. "Farrington. Hobson."

"Collins. Join us for whist?"

"I was headed to faro, but if you have four, yes. I hate waiting to play."

"We have three already," Hobson pointed out.

Collins tossed his mark negligently on the table and nodded at the other men. "Then I shall be your fourth, as long as Miss Boswell will stand between Farrington and me. She is excellent company."

"As I well know," Hobson replied.

Miss Boswell blushed at the compliment. She never acquired Miss Brooke's knack of blushing gracefully. Instead, she grew splotchy red. At the table, both Farrington and Collins smiled at her reaction. Miss Boswell watched, and smiled contentedly at her lot in life.

CHAPTER XIV

Charmaine awoke feeling rejuvenated. The ball had been a spectacular success. He managed to corner several of his contemporaries and hammer out details to assist in the Scottish banking crisis. Charmaine smiled to himself, he suspected the champagne helped his cause. And then there was Miss Brooke. He started his morning exercises and tried to clear his mind, but she was there, spinning in her rose gown. There was something fragile and ethereal about her that made him want to conquer the moon so that he could give her a better view of the stars. And then his delicate lady turned out to be a wildcat in bed. He grew hard thinking about the ferocity of her response. He was blessed.

He quickly bathed with the warm water in the pitcher and pulled himself into the clothes Wilhelm had laid out. Charmaine found breakfast waiting for him in the cramped living room. He placed a piece of melon in his mouth and attempted to grab his morning paper. The paper was stuck under a pair of unexpected boots. They were connected to long, muscular legs that tapered off into a man who looked much like a taller, lither version of Charmaine.

"Your boots are on my desk." Charmaine glared at his little brother.

Anderson leisurely pulled his legs back and stretched out further in Charmaine's chair. "Charming place you have here."

"I like the view." Charmaine grabbed his paper and sat in the other chair in the room, a sturdy but worn wingback.

Anderson glanced out the window to the brick wall of the neighboring building. "Lovely, indeed. How are you?"

Charmaine paused, trying to decide how much to tell his brother. "I am good, actually."

"Really?" Anderson raised a plucked eyebrow. "Father is dying, Mother is hysterical, and you live in squalor. Sounds divine."

"I have missed you, too." Charmaine replied sarcastically. "Father is the same as he has been for the past year. At some point you get numb. Mother has been hysterical for the past year. At some point you get numb. I have…"

"Yes, I get the idea. But being numb does not sound like 'I am good' to me. What are you not telling me?" Anderson reached forward and took the plate of food Charmaine had started on.

Charmaine shrugged. "I met a girl."

"Wilhelm told me." Anderson nodded. "When is the wedding?"

"I only said I met her, Michael, not anything else." Charmaine mock glared. "And, at the end of the Season. Her father will not give consent, so we are going to cause scandal when the gossips take their winter break."

"Not heard you speak of a woman since that deuced wanton had you calf-eyed. You might as well have the wedding invitations engraved right now."

"I suppose." Charmaine opened his paper and glanced through several pages. "How long will you be staying?"

"Just until the end of the Season. Long enough to convince Mother I have all my limbs, go over financials with you and Wilhelm, break a few hearts, and dash back to Algiers."

"I thought you were in Bombay?"

Anderson nodded. "I was. A captain is retiring on an established Gold Coast route. The Company wants to see if I can improve their African revenue." He gestured with the piece of fruit he was holding. "And I would like to be a bit closer. This does not seem the right time to be half a year away."

"Duty? From you?" Charmaine teased and held up a hand to forestall an answer. "Have you been to the townhouse yet?"

Anderson nodded again. "I supped with Mother before the ball and sat with Father during it. I got quite a lecture from her about intentionally missing the King's Birthday."

"It was surprisingly pleasant."

"You enjoyed a ball? That is more alarming than myself knowing the meaning of the word duty!" Anderson's tone was teasing, but he sounded genuinely surprised.

"Miss Brooke makes them tolerable."

"She must be an amazing woman, indeed. You hate those things."

"She is," Charmaine's voice was soft and firm. "She truly is."

Anderson bowed his head in assent. "Good. On to business?"

Charmaine nodded. "I do not suppose you have good news for me."

"No. I do not."

Charmaine frowned at Anderson's serious expression. "How bad is it?"

"Bad." Anderson placed his hands behind his head as he leaned back in the chair. "Stiles is dead."

Charmaine blinked. Captain Stiles worked for the Donahue family for longer than either of the boys had been alive. He was a kind-hearted man with patience for children that did not extend to his crew. He kept a tight, well-disciplined set of ships that always ran successful trade missions to New England. Charmaine liked him. As a child, Charmaine used to dream of life as a sea captain. He always imitated Stiles' mannerisms and followed him like shadow. Stiles death hurt. "And his ships?"

"Gone. All of them." Anderson reported, "No report on what happened. Official rumor is bad weather, but the scuttlebutt is they were sunk by the French returning from the Carolinas."

"God." Charmaine closed his newspaper and sat there for a moment. Stiles had been a good man. And then there was the revenue issue. Those ships were considered a sure thing. Their reserves were gone. Once the bankers found out about the loss, they would come collecting.

"Indeed." Anderson continued, "My venture is in and it did not do too badly. Better than we expected, even with the East India

Company's outrageous cut. But it is not enough to cover the loss of those ships, much less the profit we were expecting from them."

"How did Mother take the news?"

Anderson frowned. His brother was not reacting, rather staring expressionlessly at a spot on the wall. "I did not tell her yet. I decided it was best to talk to you first. You do not look well."

"I am fine." Charmaine's voice was flat, distant. "We have to assume the gunpowder shipment is gone as well."

"It is extremely overdue. But, not only do they have to deal with the absurd customs and closed culture of the Orient, they have to go around the Cape." Anderson did not sound convincing.

"As did you to get to Bombay and you are gone and back since they left." Charmaine's eyes narrowed slightly. "I received word for Stiles' venture under a month ago. They were returning and were pleased with the large amount of profit. I find it unlikely they were sunk off New England."

Anderson shrugged. "Scuttlebutt. Sailors lie. But the ships were sound and Stiles an experienced captain. I agree it is unlikely that a storm sunk the lot."

"No way to know." Charmaine put down his paper. "What now?"

"Unknown. Sell off parts of the country estate? Yes, we cannot sell the manor itself without permission from the King, but much of our land can be sold off. Build up enough capital to try again."

"Not only will I not sell off the land Father worked hard to buy, but such an act would only pay off our debt. We would break even at best. There would be nothing left to invest. We would be consigning ourselves to a mediocre life of poverty."

Anderson shrugged, looking uncomfortable. "Father built himself up from nothing. Surely you can do that as well?"

"It took me under two years to waste a lifetime of his work. Do not look to my skills to save us." A bit of self-deprecation crept into Charmaine's otherwise emotionless voice.

"Robert, come now. They were all good investments. People are ruined from ships sinking. We had two out of three investments fail at once. That is all. We will get through this."

"We will." Charmaine nodded at Anderson. "Do not worry, Michael. I will handle it."

The little brother frowned. "What do you have in mind? Tell me."

Charmaine glared slightly but gave in at Anderson's stern expression. "We need a large amount of money quickly. I have this illustrious title, political power, and a large, well-maintained, country estate. There are plenty of people who would pay us to take their daughters off their hands. We find one with a large dowry and I marry her."

"What about Miss Brooke?" Anderson did not like the dead note in his brother's voice.

"What about her? She is a true diamond but this is about duty. Family. Her inheritance is dependent on her father's approval, which he will not give. Thus, it is an impractical match."

"Bullocks." Anderson leaned forward in exasperation. "Happiness has a value, Robert. We can recover from this. There is no need to be melodramatic."

Charmaine raised an eyebrow, but otherwise remained distant. "Melodramatic? Do you know what will happen when news of this gets out on the street? My creditors will come a calling. I have nothing left to promise. They will take the Donahue townhouse. And then what? Where do I put Father? He is too sick to be dragged across the countryside to the hereditary estate. Should I house him here?" Charmaine gestured around the cramped, rundown apartment. "Or I should put Mother out on the street? Or, wait, I should sell off our land! Certainly, it is our only source of income, but it would get us out of the momentary collapse. Next year we will not be able to pay for clothing or food but right now we will be stable. So, pray tell, Michael, how am I being melodramatic?"

Anderson listened to Charmaine's rant, but was truly focused on watching his brother's hands. By the time the speech ended, his hands were balled tightly into fists that his knuckles were white. "Do you love her?"

"Bloody hell, Michael. What does it matter?" Charmaine's momentary passion faded, and his hands unclenched. "I will be the Earl of Donahue. Love does not factor into that."

"I could do it." Anderson looked like he swallowed a live rat. "I am not quite the catch you are, but there must be merchants who would love to see their daughters elevated to the *ton*."

Charmaine smiled slightly, the first emotion to reach his face since Anderson told him Stiles died. "You have my thanks, but I must decline. This is my mess. Besides, Africa waits for no man."

"I am serious."

"I know. But you do not think things through." Charmaine held up his hand again. "I mean no insult. But I need you out there earning revenue and influence. I do not want to fix only this moment but build a platform for the futures we desire for our wives and children. Thus, it cannot be you."

They were both silent for a long moment. Finally, Anderson spoke. "What will you tell her?"

Charmaine looked across at him. His eyes were flat and filled with hollow dread. "I know not."

Later in the afternoon a knock rattled the door of Charmaine's chambers. He ignored it, staring blankly at the wall of his bedroom. He had not moved from the spot in hours. Anderson left after mumbling pleasantries. Charmaine stared at the wall in the main room for an hour or so, but soon Wilhelm returned. He thus retreated to his bedchamber to drown in his misery. He had the most wonderful woman he could imagine, and he had to let her go.

The knock returned. He again ignored it. The door squeaked as it swung open.

"You missed Session." Farrington's voice echoed into the still room.

"Go away."

"You are never absent. And you were excited last night about some banking thing."

"Go away."

Farrington continued to ignore his friend. "Is this a new political strategy to throw your enemies off guard?"

"Goddammit, Farrington, go away."

"What has you upset?" Farrington leaned against the doorframe and folded his arms across his chest.

Charmaine unclenched his fists. "I want you to leave."

"I heard you. Your darling brother wasted no time in running to Collins, who then ran to me. Gossip thus tells me you are planning on throwing Miss Brooke to the wind to marry a shrew for her money."

"And you have come hither to gloat?"

"No." Farrington's voice was level, as always. "I went through this too, remember. I thought I loved her. But I have seen the two of you together. I was wrong. Whatever I felt was not love. It was infatuation. It was a desire to have the most beautiful woman. It was many things, but it was not love. You, however, love her."

"Yes." Charmaine turned around, his blue eyes blazing. He otherwise appeared calm. "Yes, goddammit, I love her. I want to marry her. I want to spend the rest of my life with her. I want her to have my children, I want to grow old and die with her, I bloody want her."

Farrington slightly raised an eyebrow. "But?"

"But I bloody cannot. Love is a luxury. If I had not blundered, if I had not ruined my family's finances, I could marry her. But I cannot. I mucked everything up."

"What is the major stumbling block?"

"The bloody sarding townhouse." Charmaine sighed. "And my father. The doctors say he will not survive any change in temperature, much less a trip to the country. Our London domicile is the collateral on my loans. I managed to convince the creditors that payment would come when the shipment from the New World arrived. With the ships gone, the townhouse is gone."

Farrington nodded from where he was leaning on the doorframe. "You cannot lose the residence. Could your father stay with the Stantons?"

Charmaine shook his head no. "Setting my pride aside, they do not have enough space. My father requires a bedchamber with a huge fireplace, walls with extra insulation, and an army of servants."

"Then you have your answer." Farrington sighed slightly. "I cannot help but feel sorry for Miss Brooke."

"I know." Charmaine hung his head as he turned back around. "I told her I would not do this. I swore to her I would marry her no matter what. I lied. I am one more worthless cretin after her wealth."

Farrington walked across the room and stood next to his friend. They were facing a blank white wall about a foot in front of them. "You are in good company."

"You did not go out and marry the next chit with a dowry."

"I would have. I likely should have. But I cannot let anyone get close to me right now. A wife would be a liability."

Charmaine clenched his fists again. "Is it worth this, Anthony? Your love of an ideal, my sense of duty to my family, is it really worth giving up a woman like Alison?"

"Yes." Farrington's voice was certain. "Because it is who we are. Being true to yourself is the most important thing of all."

Charmaine avoided Miss Brooke for several days. He threw himself into his work, researched schemes that might save him from his dilemma, and spent time with Farrington. They engaged in their equivalent of drinking and whoring as they rode recklessly early in the morning, played tennis after the House of Lords, and attended boxing matches in the evening. They seemed like Herculean men—strong, quick, and efficient—but inside they were both broken husks trying to carry on.

It was Miss Boswell who broke the silence. The gentlemen followed a predictable route from the Farrington domicile. They were both punctual and their rides were as smoothly timed as if they were planned by water clock. Intercepting them 'accidently' was easy.

Charmaine smiled as he spotted Miss Boswell. He cleared his throat to get Farrington's attention and cocked his head in Miss Boswell's direction. With a nod, Farrington directed New Amsterdam towards her.

Miss Boswell held her horse steady and pretended not to notice as they descended upon her. Farrington was riding the same horse she saw before, a tall brown and black one with a funny little white dot on its nose. His dark green riding jacket made him look as if he should be part of a deep wooden landscape. Charmaine looked sharp too, she supposed, his blue jacket highlighting his eyes, and his horse seemed powerful, but Anthony's boots hugged his calf so tightly. She waited until they were almost in front of her before she pretended to notice them.

"Miss Boswell." Farrington greeted her with a small bow, "A pleasure to see you."

"Lord Farrington, Lord Charmaine! You both look dashing!" Miss Boswell tried to mimic Miss Brooke in her casual morning conversation. She would have preferred to start with 'why have you been avoiding me or us?' but that seemed rather, well, rude.

Farrington raised an expressive eyebrow and Charmaine flat out laughed. "Miss Boswell, you are darling."

Miss Boswell glared at them both, lingering on Farrington. "What did I do wrong?"

"You did nothing wrong," Miss Brooke's champion answered. "At all. I have never heard you say 'dashing' before."

Miss Boswell was skeptical of Charmaine's smile. Farrington's expression settled into his unreadable stare. Suddenly confronting the two of them did not seem wise.

"I, yes, well. You are dashing, yes?" She frowned, as they both grew more amused. "Lord Farrington, may I speak with you?"

Now, it was Charmaine's turn to raise an eyebrow. He glanced at his friend and, receiving a nod, backed his chestnut gelding away. Charmaine politely stopped the horse in front of a pastry shop and tried to pretend there was an item he cared about in the window. Miss Boswell's groom, he noticed, was doing much the same thing on the other side of the cobblestone lane.

"Yes, Miss Boswell?" Farrington's expression was impassive. "How may I assist you?"

"Are you avoiding me?" Miss Boswell sounded irritated and nervous all at once.

"No." Farrington's answer was curt. "Is that all?"

"I have not seen you in over a week, you missed the Rosenhall ball, and did not attend the Haven garden party, but yet you are not avoiding me?"

"Correct."

Miss Boswell bit her lip. "Did I do something wrong?"

"Nay." It was the same curt reply. Soon after, however, Farrington seemed to relent. "Let us not speak of this."

Miss Boswell pushed down the surge of disappointment. She wanted to believe he was speaking the truth, but without a reason it was hard. The absence of his company grated on her soul. "Will you be at the Devonshire ball tonight?"

"I think not." He frowned, feeling as if he should give her more of an answer. "We may head out to the country for the weekend. There is a hunt that seems promising. We may race."

"You promised to take me to the races," Miss Boswell timidly reminded him.

Farrington's frown remained. "I did, did I not? I shall have to make good on that in the future."

Miss Boswell wished she were someone else. Miss Brooke would have a witty rejoinder, a hair flip that would break through his silence and have him spilling out his secrets. She, however, was only Brenda. She sighed and nodded with acceptance. "Then I will see you anon?"

"Sooner rather than later, I hope." Farrington half bowed as Miss Boswell turned her horse. Without even glancing at Charmaine, she started riding back down the street with her head held high. She did not even notice she turned to go back the same way she arrived.

Farrington's voice unexpectedly called out from behind her, "Brenda?"

She stopped her mare and looked over her shoulder, trying to keep her heart out of her eyes. "Yes?"

"That is the same mare you hired from the livery stables as the last time we rode, yes?"

Miss Boswell's heart sank. "Yes. She is."

"The roan's flecks match your hair."

Miss Boswell forced herself to smile. "I noticed that myself. Good day, Lord Farrington."

This time he did not call out after her. Miss Boswell was almost all the way down the block before she realized he called her by her Christian name. It took special effort not to gush all the way home.

Farrington maneuvered his mount over to Charmaine.

His friend raised an eyebrow. "Your roan's flecks match your hair?"

"They do match." Farrington's irritation was clear in his voice "You will talk to Miss Brooke."

"I am not ready." Charmaine looked away. "I did not know we were going hunting."

"I made it up. I am sure you do not intend to go to whatever ball she mentioned. I do not care if you are ready to confront Miss Brooke or not, Charmaine. The time has come."

Charmaine frowned at his horse's mane. "I..."

"I know. But you need to handle your affairs. Whining achieves nothing."

Charmaine's shoulders straightened. "Plan that hunting trip. I have the feeling I do not want to be in Town this weekend."

"We will still have to come back." Farrington absently adjusted the reins of his fidgeting mount.

"I know. I am not running away. I am..." Charmaine sighed in irritation at himself. "I am running away."

Farrington shrugged. "These things happen. You go break Miss Brooke's heart and I will see whom I can rustle up for a hunt. I hear Haven's hounds whelped this winter. He should be pleased to show them off."

Charmaine nodded and continued the ride in silence. After several blocks, he turned to Farrington and seemed as if he was about to talk. Thinking better of it, Charmaine lapsed into silence. Farrington noticed the aborted conversation and answered anyway. "I know. But it has to be done."

Charmaine nodded in answer and the two of them rode back to Farrington's residence in silence.

The Brooke townhouse grew no more welcoming no matter how long Charmaine paced in front of it. He already knew the servants had seen him, as the telltale flicker of a curtain gave them away. Yet, still, he paced. When he finally gathered his courage and walked to the impressive doorway, it opened before he finished approaching. A butler stood there expectantly. Charmaine handed him his hat and cane without so much as a by-your-leave. "I will see Mr. Brooke."

The servant nodded. "I will see if he is in, Lord Charmaine. Please wait here."

Charmaine measured the marble floored foyer as he waited. It was sixteen steps from the main doorway to the large staircase to the living areas of the residence. He paced it off nine times before the servant returned. "This way, sir."

The servant led Charmaine to the same elaborate study as before. Mr. Brooke sat inside, a large pipe resting in the ashtray before him. He raised a bushy eyebrow in hostile welcome as Charmaine walked into the room and shut the door behind him. "Lord Charmaine. What do you want?"

Charmaine ran both of his hands through his hair with a stifled sigh and began pacing the room. "My wants have nothing to do with this. I came to warn you I will be terminating my engagement with your daughter."

The older man took a pull of his pipe. "I heard about your ships. I doubt my daughter has yet. Or if she has, I doubt she understands what it means."

"I was clear money had nothing to do with my interest in her. I suspect she is not monitoring my finances." This room was only eight steps long.

"But she should have been." Brooke tapped his pipe out with an accusing look.

"Yes."

The stout gentleman leaned back in his chair. "This is why girls need their father's permission, to prevent money-hungry cads like you from breaking hearts. My staff will show you out."

Charmaine ignored Brooke's insults. "I will speak to Miss Brooke before I leave."

"Why? To lie more? I think you have done enough of that." Brooke's voice was cutting.

Charmaine glared at Miss Brooke's father. "No matter what you think of me, let us be clear, I love your daughter. If nothing else, I owe her the truth."

"A man does not abandon the woman he loves."

"Love is for dreamers and stories." Charmaine's eyes were hard. "This is a world of duty and practicality. I am sure you understand."

"I do." Brooke turned his attention to the paperwork on his formal desk. "Give your explanations and get out of my home."

Charmaine bowed and left the room. Brooke rang the bell pull, "Send for Miss Boswell. Immediately."

❧◆❧

Miss Brooke was aflutter. Word reached her that Charmaine was in the residence, so she promptly changed her gown. The dark blue velvet day dress she commissioned especially for him was too vivid of a contrast against the pastel drawing room, but Miss Brooke was convinced Charmaine preferred her in dark colors. Then again, the dress was a little severe.

She twirled in front of the mirror for a third time and frowned. Nevertheless, there was not time to change her dress again. She wracked her brain for whatever Charmaine and her father could be discussing. Maybe, just maybe, her father had consented to their marriage. Miss Brooke allowed herself the idyllic daydream as she impatiently waited.

After what seemed like an eternity Charmaine entered, towering and masculine in the delicate sea green room. His expression was drawn and dark as his eyes glowed out of his scowl. Miss Brooke had not seen him in this mood before, the conversation with her father must have gone worse than expected. His hair was askew from his normally neat queue. The reason for his dishevelment was soon clear. His hair fled its orderly style as he ran his hands through it. "Miss Brooke."

She nodded gracefully at him. "Lord Charmaine. Is there ought I can do for you?"

"No." Charmaine took in her appearance for a long moment, seemingly absorbing every small detail. Miss Brooke blushed. It had been a long time since a man looked at her with such desperate interest. "May I speak to you?"

Miss Brooke nodded again and tapped the seat next to her. "Certainly. Please, sit."

He settled in a wingback chair across from her, rather than on the chaise where she motioned. Charmaine looked at her for another long moment and then down at his hands.

Miss Brooke leaned forward and reached out to touch his chin. He took a breath and met her periwinkle eyes. Her voice was as welcoming as her gaze, "Whatever it is, you can tell me. I will not betray you."

Charmaine chuckled bitterly. No, my love, he thought, it is I who will betray you. "I have not been entirely honest with you. I could attempt to explain it in a way that justifies, but it would be a waste of time. The long and the short is I lied."

Miss Brooke shrugged and allowed her hand to drop to his knee. "Everyone lies, Robert."

"No, Alison, they do not." Charmaine's eyes reverted to his lap. "But I did. I am impoverished, Miss Brooke. I have almost nothing."

"I know."

Charmaine's eyes flashed to her face, his eyes widening in shock. "You do?"

"My servants know your servant. People talk." Miss Brooke looked earnestly into his eyes. "You are poor. I know. And if I have to give up all of this, all my fancy dresses, all the balls, the Seasons, everything, to be with you—it is worth it. We can have a wealthy daughter. You are worth poverty."

"God, Alison." Charmaine shut his eyes. She was not making this easy. "It is worse than that."

"Look at me, Robert. Do not hide from me, please." His eyes opened, and she could see the wary pain in them. "Whatever it is, we will mend it. I promise."

"I wish that was true." His deep blue eyes found her pale ones. "My last hope was extinguished. I came onto the marriage market for someone's dowry to prop up the family finances. I was courting Miss Linder the night West attacked you. After that, I stopped thinking. I thought I could make us work. I could fall in love. I could have happily ever after. I was wrong."

Miss Brooke withdrew her hand from his leg. "Why were you wrong?"

"Because, while I would be poor with you in body and rich in heart, I must support my family. I have a duty, Miss Brooke. I have to take care of my father. And that requires money." He looked away from her and stared out the window as he continued talking. "Last year, I was the primary on three shipping ventures. One returned, one is missing, and the other sunk, taking with it all my collateral. I am in debt. And without capital, I will lose everything. My family will lose everything. My father will no longer have medical care, or a place to live. And I cannot do that to them, I cannot do that to him. I cannot. I am sorry, but I cannot."

"Robert." Her voice was quiet. "Look at me." Looking at her took more willpower then seemed necessary. He forced himself to meet her eyes. "Do you love me?"

Charmaine stood, his voice angry. "What do you think?"

Miss Brooke's tone had not changed. "I do not know. Thus, why I asked."

"Yes, Alison. I love you. I want to marry you. But I cannot."

Miss Brooke's world froze as she remembered Farrington rejecting her in the park. Even the words were similar. "But you promised."

"I know!" Charmaine raised his voice. "I promised. And I love you. And I even tupped you and now I am leaving. I am a poxy bugger."

She frowned slightly. "Can you please watch your language?"

That brought him up short. "I am telling you I am ending our engagement and you are asking me not to curse?"

"I do not find it to be an unreasonable request." Miss Brooke folded her hands politely in front of her.

Charmaine took a deep breath. "It is reasonable. I beg your pardon."

"For cursing?"

"For everything." Charmaine sat in the large chair and took her hands. "I am sorry I cannot go through with this. I love you."

"We could find a way to make this work. Maybe I can help?"

Miss Brooke's calm was beginning to unhinge Charmaine. "It is impossible, Miss Brooke. I need a dowry and you do not have one. We are done."

Miss Brooke nodded. "If you say it is impossible, then it must be so." She gestured at her maid. "I am sure my staff show you out."

The maid pointedly looked at the door. Charmaine spluttered at the calm, composed lady in front of him. "That is it? The staff can show me out?"

"Yes, Lord Charmaine, it is." Miss Brooke stood and marginally curtsied. "Good day."

"Alison, I…"

Charmaine was interrupted when the maid stepped forward and cleared her throat. "My lord? May I show you the door." It was not a question.

He nodded, embarrassed to be reprimanded by the help. He stormed out of the room, only to pause in the doorway to look back at the waif in midnight blue. She was everything he ever wanted, offering to live with him however they could, asking nothing of him, and he was leaving her because of her lack of a dowry. He had become everything he hated about the *ton*. His resolve wavered as he looked back at her, but his ever-present sense of duty quickly came to the fore. Charmaine walked out without another word.

The knock on the front door of Farrington's London domicile was so loud it echoed in the study. Farrington looked from his ledger with curiosity as sounds of a vigorous exchange floated up the hallway. Listening, he could clearly make out Miss Boswell's voice but not quite what she was saying. Farrington pulled out a desk drawer and removed the false bottom. Putting away the papers he was working on, he looked around the room once more. There was nothing to indicate he was anything more than the average gentry chap and certainly nothing that would paint him as a traitor. He pulled the rope by his desk twice in quick succession to let his staff know he was willing to see the visitor.

Miss Boswell was flushed when she entered. Her hair was wild, curls flying every which way. The gown she was wearing screamed of the old Miss Boswell, patterned yellow chintz with orange bows on the sleeves. Farrington might have taken more time to admire her form but her pained octave pierced through his calm like nothing else, "Why did you not tell me?"

Farrington took a firm grip on his emotions. Being yelled at was not his preferred pastime, yet responding with anger would serve no purpose. It was best to be impassive. "Good day, Miss Boswell. What a pleasure to receive your call."

"Do not waste your words with me, Anthony." Miss Boswell's eyes narrowed as she approached his desk. "You knew he was toying with her."

Zounds, Farrington thought, how do I get myself into these situations? "He was not, madam, toying with her. Charmaine loves your Miss Brooke and, under other circumstances, would indeed marry her."

A bright copper eyebrow arched skeptically. "What circumstances?"

"His most reliable investment was recently reported as destroyed. Now his poverty is public." Farrington leaned back in his chair and considered the minx in front of him. He had never seen Miss Boswell this animated before and found her to be delightfully pretty. He hid a smile as she raised a finger to continue scolding him. She would make someone an excellent wife.

"He was in dun territory before," Miss Boswell pointed out, "so what is the difference now?"

Farrington considered before answering. He decided the truth was harmless enough and, while however unlikely, perhaps the women could find a solution. "The latest shipping venture was financed using the Donahue townhome as collateral. If Charmaine does not find another source of capital, or collateral, and soon, they will lose their residence in town."

"So? It is only a house."

"Lord Donahue cannot be moved."

Miss Boswell looked confused. "Lord Donahue?"

"Charmaine's father. He is deathly ill."

"Mother of God!" Miss Boswell's hands moved to her mouth. "How terrible! The poor Donahues! Does Alison know?"

"I have that impression."

Miss Boswell bit her lip. "Lord Charmaine is breaking off with Miss Brooke so he can marry to gain a dowry and save his father?"

Farrington nodded. "Approximately. You are leaving out Charmaine's guilt and self-recrimination because he feels the family's financial situation is directly his doing. Otherwise your summary is accurate."

"That is almost noble." Miss Boswell cocked her head, fiery curls pouring over her pale shoulder. "Why did he not tell her upfront?"

"Why should he?" Farrington asked. "Miss Brooke would never have taken a pauper seriously. She would have viewed him as another suitor who wanted her dowry. Until this recent shipping report, he was serious about marrying her nevertheless of her income."

"People should be honest with each other. Such secrets should not exist between friends."

"I am not sure they classify as friends," Farrington amended with a slight smile.

"Or suitors," Miss Boswell added.

Farrington's smile grew. "I would think those would be the most likely, and the most justified, to keep secrets."

"It is not right."

"If you say so." The topic of secrets drew Farrington's mind to the documents in his desk. Suddenly, the conversation made him lonely. "Charmaine did what he felt he had to do."

"He hurt Alison." Miss Boswell was serious.

"I know." Farrington nodded. "He knows, too. He feels he had no choice. May I ask you a question?"

At Miss Boswell's zealous nod he continued, "Are you here on your own behalf, or did Miss Brooke send you to ferret out information?"

"I am here on my own behalf, thank you very much. I would tell you if I was snooping." Miss Boswell was indignant. "I told you last time, yes?"

"You did. But I am confused on why you are here. What do you wish of me?"

Miss Boswell frowned and tried to figure out the best way to answer his question without admitting her unseemly interest. "I wish you had warned me. This was put upon me with no notice."

"If I told you, would you have been able to keep such from Miss Brooke?" Farrington asked the question as if it was rhetorical.

"Yes. I can keep a secret."

Farrington seemed surprised by her answer. "Would you not have a duty to report what you know to her?"

Miss Boswell raised an expressive eyebrow. "I am not her spy. But even if I was, you are my friend. Betraying you would be wrong."

He smiled slightly. "You and Charmaine have much in common."

Miss Boswell made a face. "I do not have a large dowry, if that is what you are implying."

Farrington laughed unexpectedly. "No, I was not." He sobered quickly as he realized how easily she could make him laugh. He did not all together like it. "Is there anything else, Miss Boswell?"

"I do not think so. You seem to have been quite effective at taking the wind out of my sails." She mock-glared at him. "Unless there is anything else I need to know?"

"If there was, I would not tell you."

Farrington's sudden serious tone caught Miss Boswell off guard. "I seem to have failed at making my point. I would like to be warned."

"I comprehend, Miss Boswell. But you seem to mistake mine. I will not warn you. I am not in the habit of extending confidences."

"I understand." In truth, Miss Boswell had no idea what had occurred. They went from a jovial conversation that defused her anger to a serious, defensive one. "I will see you anon?"

Farrington nodded, turning his attention back to the harmless papers on his desk. "Yes. I do owe you a trip to the races. I have not forgotten."

"Good day, Anthony."

The soft tone to her words made him look up. There was something vulnerable, something distinctly feminine, in her voice he never heard before. For the briefest of moments, he saw Miss Boswell as she wished. Her curly hair blazed fire against her pale flesh and her small, firm breasts rose out of a waist that begged to be spun in endless dancing. He paused, seeing his friend as a woman for the first time. "Farewell, Miss Boswell."

Miss Boswell curtsied and slid out of the room. She had the awful feeling she was leaving his life forever.

CHAPTER XV

Miss Boswell once told Farrington time heals. Yet, as she watched Miss Brooke mope around the sitting room, she began to doubt the truth of her statement. "Ali, you have to slip this sorrow. Almost a fortnight has passed. You are a hermit. Let us join the festivities this eve."

Miss Brooke shrugged. "You go. I have a headache."

"You have a headache every time I suggest anything."

"I cannot imagine why."

Miss Boswell bit her lip. "Do not air your venom on me. There is more to life than sitting in your room and supping with your father."

"There is also chasing men at balls so that I can find the perfect match and have my father refuse to give his approval. Then, they can then leave me when they find out I am not a source of easy money." Miss Brooke smoothed her skirts. "I am sorry, Miss Boswell. I am being a witch. I simply," she sighed, "I miss him."

"Forgiven," Miss Boswell replied automatically. "Ali, lots of women come on the market without dowries and most of them find husbands. Maybe we are doing this wrong?"

Miss Brooke smiled slightly, "I am not going to take that as you saying this is all my fault."

"No, no!" Miss Boswell rushed forward and sat next to her friend. "I did not say that at all."

"I know. You are saying I should find a man who does not need money and simply wants me for my looks. Or to breed."

Miss Boswell sighed. "Alison, I hate to take what is traditionally your part of the conversation, but that is what Society expects from us. We should know how to dress ourselves, run a household, and produce children. All of which you want."

"I want more than that." Miss Brooke looked at Miss Boswell. Her sky-blue eyes were intense. "Robert made me feel like I mattered. Not my money, not my father's shipping connections, nor how pretty I am, but who I am. Returning to *ton* feels like giving up that dream."

"Maybe it is still out there. Lord Charmaine only showed you it existed. Now you can find someone else."

Miss Brooke frowned. "You do not believe that."

"I know. But it is the accepted knowledge."

Miss Brooke's frown remained. "Pray, be honest with me."

Miss Boswell shrugged. "I think it is horrible and we should have a good cry about it. True love only happens once."

"Romantic." Miss Brooke wiped her eyes. "But, but what am I to do?"

"Cry. Scream. Rage. Then go back out and put on your pretty smile and go on with life. That is all you can do." Miss Boswell seemed sorrowful.

"It is unlike you to tell me to give up," Miss Brooke said.

"I know. But his reasons for leaving are valid. I know he loves you. I believe that. If he says he cannot be with you, then he cannot. I know, deep in my heart, he wants you more than anything."

"Clearly not more than anything," Miss Brooke snorted.

Miss Boswell put her arm around her friend. "Ali, would you want him to put his father on the street to be with you? There are things he cannot reasonably sacrifice and still be a decent human being."

"No." Miss Brooke frowned, her brow creasing. "Yes. But I do not want to say yes. I want to say no, I want to understand he is doing the right thing, but my heart disagrees. All I can think about is how much I want to be with him. Brenda, I have never felt anything like this!"

Miss Boswell smiled. "I believe they call it love. Have you ever told him?"

"That I love him?" Miss Brooke looked puzzled. "He has to know."

"But have you told him?"

"I suppose not. Do you feel it matters?"

The red-haired woman shrugged. "I was curious."

The conversation died briefly. Miss Brooke began to retreat into herself. Miss Boswell lightly shoved her friend. "Stop that."

"I am not doing anything but being sad. Hearts do not unbreak."

"La, Ali. They say time heals. But we should not trust it to do all the work. We should away and try to find our own joy." Miss Boswell smiled encouragingly. Miss Brooke seemed immune.

"Pray, tell me, Brenda—tell me why I should go out there, why I should lift up my chin, and why I should hunt for yet another man? Unless you have a reason, I am staying in."

"You cannot have children without a man."

Miss Brooke frowned. "I no longer only want children. I want *Robert's* children."

"I know. But you have spent your whole life wanting children and dreaming of being the mother you wished you had. Are you going to give up on that dream because you fell in love?"

"Well, no, but," Miss Brooke's frown grew deeper, "I am not the most logical creature at the moment."

Miss Boswell smiled slightly and tightened her arm about her friend. "I know. But you asked for a reason. I gave you one. Now, will you go out?"

Miss Brooke sighed and looked out the window. The bright sunny day seemed out of place with her mood. "Tomorrow. Pick an event and we can go tomorrow."

"Promise?"

"I do not promise. Brenda, this is not losing a fan or snagging a hem. This is…Oh, I miss him so," she finished weakly.

"I know. But hiding in here is not going to fix anything. At least promise we can go riding tomorrow. I want to see you out of this room."

Miss Brooke sighed. "Fine. I promise. But I will be miserable the whole time."

"If it makes you happy, Ali, you can be as miserable as you want."

Miss Brooke swatted at Miss Boswell. "The Stantons invited us to join them at the opera on Friday. Is that going out enough for you?"

Miss Boswell nodded in assent. "I suppose that means I am done bullying you, then. Do you want to play cribbage?" She scooted away from Miss Brooke and picked up a deck of cards. "I will spot you a point."

"You have to have better things to do than spend every day playing cribbage with me."

"No." Miss Boswell smiled at her friend. "I do not."

Miss Brooke smiled, her first of the day. She reached out and hugged her friend. "I do not deserve you."

"No. You do not." Miss Boswell hugged back. "Now, deal the cards. We have a game to play."

They ventured to the opera, rode together in the park, and slowly, bit-by-bit, Miss Boswell and Miss Brooke resumed their places in London Society. Miss Brooke smiled, danced, and put up a brave front. The two friends departed balls when Charmaine arrived, Miss Brooke barely maintaining a smile until they reached the carriage. One day, after retreating from Charmaine and Farrington while riding in the park, Miss Boswell broke.

After saying her farewells to Miss Brooke, Miss Boswell fumed to find Brooke. In the three years she had known him, Brooke treated her like a surrogate daughter. Miss Boswell's own father was a distracted creature who lived in his books. Brooke accepted Miss Boswell without question once she was installed as Miss Brooke's best friend. She supped with him when Miss Brooke was busy and spent hours daydreaming in the Brooke's London library. Mr. Brooke treated her with the love and acceptance she had never received at home. Perhaps, Miss Boswell thought, love is what allowed her to be so vexed at him now.

Without checking if he was present, Miss Boswell careened into the little study next to the kitchen. The rotund old man was bent over his desk, writing furiously on parchment. The quill stopped mid-stroke as the door was flung violently open. He raised a bushy eyebrow as Miss Boswell stormed in.

"This has to stop!" Miss Boswell yelled. "You cannot do this to her!"

Brooke put down his quill. "Good day, Brenda. Would you shut the door, prithee?"

Miss Boswell blushed slightly. "Yes, sir. Sorry."

He watched her shut the door and gestured for her to take a seat. Miss Boswell shuffled into a chair. "Now, my dear, how can I help you?"

"Ali is still distraught. I have never seen her like this," Miss Boswell confided.

"It will pass," said Brooke.

"It will not pass." Miss Boswell rebutted. "She is in love! That does not fade."

"It is an unfortunate situation," the gentleman acknowledged. "A pauper stole my daughter's heart. Now, I suspect, you are here to tell me I should change my mind and give my consent for her to marry into poverty."

"It does not matter how much money he has. He loves her! She loves him! What more do you want?" Miss Boswell was animated, gesturing this way and that as she spoke.

"Honesty. Responsibility. Obligation." Brooke remained calm under Miss Boswell's onslaught. "I understand Ali is currently distraught. I, no matter what you may think right now, do not want to see her in pain. Marrying a man who lied to her, who chose her for her money, and who left her when he found out her inheritance is unavailable, is not the sort of man I wish for my daughter. Nothing you can say will change that."

"They are in love." Miss Boswell was adamant.

"I do not care."

Miss Boswell shook her curls in exasperation. "How can you not care? Do you not want her to be happy?"

"A man who lied to her will not make her happy. I will not be here forever. I wish to see my daughter well provided for."

"What would you have had him done? Walked in on that horrible situation and then left? He tried to make it better and then could not. How is that not honorable?"

Brooke placed his hands flat on the table. "Lord Charmaine hurt my daughter. He lied to my daughter. Now, unless you have a different matter you would like to address, I have work to attend to."

Miss Boswell bit her lip at the clear dismissal. "She loves him. And she loves you. Cannot you see how you are hurting her? Do you not trust her?"

"I said I had things to attend to. I assume you can show yourself out."

"Yes, Mr. Brooke. It is only…"

"Go home, Brenda." Brooke cut her off. "I will see you at supper tomorrow."

Miss Boswell nodded and curtsied slightly before backing out of the room. Despite yelling, she did not feel any better. From both their points of view, things made sense. In one instance, Charmaine was honorable and caught by the duty to his family. In the other, he was a shifty money-hungry cad who abandoned his obligations. Miss Boswell sighed as she walked out the door. There was really nothing more she could do except for go home and dream of Anthony. And that, in truth, helped absolutely nothing.

Two days later, Miss Boswell arrived in a rush at the Brooke home. She banged on the door and rushed by the footman without any thought to propriety. The servants watched curiously as the tall woman raced up the stairs and ungracefully charged into Miss Brooke's room.

Miss Brooke leapt up from her correspondence desk. "Miss Boswell! What is wrong? Are you well?"

Miss Boswell nodded yes. Gasping for breath, she tossed a piece of parchment onto Miss Brooke's desk. Miss Brooke gave Miss Boswell an odd look before opening the letter. "Where is this from?"

"Lord Farrington's household sent it to me." Miss Boswell started to catch her breath. "I came as soon as I read it."

Miss Brooke opened the letter with great curiosity. It was brief,

The Right Honorable Ambler Anderson,
The 7th Earl of Donahue,
ascended to Heaven on this 13th day of August in the
Year of Our Lord, 1772
1 Thessalonians 4:13-14

She read the sentence twice before turning to her friend. "Lord Charmaine's father died?"

"Yes." Miss Boswell sat next to Miss Brooke. "What are you going to do?"

Miss Brooke gave Miss Boswell an odd look. "What am I going to do? Nothing."

"But if his father has died, then he can live in poverty and marry you!" While it was horrible to be glad for Charmaine's father's passing, Miss Boswell felt this was the answer to all their prayers.

Miss Brooke read the parchment yet again. "Lord Charmaine, pardon, Lord Donahue needs to decide that on his own. He still has his mother and his brother, as well as his estate and holdings he needs to support. His father was far from his only financial obligation."

"But…"

"Brenda, I know you want what is best, but he left me. Should you not speak to him if you feel this strongly?" Miss Brooke put down the parchment on her desk and raised her chin.

"If you want me to, I suppose I could. I thought you would want to know." Miss Boswell seemed suddenly unsure.

"I do want to know. And I do not need for you to talk to him. He left me, Brenda. I need to understand that. I do love him. I do still think he is wonderful. But I cannot hold on to nonexistent hope, mope around, or stalk him. I will not."

Miss Boswell nodded. "I suppose I understand."

"How is Lord Farrington?"

The question took Miss Boswell off guard. "I do not know. I have not spoken to Lord Farrington since shortly after your engagement to Lord Charmaine, la, I mean Lord Donahue, ended."

Miss Brooke smoothed her skirts. "Oh. That is too bad."

Miss Boswell silently agreed but outwardly shrugged. "I am sure he is fine. It was good of Lord Farrington to think of you when this happened."

"Yes, it was kind of him." Miss Brooke's frown deepened. "Grant me your leave, Miss Boswell? I find this news deeply troublesome."

Miss Boswell walked over to her friend and gave her a hug. Surprisingly, Miss Brooke fiercely hugged her back. "Certainly. I will be here if you need me."

Miss Brooke nodded into her shoulder and then let Miss Boswell go. "Thank you. For everything."

Miss Boswell smiled a bit shyly in response to her friend's outpouring of affection and slowly made her way back to her empty domicile. For a moment, she thought things were looking up, but it seemed as if they were doomed to a life of spinsterhood and misery.

Miss Brooke checked the address twice before leaving her coach. She had never been to Tower Hill before and quickly understood why. The rundown neighborhood was dreary, filled with rickety shops and tightly packed apartments. The building in front of her looked no better than any of the others. Her driver looked at her in concern. "You want me to come with you, miss?"

Despite her misgivings, Miss Brooke declined. "No. But thank you for offering."

"Yes, miss." The driver gave her an encouraging smile. "I will be a waiting."

Miss Brooke gathered the hem of her indigo day dress and picked her way over the curb. Heavy cloud cover made the cramped neighborhood seem even drearier. The door to the old brick building was slightly ajar and led into a long hallway. The numeral 7 was scrawled on the scrap of paper, so she could only assume it was further inside. Quickly adapting, Miss Brooke followed the numbering scheme up two flights of stairs to the end of a dark, unlit hallway. Taking a deep breath, she knocked on the door.

A young blond man answered. Miss Brooke bit her lip in consternation, as she had never seen him before. He looked her up and down critically. "Can I help you?"

"Yes. Would you kindly tell Lord Donahue that Miss Brooke is a-calling?" Miss Brooke fervently hoped her servants were right. How could Robert live in this dim little building? It smelled.

The door began to shut. "There is no one here by that name. You have the wrong address."

Miss Brooke put her hand on the door. "And you have the wrong accent for the lower class. Please. Tell him I am here."

"Please go, ma'am. He does not wish to see you. It will be better for all of us."

"I will see him," Amelia declared. "I do not care if I have to stand on this stoop and yell until the constables come to take me to Bedlam."

"He is in no place to be yelled at, Miss Brooke. It would be better if you left."

Miss Brooke blushed. The young man's condescending tone was unfamiliar to her. She found it exceedingly distasteful. "I have no intention of scolding him. But I will see him."

"This is not a good time." Wilhelm moved to shut the door again.

"I know," Miss Brooke said. "Have I ever done him wrong? Have I yelled or ranted or embarrassed him? Ever? Why do you think I would do so now?"

"Because you are angry and hurt. Revenge. I know not."

It was Miss Brooke's turn to roll her eyes at him. "Do not be foolish. Lord Donahue trusts me, even if you do not. Open the door."

"Demanding to be let into a man's private chambers is not very ladylike."

"Screaming for Lord Donahue is also not very ladylike. But I am on the verge," Miss Brooke warned.

"So," Wilhelm smiled, "The lady has pluck." The smile faded. "You swear you mean him no harm? I will not tolerate you bringing additional pain into our home."

Miss Brooke nodded, "I promise."

Wilhelm opened the door and stood aside. She assertively stepped through into a cramped office with nothing more than a rundown desk and two chairs. A riding coat was tossed haphazardly on the desk. The whole room had a musty, alcoholic odor.

"He is through there." Wilhelm pointed to a door on the other side of the room.

"Thank you." Miss Brooke made a guess, "You are the Honorable Mr. Michael Anderson, are you not?"

The man laughed. "Me? Anderson? Not on your life. I am Wilhelm, Lord Donahue's steward."

Miss Brooke's eyebrows shot up almost to her hairline. "You are a servant? You do not act like a servant!"

"Donahue tells me thus. But you did not come all this way to engage in chitchat with his steward." Wilhelm gestured towards the door. "Remember your promise. I would hate to have to throw you out."

Off-kilter from such a strange reception, Miss Brooke timidly walked to the door. All her bravado faded. Once her quest was achieved, she felt lost. What would she say to him? Taking a deep breath to banish her fears, she knocked lightly on the door. There was no answer. She knocked again and received no response. She looked over her shoulder at Wilhelm, who nodded for her to continue. At her hesitation, he gestured her on with another eye roll. Her irritation at the young man helped her find her courage and enter.

The room was cluttered with clothes and bottles. She had to push the door to move the clothing scattered behind it. Stepping daintily through the small space, she peered around the dingy chamber. The bedroom was tiny. Donahue's bed took most of the space, leaving little place to stand. The dark blue velvet duvet was so well worn it shined. Slumped discontentedly in the middle of the bed was the man she loved. He held a bottle of dark amber liquid in one hand and his eyes appeared unfocused. He did not seem to notice she was there.

Miss Brooke tiptoed her way through the clutter and sat next to him on the bed. His blurry stare looked on her. "Whadda want?"

"Nothing."

His eyebrow rose, "Nothing? That's not right."

"I know. And I am not going to pretend I do not want to argue with you, or I am not hurt, but I think you need me right now more than I need to yell at you." Miss Brooke put her hand on his knee. "Thus I do not want anything. I am simply present."

"I'm drunk."

Miss Brooke nodded. "Unsurprising. You have been dealt a terrible series of blows."

He laughed bitterly. "God's own truth."

"How long ago did you climb in the bottle?" Miss Brooke stood and started moving things off the bed beside him. Tidying the clutter gave her mind something to do other than focus on the pain seeing Donahue like this caused her.

"Feels like forever. Had to go to my investiture though. Sobered up for that." Donahue scoffed bitterly. "I am an Earl now."

"I am sorry."

"Me, too." He lifted the bottle to his lips but did not drink. With a sigh, he put it back down again. "I never wanted any of this. Maybe I would have if I had a choice. Never did, always family, duty, take care of Michael, then take care of Father, but never take care of me."

Miss Brooke focused on folding his waistcoat. "I am sorry."

"Makes me feel bad. Everyone else wants a title. I want to marry you." Donahue frowned at the bottle. "That makes me feel bad, too. Cause I'm not gonna. Gonna to marry some dimwitted shrew with more money than sense."

There was nothing Miss Brooke could say. Instead, she started a waistcoat pile as she picked more of his clothing off the floor. His disaster was orderly. His waistcoats were all in one area, his breeches in another, and the bottles stacked neatly by the wall. "Your chambers are quite a mess."

"Wilhelm is a bother, constantly scolding me. Told him to get out."

Miss Brooke nodded. "He is a very unusual servant."

Donahue snorted. "That is a kind way of putting it. But I cannot find fault. My father both trained him in numbers and found him an extremely prestigious placement. When my father fell ill, Wilhelm returned. He has stayed with me through this whole mess. I pay him in promises." Donahue looked back at the bottle. "Promises I cannot keep."

"You will keep them." Miss Brooke focused on the folding. Donahue needed her more than she needed to cry. "You are making the sacrifices you need to be able to fulfill your obligations."

"You mean abandoning you for a dumb shrew."

"Yes." Miss Brooke took a deep breath. "I meant that."

Donahue looked at her, his deep blue eyes finding her in his misery. "Why are you here?"

She walked back towards him and took his hand. "Because you need me right now."

He nodded. "I cannot give you…"

Miss Brooke cut him off, "As I already told you, I want nothing from you. Believe in me."

"That doesn't seem fair," Donahue frowned.

"I know. I cannot say I do not care, or I do not want to fight, but now is not the time." She sat next to him and forced his arm over her shoulders. "I thought maybe you could use a friend. Or whatever I am."

"Alison. You are an Alison. My Alison."

Miss Brooke shut her eyes and fought to keep her voice level. There was no way to stop the tears from forming. "Whomever I am, I am here."

He nodded and slumped further forward. The silence stretched between them. Miss Brooke fought to keep her composure and, borrowing a trick from Miss Boswell, counted to one hundred. She reached seventy-two before Donahue shifted beside her and looked at the top of her head. "Mind if I lie down?"

"Not at all. You look as if it has been days since you slept."

He nodded yet again and stretched out on his bed. "Feels like it. I'm falling asleep sitting next to you. I have nightmares. I let everyone down." He reached out for her. Miss Brooke came to his side without thinking about it. After a bit of hesitation, she finished lying next to him.

"You did the best you could."

He shut his eyes. "Doesn't matter. Still failed."

"Why blame yourself?" Miss Brooke's voice was muffled as she tucked herself into the crook of his shoulder. Her stays dug into her armpit but she decided that she did not care. A little discomfort was worth being here.

"Whom should I blame, Alison? Tell me whom to blame and I'll blame them." His voice was slowing down, becoming softer. She struggled to understand him as he slurred his way through the conversation.

"No one. You blame no one." Miss Brooke's tears were flowing freely now.

"A pox on life, then."

"Amen." Miss Brooke paused for a moment and lifted her head slightly. "Do you love me?"

"Mmmmhmmm. Will until my dying day, never doubt that."

Despite her tears, Miss Brooke smiled. His voice was warm, relaxed, and flowed over her like honey. "Can I tell you something?"

"Whatshat?" His voice was barely a murmur.

"I think you already know this, but, well," she paused and tried to find the right words, "I am quite fond of you. In truth, I, well, I, and I do not want you to think me saying this means I want anything right now—because I do mean it when I say I am here for you and want nothing—but," she took a deep breath. "The truth is, I love you, too."

Donahue's deep breathing was the only answer. Trapped under his arm, there was nothing Miss Brooke could do but snuggle into his shoulder. She put her head back on his shoulder and allowed her tears to pool into the crook of his arm. Against her better judgment and intent, she fell asleep.

ॐ◆ॐ

Miss Brooke awoke with a start. It was dark, and she was alone in a strange room. Adrenaline flooded her system before memory arrived. Groggily sitting up, she looked around for Donahue, but found no sign of anyone else. Somehow, her stays were twisted. She struggled to retighten the stays on her own, but it was hopeless. Giving up, she looked around the tiny room for a washstand. The water was fresh and even slightly warm. She adjusted her hair in the mirror and timidly left the room.

The public room of the cramped flat appeared to double as Donahue's office. It, like the bedroom, was devoid of another living soul. There was a plate of stone fruit and cheese on the desk. She took a piece of plum while she looked over his desk for a note. A soft step behind her caught her attention. Miss Brooke turned, expecting to see Donahue. Instead the young man from the day before stood there. His demeanor still irritated Miss Brooke.

"Where is Lord Donahue? And when is it?"

Wilhelm set a pot of tea and a cup next to the plate of fruit. He poured the tea and handed it to Miss Brooke, "He departed a bit ago. The time is slightly before midnight."

Miss Brooke gasped as she absently took the tea. "My poor driver! I have left him waiting for hours!"

"Do not concern yourself. I dismissed him after it was clear you were staying."

"He went home? My father knows I am here?" A hint of panic crept into Miss Brooke's voice.

"I am not incompetent." Wilhelm did not wait for a reply. "The driver is waiting for you at a pub down the way. I sent a runner to fetch him when I heard you wake."

Miss Brooke was a bit taken aback. The disrespectful whelp seemed to have everything well in hand. "Anything else I should know?"

"You supped with Lady Stanton tonight. She is concerned about the separation, again. You know what a pest she can be. Now, turn around and I will help you straighten up."

Miss Brooke blinked. "But, but, that is not very proper."

"And anything else you have done here is?" Wilhelm's raised eyebrow matched the sarcasm in his voice. "Turn around."

Miss Brooke turned around. Wilhelm's hands on the laces were quick and deft and soon she was tidied. With a final tug, he stepped back. "There. Good as new."

Miss Brooke turned around and paused. "Do you mind if I ask you a few questions?"

"Donahue loves you. He is currently supping with his brother." He gestured towards the door of the flat, "Anything else?"

"Is he well?" Miss Brooke's voice was quiet and filled with lingering sadness.

Wilhelm tightened his lips and looked at her critically before answering. "No. He is not."

"Is there anything I can do?"

"I doubt it." Wilhelm's condescending nature vanished abruptly. "We will persevere but he is not well."

"Maybe he needs a friend, someone to talk to?" Miss Brooke suggested.

"No. Lord Farrington, Collins, and his brother have all foisted themselves upon him," Wilhelm informed her. "He needs time. And acceptance. He let himself dream. Now he has to give that up."

"He does not have to," Miss Brooke ventured. "I would marry him even if he had nothing."

Wilhelm nodded. "Maybe you are worthy of him after all. But that would still do little good. He owes debts—to banks, to shipping agents, to the East India Company. He will not put his mother on the street. And then there is you."

"Me?"

"Yes, you." Wilhelm made a mollifying gesture at Miss Brooke's confusion. "Lord Donahue has been raised his whole life to do right by a woman. He loves you. He wants to give you the world and the stars. If he cannot give you that, he will give you nothing."

"Foolishness," Miss Brooke exclaimed, "I would take anything!"

"It is who he is."

"But, he…"

Wilhelm cut her off. "I told you that you should not have come. His mind will not change. Trysts like this will only hurt you both."

"I did not come for me."

"As you claimed before. But, Miss Brooke, your engagement is over."

Miss Brooke told herself she was not going to cry in front of the help, but the tears in her eyes would not listen. She raised her chin and prayed they would not fall. "I am aware. Is my coach here yet?"

"It should be." Wilhelm raised a tentative hand towards her arm but let his hand fall. "I am sorry. The only consolation I have is the truth Lord Donahue loves you. You will be his first, his only, and no one will ever replace you in his heart."

The tears burst forth, quietly racing down her face. Miss Brooke tried to speak, but sorrow made her incoherent. Wilhelm shifted awkwardly and Miss Brooke burst from the room without any further conversation. Once in the hallway, she dashed down the flights of stairs. Her driver found her on the landing of the first floor, bawling into her perfumed handkerchief. Protectively, he guided her to the carriage and drove her home.

CHAPTER XVI

Donahue's eyebrows touched as he scowled at the pile of papers towering over him. If there was a slight breeze, he might literally be buried in his work. The forced solitude might be welcome. The search for the funds being channeled out of England was about to bear fruit. There were only a few more reports to read. He was close. He could feel it.

He knew the picture the last bits of information painted. Truth be told, Donahue was in no hurry to discover the results, but he had no other escape except but work. His speeches were written, the next week's research was complete, and Donahue noted a distinct sense of annoyance from his Peers about his increasing zealotry for meetings and action. The House of Lords was the only place Donahue could be without obsessing over Miss Brooke.

Donahue glared at the mounds of papers covering his desk and decided he was done for the day. There was proof on his desk that Farrington was a traitor, and Donahue was not ready to find it. His mother previously asked him to visit. Condemning his best friend could wait.

❧ ◆ ☙

The walk to the Donahue townhouse destroyed any remaining good cheer. The sun was shining, the birds were chirping, and he was a horrible human being with no sense of self-worth left. Donahue smiled mockingly his own self-depreciating humor, but any hilarity crumbled as the truth of the joke sank in. He pushed his mind quickly away from his broken dreams. His mother was waiting. With a sigh, he walked the stairs to the townhouse. A footman let him in and Donahue proceeded directly to his mother's apartments. A maid scurried ahead of him. Sea trunks were stacked against the wall. Donahue gave Anderson's boxes little thought.

The open doorway of Lady Donahue's parlor showed her directing servants within. Lady Donahue was dressed in a somber, utilitarian cut she normally only wore at their country estate. Donahue cocked a bushy eyebrow, as he could not imagine what she was signaling with such a practical fashion. Lady Donahue's bearing softened as she noted Donahue's approach. Anderson was sprawled in Donahue's favorite chair. The younger brother was dressed for Town, his tight trousers the height of last year's rakehell fashion. Despite his devil-may-care dress, Anderson's expression was uncharacteristically sober.

Apprehensive, Donahue turned to face his mother. "Mother, good evening."

With a distracted nod, she dismissed the servant in front of her and turned her attention to her sons. Her eyes were filled with warmth and love. Donahue shot Anderson a confused, trapped glance, but got no answer. Both men stood as she walked towards them. She inspected each of them, pausing to fix a strand of Donahue's hair, and sat facing them on her vanity bench. Her sons sat across from her. "You both look dashing." Her expression was slightly critical as it rested on Anderson. He smiled charmingly back at her, clearly unconcerned. Donahue inclined his head.

There was an unexpected silence. Donahue turned his attention to his brother. "You are leaving?"

Anderson's eyebrow rose. "I had no such plans. Do you wish to speak to Mother in private?"

"No." Donahue shook his head sharply. "Not at all. But your trunks by the door?"

"Ah. Those are not mine. I am staying on my, your," he corrected himself with a smile, "ship."

Donhue allowed himself to smile back, although it felt forced. He could not shake the sadness of Miss Brooke's separation even among family. "You are her Captain. That makes the ship yours enough."

"My sponsor is too kind," Anderson replied with a seated bow.

Donahue shook his head ruefully at his younger brother and turned his attention to his mother. "You wished to see me?"

Lady Donahue nodded. "Indeed. And I want you to know I have given this matter much thought, so your objections will mean nothing."

Donahue frowned. "That is never a good opening. Continue."

"The trunks are mine. I am leaving Town."

Donahue's eyebrows shot up. Anderson leaned back in his chair, his long fingers steepled in front of his face. Donahue spoke first, "Mother, do not be foolish."

Lady Donahue gave him a flat, scolding look. Anderson hid a smile and replied as if Donahue had not spoken. "Mother, what a suggestion! Why?"

She gave her younger son an approving smile. "Better. I am going to spend the rest of the Season in the country. I shall redecorate the Donahue Estate to prepare it for the arrival of its new Lord and find a suitable place to build a residence for the Dowager Countess. A delightful project to take my mind from a dreadful time."

"This is unwise. During loss, you need Society the most. Isolating yourself from your friends helps nothing," Donahue said.

Anderson again ignored his older brother, "That's a lovely story for the *ton*, but what is the real reason? Surely you do not truly wish to give up a London Season! You have not been to our estate in years."

Lady Donahue nodded, also ignoring her eldest. "We all have to make sacrifices. I am going to make this one. Nothing your brother," her eyes fell on Donahue. His frown increased as the two of them chattered as if he was not present, "says will stop me."

Donahue folded his arms across his chest. "Answer Michael's question, Mother. Why?"

She shrugged prettily in answer, "If I go to the country, the townhouse is empty. It can be sold, or repossessed, or whatever horrible thing will happen to it."

"I am not selling this house. I am marrying for money. This conversation is over."

Anderson continued his pattern of ignoring his brother. "Your idea has merit, Mother, but are you sure you are strong enough to be in the country after Father's death?"

Lady Donahue nodded. "To help my son, I can mourn alone."

Anderson rose and kissed his mother on the cheek. Anderson was fuming silently in his chair. "Mother," Anderson could keep the smile off his face, "do you mind if I argue your strong-willed son?"

She smiled back. "Not at all."

Anderson turned to face Donahue. Before he could speak, Donahue interrupted with a curt, "No."

Anderson flashed a smile that normally broke hearts. "Now who is being foolish?"

"I will not allow our mother to be evicted from her home. She lives in Town year-round. She loves it here. She is my family and I will take care of her. This conversation is over." Donahue's voice was cold, firm. Lady Donahue shivered at the remote tone of his voice.

Donahue stood and walked several steps away from their cluster. Lady Donahue turned around on her stool to give her sons a semblance of privacy. Anderson stood as well, walking over to stand behind his brother. They both stared at their mother's back. "This is your duty?"

"Yes," Donahue's reply was curt.

"What of your family's duty to you?"

"My family supports me in all I do. They answer to me, they are respectful, and they trust me to guide our path." A slight note of humor entered Donahue's anger, "Mostly."

Anderson shrugged. "No one is perfect. But, and I am quite serious, there is another side of duty. You shoulder most of the weight of the family. You support us, but we also support you. Now you are at a crossroads. Mother is acting in support of you. How is that not her duty?"

Donahue sighed. "These are my mistakes, Michael. I will pay the price."

"Do not be daft, Robert." Anderson paused, his eyes narrowing. He decided to try a different tact. "Pray tell, how much do you really want to be rid of Miss Brooke?"

Donahue stood and turned to face his brother. "What in God's green earth do you mean by that?"

"Nothing is stopping you. The world has given you every reason to marry this girl. Father died, Mother is leaving Town, and I have a lucrative commission off the Gold Coast. You are hiding behind duty."

Donahue took a deep breath and closed his eyes, while the urge to pummel his younger brother flowed slowly from his system. It took a remarkable expenditure of effort before he was able to speak calmly, "I do not wish to have this discussion."

Anderson shrugged. "It is your life to ruin."

Lady Donahue turned back around to face them. "Michael," she scolded. Her light green eyes looked at her eldest son. Her expression was soft and slightly vulnerable. "Robert, will you listen to me?"

He closed the distance between them and looked at the older woman. He towered above her. "I will always listen, Mother, even if I do not agree."

"When I was young, I believed wealth and power were everything." Smile lines tightened around her eyes as she looked at him, "Sometimes I still do. But, then, the game of politics was all I knew. I was on the arm of a Duke, engaged to an Earl, the prima donna of the *ton*, and I gave it up for the most ridiculous of reasons. Love." Her eyes grew misty. "Ambler was dashing and charming, but he was unpopular, poor, and only the slightest hope of inheriting a title. I broke off my perfect engagement, the route to unbridled wealth and power, for a man who had nothing more than a smile—and my heart."

Lady Donahue wiped her eyes with elegant dignity. "The early years were difficult. But your father had a head for numbers, and several surprising events later the title came his way. But when I made my choice, I knew none of that. All I knew is I was willing to risk everything to have a chance at love. And now, now, I see my son giving up his dreams so that I can have wealth and power. Robert," she stood and took his hand, "I do not want wealth and power. I want you to know love the way I knew love. I want you and Alison to know what Ambler and I had. And if I have to give up a Season, or all of them, well, I find that a suitable sacrifice."

"Mother, I…" Donahue struggled to find words.

Anderson stood beside them. "I approve of Miss Brooke."

Donahue tilted his head in surprise. "You do?"

The younger man nodded. "Stop trying to do what you think is right by us and do what is truly right by us. Mother is in a bad way. Let her see you happy. That would mean more than all the money in the world."

Donahue turned his piercing blue gaze on his mother. "Truth?"

She nodded, tears still in her eyes. "You have your father's eyes, you know. I would give the world to see those eyes filled with joy one more time."

"This is truly what you want?" Donahue's voice was soft.

Lady Donahue smiled slightly through her tears and shrugged. "No, I want many other things. But out of the choices we have, I like this one best."

He nodded, his eyes fixed on his mother. "Then head to the estate and prepare for the wedding. If it will make you happy, I would like nothing more than to marry Miss Brooke."

Anderson interjected, "She never will believe you."

"Who? Mother?"

"No, Miss Brooke. She will think this is another ploy or deceit. You no longer have her trust."

Donahue frowned at his younger brother. Anderson was right. Trying to find a way to make Miss Brooke believe in him once again would be impossible. Lady Donahue smiled, "Then we will have to do it right. Listen, my boys, this is what we will do…"

Donahue leaned back at his desk in the Palace of Westminster, extremely pleased with the night so far. After consideration, he grudgingly admitted his mother's proposal was almost a perfect solution. Hope returned.

Deep in thought, he absently flipped through the piles of paper on his desk. His hand froze as a he noticed a ship's name on a manifold. Donahue quickly reached into his desk and pulled out the file he was building. With an explosive curse he threw the scrap of paper down. It was the irrefutable proof Farrington was funneling money to the rebels in the Americas.

Seething with silent doubt, Donahue wrote a summary of his findings. The quill fell silent and time slipped past. He could blame West for Farrington's guilt. The logistics would be simple. But then, Farrington would continue to finance rebellion. Donahue could not, would not, betray the Crown.

Trembling, he reached out and yanked fiercely on the bell pull. His manner was uncharacteristically harsh, as he demanded the servant rush the document to Lord North.

Donahue wiped perspiration from his forehead. Farrington's fate was out of his hands, now. One of Parliament's carriages took him home to Tower Hill. Donahue carefully strode inside under the uncaring gaze of the night driver. Nothing could exist to damn his family name alongside his friend.

Wilhelm greeted him with an uncharacteristically polite good evening. Donahue collapsed gratefully into his chair. Any hope of sleep or relaxation was ruined when Wilhelm latched the deadbolt. The servant's voice was a low murmur, "The door is being watched."

Donahue leaned sharply forward. Every muscle in his body tensed. His answering whisper was hoarse, "What did you say?"

"By two men. Too well dressed to be Runners. I suspect the Royal Guard, so either the Crown or Parliament." Wilhelm cocked an eyebrow while he hung Donahue's coat. "What did you do, my lord?"

"Bloody hell." Donahue ran his hands through his hair. His words were a soft murmur. "I caught Farrington and sent in the summary as soon as the ink dried. I resisted foolishness. I suspect I am being watched to see if I warn him."

Wilhelm's eyes narrowed as he nodded. "You knew this was coming. As did Lord Farrington. I am sure he has a plan."

"Which will only work if he has warning." Donahue frowned. "If he is confronted in the House of Lords he will have no chance. He will be hanged."

"You are going to risk life, limb, and family to warn your friend?"

Donahue shook his head. "I am going to risk nothing. In truth, I am to bed. But I would like to see Miss Boswell in the morning. My mother has laid forth marching orders regarding Miss Brooke, which I would like to discuss with her."

"Is this truth, my lord?" Wilhelm asked.

"Mostly. Miss Boswell is also capable of getting to Farrington, which I am not. Ensure my mother's servants and you all gossip freely about a possible reconciliation between Miss Brooke and myself. We need to put those fools outside firmly on the right trail." Donahue pulled off his boots and tossed them haphazardly by the door.

"Are you sure Miss Boswell will be prompt? A delay could be problematic."

Donahue nodded. "Never underestimate that girl's curiosity, Wilhelm. Additionally, my mother has instructions for you regarding the reconciliation I mentioned." He passed over a piece of parchment covered in his mother's elegant cursive. "I am sure you can handle it."

Wilhelm looked it over and nodded. "With pleasure, my lord. You should sleep. Several busy days are ahead."

"No rest for the weary, eh?"

"That is wicked, my lord," Wilhelm answered with a smile. "Sleep well and wake."

Donahue let out a sigh of relief. Punctual Miss Boswell was on time for their ride. If he was not mistaken, she had ridden up from further on The Serpentine rather than from the direction he expected. The bright copper of her curls tumbled out from her bonnet, giving her a wild and free appearance. The emerald riding habit she was wearing was too rigid to ever look right on Miss Boswell, but her welcoming smile expressed her warmth better than fashion could ever hope to do.

He bowed the best he could from horseback. "You look lovely, Miss Boswell."

Large, uneven red patches appeared on Miss Boswell's cheeks. "You flatter, Lord Char—oh, pray pardon, Donahue."

His eyebrows drew together as he forced a smile. "Every time someone refers to me as Lord Donahue, I find myself looking for my father."

"That must be difficult."

Donahue was unaware of his frown as he replied. "Very. But life moves on. How are you?"

"I am adequate. The weather is lovely. The Devonshire ball was most excellent. Now, if we have covered the pleasant chit chat, might I ask why you invited me to ride?"

Donahue smiled at Miss Boswell's impatience. "Could I not seek your companionship?"

"You have never asked me to ride before, therefore, I find that unlikely."

Amusement colored his voice. "I asked you to ride due to your friendship with Miss Brooke. My mother has a proposition and I would prefer to garner your opinion on it before moving forward. Do you mind?"

At Miss Boswell's nod, Donahue set his horse to a walk and explained Lady Donahue's plan to sell the townhouse and to move to the country. He was only half paying attention to what he was saying, his true focus on the people in the park. Finally, he spotted the men watching them. Once he was sure of their location, Donahue was careful to make sure they got an earful of his plans for Miss Brooke. With great care he maneuvered Miss Boswell over to a narrow stone bridge in the park. They would be perfectly visible, but temporarily out of any earshot.

Donahue did not change his smile or any mannerism, "Miss Boswell, do not show any reaction or do anything out of the ordinary. We are being followed. The conversation about Miss Brooke is true but not why I asked you to ride."

"Am I ever glad of that! I was afraid you had gone senile. You told me the same bit about your mother thrice in a row!" Miss Boswell flipped her curls, her amber eyes flashing with excitement. "Who is following us? What is going on?"

"Shuush. Not so loud. Can I trust you, Miss Boswell? More importantly, can Farrington trust you?"

Miss Boswell's world stopped. "As God is my witness, Anthony can trust me. What is amiss?"

"You must to go to him as soon as you can and tell him he has been caught. Tell him I expect him to be exposed at Session today. He will be trapped if he goes to Parliament. Under no circumstances must you go straight from me to him." The serious words sounded odd coming from Donahue's jovial expression. She realized he was acting, trying to keep the same smile from when he was talking about Miss Brooke.

She bit her lip. "Session starts late today?"

"Two and thirty."

"It is still before ten. He should have time." Miss Boswell was already calculating.

"Except we need to ride around the park and continue to discuss my plans for Miss Brooke. I cannot be implicated in this, Miss Boswell. I cannot express how much I am trusting you."

"I would never betray Lord Farrington. Or you." The last bit was an afterthought.

"You have my gratitude." Donahue selected a path that would lead them close to a watcher.

Worry clouded Miss Boswell's sherry eyes. "What will happen to him?"

"He will escape. Or hang. If he is not caught, I suspect he will go somewhere very far away. Do not worry, Farrington is quite foxy." Donahue smiled again, his expression still not matching his words. "He is sure to have a plan."

"Is there anything else I should know?"

"A million things, but I do not have time to tell you any of them." Donahue shot her a stern look. "We expect Mr. Brooke to again refuse my suit but I care not about him. Miss Brooke, on the other hand, is likely to disbelieve my offer. Wilhelm is drawing up a document to alleviate any fears your friend may have…"

Miss Boswell only half listened as Donahue droned on and on about his latest ploy to marry Miss Brooke. Her mind was racing with intrigue and danger. Yet, no matter how interesting or exciting delivering a secret message was, her mind kept focusing on one thing. Donahue was sending her to banish Anthony from her life.

By the time she realized Donahue was attempting to excuse himself, Miss Boswell had worked herself into a full-fledged dither. She turned a brilliant scarlet in embarrassment at being discovered woolgathering and hastily returned his polite regards.

Donahue's closing comments urged her to see if Miss Brooke was receptive to resuming the engagement. She assumed it would thus be natural for her to follow his advice and go visit her friend at once. She begged a trot from the spoiled mare back to the Brooke townhouse, oblivious to the man scrambling to follow. Miss Boswell slid off her horse and handed the reins to a waiting groom before dashing inside. The man following her watched as she entered the domicile and left to report that Miss Boswell would cause no real trouble.

Miss Boswell pounded on the large oak door impatiently. The butler gave her a stern look for such unladylike behavior, but Miss Boswell paid the man no attention. She dashed in and started up the large curved staircase to Miss Brooke's room before skidding to a halt before Abigail. The older woman smiled kindly at her but continued to stand in her way. "Morning ma'am. Miss Brooke ain't up yet. I can wake her if you wait?"

Miss Boswell blew out an explosive sigh. How could Miss Brooke be asleep when there were such momentous things afoot? She nodded at Abigail and returned downstairs to impatiently pace the foyer. She made four or five circles before a footman appeared. "Miss Boswell?"

"Yes?" Miss Boswell looked inquisitively. The man came from the bottom floor, not the top, so it could not be a message from Miss Brooke.

"Mr. Brooke would like to know why you are making such a racket. He is in his study." The man gestured towards the little room by the kitchen.

Miss Boswell nodded and marched towards Brooke's study. She had not considered what she would tell him, nor had she finalized what she was going to do. Miss Boswell frowned at herself, her sherry eyes closing for a moment. She could not lose Anthony. He was worth any cost, any sacrifice. If he must leave, she would go with him. And if he rejected her, well, she would have to follow him.

Brooke's harsh voice cut into her thoughts. "Girl, you are standing in my doorway with your eyes closed. Get in here."

Miss Boswell blushed and scurried inside. The room was, as always, a disaster. She picked her way over maps and piles of paper before finding what she assumed was a chair. She poked at it once to make sure it was sturdy and not a rickety pile. Delicately, she sat. Still trying to compose her thoughts, Miss Boswell smiled at her best friend's father. "Good morning, Mr. Brooke."

"Good morning my behind, Miss Boswell." Miss Boswell hid a smile at his language. "What in God's green earth is going on?"

"Nothing," Miss Boswell blushed.

Brooke gave the young woman a flat look. "Nothing. Just for nothing you barged in and ran holes into my marble with your pacing? A suitor? An elopement? Nothing? What trouble are you girls up to?"

"Trouble? Me? I am not up to anything." Miss Boswell's blush crept further up her cheeks. Her ears were on fire.

He frowned at her. "Very well. You do not have to tell me. We shall have tea while you wait for Miss Brooke. Girl had a late night. She may be a while."

Miss Boswell bit her lip. Miss Brooke could not be a while. She had to talk to her about Donahue's nonsense before she could leave to warn Anthony. Miss Boswell watched with growing impatience as Brooke rang for tea. Farrington only had hours to escape and here she was drinking tea! And Donahue said he was going to hang. Hang! If she fled with him and got caught, would she hang too? Likely, she decided.

Brooke cleared his throat and Miss Boswell's blush flared onto her ears and neck. "Sorry, I was woolgathering."

Brooke's grizzled eyes narrowed as he reached for a cigar. "This behavior is worrisome, Miss Boswell. Are you in good humor? Is there anything you need to speak upon?"

He was pressing, Miss Boswell realized. Maybe he knew about Anthony! Donahue implied they were being followed. Could Mr. Brooke be in on it? She laughed nervously at her foolish conjectures. She reminded herself the gentleman was fretting over his daughter and whatever terrible thing was unfolding.

Miss Boswell forced herself to take a deep breath and tried to focus on the conversation at hand. "Alison is fine, sir. None of this involves her. Well, only marginally. The Divine Comedy of Donahue is not yet over. There is a new proposal in the works. His mother is apparently involved. And her latest dress is ready. The dressmaker has a lovely new ribbon Alison might like. Bright green." Mother Mary and Joseph, I am rambling, Miss Boswell thought.

The older man raised an eyebrow as she rapidly talked. He cut off the tip off his cigar as he answered, "Miss Boswell, either sip your tea and talk about the weather, or tell me what is bothering you. You know our house is here for you in any way you need."

"Am I that obvious?"

Crow's feet blossomed around his eyes as he smiled. "Yes. To be fair, I know you well. You are, after all, my daughter's best friend. I should bill you for lodging considering how often you are here during the Season."

"If I was to do a completely reckless and, well, unwise thing, would you still care for me?"

"I find it highly unlikely you could challenge my affection. But, I am fairly certain I would still be at least marginally fond of you nevertheless of the beehive you stir up." Brooke set his unlit cigar aside and leaned back in his chair. His girls had spent three uneventful Seasons of failed suitors and courtship in London. This Season was different. Miss Boswell was almost frantic, a state he had never seen her in before.

"That's good." Miss Boswell nodded. "Yes. Would you tell my father I do love him, and everything is fine? No matter what?"

"You should tell him yourself, dear." Brooke made an effort to relax. Miss Boswell would tell him what was wrong as long as he did not push too hard. "You will not perish tomorrow."

"No, I will not. But would you tell him, nevertheless?"

Brooke nodded. "I might be persuaded to mention those things to him. What reckless behavior did you have in mind?"

Miss Boswell ignored his question as if he hadn't even asked it. "If you had to escape London, and maybe chase after someone, how would you do it?"

Brooke made an effort not to groan. This, whatever it was, was clearly a disaster. "Are you chasing them to the country, or overseas?"

Miss Boswell bit her lip. "I do not know. Very far away is all I know."

"In that case I would take one of my shipping vessels. In your case, you will have to charter a ship. There is a fairly expensive service that handles such charters."

"And it keeps records too, does not it?"

"Now this is a clandestine chasing." Brooke gave Miss Boswell a stern look. "I do not believe I approve of this plan."

Miss Boswell raised her chin. "You cannot stop me."

"I see where my daughter got her stubborn streak since we have been in London. I spoke not of stopping you." Brooke picked his cigar back up and looked at it critically. "Now, Miss Boswell, if you trust me, you must tell me what is unfolding."

"No." Miss Boswell's lip flared in pain as she chewed on it again. "I truly desire too but I cannot. I am sorry."

"My dear, if you cannot tell me what is happening, tell me what you need."

Miss Boswell looked askew at the older man. "Pardon?"

He sighed and lit the cigar. "Brenda, whatever this reckless disaster is, are you going to do it? No matter the consequences?"

"Yes." Her voice rang firm and clear.

"You matter to my daughter. Therefore, you matter to me. And since you apparently are not even going to speak to your own father before making this piss poor decision, the matter appears to be in my lap. Now, Miss Boswell, who theoretically trusts me, what is it you need?"

"What if..." Miss Boswell paused, trying to think of what she could and could not say. "What if helping me was really bad for you? What if I was trying to—do something bad."

"Brenda, enough is enough. Tell me what is going on or I will hire Runners and find out on my own."

Miss Boswell bit a different part of her lip. The Runners would ruin everything. They would know her every movement. They would report she visited Farrington. They would likely be able to track her back to Donahue. This part of her lip hurt, too.

Brooke took a puff of the cigar and exhaled it with a scowl. "Brenda, I swear I will not betray your secret. But I must insist."

She looked at him. Her eyes were filled with tears. "I want to trust you. But…"

"Miss Boswell. I swear on Alison's love for me that I will not betray you. I have nothing greater. Speak."

Miss Boswell's will collapsed. "Lord Farrington has to escape London before Session starts at two and thirty or he will hang. I am going with him. No matter what he says."

Brooke took another pull of the cigar to hide his surprise. This was not at all what he was expecting. He thought it would be an elopement, or more likely, an attempt to break up an elopement. But Lord Farrington hanging? That seemed a bit farfetched. "Do you know why?"

Miss Boswell shook her head no, the tears starting to leak down her face.

"Brenda, are you sure? If he is to hang, then chasing after him, or going with him, condemns you as well. This is no light decision."

"I…" Miss Boswell wiped her nose on her sleeve. "I love him. I cannot lose him. I cannot. I will risk everything."

"Be clear you *are* risking everything. Your life included." Brooke grumbled inwardly. He had not even known Brenda was interested in his daughter's former suitor.

She rubbed her hands on her face and took a deep breath. The tears slowed. "I understand."

"If he is going to be denounced at Session then there is already proof against him. That means he is already being watched. His chances of escaping are poor, at best." Brooke's voice had only a hint of concern, a businesslike edge otherwise predominated.

"I have been assured Lord Farrington has an escape plan," Miss Boswell offered.

"Which we should assume has already been compromised. Girl, this is your life we are talking about here. You should have a better plan than assuming he has one." Brooke scolded.

"I…" Miss Boswell stuttered. "I have not known about this situation for long, Mr. Brooke. I feel you are being marginally unfair."

"Reckless does not have to equal stupid, Brenda. Nor does undertaking fast action."

Miss Boswell's eyes flashed. "Are you going to help me or insult me?"

"Both." He waved a hand at her in dismissal. "Go talk to your friend. Return here before you depart."

Brooke's voice grew stern. "I understand this is a hard command but tell my Alison nothing of this. I will not have your actions harm my daughter. Whatever your lord is hanging for will not tarnish this house."

Miss Boswell stood and curtsied. "Yes, Mr. Brooke."

She carefully lifted her skirts over the piles of papers on the floor and exited the room. She had butterflies in her stomach and thought she might vomit. What if she betrayed Anthony? Were there messengers being sent to Parliament right now? Before she had a chance to panic, a servant appeared to tell her Miss Brooke was awaiting. Miss Boswell tore up the stairs without a second thought. Time was of the essence.

Miss Brooke laughed as her friend tore through the doorway. Miss Boswell looked more askew than normal. Her riding habit was covered with twigs and her curls were pointing every which direction. "Good morn, Brenda. What brings you over in such a rush?"

Miss Boswell fought the urge to tell her best friend everything. Remembering her promise to Mr. Brooke, she forced an answering smile on her face and regurgitated the story Donahue told her. "A ride with Lord Donahue demands the rush!"

Miss Brooke's smile fell. "I see. And he is why you came?"

"Indeed. He is going to offer for your hand again. A formal offer!" Miss Boswell's mind was elsewhere. How was she going to get to Anthony's quickly? She could take a hack. But why was she going there?

"What difference will a formal offer make?" Miss Brooke crumpled into her chair, dejected. "He cannot marry me. We both know that."

"But his father died. Everything has changed!"

Miss Brooke shrugged, blond curls falling over her bluebell dressing gown. She gave up dark colors when Donahue gave up on her. "Everything has not changed, Miss Boswell."

"Oh, Ali. Can you not give him another chance?" Oh! Oh! She could be going to Farrington's to warn him Donahue was going to propose to Alison again! Perfect!

"No." Miss Brooke's pastel eyes filled with sorrow. "Losing him was more than I thought I could stand. I cannot live with these waves of hope and desolation. Mary's truth, Brenda, suddenly I understand why women swoon and have fits!"

"I advise for you to give him another chance. You love him. You told me once if I loved someone I would do anything for them and that I did not understand what love was." And now I do, Miss Boswell thought to herself. "Is that not true for you? Does doing anything for love include giving him yet another chance?"

"I did. I accepted him in poverty." Miss Brooke sat at the window and faced away from Miss Boswell.

"Will you consider it? Can he do nothing to mend your broken heart?" Miss Boswell prayed the servants were listening. She needed everyone to know why she was here.

"Brenda." Miss Brooke took a deep breath. "I love you but I simply cannot keep having these conversations."

She turned back around to face her friend and continued speaking. Her cheeks were dry, but Miss Boswell could see the rivulets where the tears had been. "I must beg your pardon, my friend. Perchance we could ride after luncheon? I am not feeling up to conversation right now."

Thank the Good God, Miss Boswell thought to herself. "If you wish, Ali. I am sorry to have upset you."

Miss Brooke smiled sadly. "Do not trouble yourself. I will be fine."

Miss Boswell walked over and gave her friend a kiss on the cheek. "You are my best friend. And an amazing one."

"That is an unexpected compliment." Miss Brooke smiled at her. "But very welcomed. Come after luncheon, then?"

"With certainty," Miss Boswell lied, "I would not miss it for anything."

Miss Boswell considered charging in to see Mr. Brooke but decided a second visit to the study needed a reason to defray suspicion. She knew the tiny, cramped room Mr. Brooke favored was almost impossible to spy on. The room shared a wall with the kitchen ovens, filling the room with heat and noise from the fire. Miss Boswell frowned and searched for an excuse to return to Mr. Brooke's office. Seeing Abigail inspired her.

"Abigail," Miss Boswell approached Miss Brooke's maid. "I worry about Miss Brooke."

Abigail nodded. "The cur broke her heart good."

"Take care of her, please?" Miss Boswell tried to make her face appear as if a thought dawned upon her. "I will speak to Mr. Brooke about it again. Maybe he will yield."

"It don't snow in August, ma'am. Suppose it would do no harm, though. Poor Ali is dreadful upset."

Miss Boswell agreed with Abigail and headed towards the small study. She knocked once and then let herself in. She looked around in surprise, as the room was empty. The cigar smoldered in the ashtray. Deciding to wait, she picked her way back to the pile that served as a chair. Soon, Brooke hobbled in behind her.

"That was fast," Brooke noted by way of greeting.

"I made her cry. I am quite certain I will feel most horrible about it soon."

"Anything worth knowing?" he asked as he maneuvered his way to his desk.

Miss Boswell shrugged. "I already told you. Donahue is coming to make a formal offer tomorrow. Apparently, his mother has decided to move back to the country so that they can sell the townhouse and Donahue can marry Miss Brooke. I was not really listening when he told me. I was slightly distracted."

"I will handle the whelp." Brooke held up his hand to cut off Miss Boswell's objections. He handed her a stack of papers. Miss Boswell folded them and placed them in her reticule without so much as a second glance. "I am giving you a gift. A fairly large one, so remember to thank me in your prayers. The Graceful Sea is moored on the east side of the wharf. She is one of my trading vessels and can leave with the tide. The dockmaster raised rates for moorage recently and I am known far and wide for my cheapskate nature. Leaving early will raise no eyebrows. When you say go, she goes."

Miss Boswell nodded. "I am grateful."

"How you get to the ship is up to you. Assume you are being followed. And if that boy of yours gets caught, you have to let him go. Yelling or chasing after him will do nothing. I will not defend or save you. Do you understand me?"

Miss Boswell nodded again.

"Now, go. You are rapidly running out of time."

"Can I borrow a carriage? Walking to Lord Farrington's will take forever."

Brooke gave her a flat look. "I am not keeping your horse while you go off and have an adventure. Do you wish to paint a sign of guilt upon my home?"

"Oh! I rode here! I forgot!" Miss Boswell blushed. "I have much on my mind."

"Pull it together, girl. You are smart enough to pull this off, but only if you pay attention. Now, go."

Miss Boswell stood, curtsied, and traversed to leave. She paused with her hand on the door. "Thank you ever so much."

"You girls and your endless gratitude. Get out," Brooke replied gruffly, "I have work to do. And do not gallop to that boy's estate. Walk."

Miss Boswell curtsied and left on quick, quiet feet.

CHAPTER XVII

Mr. Brooke's command to hold her horse to a walk reverberated through Miss Boswell's mind. She wanted to spring into action and race all the way to Farrington's domicile. When the bells tolled for noon, she almost leapt clear out of her skin. By the time she reached the sprawling grounds of Farrington's London home, she was a nervous wreck. She cast a suspicious eye about for the people watching the grandiose mansion but she found it impossible to tell normal individuals from potential covert operatives.

An outpouring of servants greeted her as she approached. One sharply dressed young man held her horse, while another held a dismounting block steady. Two more matching individuals appeared to steady her dismount. She thanked them all politely and headed to the front door. The entrance was, she noticed, in listening range of the street if she spoke loudly enough.

A servant in Farrington's livery promptly answered her knock. He gave her appearance a skeptical glance that made her wish that she wore Indian silks and diamond buckle shoes. Her sensible cotton riding habit suddenly felt out of fashion and dirty. Even the man's voice was condescending. "Can I help you?"

"Please inform Lord Farrington that Miss Boswell is calling." Miss Boswell raised her chin in challenge.

"I am sorry, madam, but My Lord Marquis is not at home."

Miss Boswell looked at the servant blankly. That was an unacceptable answer. Belatedly, it occurred to her he was getting ready for Session and his staff would turn away callers. "That cannot be. Please tell him I am here."

"I am sorry, madam, but without a reason I cannot do that."

Miss Boswell was suddenly filled with affection for the officious butler. She had been searching for a way to give any potential eavesdroppers a way to hear her why she was at Farrington's. "If I must. This is urgent." Miss Boswell pretended to drop her voice into a stage whisper, which sounded more like a shout. "Lord Donahue is going to formally offer for Miss Brooke again! Your master must be warned!"

The servant's disapproving look grew but he reluctantly stepped out of the doorway. "If you will wait in the foyer, I will see if His Lordship is at home."

Miss Boswell breathed a sigh of relief and stepped inside. Even if she had to scream like a banshee, she knew she would be able to get to Farrington now. She had experienced a moment of true fear when the butler reported he was not at home. Miss Boswell glanced around to see if anyone would be able to overhear conversations. There were servants everywhere! Keeping secrets in this house would be impossible. She paced the foyer and desperately plotted how she would convey his need to escape.

After what seemed like far too long, the self-important oaf returned and officiously informed her Lord Farrington would see her in the study. Miss Boswell practically flew up the stairs. She careened to a halt in front of an open door. Making an effort to adjust her effervescent curls, Miss Boswell took a deep calming breath.

The first step through the doorway was unexpectedly hard. When she entered, Farrington was standing at a window with his hands touching behind his back. The sight of him took her breath away. His dark hair was unclasped and lightly curling over his shoulders. He was only wearing a shirt and the breadth of his shoulders was clearly visible. He turned to face her, and a small smile creased his stoic facade. If Miss Boswell had any doubts previously, his welcoming smile banished them. She would follow this man anywhere. She took a deep breath and prepared to put on the act to save their future.

"My God, Anthony," Miss Boswell rushed across the room. "You will never believe what has happened!"

Farrington raised an eyebrow at her theatrical approach. "Good day, Miss Boswell. Pray tell, what great tragedy has occurred?"

"Lord Donahue is going to formally offer for Miss Brooke. Again!"

The slightest furrow of confusion appeared between Farrington's brows. "I find that unlikely. I spoke to him earlier this week. He was firmly set in his ways."

Miss Boswell shook her head and spoke in a conspiratorial voice. "His mother has decided to give her blessing to the marriage and is moving to the country so that the townhouse can be sold!"

Farrington looked at her. "Interesting."

"And you will never believe the best part!" Miss Boswell leaned up to whisper in his ear, much like a schoolgirl telling a secret. Her voice was serious and contained none of her previous bubbly nature. "I need to speak to you. Without any chance of being overheard." She came back off her tiptoes and resumed her presentation of melodramatic gossip. "Can you believe it?"

Farrington's eyes narrowed. "That is startling enough to call for a brandy. Would you join me for one?"

Miss Boswell bit her lip for a moment, wondering if Farrington understood the urgency. She nodded affirmatively. "A little restorative would be delightful."

"In my office." Farrington opened a door at the back of the study and ushered her into a room dominated by towering bookcases. He lifted a large brandy snifter off a shelf and frowned at it slightly.

"By your leave, I will obtain glassware." He stepped back into the study, picked up two glasses from a side table, and entered the office again, this time closing the door behind him. He raised an eyebrow at the sprightly woman next to him. "This room is lined with cork. You may say anything you need here."

"Good." Her manner became still and serious. "Lord Donahue sent me. He said you will hang if you attend Session today."

Farrington froze. "Were you followed?"

"Likely, but I went to Miss Brooke's first. We had a charming conversation about the proposal. Then, I came here to warn you."

"Does anyone else know?" The questions were coming rapidly, one after another, without any pause between.

"Mr. Brooke."

Farrington frowned. "That is one too many."

"He will not betray us. He says your escape routes are likely compromised. His ship, the Graceful Sea, is ready to sail now."

Farrington paused. "He is helping me?"

Miss Boswell's voice was quiet. "No. He is helping me."

Farrington placed a hand on her shoulder. "This means more to me than I can express. But I am afraid you must depart with all haste. I must away myself."

Miss Boswell steeled herself. "That is not possible. I am going with you."

"What?" Farrington looked at her in exasperation. "Miss Boswell, I have no time for your humor. Session is in less than two hours."

"If you have no time for my humor, then you have no time to argue. I am going with you, Lord Farrington, or I am chasing after you. It is as simple as that." Miss Boswell's voice was steady.

"Why?"

Miss Boswell took a deep breath before answering. "Because I love you, Anthony. I have loved you from the start. And my world is not good enough without you." A quiet dignity settled into her bearing as she exposed her heart.

Farrington paused. His body was still crunched in the position of a frightened animal ready to run. "Miss Boswell, while I admire you deeply but do not return the depth of your affection."

"I know. I have made no such requests. You asked why I was going with you. I answered. I have loved you for months with no expectation of it ever being returned. Why should you expect different of me now?"

Farrington's voice was rapid, a bit frantic, but his expression was steady. "Miss Boswell, I cannot be burdened with this now. I have to flee or perish. I cannot attend to both of these matters at once."

"I know." Miss Boswell was as calm as if they were discussing last week's ball. Rather than being the nervous wreck she expected, the conversation was easy. She knew what the outcome would be, and only needed to walk Farrington through the process. "That is why I will go with you and we can attend to this later. Wherever we go, all I ask is that I be your friend."

"Miss Boswell, I am not traveling on a ship with a woman who is not my wife. That would tarnish both our reputations beyond repair."

Miss Boswell raised an eyebrow and allowed herself a slight smile. "You are about to be hanged and you care about tarnishing reputations?"

"Miss Boswell, this is no…"

She cut him off. "No time for humor. I know. Then let me hurry this along. You cannot afford to leave me behind. For, Lord Farrington, I will chase you. I know the ship you will be on, I can guess by the name of your horse where you are headed, and I will move the earth itself to follow you. I have no experience in chasing a man across the ocean. I am sure I will make inquires and raise quite a racket as I do so. You can trust I will not betray you, but can you trust I will not be clumsy in following you?"

Farrington looked at her for a long moment. His expression was unreadable.

Finally, Miss Boswell could stand it no longer. She whispered, "What are you thinking?"

"I am making a hard decision," he whispered back.

"Betwixt which?"

"Murder and marriage." He sighed and hung his head. "And I find I cannot kill you, Miss Boswell. I will kill for my ideals but I cannot raise a hand against one who wants only to save me."

Both of Miss Boswell's eyebrows flew to her hairline. "That is a rather unexpected set of choices. You would kill me?"

"Apparently not. Will I kill a Bow Street Runner who tries apprehend us?" Farrington's gaze blazed. "Yes. I will. And you will be married to a murderer. Do you still wish to come with me?"

"Anthony," Miss Boswell sighed, exasperated. "I want to spend my whole life with you. I do not care what you have done or what you will do. I love you."

"Enough to force me to take you with me? To force me to marry you against my will?"

She answered with her heart in her sherry eyes. "Yes."

He grimaced slightly at her. "You are a hard woman, Miss Boswell."

"I am your woman."

"Yes." Farrington softened. "I suppose you are. I need you to get to Mr. Brooke's ship…"

"…the Graceful Sea…"

"…the Graceful Sea without me. Wear your most boring day dress, allow not a drop of your hair to show, and arrive without being followed. Tell the porter who works at the docks that you have gone shopping and are expecting packages. Have them sent to your quarters at once." He gave her a stern look. "Please do not allow me to suffocate."

"You will be in the boxes?" Miss Boswell clarified.

"Hopefully only one box," Farrington answered. "Once the boxes are on the ship, you may tell the Captain we can leave. This will be a hard life, Miss Boswell. Where we are going, I will be neither rich nor a lord. Are you sure?"

"Certain, Anthony. A million times over, I am sure." Miss Boswell smiled at him. "Mr. Brooke also gave me these." She pulled out the papers and handed them to him. "He told me not to lose them, but I have not yet had the moment to pursue them. They may be relevant."

Farrington's eyebrow inched ever upwards as he scanned the parchment. "I should be the one begging you to marry me, Miss Boswell. These are the ownership papers for the Graceful Sea and everything on it."

"Will not that implicate Mr. Brooke in our escape?"

Farrington shook his head negatively. "No, we will use these to prove ownership in the New World. England need never know. But it is quite a gift."

"He mentioned that." Miss Boswell smiled at Farrington, her spirits soaring. The future—if only they could survive the next few hours—suddenly looked glorious. "We should away. There is not much time."

"Aye. You remember your instructions?" He asked as he handed the papers back to her.

Miss Boswell nodded. "Are you sure you will be safe?"

Farrington nodded confidently. "I have been preparing for this moment for quite some time. I am going to send my other ship, the one I was planning on escaping on, out as a decoy. If we can get to Brooke's ship, and if he does not betray us, our safety should be assured."

"You think he will betray us?"

"No. The document you carry could be argued as proof he knew you were attempting to help me escape. He would be hard-pressed to argue how you came to own the Graceful Sea. His gift ensures you will not be a poor farmer's wife, but it also proves his intent to aid me."

Miss Boswell furrowed her brow. "Do you even know how to grow plants?"

"Not in the slightest." Farrington put his hand on the door and looked at her. "Are you ready?"

"One more question. When we get on the ship, will you tell me what all this is about?"

"All what is about?"

She gestured vaguely with her hand. "All of this. Why Parliament wants to hang you?"

Farrington's eyebrows rose yet again. "Pardon? You do not know? You are full of surprises. I will tell you everything when we are on board. After all, if you come with me, you should at least know why the Crown will hunt you. And, let me be clear, it *will* hunt us."

Miss Boswell's curls shook as she nodded. "Then we should be away."

Farrington nodded back and opened the door mid-word, "…ison is fond of making bad choices. There is nothing I can do to help either of them at this point."

Miss Boswell walked into the study. "But you are his friend. Should you not warn him she is going to reject him again?"

"Lord Donahue has heard plenty from me. As I told you, he banished me from his rooms less than a week ago. I am sorry, Miss Boswell, but there is nothing I can do."

"I thought you would at least try," Miss Boswell pouted.

"I thank you for your information, Miss Boswell, and I wish you an excellent day. I am afraid I must prepare myself for today's

Session of Parliament. By your leave?" Farrington bowed flawlessly at her.

Miss Boswell curtsied automatically. "Lord Farrington."

She almost squealed in joy as she walked out of the room, only to encounter a gaggle of servants in the hallway. Putting on her best fake scowl, she stalked through the hallways and towards the front door. The same detachment of servants helped her mount her horse. Grinding her teeth, she again forced herself to maintain a leisurely gate the whole way to her house.

The unhurried pace continued at her rustic townhome. She took her horse around to the stable and impatiently waited. A groundskeeper came over to help her dismount and take care of the animal. Miss Boswell let herself into the domicile and walked down a tapestry-filled hallway to her bedchamber.

Frowning, she considered her dresses. There was nothing she would consider plain or unassuming. Everything was either a bright color or a wild cut that caught her eye. She never dressed with the intent to be unnoticed. Finally, inspiration struck. Miss Brooke had long taken to leaving a gown or two at Miss Boswell's (as Miss Boswell had several gowns at Miss Brooke's). One of them was likely to be normal enough to blend in with Society. And, if there was a hat with it, she could hide her hair and be any noblewoman at all. Excited, Miss Boswell summoned a maid and quickly got dressed.

When they were finished, she dismissed the maid and walked around her room one last time. She placed all her pin money in her reticule and thought desperately of what else she should take. She packed the mourning locket with her mother's hair, her single strand of pearls, and the first dance card of hers that Anthony had signed, but could not settle on anything else. There were no memories of her current life that she wanted to take with her. The only thing she would truly miss was Miss Brooke. Her father was unlikely to notice she was gone. When he did he would likely be relieved he could return to the country.

She sent a note to Miss Brooke begging out of riding that afternoon. Donahue's formal proposal would hopefully distract Miss Brooke for a few days. Miss Boswell hated to deceive her friend, but Mr. Brooke was right, nothing could link Miss Brooke to Farrington's crime. Miss Boswell informed an uninterested maid she was going out for the afternoon and headed to the docks. The quality of the neighborhood decreased quickly on the long walk. Skittish, Miss Boswell decided to take a hack for the rest of the journey.

The docks were crowded, filled with burly men working on ships, screaming women selling bits of food, and urchins running throughout looking for something to steal. The hack driver reached out and cuffed a boy who ran close to the carriage.

"You, there. Which ship is the..." he looked back at his passenger. Miss Boswell whispered the name forward. "...Graceful Sea?"

The ragged boy looked about to object but the driver showed him a coin. The boy responded by pointing. "'Tall ship on the end, gov'nor." The Graceful Sea looked lovely to Miss Boswell, but she knew less about ships than she did about why she was fleeing the country in the first place. The Union Jack flapped proudly on its mast.

The hack took her as close as possible and sent another urchin to notify the ship of her arrival. The boy returned with two burly men.

Miss Boswell looked askance at the hack driver. "Is this precaution necessary?" She could not say she was trying to be clandestine but the extra attention highlighting her presence was unwelcome.

The driver nodded. "Docks are a rough place. Not the right place for a Lady of Quality."

She smiled at him, thinking of the reason she invented for being there. "They say the best selection of silks comes right off the boats."

"Yes, milady. These boys here will see you the rest of the way." The driver gestured at the large men waiting for her to exit, before holding out his hand for her fare.

Miss Boswell paid him and gingerly accepted help out of the hack. The two men both tipped their hats at her, silently escorted her onto the ship. A well-dressed workman approached Miss Boswell and offered her his hand. Well-dressed was about the kindest thing she could think about him. His lip had been split in an earlier conflict and his nose looked as if it was broken thousands of times. Hesitantly, she placed her hand in his. His rough calluses snagged at her satin glove. "Captain Zackary Parsons. Let us get you below deck, lass."

Miss Boswell quickly followed the slender man, grateful to be away from prying eyes. "Captain Parsons, I am expecting packages from my recent shopping trip. When they arrive, I would be grateful if they would be sent to my berth."

The Captain grinned. She grimaced as she noticed his jagged teeth. "Already arrived and delivered to your quarters, last I recall. Waiting only on you."

"Why, thank you." That sounded positive. Miss Boswell looked around at the dark hallway that led below.

"Down you go." The man gave her another frightening smile. "My bosun will show you the rest of the way."

Miss Boswell made her way down the dim staircase, where another man awaited her. He also smiled at her but, much to Miss Boswell's relief, he had most of his teeth and no major scarring. She smiled timidly back.

The bosun chuckled, "Don't let the Captain afear you. He's a might scary looking, but only 'cause he loves the fisticuffs. Best fighter this side of the Atlantic." There was a note of pride in his voice.

"He did not bother me at all!" Miss Boswell lied. "He looks quite fierce."

"He is, milady. But a good captain. We'll have an easy trip with him at the helm. Now, Mr. Brooke indicated we wanted to make good time out of the Pool of London. Tides in our favor, so we be leaving 'erelong. You need anything 'fore we are off?" The man gestured towards a small door at the end of the hallway.

"No, no. I am quite content." Miss Boswell gave him a timid smile. Things were much more intimidating now that she was on the ship.

"Aye, ask if that changes, milady. This be the owner's suite. You make yourself at home now. We'll let you know when we clear the harbor." He walked off with a half bow.

Miss Boswell took a deep breath and let herself into the room. The wood-paneled chamber was much more welcoming than the dark hallway outside. The room was small but not nearly as cramped as she expected. There was even a window on the back wall. Her inspection of the room came to an abrupt halt as she noticed Farrington sitting on the bed. His tan breeches and loose white shirt were more casual than anything she had previously seen him wear. His dark eyes were focused on her. She blushed brightly under his scrutiny.

He nodded at her in welcome and held out his hand. She bounded across the room without hesitation and put her hand in his. "I have a gift for you." His voice sounded as different as his new wardrobe. His low and warm cadence was music to her ears.

She smiled at him. Her reply was forgotten as she noticed blood by his ear. She tentatively touched the side of his head and he winced away. "Sweet Mary, what happened?"

"Someone took a shot at me while I was on the other ship." Farrington took her hand in his, removing it from its inquisitive poking of his recent wound. "The shot only grazed me. I am fine. I owe Donahue and Brooke a greater debt than I realized. There was a significant amount of surveillance placed upon me. I can only hope my ship and sailors escape the wrath of the Crown. My escape plans were not as flawless as I would have liked."

"I am sure they will be safe." He appeared unconvinced and she frowned at his worried expression. "And us? Are we safe now?"

"As far as I can tell, yes. Once we are on the high seas, we should be clear of any immediate danger. I had a few words with this captain of yours."

Miss Boswell made a face. "He is very…"

Farrington nodded in agreement. "Indeed, he is. Apparently, the Graceful Sea has seen its fair share of pirate activity. Your Captain

Parsons has fended them off quite successfully. His looks have suffered accordingly."

Miss Boswell thought about it and then smiled slightly. The ship swayed as it undocked. "That makes me feel better."

"I thought it might. Although…I have a speculation…"

"Really? What?" Miss Boswell leaned forward, interested.

"A ship Captain Parsons mentioned as a pirate had a similar name to a ship belonging to a certain Mr. West." Farrington gave Miss Boswell a significant look. "I do not think he gained all of those scars defending pirates."

She considered the information. "Good. Anyone who hurts Ali deserves to have his ships sunk."

"I am sure West's sailors did not share your viewpoint. But, no matter, if you are done interrupting, I still have a gift for you."

She smiled at him. "Consider me chastised."

Farrington took a deep breath and then stood himself. He reached out and pulled out Miss Boswell's hatpin before uncovering her head. Her copper hair spilled around her face and bounced onto her shoulders. It distracted him from the task at hand, "Has anyone told you how lovely you are?"

Miss Boswell blushed a brighter scarlet than her hair. "Alison. But it sounds much better coming from you."

"I should hope so." Farrington took another breath.

Miss Boswell noted his nerves. Rather than relieving her, it made the situation worse. What was he going to say?

His words cut off her speculation, "Miss Boswell. Brenda. We both know you forced my hand in this matter. While I wish you had not done so, I can honestly say I am not disappointed you are here." He took another deep breath. "I promise I will always be by your side. I will take on your fights. I will never forsake you. I am not an easy man and I am not in love with you, but I promise to try. I cannot even give you a church ceremony. But I can give you an oath before God to honor and care for you always. Is that enough for you?" He paused uncertainly. "It is all I have."

Miss Boswell smiled radiantly at him. "It is all I could have ever asked for and more."

He reached for a small box sitting on the bed next to him. "My grandmother's," he offered as way of explanation. Inside sat a grand

286

ring, consisting of a brilliant ruby encircled by diamonds. "Mayhap a bit ostentatious for our new life, but…"

Miss Boswell cut him off with a squeal of pure joy. "Oh, Anthony!"

He stopped talking and smiled at her. "You like it?"

"Almost as much as I like you."

Miss Boswell thrust her hand forward at him expectantly. Farrington frowned as he carefully maneuvered the ring onto her finger. "A bit big."

"I'll grow," came Miss Boswell's unconcerned reply. She looked into his brooding expression as the ship took them further out to sea. "Does this mean we get to live happily ever after?"

"Why yes, Marchioness Farrington, I believe it does."

CHAPTER *XVIII*

Miss Brooke spent her morning making calls and catching up on gossip. The end of the Season was fast approaching, and the marriage market was in full swing. She returned home with a headache from all the last-minute matchmaking and speculation. Days without Miss Boswell's company irritated. Apparently, Mr. Boswell had fallen ill and she did not trust anyone else to nurse him. Miss Brooke felt guilty about her annoyance at her friend for being a dutiful daughter, but Miss Boswell's company would have been much improved the day.

Miss Brooke walked in her bedroom door to find several of the maids impatiently waiting for her arrival. Abigail abruptly ushered her to the vanity. With only the briefest greetings, Miss Brooke felt her hair being adjusted and dress straightened.

"Abigail, good grief, what is going on?" The rushed touch-up flustered Miss Brooke.

"Gossip came this morn' that Lord Donahue is coming. Bringing his mother and everything. His man came and told all the servants to peek in on the encounter. Boy claims it be juicy rich gossip." Abigail tightened Miss Brooke's stays another inch. Miss Brooke grabbed the desk momentarily afraid she would faint.

"That is tight enough, Abigail. Lord Donahue has seen me plenty of times." Miss Brooke frowned at her hands. "He has already rejected me. What more could he want? Why should I dress up for him now?"

"Shush, miss. I already chattered too much. They'll be here soon. I was worried you'd not make it back in time. Right disaster that have been!"

Miss Brooke nodded at Abigail's prattle, no longer listening to the maid's words. Abigail's reactions made no sense. The maid's feelings seemed to have changed regarding Donahue. After all, it had been Abigail who warned Miss Brooke Donahue was seeking her only for her dowry, it had been Abigail who told her how poor he was, and it had Abigail who repeatedly urged caution and not to be at Donahue's beck and call. Something was afoot. The servants knew more than they were telling.

She turned to query Abigail when a loud, booming sound echoed throughout the residence. Miss Brooke needed a moment to identify the doorknocker, as it was operated with more force than she ever heard before. She quickly jumped to her feet, but Abigail motioned for her to wait.

Donahue's voice, cold and imperious, carried up the stairs. "I will speak with Miss Brooke."

Miss Brooke could hear the butler give a polite reply and scurry off. Miss Brooke walked into the hallway so that she could better eavesdrop. She was slightly surprised to see many of the house servants clustered in the hallway and attempting to peer into the foyer below. Miss Brooke cleared her throat and the gaggle disbursed, embarrassed.

The footman crested the top of the elegant staircase and bowed at Miss Brooke. She nodded in acquiescence and he returned downstairs. She waited until the footman informed Donahue that she would see him and then counted to forty. Donahue must not think she had been waiting.

As Miss Brooke stepped onto the top landing of the stairs, the library door burst open and her father stormed out. It was like the opera, Miss Brooke thought. The players were all perfectly placed. On either side of Donahue stood his brother and mother. His manservant, Wilhelm, was standing behind in the shadows. Her father was entering from stage right. The house servants clustered in alcoves, providing the chorus. Her father's bellow cut her comparison short, "Lord Donahue, what are you doing here? You are not welcome in my home."

The lovely elderly woman answered before Donahue had the chance. "Forgive the garish intrusion, Mr. Brooke, but our family humbly request a moment of your time."

Brooke bowed. "Lady Donahue. My apologies and sympathy on your loss. Yet neither your request nor circumstances change my stance on this man. I want him removed." Brooke looked over to his footmen. They leaned forward ominously.

Donahue stepped forward and spoke to Brooke without looking at him: "After a moment."

His gaze was focused on the top of the staircase where Miss Brooke was watching the show. She was radiant in heather muslin with her hair piled in graceful waves on top of her head. A single strand of golden hair fell, curved around her neck and forced his eyes to the upper hemline of her dress. Donahue bowed to the glorious creature in front of him. Miss Brooke did not so much as incline her head.

"Miss Brooke, you said once you would marry me if I had nothing. My duty forbade my acceptance. My father," Donahue gestured slightly at his mother, "was alive and required care. I could not abandon him. Forgive me."

Miss Brooke gave no indication she heard but Donahue continued nevertheless. "The situation has changed. My father no longer has earthly cares. My family reminds me there is more to this world than wealth and power. I have no funds and only fleeting political power. In truth, I still have nothing. But I love you, Miss Brooke."

Donahue paused, the words hiding in his throat. His carefully prepared speech fell apart on him. "And, and, I would like it, very much, if you would, once again, consent to be my wife."

Brooke cut in, "You will not see a hapenny of her inheritance no matter what disgusting hovel you drag her to."

The taller man to Donahue's left spoke. Anderson's normally flippant expression was serious. "There are more important things than money, Mr. Brooke. My brother loves your daughter. That is worth all of the spices in India."

Brooke shook his head. "You have played this song and dance before. I know how it ends. Get out."

Donahue was still staring at Miss Brooke. He had not moved since he asked for her hand in marriage. Wilhelm stepped forward. "Good sirs, forgive me for being bold. I have here a document that may relieve Mr. Brooke's concerns. This document outlines the liens Lord Donahue is willing to put on his property and investments. We propose quite drastic consequences if Lord Donahue fails to marry Miss Brooke at the proposed Christmas Day wedding."

Wilhelm handed the document to a nearby servant but his eyes remained on Miss Brooke. He bowed deeply as she lowered her gaze to examine him.

"Is this true?" They were the first words Miss Brooke spoke since the Andersons had arrived. "Wilhelm?"

Wilhelm bowed again. "Yes, mistress. The Dowager Countess assumed you may have difficulty accepting yet another proposal from her son. We offer liens on our property as reassurance."

Miss Brooke's gaze found her father. "Father? Is this true?"

Brooke glanced up from the document he was reading. "It appears to be as they say. But this changes nothing. You do not have my approval to marry this man and that is final."

Miss Brooke curtsied at her father in reply and slowly descended the stairs to end in front of Donahue. She looked at the man she loved with her heart in her eyes. Her smile was as bright as the sun she answered her father, "Then you will have an extremely wealthy granddaughter."

A radiant smile lit Donahue's face as he gathered Miss Brooke in his arms and twirled her around. He kissed her soundly on the lips and placed her lightly next to him facing the assembled household. Wilhelm winked over to Abigail and the two of them lead the servants in a round of applause. From behind all the uproar, unnoticed in the sea of excitement, Brooke allowed himself a small smile.

Donahue was quick to insist on taking the traditional carriage ride that would re-announce their engagement. He placed her in the carriage he borrowed from Collins and climbed next to her. Taking the reins, he waited for his brother to mount up. Their mother had bullied Anderson into providing an appropriate escort. He would ride behind the carriage and give the newly engaged couple a semblance of privacy. Anderson gave Donahue an approving nod and the three of them were off. Wilhelm and Lady Donahue would settle the affairs of the marriage with Brooke and return to the townhouse later.

Miss Brooke leaned her head on Donahue's broad shoulder. She let loose a happy sigh. "Odd the sky is cloudy today. The day you left me it was vivid blue. I suspect that means it will rain on our wedding day."

"Because the weather is backwards from our moods?" Donahue smiled at her. "Then it will not rain, it will hail, lightening, and be the worst storm London has ever seen. Speaking of, do you mind if we are wed at my country estate?"

"Not at all. Is there a reason why?"

"My mother needs a task while finishing out the Season in the country. I am hopeful planning the wedding will keep her distracted from the recent troubles within the family."

Miss Brooke nodded agreeably. "We will be wed on Christmas Day?"

"Unless you object? My Mother claims Christmas is a fashionable time for weddings. She desires us to have an *event*."

"As much as I would also love to have a large gathering, I admit I am concerned about waiting five months. You will likely find a way to bankrupt yourself again!" Miss Brooke's cheek twitched at the joke.

Donahue laughed easily. "Indeed. I admit to willingly suffering through poverty, if you are my cure."

He turned the horses towards Hyde Park, preparing to make the late afternoon loop that would inform the Polite World that Lord Donahue and Miss Brooke were again engaged. They barely turned onto the main strip when a man in the Palace of Winchester's uniform rushed towards the carriage.

"Lord Donahue, you are needed at Parliament." The man panted for breath.

Miss Brooke looked at Donahue in alarm. "Robert, what is going on?"

Donahue sighed and ran his hand through his hair. "The matter is complicated. I must away, my love."

"Away? Now of all times? The drive, the re-engagement, and…" Miss Brooke's words trailed off as she looked at Donahue with confusion. "Can it not wait?"

The liveried man shifted his weight from foot to foot as Donahue shook his head at Miss Brooke. "No."

Creases furrowed her brow as she nodded agreement. "Pray, then, at least tell me why you must go?"

There was a pause and the messenger scuffed his feet again. Frowning, Donahue yielded. His voice was clipped and concise as he began to descend from the carriage. "Lord Farrington has been found a traitor to the Crown. He is currently missing. As I am familiar with the traitor, I am leading the hunt against him. I can only suspect something new has occurred."

Miss Brooke's mouth flew opened. "Anthony a traitor? Impossible! You must be mistaken."

"I assure you, Alison, I am not." Donahue turned and gestured. Anderson rode up promptly. "Michael, I must return to Parliament. Will you see the lady home?"

Anderson nodded. "Take the horse. You will make better time with him." He directed his attention to the man in livery before them. "Tell North that Donahue is on his way. Go."

The man departed at a run. Donahue turned his attention to his betrothed. "I am sorry, Miss Brooke. We can do this…" Donahue considered his schedule with a frown, "some other time?"

She nodded absently. "Lord Farrington cannot be a traitor. That makes no sense. They must be wrong."

"I wish that were true." The horse flicked its ears as its riders changed. Donahue continued, "I truly must go. I will return to your side as soon as the Crown allows. Forgive me?"

"Without pause or question. Have you known long?"

He paused, gathering the reins tightly in his hands. The horse pawed at the cobblestones impatiently. "I have suspected for most of this Season but confirmed his treason two days ago. The King himself wants Farrington hanged." Donahue half bowed at her again. "I must away."

Miss Brooke gave Donahue a little wave with her fan as he trotted off through Hyde Park. She turned her attention towards the new driver of the carriage. "They are really putting Lord Donahue in charge of hunting Lord Farrington? Are they not best of friends?"

Anderson smiled a bit mockingly. "You do not yet know my brother's sense of duty. If anyone will catch Farrington, it will be him. Lord North's logic in appointing him to the task is sound. My brother knows how Farrington thinks, knows his estates, and found the evidence to convict Farrington. He even wrote the report stating Farrington's guilt."

"Donahue brought charges against his best friend? That is— wretched." Miss Brooke's unhappiness grew the more she considered. "I could never do that."

Anderson shrugged as he urged the horses forward. "Donahue views the world simply: country, family, and then friends. Where do you wish to head? I suspect you do not wish to take a turn in the park with me." He smiled playfully at her. "Although, think of the gossip!"

"Rumor has it you are quite the rake." Miss Brooke smiled wanly back. She was uncertain what to think regarding Farrington but was determined not to let the news ruin her ride.

"A pristine woman like yourself should not consort with the sort of people who know such things." Anderson slouched into the backrest.

"Collins told me such, if you must know."

"See? Trouble of the worst sort," Anderson shot back.

Miss Brooke shook her head at the whimsical nature of the man beside her. "If you do not mind, I would like to call upon Miss Boswell's. If anyone should know of Lord Farrington's betrayal, it would be her. The three of us will be able to ride in the park without comment."

Anderson grandiosely removed his hat and inclined his head from his slouched position. "I am at your leisure. I do not suppose this friend of yours is attractive?"

Miss Brooke hit Anderson with her fan.

The ride to the Boswell townhouse was uneventfully pleasant. Miss Brooke was forced to admit Anderson had an excellent hand with the horses, even if he drove a bit more dangerously then she preferred. When they arrived in front of the old estate, the young rake wrinkled his nose. "It looks like something we would own."

Miss Brooke looked at him in disbelief. "Be polite."

He smiled at her. "Never. Now, wait here while I fetch your friend."

Anderson handled the unusual household with ease, gesturing for a gardener to hold the horses. Staring off into dismal sky, Miss Brooke allowed herself to be happy. She and Donahue would finally be wed. The only dark cloud was Lord Farrington. Poor Brenda. She would be crushed.

Anderson returned to the carriage with a concerned countenance. Without speaking, he pulled himself up and set the horses off at a trot. Miss Brooke waited a moment for him to speak and after being met only with silence inquired, "What has transpired? Where is Miss Boswell?"

"Miss Boswell, according to her staff, is with you. Rather than argue with them, I decided it was politic to accept their answer and leave," Anderson replied.

"But Miss Boswell is not with me," said Miss Brooke.

"I know." Anderson was also frowning, catching his lower lip between his teeth. "They say she rode with you yesterday afternoon and spent the night at your townhouse as is her custom."

"No, she canceled riding with me yesterday. I have not seen her since she warned me of the proposal." Miss Brooke blushed slightly.

"Do not fret. I did not hear you betray your friend for gossiping about my brother." Anderson was now fully chewing on his lower lip. "I have a sinking feeling. You mentioned being friends with the Stantons?"

Miss Brooke fluttered her fan to indicate uncertainty. "I would not say friends but we are well acquainted. They think I should marry Lord Donahue, and Lord Stanton seems quite fond of Miss Boswell."

"Then we will go there. They will know what is going on."

"Why would they know what is going on?" Miss Brooke asked. Not only was her life a constant farce but also the cast of characters was much too large. Turbulence required privacy or it grew to scandal.

"They know everything," Anderson confided. "Collins was the nosiest child imaginable and the creature he married is worse. If something happens in Polite Society, they know about it."

"You sound like you dislike them."

Anderson shook his head no with a large grin. "I happen to quite enjoy Collins. Do you know the tale of the time Robert broke Collins' leg?"

"No, I do not believe either of them has."

"Then let me enlighten you." Anderson animatedly told a story from their youth. They arrived at the Stanton home slightly before the end of the story. Anderson was still regaling her when they were seated in the parlor and Collins arrived.

"God's teeth, Michael! You are not telling that awful story again?" Collins exclaimed by way of welcome.

"With gusto. It is a favorite." Anderson replied. "We were at the part where you promise Donahue anything, anything at all, if he would go get your parents."

"And you suggested I be his slave for a week. Yes, I know." Collins' eyes narrowed as he frowned at Anderson. "I was there."

"Miss Brooke was not." Anderson cheerfully replied. "By the by, there is new excitement."

Collins sat on the cream couch. "Is there not always? Elizabeth will be here shortly and we can all discuss what we know. Until then, sherry?"

Miss Brooke accepted the sherry gratefully. She was in sore need of a restorative. Anderson looked askew at the offer. "Do you have anything stronger?"

"You never change, do you?" Collins rang for a servant and gave quiet instructions.

"That is a false statement. This lovely lady was in my keeping for at least an hour and I have yet to ravish her." Anderson flashed his devil-may-care smile at Miss Brooke.

"Michael, she is your brother's former intended," Collins noted with exasperation.

"Tsk, Collins, so behind in gossip! Current intended," Anderson corrected.

"No!" Collins looked between the two with amazement. "Tell me."

"My mother decided it was time to step in..." Miss Brooke stopped listening as Anderson began telling Collins the tale of her most recent engagement. She fought down her rising irritation. They came here for answers but all they were doing was gossiping and drinking.

Miss Brooke was quite upset by the time Lady Stanton entered the room. Lady Stanton took one look at her and ignored the two men all together. She poured herself a glass of sherry and refilled Miss Brooke's.

"Thank you," Miss Brooke replied automatically. "Lady Stanton, what is going on?"

Collins looked at the sound of Miss Brooke's voice and spotted his wife. "Elizabeth, you will never believe, Miss..."

Lady Stanton cut him off with a curt wave of her hand. Her full attention was focused on Miss Brooke. Lady Stanton started rattling off information.

"Lord Farrington has been declared a traitor to the Crown for financing the rebellion in New England. Lord Donahue is in charge of the investigation and has most of the harbor shut down. The Runners and Guard are everywhere. Miss Boswell is missing. There is no trace of her. Your household reports seeing her on her way to Farrington's in the late morning. It is assumed she is with him." Lady Stanton looked over at Collins. "Did I forget anything?"

"Miss Brooke and Donahue got re-engaged," Collins answered.

Lady Stanton snorted. "Poor timing. What would have once been gossip worthy of inclusion in Society's letters is going to be completely overlooked."

"Pardon?" Miss Brooke's confused voice cut in. "Miss Boswell is with Lord Farrington? You think—but. I am not even sure where we think Lord Farrington is."

"He is missing. Either he went to ground here in Town, or he managed to escape before the blockade of the harbor." Lady Stanton answered promptly.

"Rumor in Parliament is he escaped on one of his ships. The Royal Navy is chasing it now." Collins added.

"And Miss Boswell is on that ship?" Miss Brooke slowly pieced together the puzzle.

Collins nodded. "Love causes drastic action, my dear. Too bad. I was fond of that girl."

"Why is it too bad, Lord Stanton?" Miss Brooke took a large gulp of her sherry.

"Unless she was kidnapped, which seems highly unlikely, she has thrown her lot in with the traitor. Unless the ship surrenders, they will likely sink it without a second thought." Collins pouted excessively. "Which is, indeed, too bad. Farrington made his bed. Miss Boswell was caught up by a desire to be in it."

Miss Brooke let out a whistling breath between her teeth. "We have to do something. We have to help Miss Boswell."

There was an uncomfortable silence after Miss Brooke's proclamation. Miss Brooke looked back and forth between the three of them. Finally, Collins spoke. "Miss Brooke, this house stands with Lord Donahue. Lord Donahue has declared Lord Farrington a traitor. If Miss Boswell is with him of her own will, there is nothing we can do."

"My affianced doomed my best friend?" Miss Brooke put her sherry down.

Anderson nodded. "And his own best friend."

Miss Brooke was staring at the Stantons in horror as the conversation from the picnic returned to her. Suddenly, it became clear the discussion of Lord and Lady Stanton's hypothetical affair was an allegory for Donahue's loyalty between Farrington and the Crown. Miss Brooke leaned back in her chair and took a long look at the ceiling. The world was complicated.

"What do I do now?" she asked the room.

There was an incomprehensible wave of chatter as all three of them attempted to answer at once. Anderson claimed control of the conversation by slamming his brandy glass firmly on the table. Liquid spilled everywhere but he ignored it. He unflinchingly met Miss Brooke's gaze, "You support my brother. Unconditionally."

"Even though he contemned Miss Boswell?" Miss Brooke asked as Collins nodded agreement with Anderson's statement.

Lady Stanton shook her head. "He did not condemn Miss Boswell. He condemned Farrington. Miss Boswell chose to link her fate to Farrington's. Do you blame Lord Donahue for that?"

"I suppose not. But it does not make me happy."

Collins looked at Miss Brooke with a serious expression. "Miss Brooke, none of this makes any of us happy. We all cherish Miss Boswell. But, we must play the cards we have been dealt."

"For the record," Anderson cut in, "I have never met Miss Boswell."

"Silence, Anderson." Collins answered without looking at him.

Miss Brooke picked up her sherry and took another large swallow. "What do I do tonight?"

"Tonight?" Lady Stanton seemed surprised by the question. "Tonight, we do what we do best. We go to a ball! We gossip. We allow you to be seen, to make it clear you support Lord Donahue, and know nothing about Miss Boswell's actions."

"Lord Donahue will certainly miss the start of the event, if not the whole thing. The young Anderson can escort you," Collins added dryly. "He has to be good for something."

Anderson glared at Collins before turning to give Miss Brooke an elaborate mock bow. "I would be honored."

Miss Brooke inclined her head automatically in return. "Robert will not attend?"

"We cannot plan on him." Collins replied. "Parliament is in session. There is no way of knowing when he will be free."

Anderson stood and offered Miss Brooke his hand, "I hope, my brother's most glorious flower, I can provide a suitable escort."

Ignoring Anderson's ridiculous statement, Lady Stanton nodded with satisfaction. "Good. Mr. Anderson, you will meet us here at nine and we will pick up Miss Brooke by ten. This is one ball we wish to be relatively on time for."

Lady Stanton, Miss Brooke thought, looked much like a preening bird excitedly hunting a mate. Her support was welcome, but, Miss Brooke thought with irritation, Lady Stanton did not have to look so pleased at the dramatic farce life had become.

Dressing for the ball was difficult. Miss Brooke could not settle on the right dress and it was lonely. Miss Brooke had always taken Miss Boswell's company for granted. She found herself attempting to ask Brenda's opinion on a brooch or how high she should wear her hair.

As Miss Brooke made the final turn in front of the long, polished mirror, the terrible realization her best friend was likely gone forever sunk in. She shut her eyes and prayed. If Miss Boswell loved Farrington half as much as she loved her Lord Donahue, then Miss Brooke understood her decision. Understanding did not stop the selfish part of her from wishing her vivacious friend had stayed. Her step was heavy as she made her way down the stairs to meet Anderson.

He was waiting for her in the foyer, examining the art with an absent eye. His breeches were cut tightly to show off his firm thighs. In fact, Miss Brooke thought with slight disapproval, all his clothing showed off his tall, lithe frame without care for propriety. He would never be a member of Almack's, she thought with a sniff. Then again, she corrected herself, neither was she, so perhaps she should not be so high on the instep. Anderson flashed her his rakish smile, which advertised the fact he enjoyed, and used, the female form. As his eyes examined her, Miss Brooke felt herself fighting a small blush. Those bright eyes were both critical and approving. Even his gaze managed to be improper.

Anderson, in truth, was having asexual thoughts. Miss Brooke looked exactly as he wished the next Countess of Donahue to appear. She was slightly out of fashion in navy with woad blue trim. Her gown was dark, dashing, and matched his brother perfectly. The strands of blue beads woven through her wig set her apart from the flowers and feathers that adorned most of the heads of the *ton*. The colors of the gown gave her a mysterious air that would only help fuel the gossip.

Anderson worried as he noticed how drawn she looked. Hopefully, she was prepared for the stress of the next few days. With his brother busy, Miss Brooke would take the brunt of Society's curiosity and gossip. Anderson promised himself that he would be vigilant in supporting the frail beauty. At least, he corrected himself, until one of his mistresses showed up.

Watching Miss Brooke's perfect descent down the stairs moved Anderson's thoughts away from a certain young widow's breasts and back to the matter at hand. He bowed, she curtsied, and they were out the door without a word. The normal polite chitchat seemed unneeded. The Stantons' silver carriage waited outside. Anderson helped Miss Brooke in and instantly the chatter of Lord and Lady Stanton overwhelmed her. She allowed the latest gossip to wash over her as she mentally prepared for the evening.

Arriving on time for a ball was a new experience for Miss Brooke. The crush of carriages was almost nonexistent and it was possible to hear one's own thoughts in the main room. Even with the slight attendance so early in the evening, it took no time at all for parts of Miss Brooke's group to form around her. Any earlier exclusion faded away as everyone sought a piece of the latest gossip. She found herself quickly regaling them all with the narrative Lady Stanton told her—Farrington was missing, most likely on a ship, the Royal Navy was in pursuit, and Miss Boswell was also absent.

The story quickly spread throughout the room and, by the time Miss Brooke was tired of discussing the subject, the ball was underway. Miss Brooke noticed Mr. West watching her as was his custom, but she could not dredge up the energy to be concerned. The event that dominated her nightmares was less pressing than the disappearance of her best friend.

Anderson twirled her through a dance, and her friends were filled with conversation, but the ballroom seemed empty. Miss Brooke tried to pretend to herself that Farrington and Miss Boswell were merely in the card room or lost in the crush on the dance floor, as had happened so many times before. Things were different now,

Miss Brooke reminded herself. Her grief welled as she took in Miss Boswell's empty spot next to her.

The bright colors of the assembled gaggle did not match her mood. Anderson noticed the sheen in her eyes and was kind enough to escort her to the back balcony overlooking the gardens. He stood off to the side in the shadows of the veranda while the sliver of light from the French doors fell like a spotlight on Miss Brooke. The summer night was humid and stifling, filled with the smell of dying flowers.

Anderson frowned at her pensive behavior. "Do you wish to talk?"

Miss Brooke shook her head negatively. "There is nothing to say. The ball feels empty, reflecting the hole in my life will never again be filled."

Anderson raised an eyebrow as he glanced back into the overflowing room they had left. "If you say so. While I understand what you mean, I do not know how you could even distinguish one person from another in that throng. I have not seen an event this packed in years."

"That is only because you have been on a ship." Miss Brooke retorted with an attempt at a smile. "The Haven ball at the beginning of the Season was better attended and everyone was at the King's Birthday. This place is small. It makes the crush feel larger."

"I am surprised you found an empty berth." Anderson gestured around them.

Miss Brooke shrugged. "I am not. There are always empty alcoves at these events. The more desperate the family is to marry of their daughters, the more dark corners exist. The Conyers have nothing but daughters in that windy haunt of theirs. I am sure they would be pleased to marry off several of them this Season."

"Several?" Anderson's response sounded amused. "Prolific."

"There is a set of twins and a younger daughter here this Season." Miss Brooke stared over the grounds, paying as little attention to the conversation as Anderson was.

"Twins, huh? I should go introduce them to an alcove or two."

Miss Brooke swatted Anderson with her fan. "Do not be crude."

"Yes, Mother dearest."

She frowned at Anderson. "Do not imply I am being a prude for objecting to your—whatever that was."

Anderson half bowed and turned his gaze over the gardens as well. "Do you intend to stay out here long?"

"I apologize, am I boring you?"

He nodded. "I do not mean to be unfeeling, but I would like to return to the ball. I return to sea in a few weeks."

Miss Brooke waved him away with her fan but he remained.

"Perchance we can compromise? You seem to need some quiet."

"I also mean no offense, but I cannot feed the gossips tonight. A whisper in the wrong ear could mean grave consequences." Miss Brooke hugged her arms around herself as if she could physically suppress her grief.

"If you do not mind, I shall stand right inside the doors. Then I will still be in eyesight, but not underfoot." Anderson gestured to the French doors next to them. The wrought iron frame held a slightly smoky glass through which the dancers in the ballroom twirled.

Miss Brooke considered for a moment and then nodded. "I would appreciate a moment. I shall be inside shortly." She wrinkled her nose. "So much has happened so fast."

"I understand." He gave her a reassuring smile. "I am not quite as callous as I may appear."

"I do not find you callous at all." She tried to match his smile. "In fact, I find you oddly charming."

Anderson winked at her. "Then perhaps I shall find those twins and attempt to convince them of the same thing."

Miss Brooke shook her head in wry amusement as the young rake disappeared back into the ballroom. She stared out over the gardens and allowed her distress over Miss Boswell's fate to wash through her. Miss Brooke paced into a dark corner of the overlook so no one would see her sorrowful mood. She should be happy, she was engaged to dear Donahue, but it was difficult to imagine a world without her best friend.

She could not bring herself to wish Miss Boswell safe wherever she was. The closest Miss Brooke could muster was a strong desire for her friend back. Disappointed in herself, Miss Brooke tried to return to the ball. She collided into a solid figure in the darkness. The bright colors of the ball hid the figure's face.

The man spoke. The voice was familiar. It tormented her in nightmares she never admitted to having. "Why the big sigh, pretty puss?" West asked.

"Get away from me." Miss Brooke looked for a way around him. His large frame blocked most of her view.

West walked closer, towering over her. "No. And do not bother looking for your hero. He left you to the wolves."

"That's fine," Miss Brooke responded much more confidently than she felt. "I have a stand-in."

West's smile crept into his voice, warm and malicious. "The youth by the door? He chased after the first pair of comely ankles that swished by." He held something in front of her. Miss Brooke had to squint to make it out in the darkness. It was the key for the French doors. "We are quite alone."

Miss Brooke tried to take a step back, but her heel caught the railing of the balcony. "What do you want?"

"I think you can figure that out, Alison." He stepped closer. His putrid breath washed over her face. She was surprised it did not have the slightest trace of alcohol on it. Looking up, she could see his eyes were bright and clear.

"But why?" Miss Brooke realized she was trapped, but hoped she could buy time, or, by some miracle, talk her way out of this.

"Eighty slaves, pretty puss." West's expression was grim. "Eighty slaves 'rescued' in the night. Six ships sunk of the coast of the Carolinas in two months. A mining venture collapsed due to lack of funding. I could go on, if you would like."

"What does that have to do with me?" Miss Brooke protested.

West reached out and pulled a powdered curl down from Miss Brooke's elaborate coiffure. "At first, I had no reason to think it did. But then I noticed striking coincidences. Your father bankrolled the mining venture and pulled out. That one was obvious. Tax agents

Donahue indirectly controls seized an entire transport of sugar. And most damning, Farrington's ships were seen near Fort Mosé days after my slaves vanish." West wrapped the curl around his finger. "Seems like a pretty little girl is calling in favors and trying to direct my downfall. Could not leave well enough alone, hmmm?"

Miss Brooke shivered at his tone. "What do you want?"

West released the curl and watched it bounce. "Your lack of denial is an admittance of guilt." He closed the rest of the distance. There was not more than a handbreadth between them. "You are punishing me, puss. Stealing my goods, drowning my men, scaring investors away, using your father and your boys against me. Why, Alison?" He leaned down to whisper in her ear. His breath felt like moldy, wet parchment. "What are you punishing me for?"

She defiantly raised her chin. "You know quite well."

His eyes narrowed as he pulled back to look her in the eye. "But, you see, Alison, you are punishing me for something I did not do. If I am to be punished, I shall at least taste the forbidden fruit. If I am to be a villain, then, by God, I will earn my villainy."

Miss Brooke spent the time during his monologue turning her fan around in her hand. As West leaned in to smash his lips against hers, she stabbed the bone spokes into his face. The fan flew out of her hand as West smashed her against the stone. His warm blood dripped onto Miss Brooke's face. He pried her jaws apart and used his thumb to press her own cheek between her teeth. Then, he snaked his tongue into her mouth.

Not caring who heard, she tried to scream, but her voice was muffled into the hungry mouth of the monster in front of her. Miss Brooke's legs were pinned in her large panniers, taking even the chance of kicking him from her. Her eyes widened with terror as she realized she was trapped. West chuckled at her fear. Keeping his thumb jammed in her jaw, he moved to whisper into her ear.

Miss Brooke never found out what West intended to say. Before he could speak, he flew back across the balcony. Her Donahue was there, blazing in fury. The French doors hung askew behind him. He paid no more attention to the destruction than he did to Miss Brooke. Donahue was focused on West, murder in his eyes. Donahue grabbed the taller man by the lapel and smashed his forehead into his nose. Blood flowed from the fan-wide puncture on

West's cheek. He jerked back out of Donahue's grasp and responded with a right hook of his own. Donahue stumbled back from the blow but came up swinging. His fist connected with West's jaw. As West was reeling from the blow, Donahue continued with a series of short, quick jabs. He only got four or five punches in before strong hands pulled him off West.

Donahue allowed himself to be guided away. He looked a mess. His formal wig was missing, his coat was covered in glass shards from the shattered French doors, and his fists were bloody from bashing West's face. In his wrath, he could barely recognize the one of the men pulling him back as Collins. The smoldering rage on his friend's face told Donahue he had his support. The painted parade of the court poured out from the ballroom and into every nook of the balcony.

West got to his feet and wiped the blood from his face. With a mocking smile, he raised his fists and beckoned Donahue forward. Donahue was sorely tempted, but the way West recovered quickly gave him pause. It was time to take this on right and proper ground.

Raising his voice so the assemblage could hear him, Donahue spit words at the other man, "I will see you at dawn."

West's smile grew. "Gladly. Choose your second."

Collins spoke before Donahue could respond. "I am Donahue's second. I find it unlikely someone will stand for a cur like you." Collins gave a meaningful look at Miss Brooke's disheveled form.

A man Donahue did not know spoke from behind them. "I will second Mr. West."

Collins nodded. "Then it is done. I suggest you leave." Miss Brooke had never heard Collins' voice like this, low, harsh, and menacing.

West bowed mockingly at the two men. With a slow, deliberate wink at Miss Brooke, he turned on his heel and walked with the other man back into the ballroom. Gossip exploded as they passed. Collins ignored it all and walked over to check on Miss Brooke. She smiled at him weakly and looked at Donahue. He was shaking, his bloody knuckles white from being clenched with rage. He was incapable of words. Collins took over.

"What happened here?" Collins asked quietly.

Miss Brooke moved towards the railing of the balcony. Both Collins and Donahue moved in close to shield her from the gossiping eyes. "West found me alone on the balcony. He said I was punishing him for what he almost did to me. If I was going to punish him for it, he might as well do it."

Donahue's rage-filled eyes took in the state of Miss Brooke's dress.

"Nothing really happened," Miss Brooke clarified, "except he made me feel helpless."

"He will not do it again." Donahue spit the words out.

Hobson spoke from behind them. Miss Brooke was a bit surprised the friend found his way out here. Normally, Hobson was involved in nothing more than frivolous fashion conversations. "Are you sure you wish to move to pistols, Lord Donahue? West is an excellent marksman."

Donahue's eyes blazed at Hobson but he did not otherwise reply. Collins replied instead, "So is Donahue."

Hobson appeared to be about to speak again when Donahue's violent gaze swept around the balcony. His gaze fell on Miss Brooke. "Why were you out here alone?" he accused.

"I was not," Miss Brooke stammered. "Or, not really. Anderson was, was escorting me. He was there, right inside. I—I was distraught. Miss Boswell, and treason, and our engagement, and scandal, and, and—it is too much!"

"Where is he now?" Donahue barked.

Shrugging, Miss Brooke wrapped her arms around herself. Her chin was still raised in a proud manner but the harshness of Donahue's voice chilled her inside. "I do not know. West said he was off chasing skirts, but he could have been lying."

Donahue gave Collins a look Miss Brooke could not read. He then walked towards her and smoothed the disheveled curl on her forehead. "May I leave you for a moment? I have things to attend to."

Miss Brooke nodded more confidently than she truly felt. "I will be. I hope you are too."

"After I kill West I will be." Donahue placed a surprising gentle kiss on her forehead. He turned his attention to Hobson. "Watch over her."

Miss Brooke was surprised at how quickly Hobson agreed. There was rough danger lurking in Donahue's voice and the normally flippant Collins radiated a flinty anger. Hobson's response was automatic obedience. "Yes, Lord Donahue."

Collins and Donahue walked out of the balcony without a single word or backwards glance.

Hobson offered Miss Brooke his arm with a courtly smile. "Miss Brooke, may I see you home? I have both a carriage and a charming niece willing to escort us safely away from this ruckus."

"Please, Mr. Hobson," Miss Brooke's voice grew stronger with every word. "I have never been so delighted to retire."

Donahue stormed across the floor of the ballroom with Collins close on his heels. He tore through the main hall, the foyer, and several smaller resting rooms, before halting at the entrance to the card room. He overheard a breathless servant tell Collins something about Miss Brooke and a safe departure but could not focus on the words. His anger was blinding. Collins grabbed his arm and tried to speak reason, but Donahue was uninterested in whatever his friend had to say. Across the room he found his target.

Anderson was playing faro, his light brown hair animatedly falling into his face as he laughed. His eyes flashed with mirth as he responded to the advances of the woman next to him. Donahue thought of another pair of light blue eyes, Miss Brooke's, but they were filled with pain. He moved with deliberate focus. Nothing existed to Donahue except for his little brother. Time slowed as he marched across the room.

Anderson looked with a smile for his sibling and made a welcoming gesture over to the gaming tables. His carefree mood vanished as he saw Donahue's glowering expression. Anderson managed to get to his feet by the time Donahue crossed the room. He made an attempt to reason with the furious man, but Donahue was not listening. His bloody fist hit Anderson firmly in the middle of his chest and the younger brother doubled over.

The flirtatious woman next to Anderson started screaming, a high-pitched annoying wail. Donahue's second punch caught Anderson across the jaw as he was crouched over in pain. The punch flung Anderson forward and sent him sprawling on top of the card table. For the briefest of moments, it seemed like the violence was over. Then, Donahue grabbed the edge of the faro table and capsized it. Drinks, cards, and Anderson crashed onto the tiled floor.

The shrill screeching of the women fleeing the scene overpowered the crescendo of glass breaking. Donahue walked through the chaos to stand over his brother. Anderson's eyes opened, blinking at Donahue. He again attempted to speak, but Donahue shook his head in disgust.

Donahue reached for Anderson, but Collins laid a restraining hand on his arm. "Come. This is over." Donahue shrugged off Collins' grip. Collins stepped in front of Donahue and tried again, "Let us away."

Donahue looked through Collins at Anderson before finally nodding. He turned on his heel and marched out of the card room, blindly trusting Collins would follow.

Surrounded by broken glass and hysterical women, Anderson crawled into a seated position and watched his brother leave. Wiping blood from his eyes, he picked up a partly shattered glass of whiskey and took a drink.

CHAPTER XIX

The morning dawned foggy and cold. A select group of nobles found themselves awake before they would normally be abed.

Miss Brooke spent the rest of her night pacing the halls. Her antics finally irritated her father enough to inquire as to the cause of her nerves. After prying the story from his frantic daughter, Brooke sent her to the most likely place where the news of the success (or failure) of a duel would arrive first. Brooke watched his daughter ride off to the Donahue townhouse with a frown of disapproval on his face and a heart aflutter with worry.

Anderson slept for only a few hours before emerging from the captain's suite of his ship. Dressed in plain workman's clothing, he roused select members of his crew. Scuttlebutt about West's tactics left him uneasy. His men gave no objection as he briefed them on the morning's plan. Wordlessly, they faded into the fog.

Elizabeth woke with Collins and helped him dress. There was a desperate sincerity in her movements. She held her husband tightly as he reassured her everything would turn out for the best. He left, riding off into the fog on his favorite black stallion, and Elizabeth stood at the window ringing her hands. She found it impossible to wait alone. Not caring about gossip, appearances, or propriety, she grabbed her reticule and summoned her carriage. Within minutes she was outside of the Donahue townhouse.

Lady Donahue spent the evening quietly supping with a few friends before retiring to oversee her final preparations to move to the country. The unexpectedly cold August evening hurt her arthritis, falling asleep was challenging. As sleep finally overtook her, the knocker banged loudly.

With the help of her maid, she threw on a robe and hobbled downstairs to see what on earth brought someone to her door at this time of night. Lady Donahue stopped short when she found Miss Brooke and Lady Stanton standing side-by-side, fidgeting on her doorstep. Both of them were trying to bully her recalcitrant footman.

"Oh, Lord." She whispered fervently as she approached. "You two," she sternly commanded, "had better come in. Mr. Summers, bring sherry. I feel I should know what has happened."

Wilhelm woke his lord an hour before dawn. Donahue went through his morning routine with as much semblance of normality as he could. His anger was hard to banish. He knew he needed to be calm and focused to be a superb marksman, but all his attention was on how much he wanted to harm West.

When Collins finally arrived at the rundown rooms Donahue had worked himself into a state of extreme ferocity. He marched downstairs and mounted the gelding Collins brought for him.

Collins gave him an assessing look, "Are you sure you wish to do this? Hobson has a point. West is a fair shot."

Donahue settled himself on the horse. "I am more than a fair shot. And I most certainly wish to do this."

Collins nodded and relayed the meeting point for the morning. They were headed to a rundown park not far from Donahue's dwelling. The duel's location was on the edge of civility, economically stable enough so the peerage could play without fear of pickpockets, while still pretending they had left Town. Once, this was a lovely area where small cobblestone streets came together to form a communal green space. Now mounds of horse dung sat unattended in corners.

The choice of location irritated Donahue. It hit too close to home, as it seemed representative of his fall from grace. Noticing his friend's expression Collin's asked, "What are you thinking about?"

"Nothing. Reminiscing, I suppose." Donahue corrected. "I would live in these streets all my life if it meant Alison could be with me."

Collins shrugged. "You still might. There is nothing says the gentry must be wealthy. Plenty of us are shunted off to the country to die."

"Delightful topic." Donahue looked out over the fog. "Today will be a good day."

Collins looked at him curiously. "How so?"

"The weather is miserable."

"That makes no sense."

Donahue smiled through his anger. "A private joke between Alison and myself. The weather has been lovely on our worst days and terrible on our best. Near frost in August bodes well."

"You exaggerate the cold," Collins answered absently. Looking at a street sign, he nodded at Donahue. "This is it. We will leave the horses here and walk down that alley. It opens to the park after a few turns. Last chance for second thoughts."

"I have none, Collins. This man needs to die." There was a quiet determination to Donahue's voice.

Collins nodded. "Let us get on with it. Dawn approaches." Collins took Donahue's horses reins and headed over to a sleepy youth halfheartedly begging on the side of the street. He bribed the young boy to hold the horses and turned to follow Donahue. Donahue, however, did not wait. He was already disappearing into the fog. With expression of irritation at his reckless friend, Collins quickened his step.

Collins was so intent with worry for Donahue he overlooked the sound of gathering footsteps behind him. He did notice the sharp pain in the back of his head. The muddy cobblestones rushing at his face received his full attention. After that, he noticed nothing.

With great impatience, Donahue stopped before the turn in the alley and waited for his lollygagging friend. The fog was so thick he could barely see twenty feet in either direction. As seconds crept by, Donahue deduced something was amiss. He strained his ears but could only hear the clatter of what appeared to be early morning street noise. Donahue paused for a moment, considering his options. He could go backwards and see what delayed Collins, or he could make his dawn appointment with a man who desperately needed to die.

With a silent apology to Collins, Donahue drew his pistol and continued onwards. Soon, Donahue could see the figure of West outlined in the fog. He took a deep breath to prepare for witty repartee and the ritual of the duel. He stopped in disbelief as he spotted West holding a flintlock pistol pointed directly at him. Donahue would have no time to fire an answering shot before he died.

Donahue cautiously raised his hands towards the sky, turning the pistol to show the hammer was uncocked. He did not need to see West's sardonic smile to know he was in trouble. The reason for Collins' disappearance became clear. The meeting was a trap and he had walked right into it. West was alone. His second must have dispatched Collins. Donahue wracked his mind for an escape route, or any form of plan at all, and came up with nothing. The street behind him was too far away to stage a retreat.

West's smile grew. "Any last words, hero?"

Each one of Donahue's senses heightened. Time seemed to slow, and he felt as if he could do anything. Yet, even slowed time provided no answers to the gun pointed at his chest, nor even provided witty repartee. "This is no way to duel, West. There is no honor in this."

West's eyebrow cocked at Donahue's statement, "Honor, Donahue? From a man who sinks my ships in the night?"

Donahue's nostrils flared. "I would rather sink ships in the night than force women."

West's finger tightened on the trigger. "Kill upwards of thirty men to launder a small stain on a lightskirts' reputation?" His voice dripped with sarcasm. "Two wrongs make a right and all that. Such logic." West's expression grew deadly. "My sailors died. You gutted my plantation, stealing my labor and burning fields. My estate is worthless thanks to your heroics. You come hither to defend the honor of a strumpet who plays you like a fiddle. I come to avenge the memory of the lives you ruined for her fancy."

Donahue refused to be drawn. West spoke of impossible things. The Donahue's lacked any form of fleet capable of sinking West's ships. He had no idea how to go about freeing a plantation-worth of slaves. "Then seek vengeance through the rules of honor. We are here to duel."

"Just as you have acted honorably while attacking ships flying the Union Jack? Or abusing the power of your office for personal vendettas?" West scoffed. "You may have come to duel, but I came to watch you die."

West raised his gun to look down the sight at his foe. Donahue tensed, preparing for a bullet. West fired. The booming sound of a shot filled the damp air. Donahue crashed onto the cobblestones.

Anderson wedged into a small space between two buildings only moments before Donahue encountered West. The fog ruined visibility. Anderson sent his sailors to keep watch as he tried to get closer. After climbing a fence and shimmying between two buildings he managed to be only feet away.

Finished creeping forward, Anderson crouched behind a pile of trash. If he jumped into the alley, he would have a shot on West. However, he could get no farther forward without revealing his presence. Anderson settled in to wait and allowed himself the luxury of listening to the conversation.

The discussion made no sense. Anderson knew their overstretched shipping fleet was not sinking ships, nor were they involved in the slave trade.

Anderson pulled himself out of the pointless conversation. The facts that mattered were clear: West had no intention of obeying the rules of the duel and Anderson had no intention of seeing his brother shot. He watched West cock the gun.

As West fired on Donahue, Anderson leapt from his hiding place with his own firearm. The racket of Anderson's sudden appearance caught West's attention and he instinctively turned his head to look. The shift of West's shoulders changed the aim of his pistol. Anderson could only hope it changed West's aim enough to save Donahue's life. His shot fired at almost the same time as West's. Two bullets crashed into two different men. West flew backwards into the darkness with a wet, hollow thump.

Anderson glanced quickly around the alley as he walked forward. Already, his men were swarming over his brother. He forced himself to trust his men. Donahue would live, must live. Anderson could not imagine a world without him. It would involve things he was not ready for yet, things like being the Earl or, worse, growing up. Pushing such thoughts aside, he marched towards West. He was splayed on his back, blood pooling beneath him. Anderson pulled his second gun from its holster and shot him again in the chest. There was no sense in being careless.

The shot caused a pile of trash to startle. Several of Anderson's sailors already had their pistols aimed before Anderson even turned his head. "Who is there? Show yourselves."

A young boy's voice reverberated through the fog. "It ain't no one, guvnor. Please don't shoot."

"Come out where I can see you. All of you." A sailor handed him a reloaded flintlock. Anderson pointed that gun at the trash.

Two small urchins crawled out from behind refuse. While they were small in stature, they gave the impression of being in their mid-teens. The taller of the two spoke. "Just us, guvnor. We ain't seen nothin'."

"You work for that man?" He pointed at the dead body in front of him.

"Not'all. Never seen 'im 'fore." The taller boy pushed the other child behind him.

The littler one piped up from behind his brother. "We live here. Our park." An emaciated arm pointed down the ally.

"Then you will want to dispose of the body. That filth should have coin enough to make it worth your while." Anderson had little fear the street rats would turn him in to the constabulary. Even if they did, it was more likely they would be blamed for the murder even in the face of overwhelming evidence to the contrary. He began to turn away and walk towards his brother. The little urchin's voice stopped him.

"We could take his money and leave the body."

Anderson turned back to face them. "Outside your nest?"

The older boy mumbled apologetically, but the younger pushed around him and continued the confrontation. "Someone'll come get 'im."

I have no time for this, Anderson thought. "A shilling. Remove the body, I care not what happens to it, only that I never want to hear of this again."

The urchin wrinkled his soot-covered brow. "A shilling for us both and you won't."

Anderson reached into his waistcoat for the money and realized with frustration he had no small coins. With extreme irritation, he tossed the children a guinea. They looked at it in shock and groveled as they eagerly snatched up the coin. The older teen raced towards the body and started looting while the younger saluted the departing gentleman. "Nothin' to link ya to this one, guvnor. Promise!"

Anderson nodded without turning and trotted towards his cluster of sailors. They were already moving down the small streets and had only left one man behind to wait for their Captain.

The scar-faced sailor nodded respectfully at his captain. "Men found the other lord down the alley they came up. Taking 'em both to the townhouse as you ordered, Captain. Bosun suggests you ride ahead. Lord Donahue don't look good."

The next few hours were a blur for Anderson. Somehow, all the women in his brother's life were at the townhouse, each full of frantic concern. His time captaining a ship with the East India Company was of great use. Panicked people responded well to orders.

Within a short amount of time Collins was in the guest room, Donahue was in his father's suite, and the women were at their sides. Lady Donahue was calmly sitting in the parlor, drinking a cup of tea.

Anderson approached his mother with a frown. "How can you be so calm?"

"Calm?" Lady Donahue smiled indulgently at her younger son. "I promise you, my dear, I am the utmost in nerves. But it is Miss Brooke's place to sit with Robert. I would be in the way." She placed her teacup down delicately. "That does not mean, however, I am not frantic."

"You look calm." Anderson begrudgingly responded. "I am not calm. I wish West would come back to life so that I could kill him again."

"Tut, Michael. You must not say such things. This is not the Orient. The gallows await murderers. It is one thing to duel, but quite another to murder." She sipped her tea again. "Speak no more of this ghastly affair. To anyone. Do you understand me?"

"Yes, Mother." There was no point in arguing. Anderson fell silent as the doctor entered the room. He was well familiar with the Donahue family after caring for their deceased lord. He appeared weary.

"Doctor, how is he?" Anderson asked.

"Not well." The wrinkled man sat without waiting for an invitation. "The good news is the bullet missed his lungs and lodged in his shoulder. The bad news is it shattered his collarbone. I dug it out, but it is still anyone's guess if his lordship will make it."

Lady Donahue nodded, "Is there anything we can do?"

The doctor shrugged. "Keep him warm, lots of fluids, and change his poultice daily. If fever fails to set in, Lord Donahue should have a chance. If it does, well, then it is in God's hands."

"And Collins?" Anderson inquired.

"Just a bump on the head." The doctor found a smile from deep in his weary bones. "I had to trick the spitfire into drinking laudanum."

"We are grateful, doctor." Lady Donahue graciously inclined her head.

The white-haired man rose and bowed. "I wish I could do more. I will return this afternoon." Lady Donahue and Anderson watched him leave.

Lady Donahue turned her attention to her younger son. "Would you retire, son? I would like to be alone."

Anderson nodded and exited the room. He paced nervously around the grounds. Finally, bubbling over with impatience, he departed to visit his mistress. Perhaps, he hoped, a bit of slap and tickle would clear his head.

Anderson returned to home with a slow step. A vigorous workout with his mistress had relieved the nervous energy pent up inside of him since the shooting, yet nothing stopped the racing of his mind. The eerie silent bustle of the household reminded him of when his father first fell ill. They lost one Lord Donahue in this townhouse. Anderson feared they would soon lose another.

Very little scared Anderson—not weather, pirates, or the violence of men, but fever and illness terrified him to his core. Here, he was helpless. At least in a storm he could stand at the helm of the ship and scream into the waves. Now he could do nothing.

The inside of the townhouse was lit with a false cheer. Lady Donahue had a fire roaring in every fireplace and candles in every alcove. Anderson shuddered at the cost of the candles. He had a suspicion his mother had no idea how expensive keeping the house lit truly was.

Even a year ago he would have no concern about things like the mundane price of candles. Now, however, their world seemed to revolve around each hidden expense. With a scowl, Anderson doused candles as he walked to the room where his father had died. His brother lay broken inside.

He slipped through the arched entrance with nary a sound and found both Donahue and Miss Brooke asleep. Donahue was wearing the long white gowns the staff dressed their father for the last year of his life. The similarity only increased Anderson's unease. Miss Brooke was curled uncomfortably on a wicker chair, her legs tucked under her and her torso resting on the foot of Donahue's bed. Collins and Lady Stanton had long since left the Donahue estate, but Miss Brooke clearly felt this was her place. Good lass.

Anderson gave her a sympathetic smile as he checked on his brother. His pulse was slow and steady and the wound looked clean. Anderson replaced the bandage.

"How does it look?" Miss Brooke's voice was quiet.

Anderson glanced over at her, startled. "You are supposed to be asleep. In a more comfortable position, but still."

She nodded. "I know. What time is it?"

"One or two hours until dawn."

"When will he recover?" She sounded fairly certain.

"I am not sure. The wound was stitched well—as you likely surmised, our doctor is excellent—and he has no fever. But he should be awake." Worry crept into Anderson's voice.

"He has been through a large trauma," Miss Brooke responded reasonably, "Whenever I am sick, I need lots of sleep."

Anderson nodded, acknowledging her point before disagreeing with it. "He is not ill. He has been shot. I have seen enough wounds to know he should be awake."

"The doctor…"

Anderson cut Miss Brooke off. "Would have told you nothing useful. Protecting the weak woman folk and all of that."

"I would hope I would be the first to know of any change in his condition," Miss Brooke ventured.

Anderson nodded. "I agree. Not all do." He raised a manicured hand and a servant scurried over. There was a whispered exchange and then Anderson turned his attention back to Miss Brooke. "Do you need anything? Are the servants treating you well?"

She gave him a wan smile. "I thought you were supposed to be the irresponsible rakehell. Yet, here you are, caring for your brother and your brother's problematic fiancée."

He winked at her. "I did drink and whore tonight."

Miss Brooke blushed, taken aback. "Ah. Oh."

Grinning slightly, Anderson came to her rescue with a new topic. "You seem remarkably unconcerned about Robert's condition."

"I am. He will be well."

Anderson gave her an odd look. "How can you be certain?"

"Because the alternative is too awful to even consider. The world is not cruel enough to take both my best friend and the man I love from me in the same sennight." Miss Brooke could not explain how certain she was of the life she would have with Donahue. She could see their future together clearly. It did not end here.

The butler interrupted their conversation with his quiet approach. He began to whisper softly to Anderson but the Captain cut him off.

Anderson gestured towards Miss Brooke, "Please, loud enough for us both. Miss Brooke has every right to know the status of my brother's condition."

The servant inclined his head. "Yes, sir. The doctor expressed concern over Lord Donahue's lack of consciousness. The wound itself seems to be healing. The doctor expressed how lucky your brother was. A bit more to the right and he would no longer be with us."

Anderson nodded, "We are out of danger of fever now, correct?"

"Yes, sir," the servant answered. "Excluding the unexpected, we should be fine on that front. The doctor does not know why he is not awake."

Miss Brooke interjected timidly, "Could he have gotten what his father had?"

"Unlikely, milady. The Lord Donahue does not open his eyes. Their conditions were different. The word the doctor used was coma."

Anderson frowned and waved a dismissal. As an afterthought he glanced at Miss Brooke, "Unless you have any questions?"

Miss Brooke shook her head negatively and the servant retreated. She looked at Anderson with big eyes. "What do you think?"

"I think you should keep your confidence, Miss Brooke." Anderson looked at his brother. "One of us needs it. By your leave?"

She ignored his request, "You are worried?"

He folded his hands on to the top of his head. "Yes. Yes, I am worried. I will leave word the doctor should keep you informed. I should have thought of that previously."

"For which I am grateful." Miss Brooke hid a yawn. "If you do not mind, I believe I will try to get more sleep." Her eyes shifted to Donahue's wound. Worry creased her brow. "And pray."

"I am not normally one to advocate religion, but," he glanced at his brother's unresponsive form, "this might be the time for it. Good night, Miss Brooke."

She forced a slight smile. "Good night, Mr. Anderson."

Anderson saw himself out of the still brightly lit estate. The discussion with Miss Brooke did little to put his mind at ease. Her confidence was based purely on faith in love. Anderson had no such illusions. Robert would live or die based on the whim of fate. His father's illness left Anderson with a bitter outlook of the medical profession. Anderson was fairly sure the word 'coma' was another moniker for 'I do not know.'

With a bleak scowl, he set off to find Wilhelm and drag his childhood compatriot to the ship. This was no time for the household to be dispersed.

Three days crawled by before anything else of note occurred. Miss Brooke spent the days at her home and her evenings sitting beside Donahue. The Brooke domicile received many callers but her staff was vigilant about turning everyone away. The only exception was Wilhelm. He showed up on the doorstep of her bedchamber on a dreary Thursday afternoon.

Miss Brooke startled when she spotted him. "Wilhelm! If you are going to be our servant, you will simply have to learn basic manners!"

"Like being announced?" Wilhelm shrugged as he walked in. "If I am your servant, why would I need to be announced?"

"Because this is my bedchamber." Miss Brooke looked at him like he was daft. "And, besides, you are not my servant."

"Yet."

Wilhelm sat on a dainty chair across from where Miss Brooke was sitting. She stared at him in frank disbelief before giving up. "What do you want? Why are you here?"

He shifted uncomfortably at her aggravation. "I promise I will try to be what I am supposed to be when we are out of this mess. Would that suit?"

She nodded. "I would like that. I know you have done the world for Lord Donahue, but…"

"But, I am a terrible servant. I know." Wilhelm did not seem the least bit insulted. "My lords have never truly cared. You do. If you guide me, I will adapt."

Miss Brooke forced herself to smile reassuringly at him. "I suppose that may work."

"Now, as your not-yet-husband's steward, I have updates I think you would be interested in."

"Updates?" Miss Brooke interrupted. "Updates about what? Is Robert…?" Miss Brooke left the question hanging.

"He is the same. As you may be aware, I serve as Donahue's butler, valet, secretary and boot boy, yet my intended focus is economic. This morn, I have an update on the Donahue fiscal status."

Miss Brooke found humor in her weary sorrow. "Poor as church mice, with a side of debt?"

Wilhelm's eyes were bright as he shook his head no. "The ships came in, Miss Brooke. They actually came in."

Miss Brooke shook her head in confusion. "What ships?"

"The ships we sent to the Far East almost a year ago. We assumed they were a total loss. They came back! Filled with gunpowder, spices, silk, and things we have never seen out of the East before." Wilhelm gestured expansively, everything about him showing his true excitement. "They were late because the Captain fought for all the permits, all the permission, and legally exported the most amazing things."

Miss Brooke watched Wilhelm's joy with a strange curiosity. She bit her tongue before she could ask him why he was telling her all of this. She understood. This was what Wilhelm and Donahue were waiting on. Now that it finally happened, Wilhelm was unable to share the joy with Donahue. She was the next best thing. Miss Brooke guessed at how she was supposed to reply, "Wonderful. How much is the cargo worth?"

Wilhelm pulled out a little black book Miss Brooke had seen on Donahue's end table. "Quite a bit, let me show you." Wilhelm opened the ledger and started explaining columns of numbers. "I decided it was best to be conservative with the estimates of what we will be able to sell the goods for. Anderson is pricing the market."

Miss Brooke listened intently as he explained the variance in prices of silk. Wilhelm reached the summary lines: "This here is our current debt."

Miss Brooke blew a silent whistle at the number. They did need her dowry!

Wilhelm continued, "This is the low estimate of the profit from the venture, this is the high estimate. As you can see, it is probable these two numbers will zero out, leaving us relatively free of debt."

"And this is good?" It sounded positive to Miss Brooke, although barely out of debt still seemed rather poor.

"More than good," Wilhelm confirmed with a nod. "It is fairly standard for most estates to carry debt as they finance ventures. Our goal is to be able to operate without any debt and build up our resources." Wilhelm tapped the book. "This does not include the entailment or upkeep funds. The estate has a separate fund we use for maintenance and tenant needs. Donahue refused to touch that, to ensure we do not lose the land."

Miss Brooke furrowed her brow. "This is, in fact, quite good. The wolf is no longer at the door?"

"As the saying goes, yes." Wilhelm smiled. "We are wolf-free. There is no need to sell the townhouse and we can settle with our more persistent creditors. Life will be normal again."

"As long as Donahue recovers." Miss Brooke's voice was soft.

"Well, yes." Wilhelm deflated. "As long as my lord recovers."

"You believe he is going to get better?" She previously assumed she was the only one with such an opinion.

Wilhelm looked uncomfortable. "It seems unlikely, ma'am."

"If he does not recover, I will not be your future employer, and these numbers will mean nothing to me." Miss Brooke pointed out.

"But if Lord Donahue does wake, he will not find his world neglected. That includes you." He stood. "I should be off. Lady Donahue mentioned going to tea with friends. None of us wishes him left alone."

"I can go," Miss Brooke already started to gather her things, the mention of Donahue being alone driving anything else from her mind.

"You should sleep. Besides, sitting with him makes me feel useful."

Miss Brooke nodded and sat back down. Suddenly, Wilhelm's zeal made sense to her. She hated the feeling of being able to do nothing and leaving her whole future and happiness to the whim of fate. At least sitting with him was something to do, some way to feel connected. She suspected Wilhelm's diligence with Donahue's finances was similar. "I understand. As an aside, I would suggest speaking with Lady Donahue before you take the townhouse off the market."

Wilhelm frowned. "Why? Now we have the capital, Lady Donahue can stay in London for as long as she likes. Lord Donahue would not begrudge her that."

Miss Brooke considered her words carefully. "If I were Lady Donahue, I may not mind the opportunity to rid myself of the place where my husband died."

"I would not have thought of that," Wilhelm admitted. "I will ask her."

"Good. Now, if there is nothing else, I will see you anon." Miss Brooke smiled at Wilhelm. "Try not to scandalize my whole staff on the way out."

He waggled his eyebrows at her before departing with a bow.

The Donahue estate fell into a mournful routine. Each morning Lady Donahue took up duties by her son's side and a carriage took Miss Brooke back to her estate. Each evening, Miss Brooke exchanged places with Lady Donahue. The doctor came three times a day to purge Donahue, but there was no change. Anderson was oft about, visiting at ridiculous hours. Each day, the household became increasingly waspish. As Donahue failed to improve nerves frayed, and tempers clashed. The climate in the household was strained. Each member watched Donahue with fear and worry.

On the sixth day, Wilhelm arrived shortly after dawn. Miss Brooke looked like hell. Her bloodshot eyes showed her weariness. He never caught her sleeping while sitting through the night at Donahue's side.

Wilhelm frowned as he came through the archway. Perhaps this was not the best time to bring her tumultuous news? Before he could reconsider, Miss Brooke spotted him. She gestured him into the open room with a weary smile.

"How is he?" Wilhelm asked in the whisper commonly used around the sick.

Miss Brooke smiled sadly and brushed back a strand of hair from Donahue's brow. "Same as yesterday."

"What did the doctor say?"

"Same as yesterday." Frustration leaked into her voice. "Keep purging and hope for the best."

Wilhelm's scowl matched hers as he looked at his lord. His expression stayed foul as his gaze moved back to Miss Brooke. "I have news."

"Tell me it is good, otherwise I do not wish to hear it."

"Then I shall remain silent."

"Gadzooks, Wilhelm." Wilhelm's eyebrow raised as the formal lady cursed. "Spare me your wit and speak."

"Word came for Lord Donahue from the Royal Navy." Wilhelm straightened his shoulders before continuing. "The ship Lord Farrington escaped on has been sunk. Lord Farrington was seen leaving the Pool of London onboard that ship, and the Navy is positive they got him. The Crown is convinced, as well. A group of runners chased Lord Farrington to the ship and shot at him as the ship departed."

Miss Brooke's face was vacant of emotion or thought. "And Miss Boswell?"

"Neither her nor Lord Farrington are listed among the survivors. The ship was chased soon after it left the Pool. No one got off before it was sunk. I am sorry."

Miss Brooke's expression did not change. "Thank you, Wilhelm. You may go now."

Wilhelm bowed. "Might I see you home? Your father has also been informed."

"Thank you, Wilhelm." Her pale blue eyes looked straight at him, but Wilhelm had the disturbing notion she did not see him. "That would be lovely."

"The carriage is waiting." Wilhelm grabbed a warmed blanket from beside the fireplace and draped it around Miss Brooke. "It is chilly outside."

Wilhelm guided her through the residence like a child. She continued to respond appropriately to conversation, but it was as if she was not there, or as if she was in shock. Lady Donahue watched them leave with a sad, drawn expression and slowly climbed the massive staircase to start her daily vigil beside her son.

Miss Brooke did not know how she got home, or how she got to her father's study. All she knew was Brenda was gone, more than gone. Brenda was dead. Anthony was dead. And Robert, Robert was dying. The doctor reported the same things day after day, but it was clear he too had given up hope. Miss Brooke wanted to cry, to bawl, to rip out her hair and scream, but nothing would come. She had cried all she could, only pain and emptiness remained. Miss Brooke curled deeper into the wingback chair and looked around at the small, warm room.

The study was cleaner than usual. Many of the random stacks became neat, orderly piles. A decanter of brandy sat on the table and Miss Brooke briefly considered pouring herself a stiff drink. She decided against it. Drinking would not help this pain. It filled every aspect of her thinking and seeped into her soul.

She was thankful Wilhelm sent her home. At least she still had her father. As if her thought summoned him, he shambled into the room behind her. His limp was pronounced. Brooke lit a cigar instantly upon sitting behind his desk. His daughter smiled wanly at him in greeting.

"There is something I have to tell you," Brooke started without preamble, "but it must remain a secret between us. You must be a consummate actress. I would prefer if you asked a minimal number of questions."

Miss Brooke simply nodded. There was nothing left to say.

"Brenda was not on that ship," Brooke said.

"What?" This was not what Miss Brooke was expecting. "But every piece of gossip says she was with Anthony!"

Brooke nodded. "She was. But they were never on that ship."

"She is alive?" Miss Brooke's whole world lit up. She straightened herself in the chair and leaned forward eagerly. "How? Wait." Miss Brooke's mind quickly put the pieces together. "Lord Farrington is not dead, either. But the Crown thinks he is, so he is not being hunted?"

Brooke nodded again. "Yes. The Crown lacks reason to suspect they live. Do not give them one. Be appropriately upset."

"I promise you, Father, I can be appropriately upset. I was not sure I could be any more upset until this morning. Then it was," Miss Brooke stumbled as she looked for a fitting phrase, "like finding a wasteland in myself."

There was nothing he could say to that. "How is Donahue?"

Brooke puffed on his cigar as she answered, "The same. Nothing changes. I—I am worried."

"As you should be, Ali. Sometimes people do not wake from things like this." Brooke's voice was soft, but he felt he needed to be honest with his daughter.

"I know. Michael is terribly worried. I think he has already given up hope." Miss Brooke clenched her delicate hands together to stop from fidgeting. "I have not. I will not. But, I feel as if I am the only one who still believes." She relaxed her hands and flashed her father her best fake smile. "How goes the rest of the world?"

"The same. Nothing changes." He gave her a gentle smile in return, worry in his eyes. "Full of gossip, actually. Rumor seems to adore your Lord Donahue. Some of the *ton* thinks he was shot in the duel, others think the duel never happened and he was shot while hunting Farrington here in the city, and yet another group believes Farrington and Donahue dueled in a dark alley by the docks. No one can decide what happened, but everyone knows it was grand."

"And West?" Miss Brooke asked with only mild curiosity. Somehow it all seemed meaningless with Donahue lying near death.

"Found naked behind a brothel with the trash. Two heavy pistol shots tore through his chest at close range. Thus, most think the duel did not happen," Brooke replied.

"So ridiculous! Donahue was most certainly shot dueling West."

Brooke took a long draw off his cigar. "Gossip rarely makes sense. But I believe you are caught up on the things you care about. I had your Society papers set aside if you wish to read them."

"The thought is kind but my mind is elsewhere." Miss Brooke leaned as far back in the chair as her stays would allow. "How do you know Brenda was not on that ship?"

"I was hoping you would overlook that, Ali."

Miss Brooke watched her father fiddle with his cigar as she considered her answer. "I can, if necessary, but I would prefer to know."

"Brenda came here on her way to Farrington's. It is possible I gave them assistance."

Miss Brooke smiled brightly, her first real smile in days. Her father really did fix everything. "Then you know how to reach them? Are they well?"

"I do, and it is likely they will be fine." He held up a restraining hand. "However, considering your Donahue is leading the investigation against Brenda's Farrington, I feel it is prudent to withhold such information."

"Wise. Are you going to tell her father?" Miss Brooke asked curiously.

"No." Brooke scowled at his cigar. "If Donahue was healthy, I would not even have told you. Too many people know the secret already. But," he waved the cigar at her, "I felt the knowledge may provide comfort in your sorrow."

Miss Brooke nodded. "Thank you. While I do wish you would have told me sooner, I understand how precious this secret is." How could she be angry with her father for keeping secrets when Miss Boswell was alive? And he gave her friend aid?

Brooke smiled at his daughter. "Since your mood seems to be lifted for the first time in a week, you should try to sleep. I will leave word to wake you if a messenger comes."

Miss Brooke beamed back at him. "Brenda is alive! How could I sleep?"

"I think," Brooke, answered wryly, "you will be surprised. You look like you have not slept in a fortnight."

"What an dreadful thing to say!" Miss Brooke objected.

"I am an dreadful man," her father agreed with a loving grin.

Three days later, Collins arrived at the Donahue estate on his way home from a night on the town. It was a preposterous time to call on the household, but Donahue would not leave his mind. The staff let him in without comment.

Miss Brooke was staring into the fireplace, halfheartedly working on embroidery while Donahue slept on behind her. Collins sauntered into the room as the servants rushed to bring in another wicker chair. Miss Brooke forced a smile at his appearance. Even by firelight, his chartreuse outfit shown like the sun.

Collins bowed slightly at Miss Brooke before slouching into the wicker chair the servants placed behind him. "How are you, my dear?"

Miss Brooke returned his bow with a slight nod. "As can be expected, Lord Stanton. We appreciate your visit. How was your night?"

"Distracted." Collins's expression soured as he looked over at his boyhood friend. "Any change?"

"None."

The ostentatious man bit back a curse. "Unfortunate."

"Indeed." Miss Brooke agreed with a nod. "And, how are you?"

Collins touched the back of his head. A dismissive wave accompanied his statement. "This? It is nothing. A small bump, quickly gone." Regret echoed in his voice. "I wish it could have been more."

A quizzical eyebrow lifted. "I disagree. A bump on your head is rather enough."

He smiled at her, his cheery expression returning despite the topic. "If I was there, rather than face-down in the mud, Donahue would be whole and hale."

"You worry needlessly, Lord Stanton. If you had not been felled, West may have shot you both without preamble. This way another was able to intervene."

Collins' wig bobbed as he nodded. "Michael's timing was fortunate. Is he here?"

"Off and on. He is spending most of his time at the docks. He and Wilhelm are sorting the new goods and lining up buyers. They seem excited."

"As well they should be. Apparently, one of the holds is brimming with magnificent silks. Wilhelm already delivered a bolt of shimmering aquamarine the precise color of the Caribbean Sea." He flashed his flamboyant smile at her. "I informed my tailor his book is full."

"That most well."

Collins made a face at Miss Brooke. "Please, Miss Brooke. You cannot give in to apathy and the doldrums. Come out to the opera with us, do something, anything, except sit in this blindingly white room. Such isolation is not healthy."

"It is my place," Miss Brooke said simply.

"No one disagrees. Yet, as I worry about Donahue, I worry for you as well. Your smile is lost," said Collins.

"I appreciate the concern, Lord Stanton. There is little reason to smile, lately." She knew he had her best intentions at heart but she found the encouragement to leave Donahue's side wearisome.

Collins nodded his head in acknowledgment. "A horrific few weeks. Nonetheless, one should not stay in and mope. Come have a night on the Town!"

Miss Brooke snipped the thread of her embroidery and inhaled to retort. Donahue's raspy whisper interrupted, "What are you two arguing about? I was sleeping."

Both Collins and Miss Brooke froze and stared at the man on the bed. Donahue had not moved but one eye was slightly open and peering at them. Miss Brooke put down her embroidery and rushed to his side as Collin's answered his friend's question, "Miss Brooke's lack of fashion, mate. Water?"

Donahue nodded weakly, "Please."

Collins poured a cup from the nightstand and lifted Donahue so he could drink. When they finished, Donahue slouched further into his pillow. Miss Brooke hovered quietly over him. Donahue smiled weakly as he gazed upon her. "Are you well, love?"

Miss Brooke nodded. "Perfect. You?"

Creases appeared on Donahue's brow, "There is pain, perhaps, sleep."

Collins poured more water and added a dollop of laudanum. Miss Brooke kissed Donahue tenderly on the cheek. Donahue peered at her through desperate eyes. "Be here when I wake?"

Collins' voice was warm as he again lifted his friend to drink. "Robert, she has barely left your side."

Miss Brooke was solemn as she watched Donahue gulp at the water. "There is nowhere else I would rather be."

Donahue flexed his fingers in her direction. Miss Brooke quickly placed her hand in his and stared longingly into his eyes. Collins slowly withdrew.

As he backed into the hallway, he encountered Lady Donahue standing in the shadows of the doorway, watching Donahue and Miss Brooke. Collins nodded to Lady Donahue and whispered, "So, things will be well?"

Lady Donahue smiled at the scene in the room as she answered, "Things are more than well. He will recover. After all, he has a Christmas wedding to attend."

EPILOGUE

Brooke shook his head ruefully at the letter hidden in his latest trade dispatch. Fugitives sending letters back home was the height of foolishness. Nevertheless, he unfolded the letter in relief. He had only known the Graceful Sea escaped the harbor safely. He smoothed out the crumpled parchment and strained to read the spidery scrawl.

Mr. B -

Through threats and bribery, I convinced Mr. F to let me send this letter. Life here is well, although different in every way. Why throw balls or attend parties when there is a whole world to help build? New ideas are everywhere. My darling fits right in, always in the center of things.

We married on the ship and are doing wonderfully. I am expecting in the spring! Ali always dreamed of being an amazing mother and her eagerness must have rubbed off on me, I am quite enthusiastic. Mr. F is a bore about the whole thing. Suddenly, he is against me traveling to meetings. Ridiculous nonsense. We will have a true daughter of the revolution! Certainly she should be at meetings!

I am positive we will have a little girl. My skin is spotty and the midwife says my face full of bumps is a sure sign of a daughter. If the babe is a girl, which she will be, we plan to name her Grace after your wedding gift. I wished to claim we named her after our ship, but A renamed the Graceful Sea to the Four Friends. I am unconvinced that the new name is more clandestine.

I miss you all more than I can express, Ali especially! We are happy here, but I wish we could share our joy with the people we love. Mr. F says his old friend is obligingly barking up the wrong tree—I do not feel dead!—but the obfuscation will not hold for even the briefest of visits.

I wish I could attend Ali's wedding! I know it hurts her that you will not give her marriage your blessing. I wish you would reconsider! I cannot see how it would cause you grief. Your support would delight her.

With all my love,

B.F.

Brooke leaned back in his chair and contemplated the scrap of parchment. The letter left him awash in emotion. Miss Boswell, now Belinda Floyd, was healthy and well.

He smiled at the small scrap of parchment one last time. Miss Boswell's writing took up every available space. Brooke shook his head ruefully. As delighted as he was to receive word Miss Boswell and Farrington were doing well and had established themselves in the American Colonies, he wished the girl would show more restraint. Brooke tossed the letter into the fire and watched it burn.

The boisterous chattering from the drawing room drew him awkwardly out of his small study. Brooke paused in the doorway to analyze the assembled guests. Collins and Lady Stanton were perched on the far couch telling an outrageous story. Brooke could not hear the words, but from Collins' wild gestures, and the skeptical expression on his daughter's face, he could only assume the tale was absurd.

Miss Brooke looked lovely, he thought with a tinge of pride. She had always been a pretty girl, but the happiness she found with Donahue made her glow. Lord Donahue was wrapped tightly in blankets and reclining on a couch next to Miss Brooke. The fire in the room was blazing.

No one mentioned the oppressive heat. The injury was three months old. Donahue claimed health, but the group embraced the doctor's orders of keeping him warm and restful with a zealous passion. Brooke almost pitied the strong-willed man. Donahue was clearly unused to being cosseted.

Miss Brooke tore herself away from Collins' tale telling to grace her father with a smile. She warmly beckoned him into the room. Donahue watched Brooke enter with a blank expression. The two men had not yet settled their differences. Brooke settled himself into a cushioned chair across from the lot of them.

The group fell silent at his arrival. Brooke cleared his throat uncomfortably, looking for a place to start. "Thank you all for attending me today. There are things I wish to inform you of."

Miss Brooke glanced around uncomfortably. She placed her hand on Donahue's arm. "Is this bad news, Father?"

Brooke smiled despite his nervousness. "I am not going to further object to your wedding, if that is your concern."

"Good," Donahue cut in. "I admit I am still in no condition for another duel, but for that I might make an exception."

"La, Lord Donahue, you are a dreadful bore," Lady Stanton tisked. "Do go on, Mr. Brooke. I, at least, am interested."

Brooke nodded. "Each of you was instrumental in the events of this summer. There are others I wish were present, but unfortunately, it was a difficult Season."

There was a heavy moment as Miss Boswell's absence was sorely felt. Intentionally misunderstanding, Collins broke the melancholy, "I feel no remorse for Anderson. He is likely hip-deep in women and riches off the African coast. All we have is ash and the hint of snow."

Brooke pointedly ignored Collins. "My rejection of my daughter's suitors has been a cause of interest and gossip. I will seek to explain my position." He glanced out the cold slate clouds before continuing. "My mother, Miss Brooke's grandmother, Beverly, married for love. I did not. My mother firmly believed my marriage to Grace was a mistake. On her deathbed, she made me promise Miss Brooke would not marry for money or political gain, but only for love."

Brooke frowned, remembering his mother's death. "I was unsure how to accomplish this. Not only did I disagree with her decision, I remembered once thinking I was in love. I was not. As Miss Brooke grew, she became prettier and prettier. Soon, she was so fair of face offers for her hand would have poured in even without my money. As she grew prettier and prettier, I grew richer and richer. I had to find a way to make suitors want Miss Brooke, rather than my money." Brooke smiled ruefully, "There was little I could do about her pretty face."

"And, thus, why you linked her inheritance to your approval and then refused to give it." Donahue interjected without any inflection in his voice.

"Yes. My logic was a man who loved Miss Brooke, and whom Miss Brooke loved in return, would marry without my money, or would find a way to convince me that he truly loved her. Once we came to London for Miss Brooke's Seasons, the offers for her hand started trickling in. Some wanted her money, some wanted my connections, and one was caught by honor and duty. I never felt, in any case, they offered out of love."

Brooke held up his hand to forestall a volley of objections. "I do not now doubt that Miss Brooke and Donahue love each other deeply. But, when Donahue first informed me he would marry my daughter, it was not due to love. He was caught by duty and the need for her portion. Only later would love blossom between them."

The room was silent. Finally, Lady Stanton spoke. "Why tell us this now?"

"This is backstory, Lady Stanton. There is only one thing I have to say and only one thing I want." Brooke looked at his daughter. Her light blue eyes were thoughtful as she listened to the tale. "Alison, I want your forgiveness. I wanted you happy. I want you happy."

"Oh, Father." Miss Brooke rose from Donahue's side and placed a kiss on the old man's cheek. "There is nothing to forgive. Wishing me happiness is never wrong." She smiled gently at him. "Although, you were a bit high-handed about it."

"I did not want you to marry the first, or second, suitor who came along." Mr. Brook said. "The second had a pretty face and a fondness for sonnets."

"Can I tell you something, Father?" At Brooke's nod, Miss Brooke whispered confidentially, "I do not even remember that man's name."

Miss Brooke shot her father a smile and walked back to sit at Donahue's side. Donahue was still expressionless. "What now?" he asked. "Are you giving Alison and myself your consent to marry?"

"There is no need," Brooke answered. "As you have noted repeatedly, she is over one and twenty."

Donahue frowned. "But the inheritance?"

"A lie," Brooke said. "Needing my approval to gain her inheritance was a lie. If she did elope, or otherwise defy me for love, it would be illogical to punish her. Money does not guarantee happiness, but it provides a strong foundation."

"But we looked into that..." Donahue let the sentence trail off.

"I am certain you did," Brooke replied, seeming outwardly calm. Inwardly he was tense, waiting for Miss Brooke's anger. "And you saw what I wanted you to see. I have had plenty of time to plan, after all."

Miss Brooke frowned. "A lie? All of it?"

"Yes, dear." Brooke looked at his daughter. "I am sorry. I did both what I thought was best and what your grandmother made me promise. I will understand your hate or anger."

"No, I do not hate you, just..." Miss Brooke's brow was furrowed. "I spent many sleepless nights wondering how and why you would deny me happiness. And then there are all those men who left because they could not have my dowry but they could have had my portion anyway if they married me." She paused. "I am overwhelmed. But, no, I do not hate you. I do not even think I am mad at you."

"I am," Donahue interjected. Miss Brooke gave Donahue a hurt, surprised look. Donahue shrugged and winced slightly in pain as his collarbone objected to the movement. "What? I am. I had to commit to an endless amount of sacrifice to marry the woman I love and now I find out it was all needless."

Collins interjected, "It was all needless anyway. You are not poor any more, remember?"

Donahue scowled at his friend, "That is not the point."

"Let's have less philosophy and more champagne," Collins replied with an unconcerned smile. "Hypothetical arguments are the sign of a weak mind."

Miss Brooke returned the smile as Donahue's glare increased. The friendship between Collins and Donahue was stronger than Miss Brooke had ever seen it. Donahue confided how relieved he was to have his childhood friend back. Their friendship, however, often led to inelegant banter. Miss Brooke was still not sure how to handle the uncouth dialogue, but she could not deny it made her smile.

"So, is this it then?" Lady Stanton asked, sipping her tea.

"Is this what?" Brooke asked, confused.

"Happily ever after." Lady Stanton clarified. "I want to make sure."

Miss Brooke looked at Donahue with a timid smile. Was it? Without her best friend? Miss Brooke fought back sorrow and forced her smile to grow. Brenda was well and would want her happy. Donahue reached out and firmly took her hand. Donahue's gaze fell on every person in the room, pausing for a brief moment on Brooke.

Donahue's expression softened as his gaze settled on Miss Brooke. "Yes. Yes, this is happily ever after."

"Excellent!" Lady Stanton exclaimed. "Because I already ordered my dress for your wedding and I would simply *die* if I had to waste that fabric. Whatever would I do?"

Miss Brooke would have laughed, but she was too busy kissing Donahue.

fin.